Lilla the Accidental Witch

Lilla the Accidental Witch

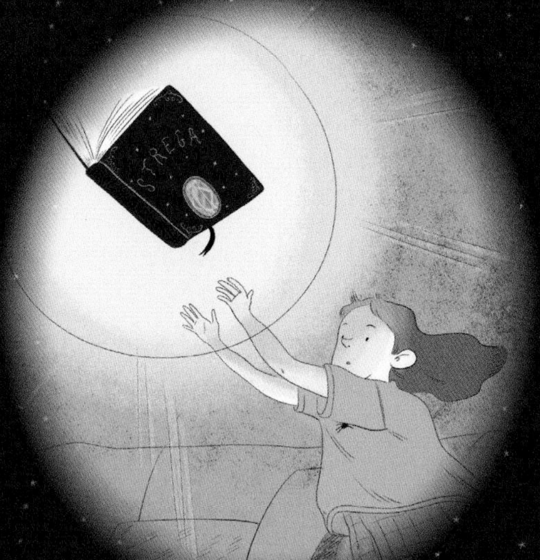
STREGA

Eleanor Crewes

LB

Little, Brown and Company
New York Boston

About This Book
This book was edited by Andrea Colvin and designed by Ching N. Chan. The production
was supervised by Bernadette Flinn, and the production editor was Lindsay Walter-Greaney.
The text was set in Sunbird, and the display type is Wanderlust.

Little, Brown and Company
Hachette Book Group
1290 Avenue of the Americas, New York, NY 10104
Visit us at LBYR.com

First Edition: July 2021

Little, Brown and Company is a division of Hachette Book Group, Inc.
The Little, Brown name and logo are trademarks of Hachette Book Group, Inc.

The publisher is not responsible for websites (or their
content) that are not owned by the publisher.

Library of Congress Cataloging-in-Publication Data
Names: Crewes, Eleanor, author.
Title: Lilla the accidental witch / Eleanor Crewes.
Description: First edition. | New York: Little, Brown and Company, 2021. |
Summary: "Shy thirteen-year-old Lilla discovers a book of magic that reveals she is a witch,
but also draws the attention of an ancient evil hidden in the woods"-Provided by publisher.
Identifiers: LCCN 2020035366 | ISBN 9780316538848 (hardcover) | ISBN 9780316538824
(trade paperback) | ISBN 9780316538831 (ebook) | ISBN 9780759555792 (ebook other)
Subjects: CYAC: Graphic novels. | Witchcraft-Fiction. | Magic-Fiction. | Sisters-Fiction. |
Aunts-Fiction. | Sexual orientation-Fiction. | Graphic novels.
Classification: LCC PZ7.7.C746 Lil 2021 | DDC 741.5/973-dc23
LC record available at https://lccn.loc.gov/2020035366

ISBNs: 978-0-316-53884-8 (hardcover), 978-0-316-53882-4 (pbk.),
978-0-316-53883-1 (ebook), 978-0-7595-5580-8 (ebook), 978-0-7595-5582-2 (ebook)

PRINTED IN CHINA

1010

Hardcover: 10 9 8 7 6 5 4 3 2 1
Paperback: 10 9 8 7 6 5 4 3 2 1

For all witches x

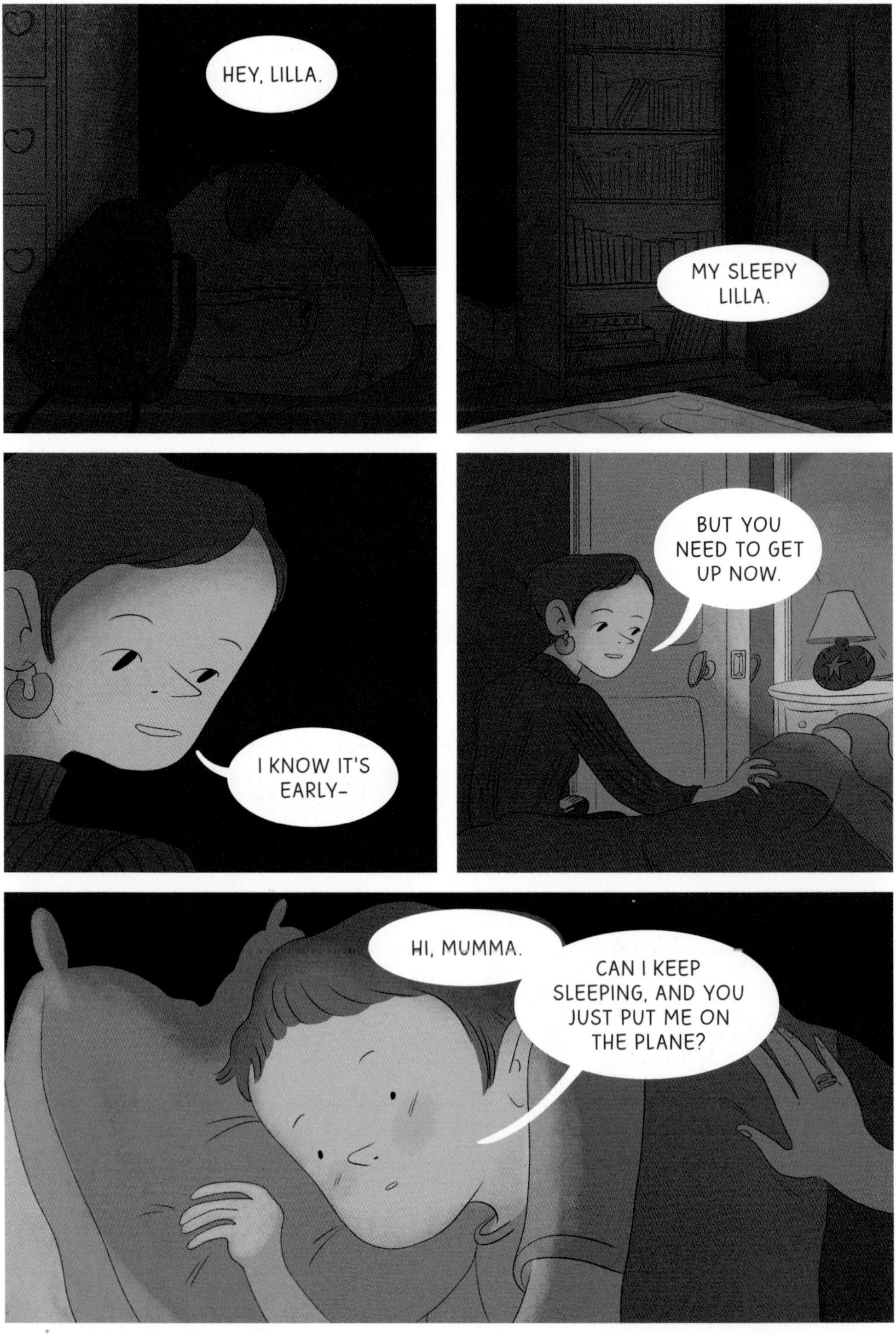
HEY, LILLA.
MY SLEEPY LILLA.
I KNOW IT'S EARLY-
BUT YOU NEED TO GET UP NOW.
HI, MUMMA.
CAN I KEEP SLEEPING, AND YOU JUST PUT ME ON THE PLANE?

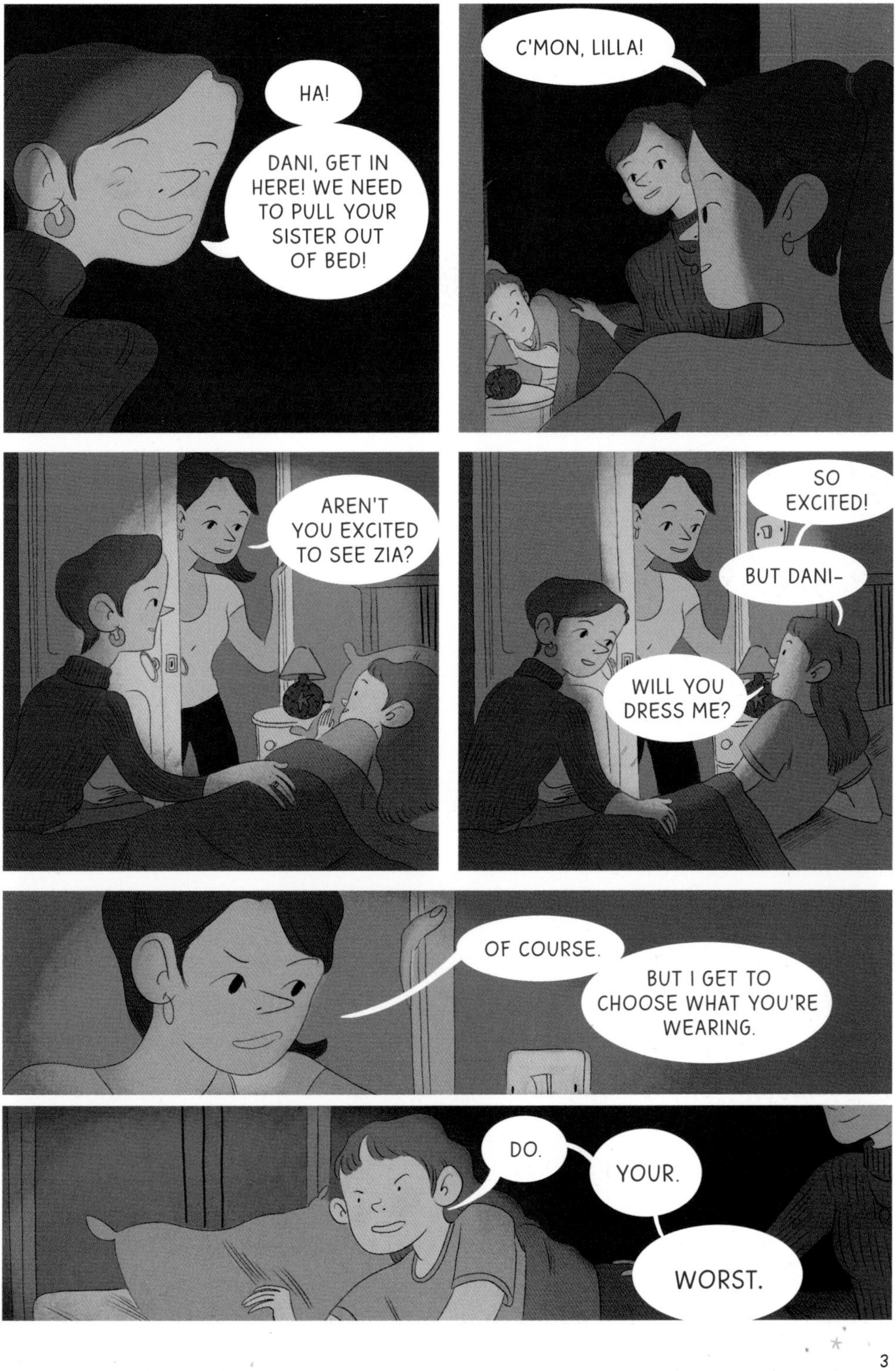
HA!
DANI, GET IN HERE! WE NEED TO PULL YOUR SISTER OUT OF BED!
C'MON, LILLA!
AREN'T YOU EXCITED TO SEE ZIA?
SO EXCITED!
BUT DANI-
WILL YOU DRESS ME?
OF COURSE.
BUT I GET TO CHOOSE WHAT YOU'RE WEARING.
DO.
YOUR.
WORST.

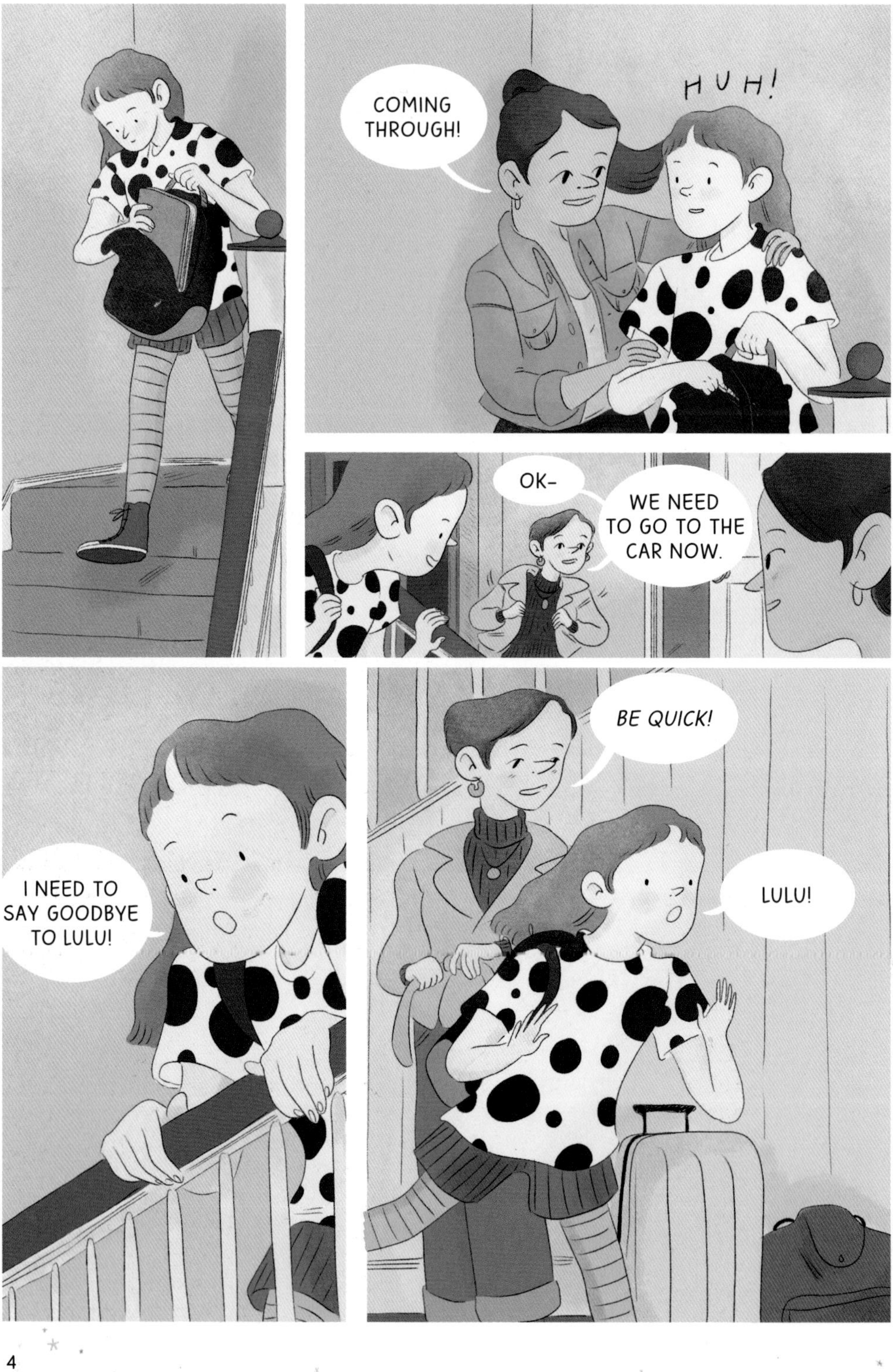
COMING THROUGH!
HUH!
OK-
WE NEED TO GO TO THE CAR NOW.
I NEED TO SAY GOODBYE TO LULU!
BE QUICK!
LULU!

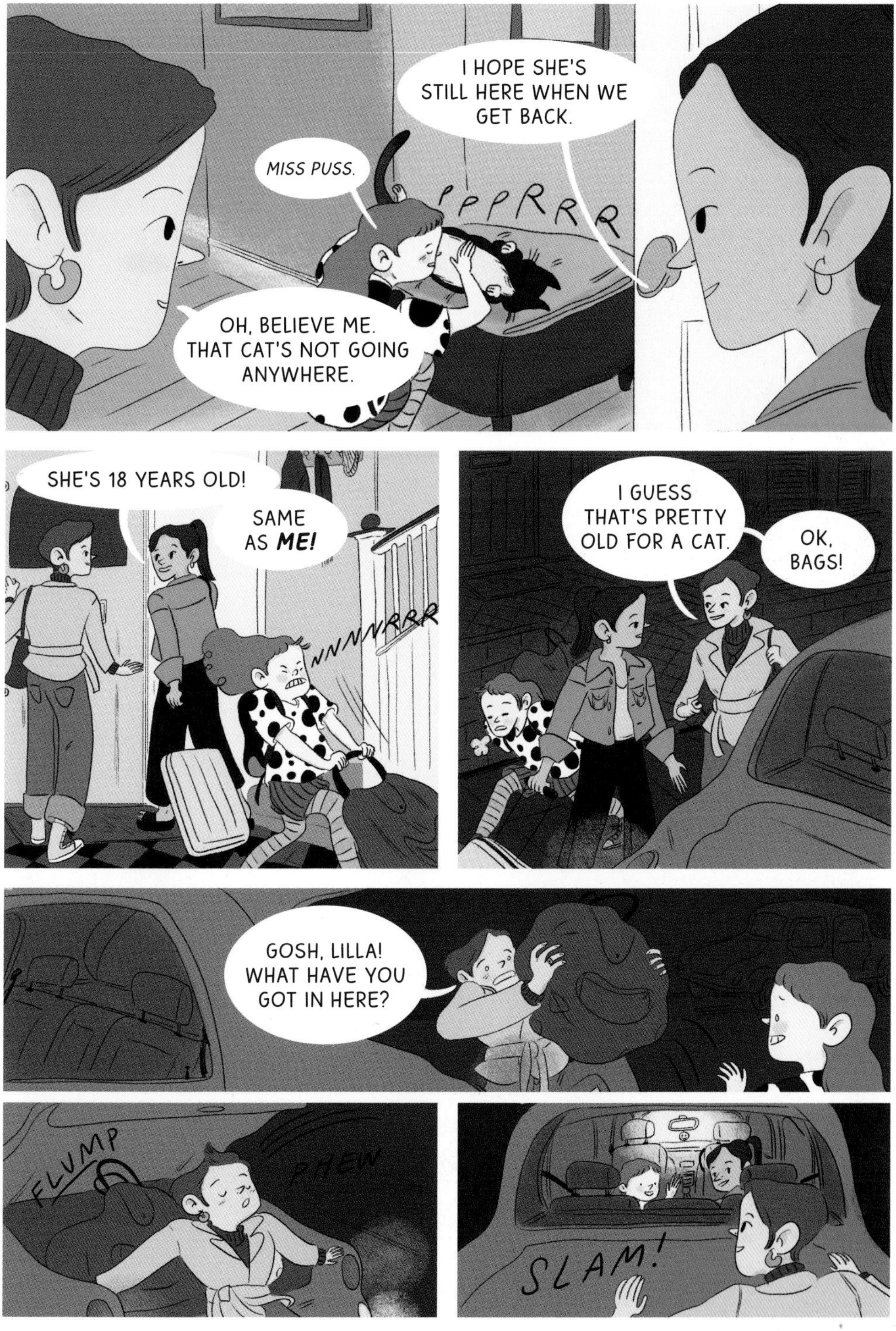
I HOPE SHE'S STILL HERE WHEN WE GET BACK.
MISS PUSS.
PPPRRRR
OH, BELIEVE ME. THAT CAT'S NOT GOING ANYWHERE.
SHE'S 18 YEARS OLD!
SAME AS ME!
NNNNNRRR
I GUESS THAT'S PRETTY OLD FOR A CAT.
OK, BAGS!
GOSH, LILLA! WHAT HAVE YOU GOT IN HERE?
FLUMP
PHEW
SLAM!

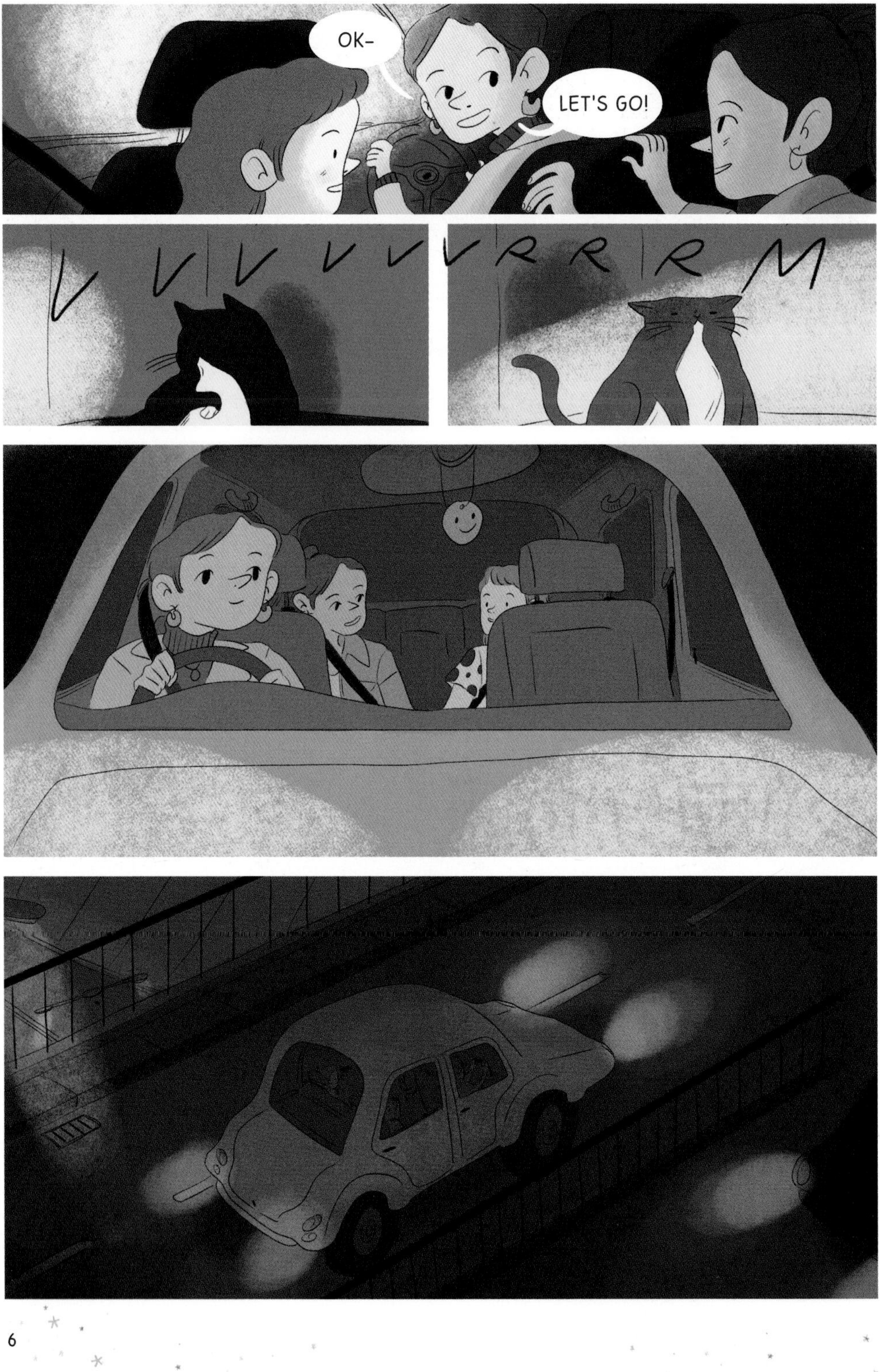
OK-
LET'S GO!
VVVVVVRRRRM

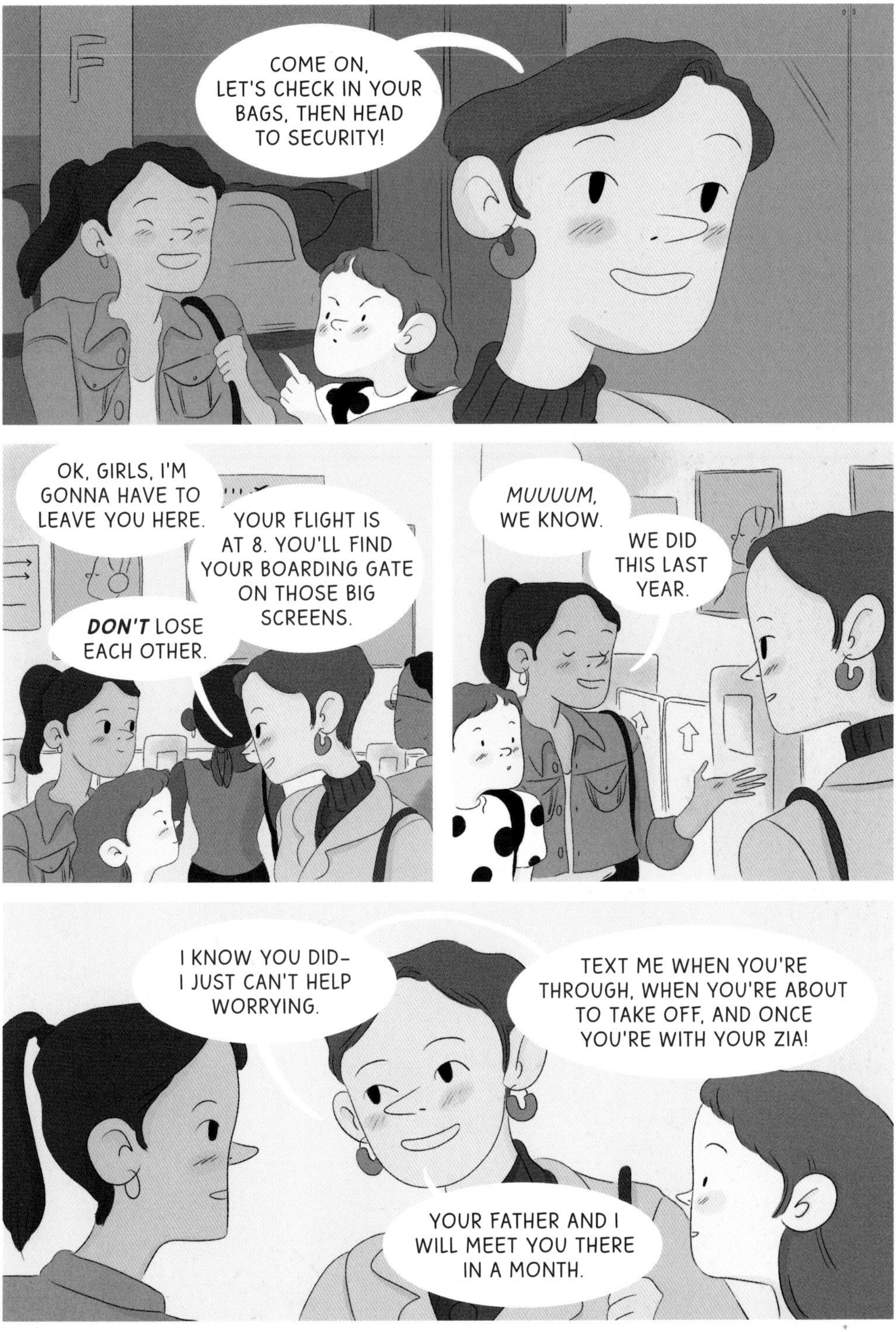
COME ON, LET'S CHECK IN YOUR BAGS, THEN HEAD TO SECURITY!
OK, GIRLS, I'M GONNA HAVE TO LEAVE YOU HERE.
YOUR FLIGHT IS AT 8. YOU'LL FIND YOUR BOARDING GATE ON THOSE BIG SCREENS.
DON'T LOSE EACH OTHER.
MUUUUM, WE KNOW.
WE DID THIS LAST YEAR.
I KNOW YOU DID-I JUST CAN'T HELP WORRYING.
TEXT ME WHEN YOU'RE THROUGH, WHEN YOU'RE ABOUT TO TAKE OFF, AND ONCE YOU'RE WITH YOUR ZIA!
YOUR FATHER AND I WILL MEET YOU THERE IN A MONTH.

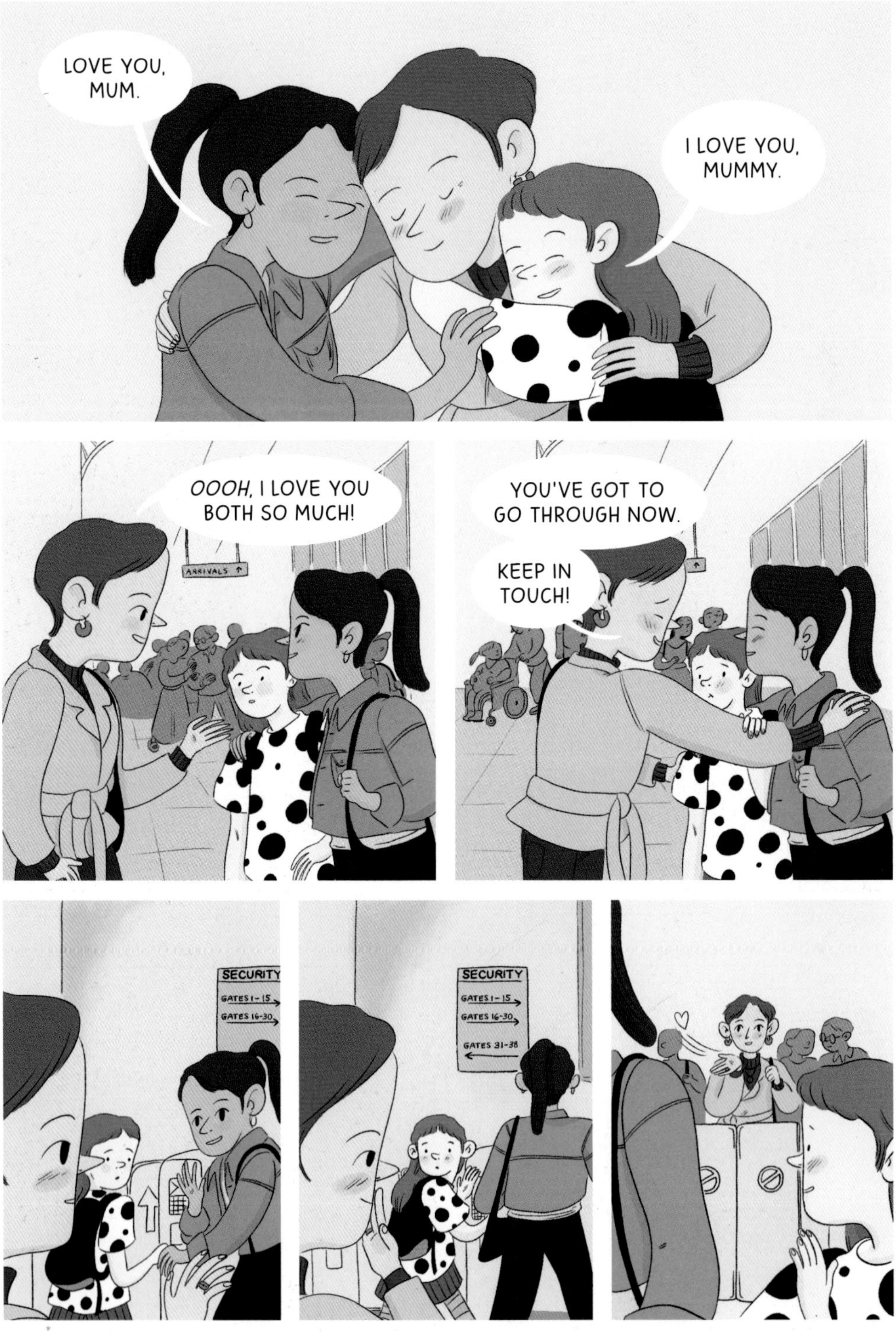
LOVE YOU, MUM.
I LOVE YOU, MUMMY.
OOOH, I LOVE YOU BOTH SO MUCH!
ARRIVALS
YOU'VE GOT TO GO THROUGH NOW.
KEEP IN TOUCH!
SECURITY
GATES 1-15
GATES 16-30
SECURITY
GATES 1-15
GATES 16-30
GATES 31-38

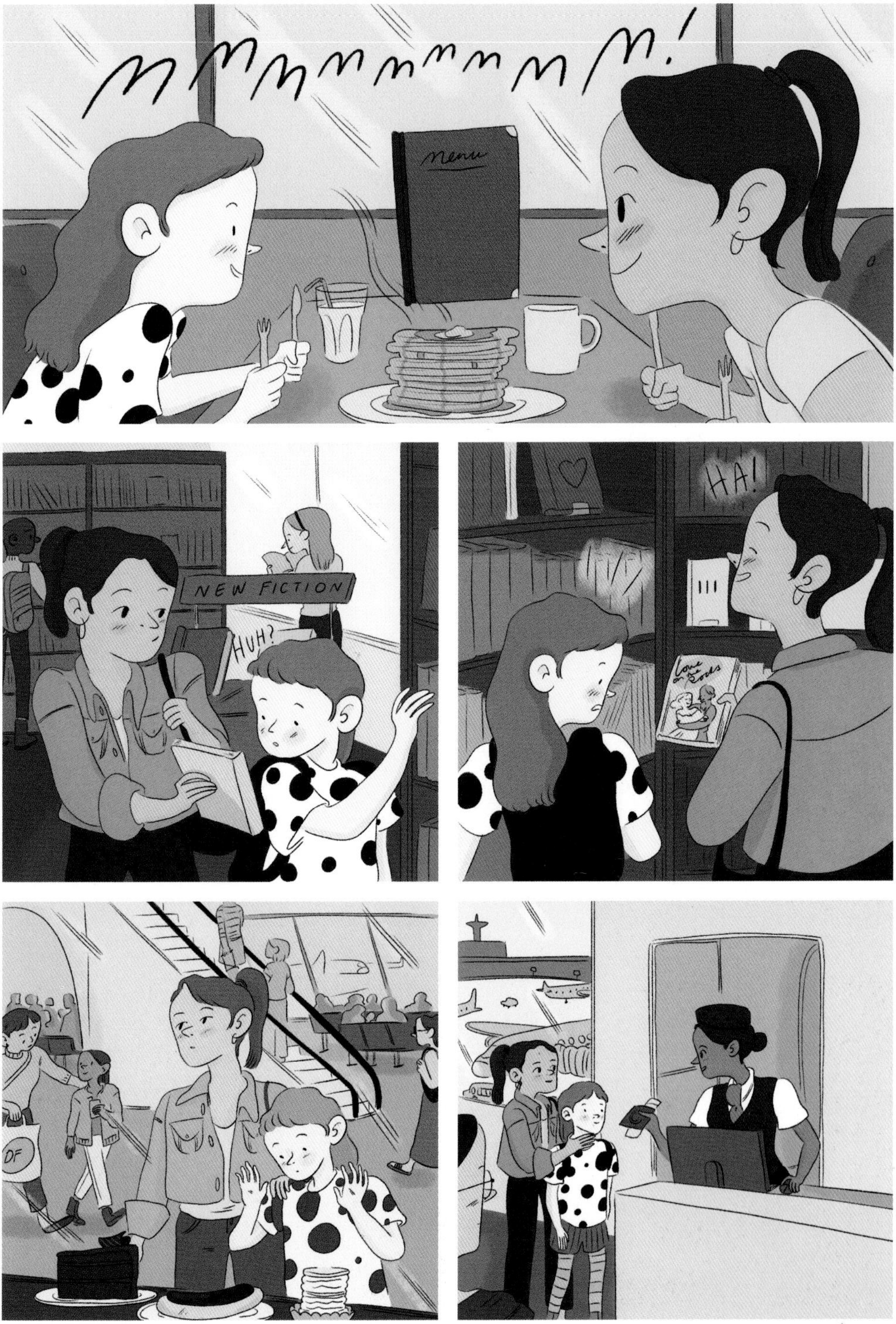
MMMmmmmMM!
menu
NEW FICTION
HUH?
HA!
Love on the Rocks
DF

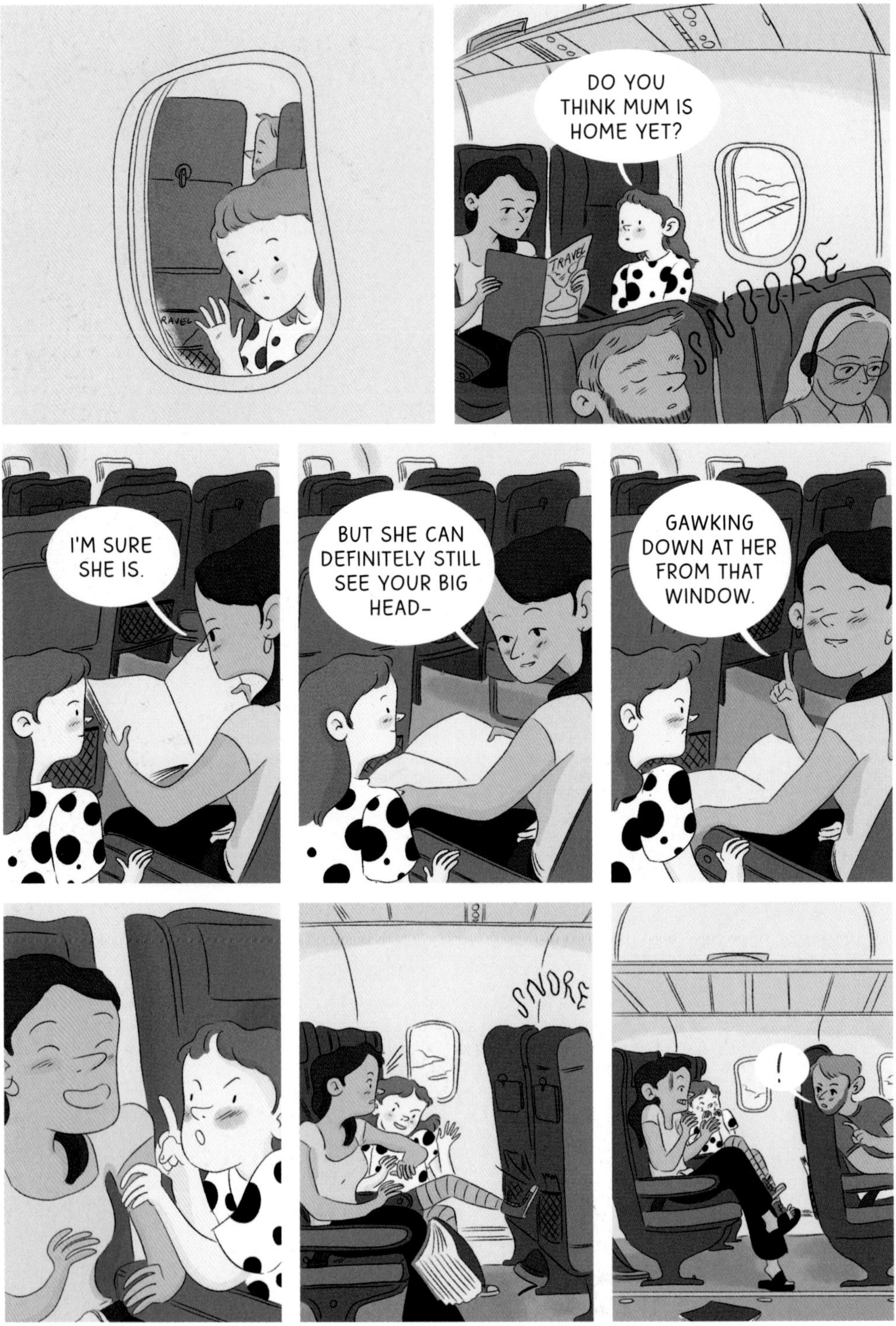
RAVEL
DO YOU THINK MUM IS HOME YET?
TRAVEL
SNOORE
I'M SURE SHE IS.
BUT SHE CAN DEFINITELY STILL SEE YOUR BIG HEAD-
GAWKING DOWN AT HER FROM THAT WINDOW.
SNORE
!

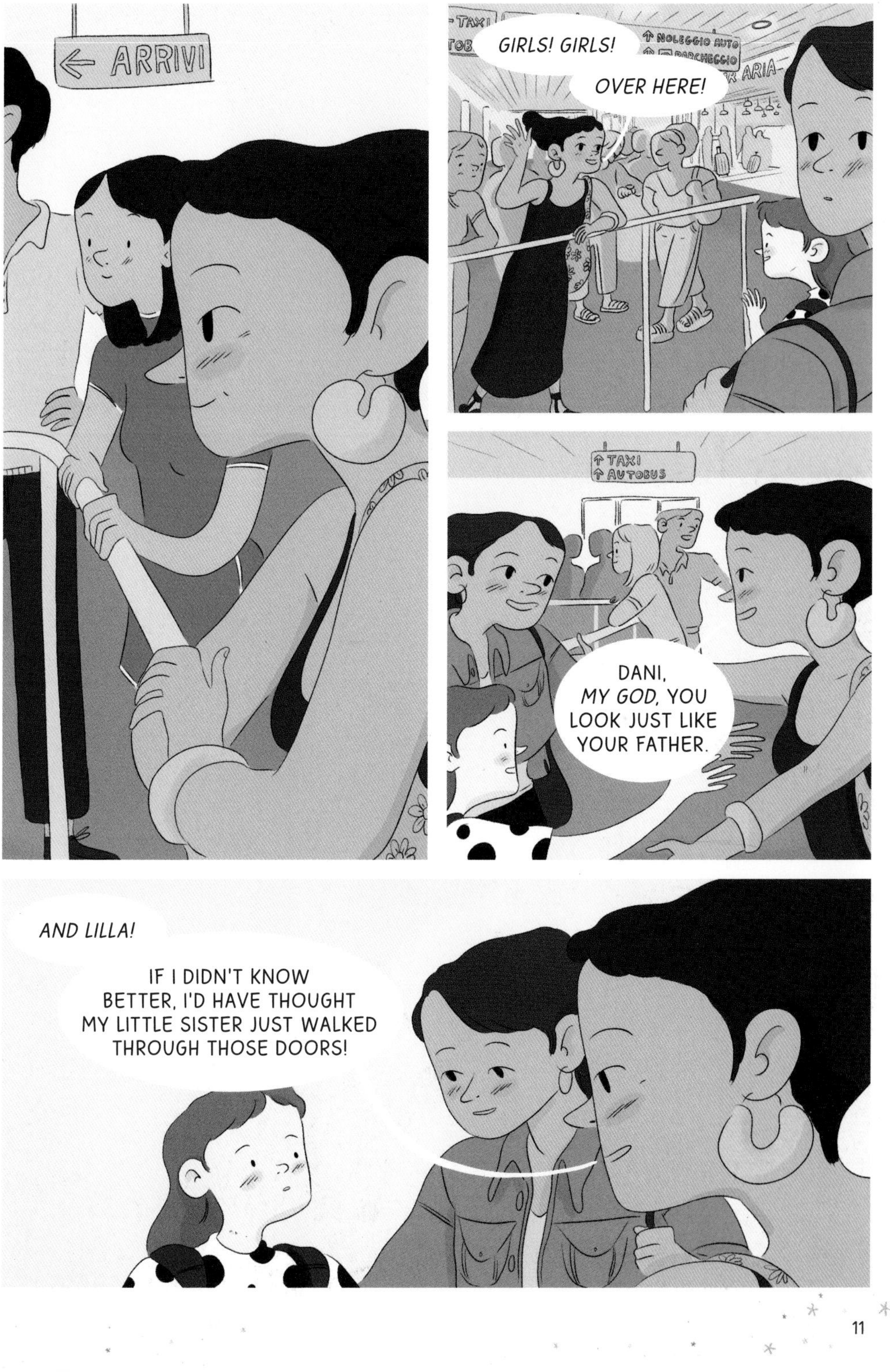
ARRIVI
GIRLS! GIRLS!
OVER HERE!
NOLEGGIO AUTO
TAXI
AUTOBUS
DANI, *MY GOD,* YOU LOOK JUST LIKE YOUR FATHER.
AND LILLA!
IF I DIDN'T KNOW BETTER, I'D HAVE THOUGHT MY LITTLE SISTER JUST WALKED THROUGH THOSE DOORS!

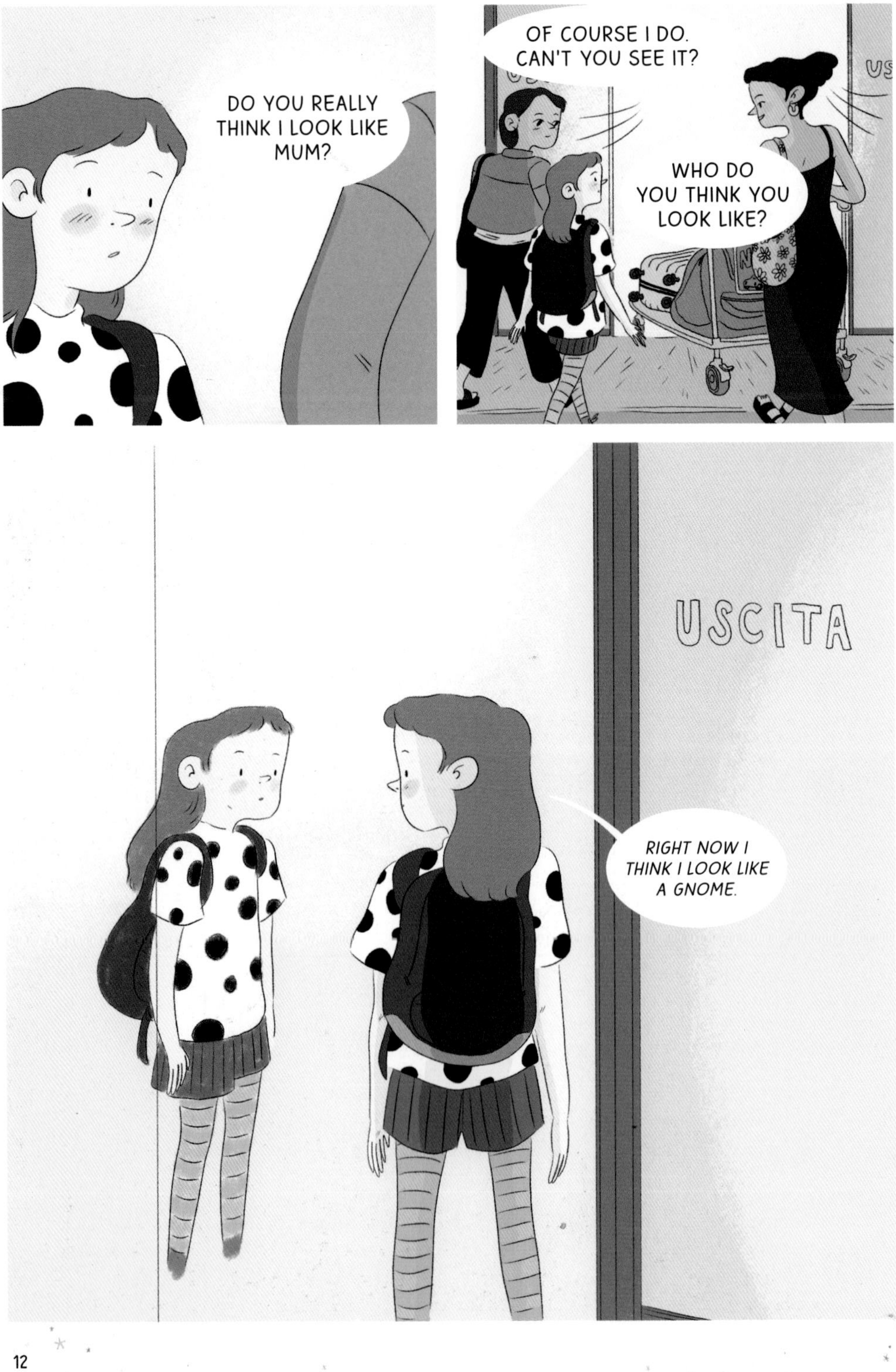
DO YOU REALLY THINK I LOOK LIKE MUM?
OF COURSE I DO. CAN'T YOU SEE IT?
WHO DO YOU THINK YOU LOOK LIKE?
USCITA
RIGHT NOW I THINK I LOOK LIKE A GNOME.

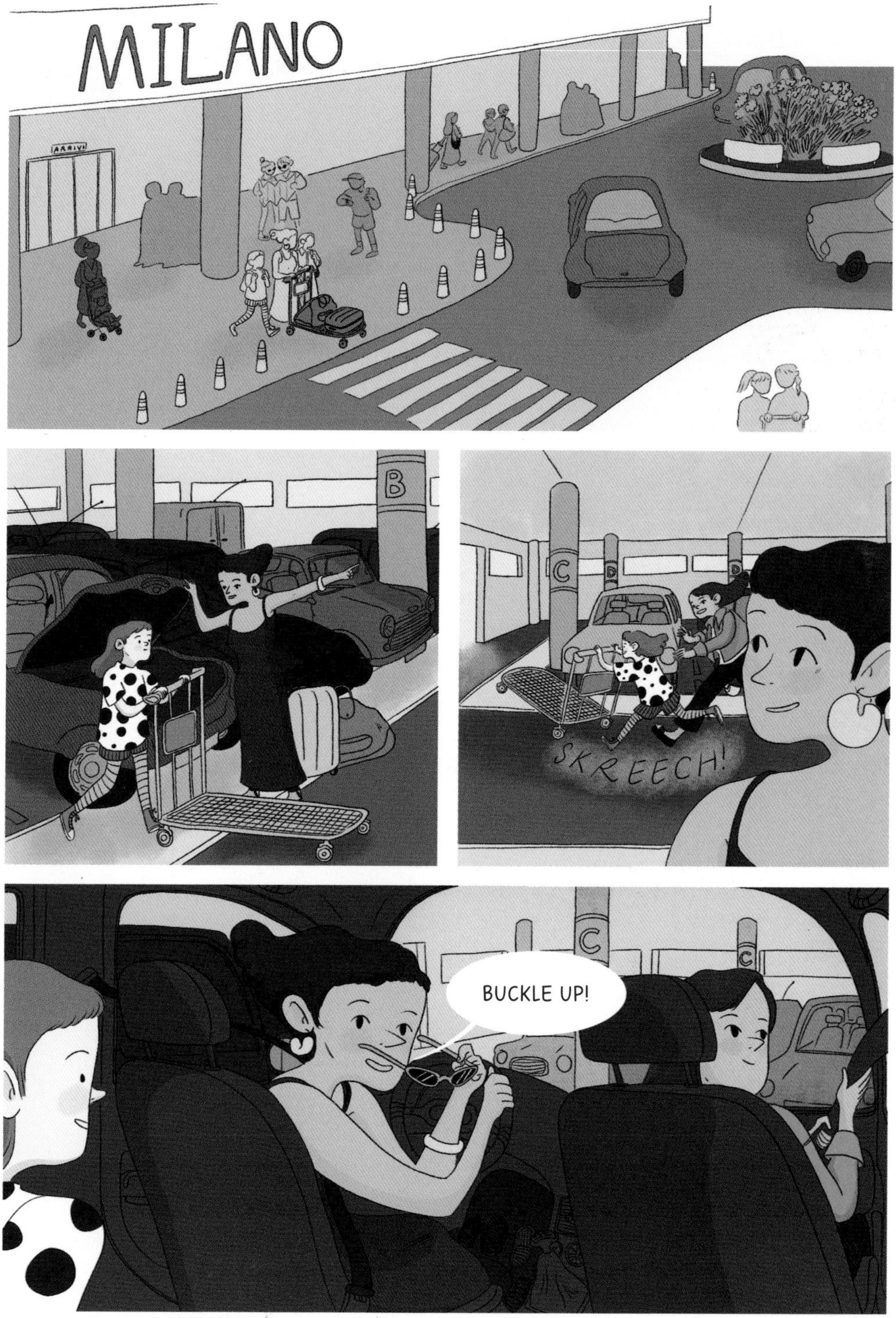
MILANO
ARRIVI
B
C
D
SKREECH!
BUCKLE UP!

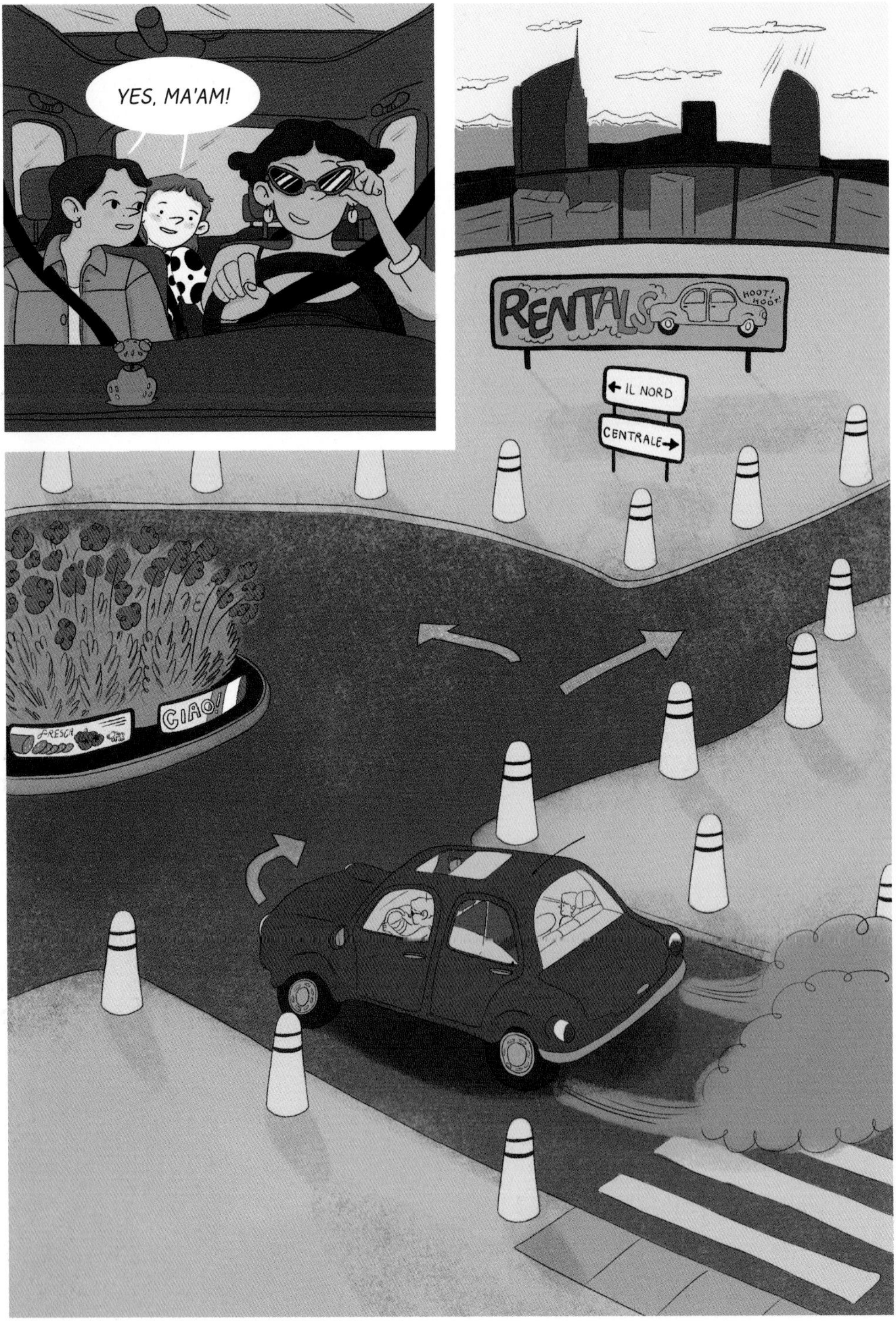
YES, MA'AM!
RENTALS
HOOT! HOOT!
IL NORD
CENTRALE
CIAO!
FRESCA

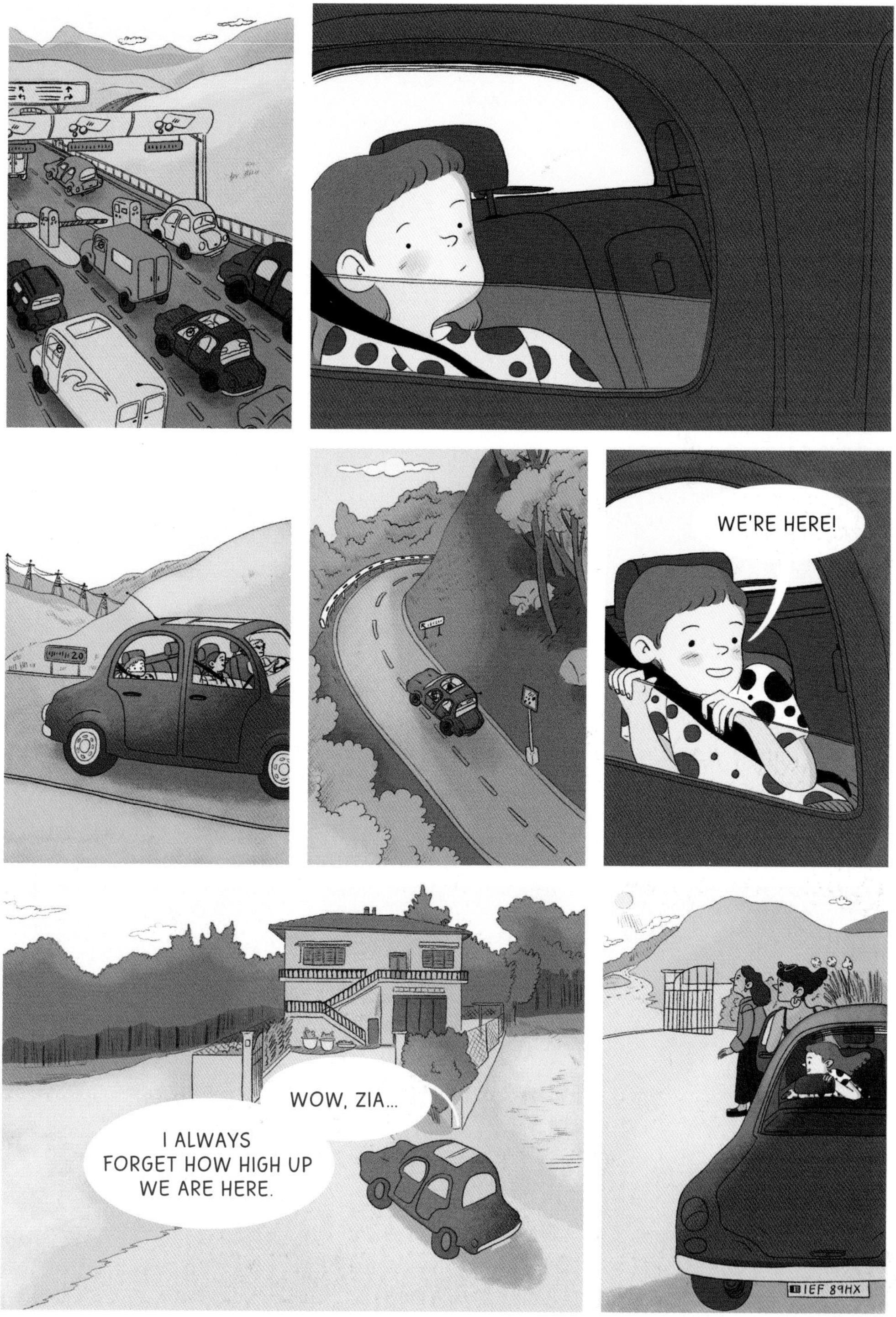
WE'RE HERE!
WOW, ZIA...
I ALWAYS FORGET HOW HIGH UP WE ARE HERE.
IEF 89HX

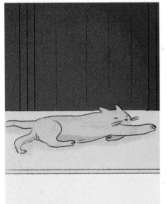

OH MY GOSH!

LOOK AT THAT CAT!

IT'S MORRIGAN!

MORRIGAN?

HE'S MY FRIEND.

I FEED HIM EVERY NOW AND THEN. AND SOMETIMES—WHEN ZIO ISN'T HERE—I LET HIM COME INSIDE THE HOUSE.

HA!

HI, MORRIGAN.

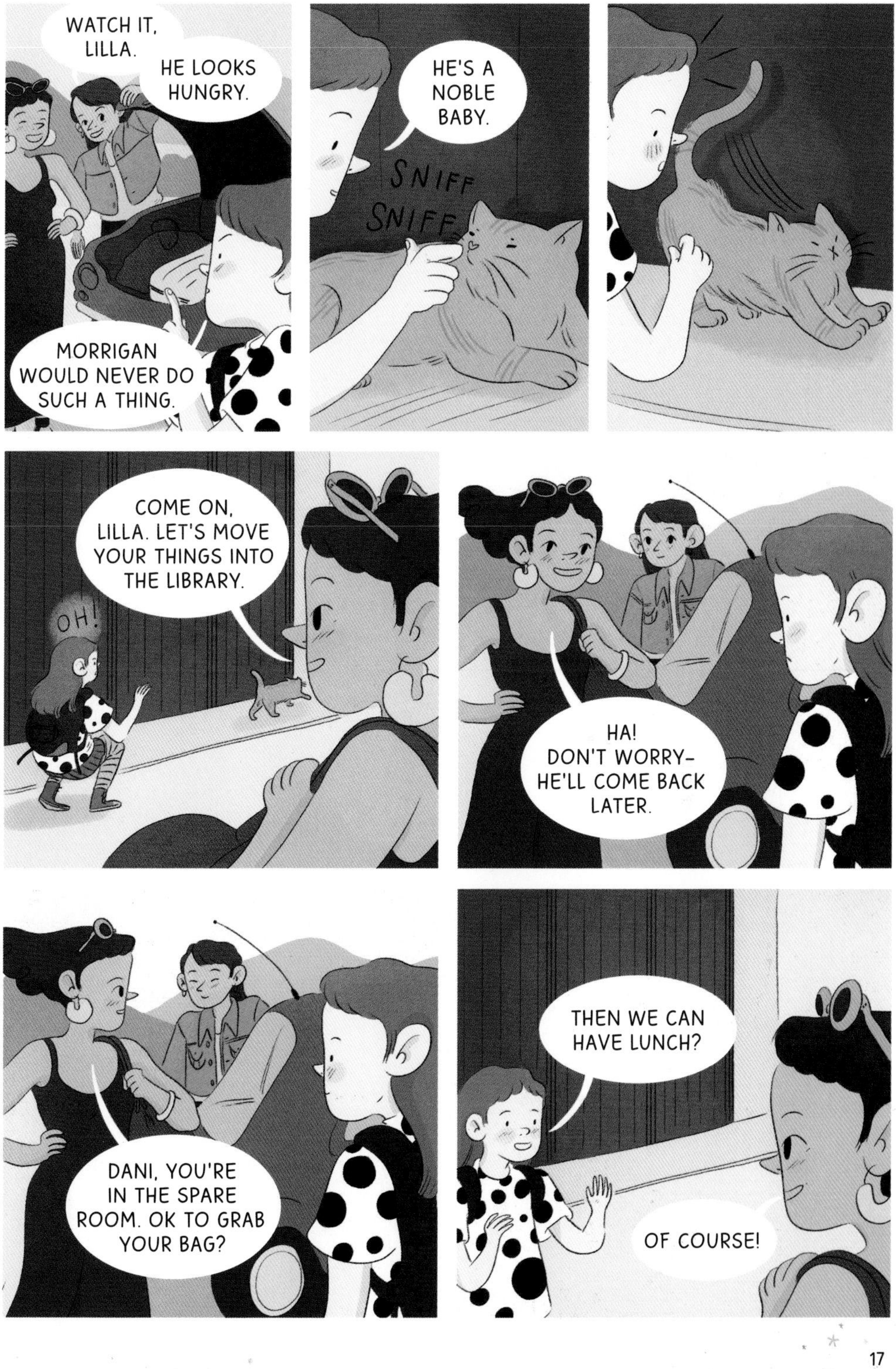
WATCH IT, LILLA.
HE LOOKS HUNGRY.
MORRIGAN WOULD NEVER DO SUCH A THING.
HE'S A NOBLE BABY.
SNIFF SNIFF
COME ON, LILLA. LET'S MOVE YOUR THINGS INTO THE LIBRARY.
OH!
HA! DON'T WORRY- HE'LL COME BACK LATER.
DANI, YOU'RE IN THE SPARE ROOM. OK TO GRAB YOUR BAG?
THEN WE CAN HAVE LUNCH?
OF COURSE!

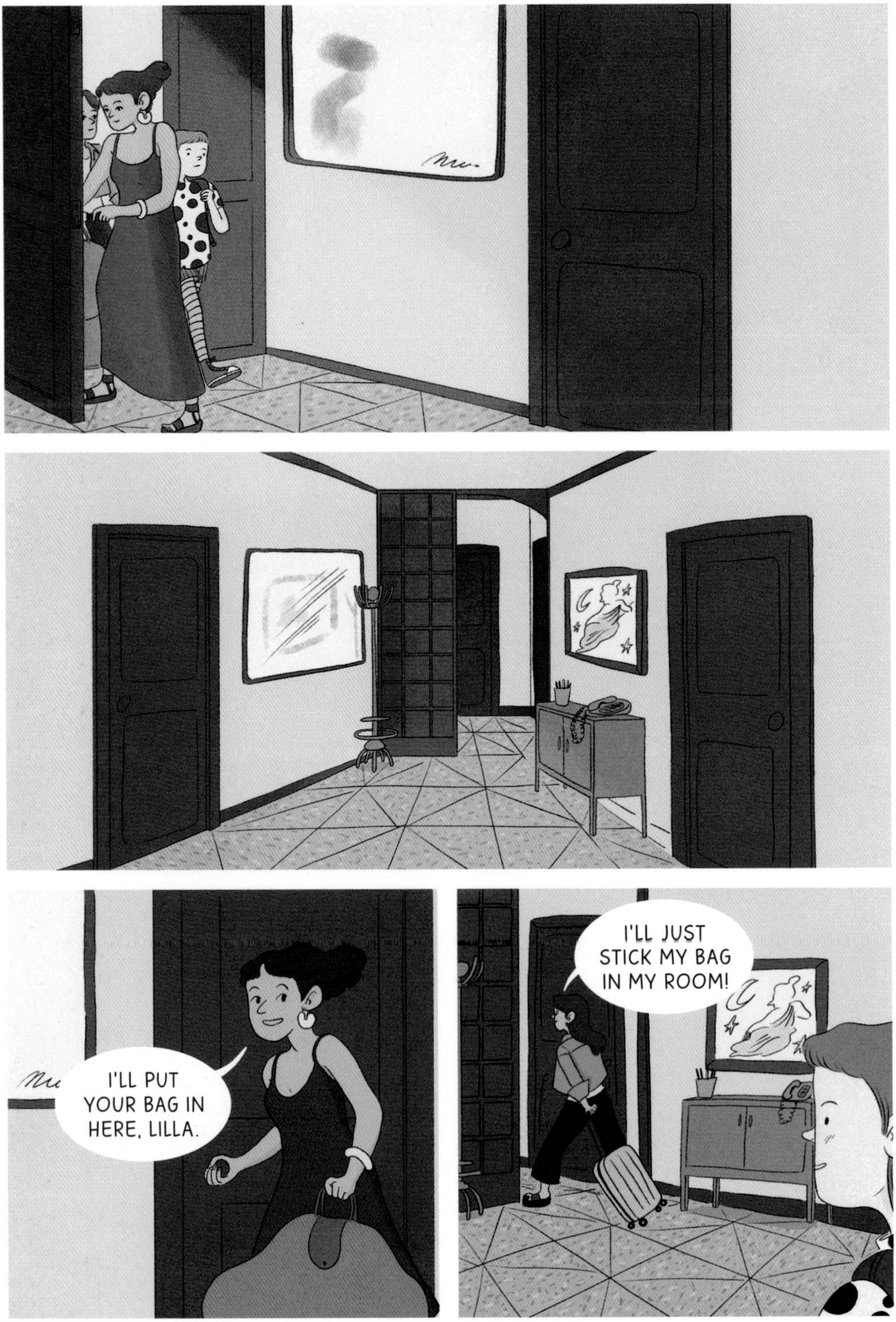

I'LL PUT YOUR BAG IN HERE, LILLA.
I'LL JUST STICK MY BAG IN MY ROOM!

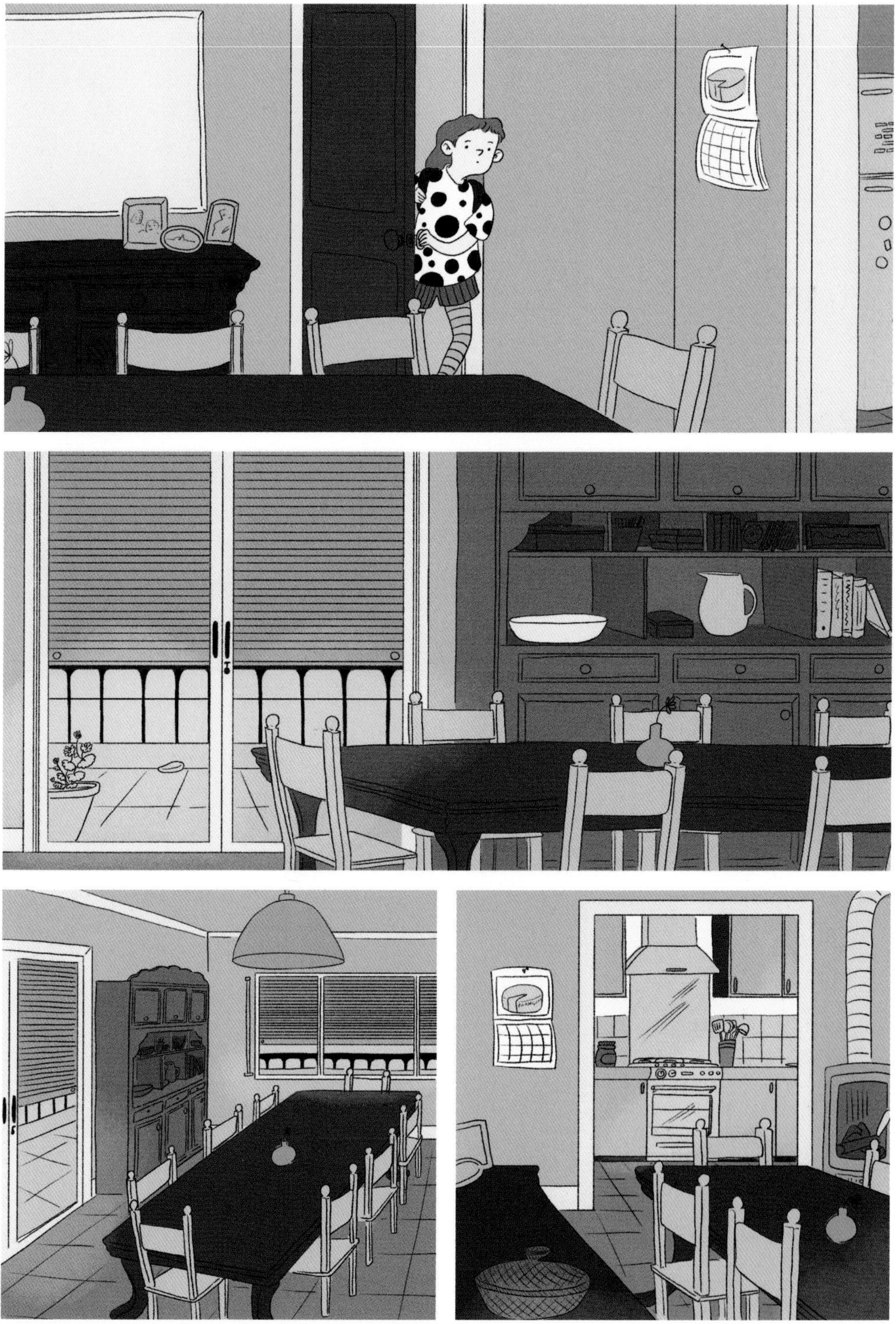

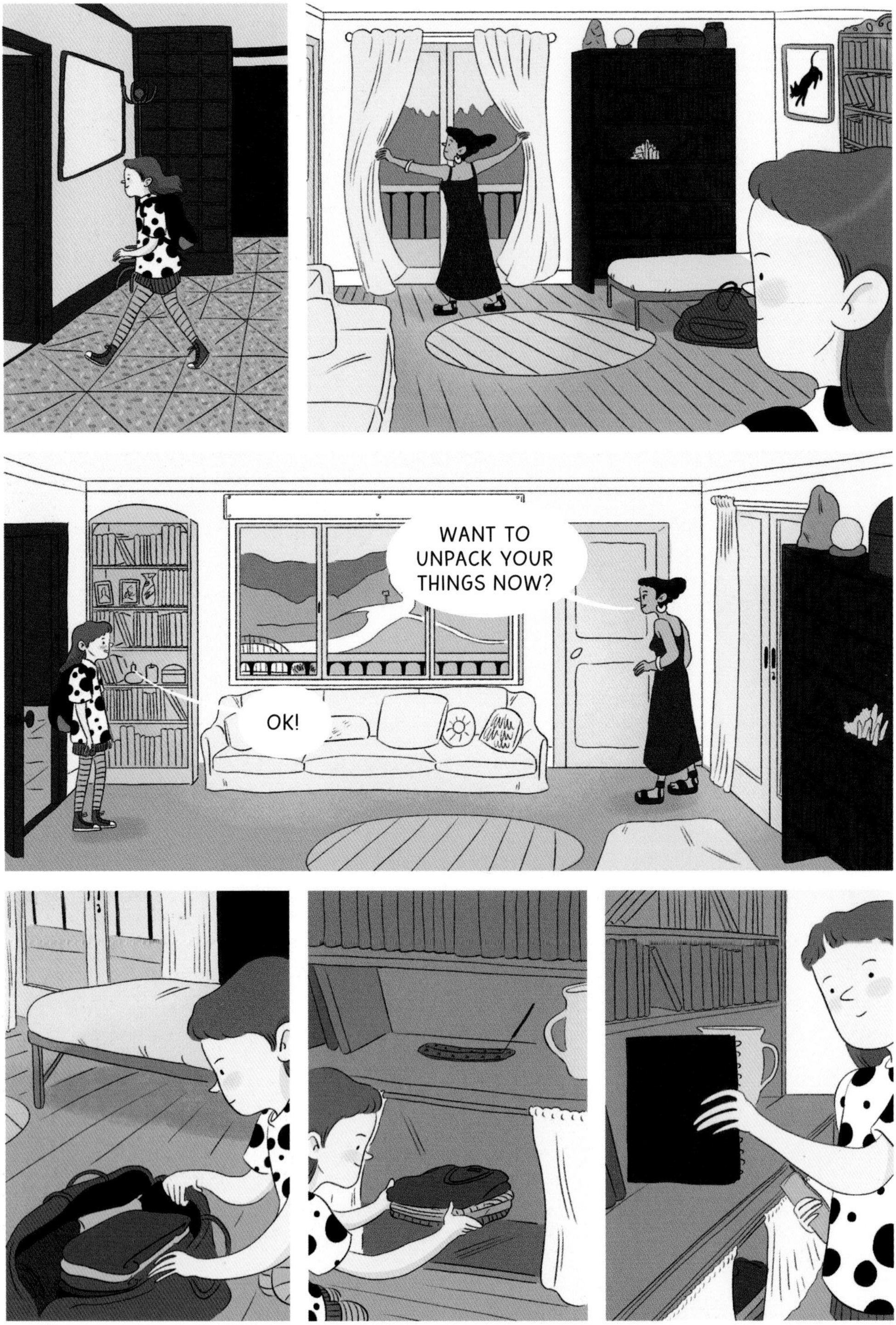
WANT TO UNPACK YOUR THINGS NOW?
OK!

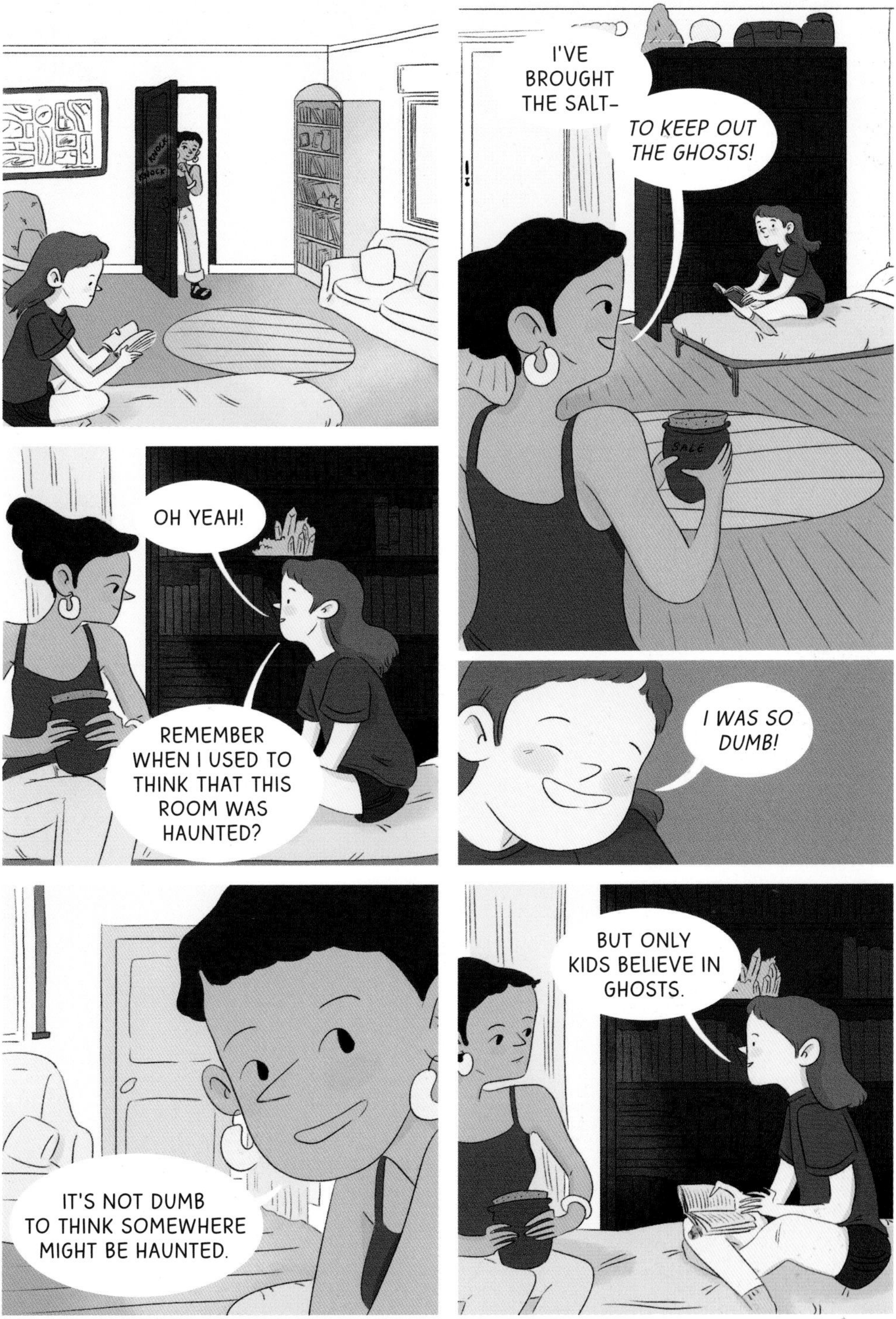
KNOCK
KNOCK
I'VE BROUGHT THE SALT-
TO KEEP OUT THE GHOSTS!
SALE
OH YEAH!
REMEMBER WHEN I USED TO THINK THAT THIS ROOM WAS HAUNTED?
I WAS SO DUMB!
IT'S NOT DUMB TO THINK SOMEWHERE MIGHT BE HAUNTED.
BUT ONLY KIDS BELIEVE IN GHOSTS.

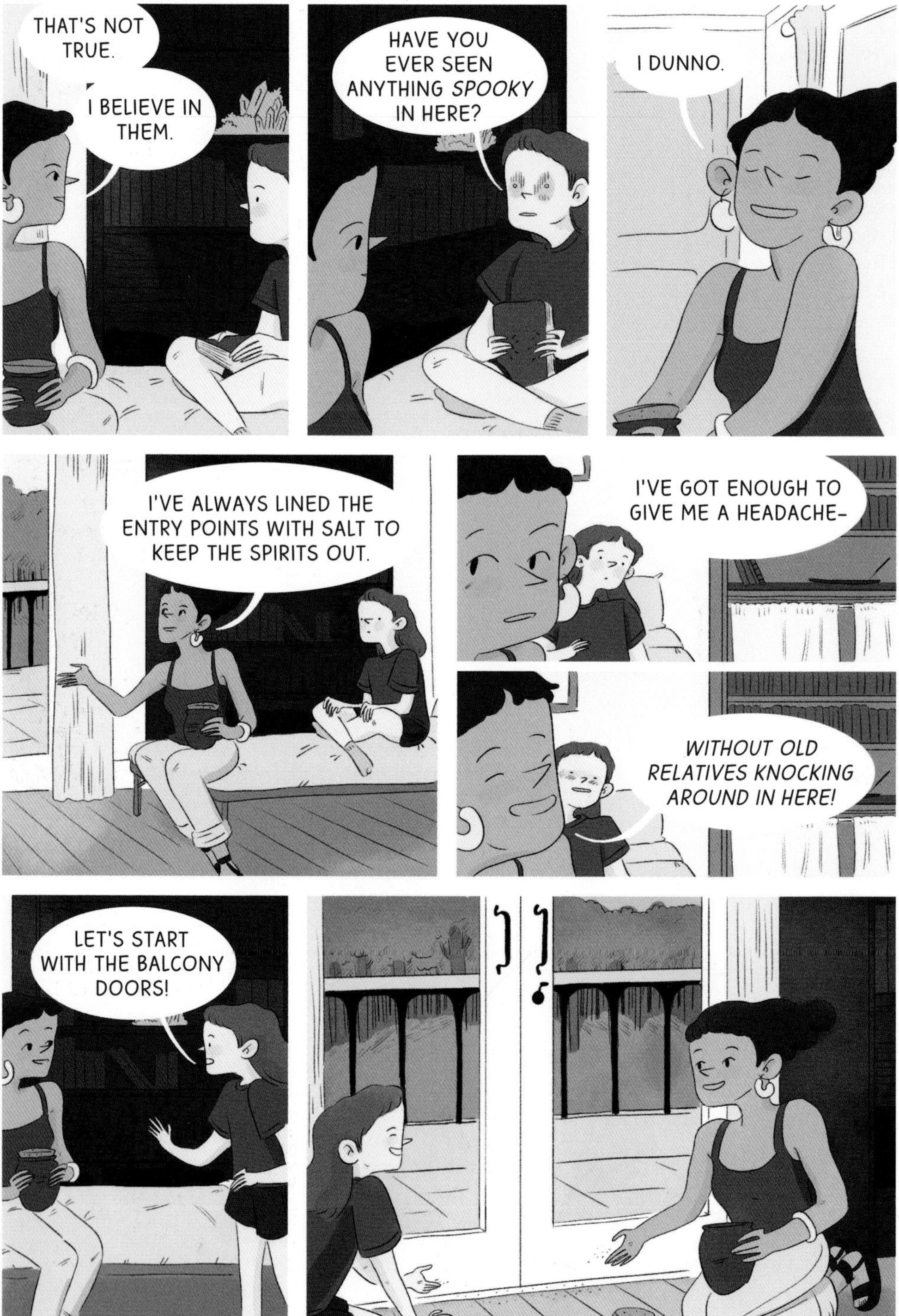
THAT'S NOT TRUE.
I BELIEVE IN THEM.
HAVE YOU EVER SEEN ANYTHING *SPOOKY* IN HERE?
I DUNNO.
I'VE ALWAYS LINED THE ENTRY POINTS WITH SALT TO KEEP THE SPIRITS OUT.
I'VE GOT ENOUGH TO GIVE ME A HEADACHE-
WITHOUT OLD RELATIVES KNOCKING AROUND IN HERE!
LET'S START WITH THE BALCONY DOORS!

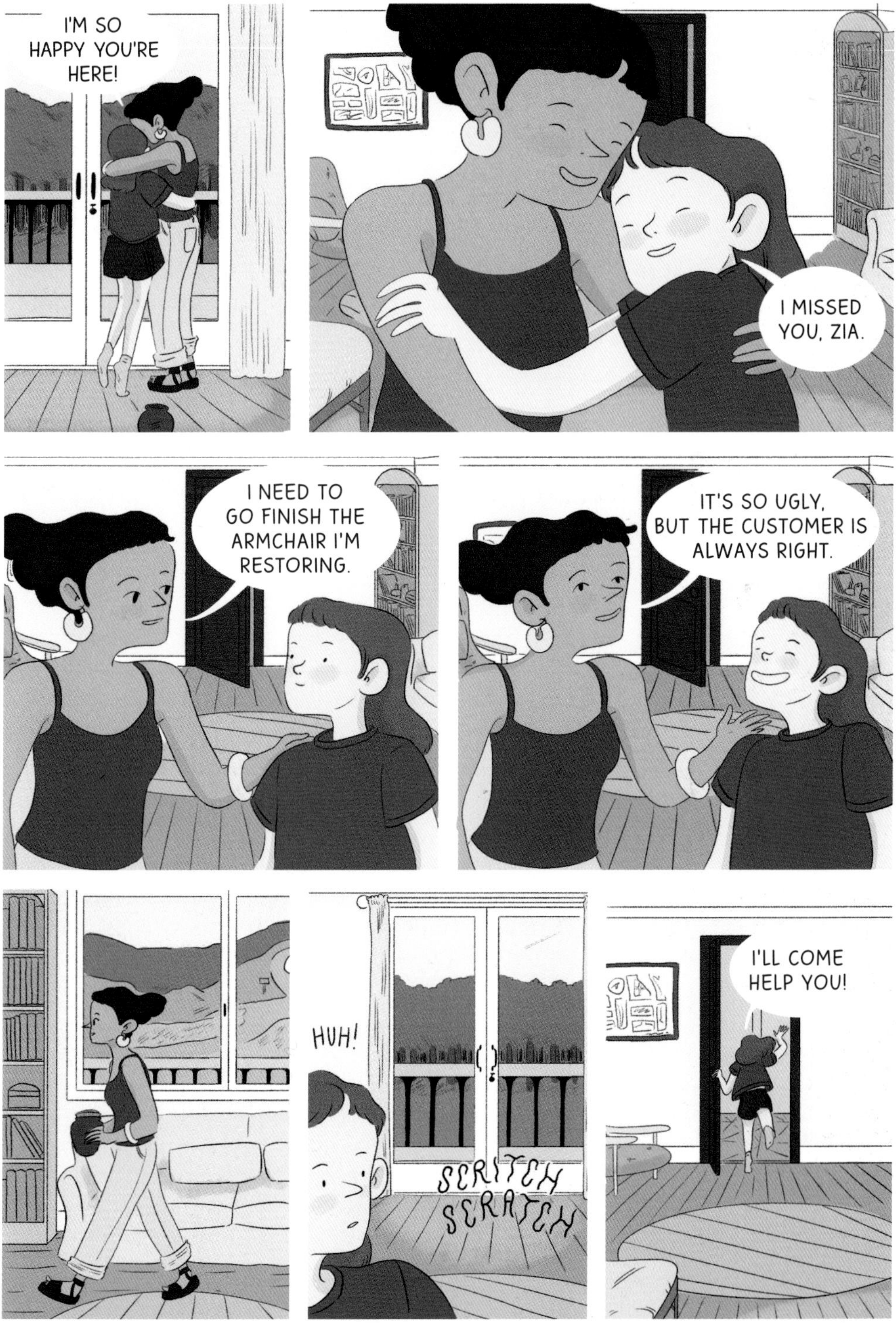
I'M SO HAPPY YOU'RE HERE!
I MISSED YOU, ZIA.
I NEED TO GO FINISH THE ARMCHAIR I'M RESTORING.
IT'S SO UGLY, BUT THE CUSTOMER IS ALWAYS RIGHT.
HUH!
SCRITCH SCRATCH
I'LL COME HELP YOU!

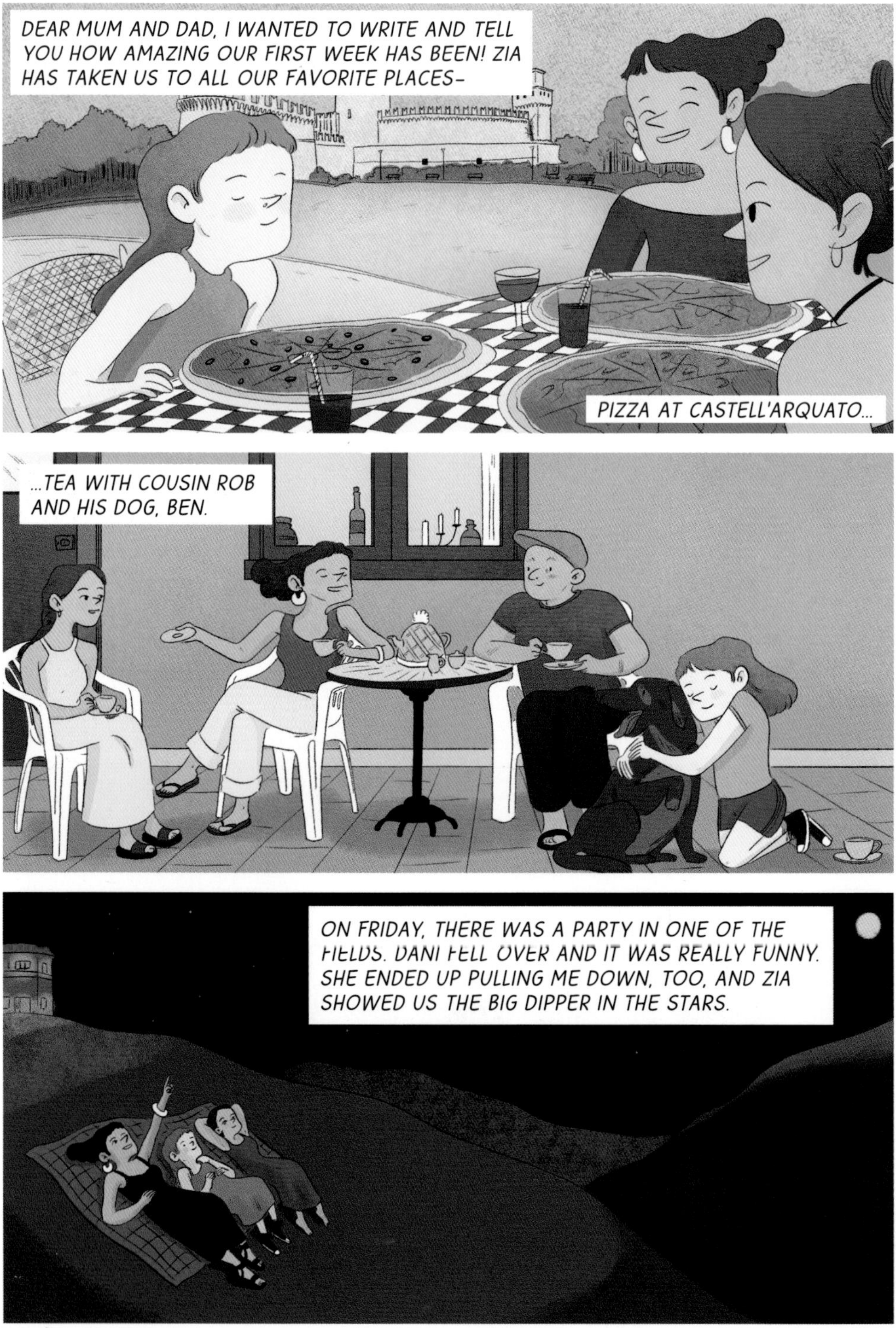

DEAR MUM AND DAD, I WANTED TO WRITE AND TELL YOU HOW AMAZING OUR FIRST WEEK HAS BEEN! ZIA HAS TAKEN US TO ALL OUR FAVORITE PLACES–
PIZZA AT CASTELL'ARQUATO...
...TEA WITH COUSIN ROB AND HIS DOG, BEN.
ON FRIDAY, THERE WAS A PARTY IN ONE OF THE FIELDS. DANI FELL OVER AND IT WAS REALLY FUNNY. SHE ENDED UP PULLING ME DOWN, TOO, AND ZIA SHOWED US THE BIG DIPPER IN THE STARS.

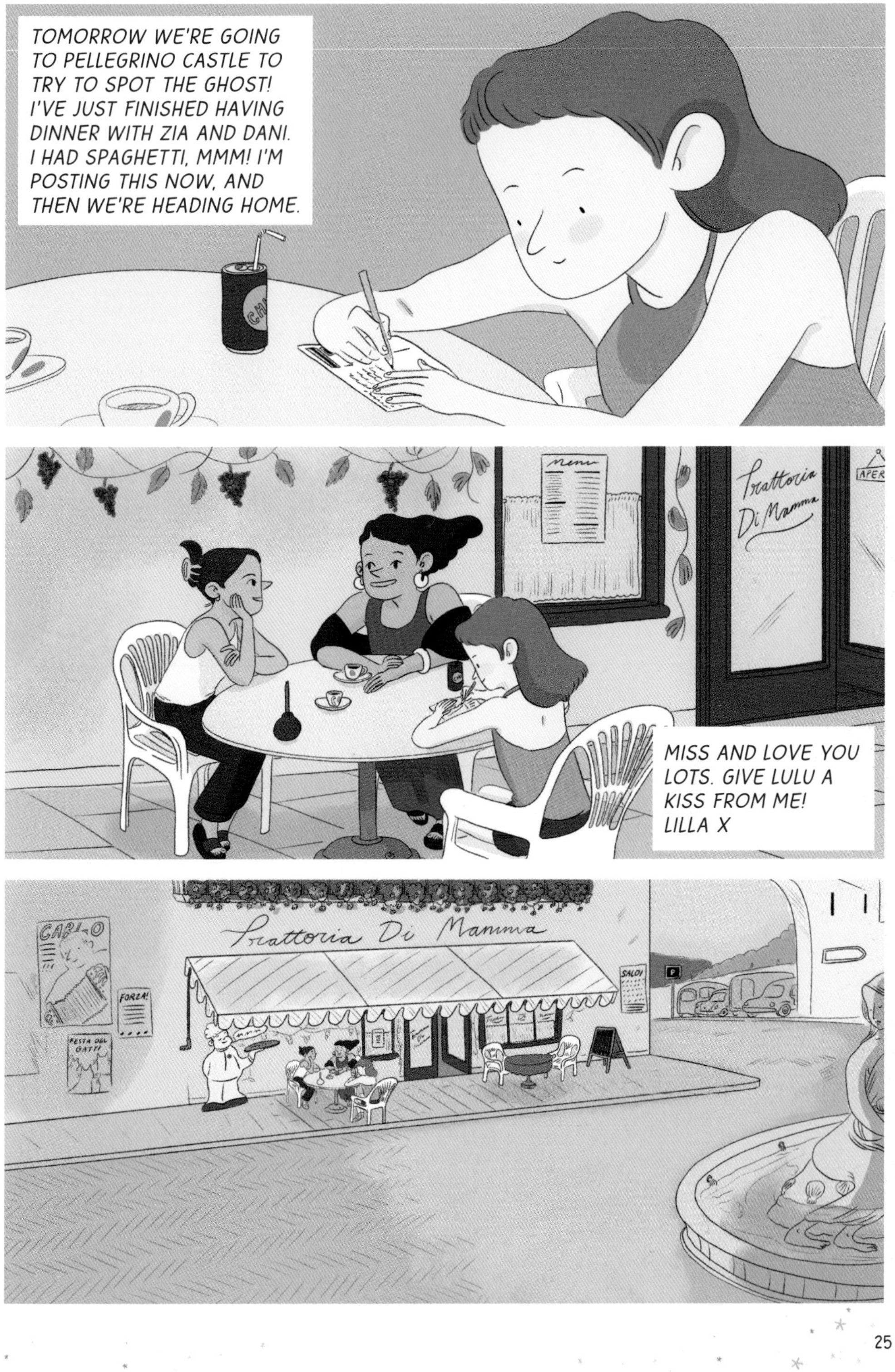
TOMORROW WE'RE GOING TO PELLEGRINO CASTLE TO TRY TO SPOT THE GHOST! I'VE JUST FINISHED HAVING DINNER WITH ZIA AND DANI. I HAD SPAGHETTI, MMM! I'M POSTING THIS NOW, AND THEN WE'RE HEADING HOME.
Trattoria Di Mamma
MISS AND LOVE YOU LOTS. GIVE LULU A KISS FROM ME! LILLA X
Trattoria Di Mamma

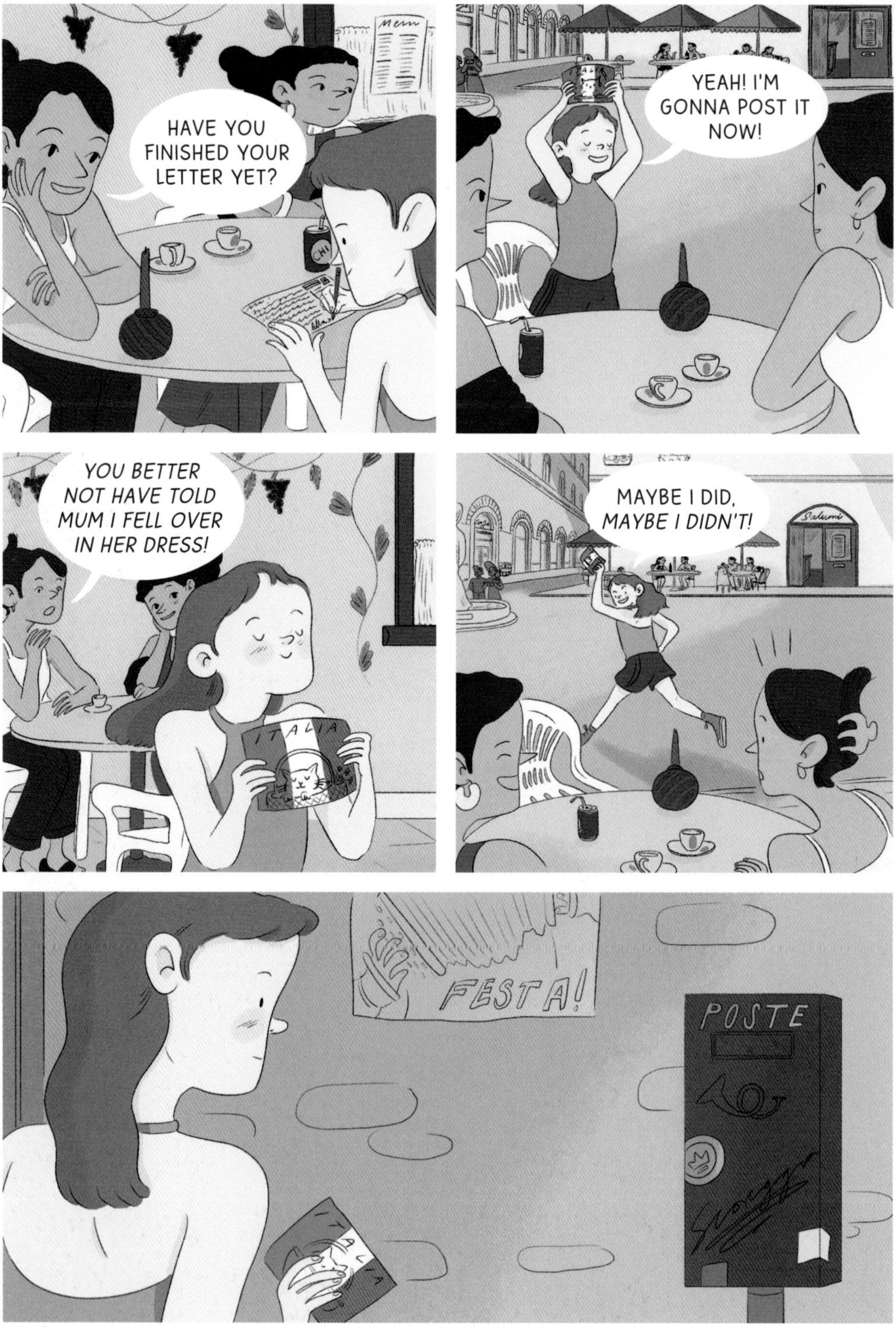
HAVE YOU FINISHED YOUR LETTER YET?
YEAH! I'M GONNA POST IT NOW!
YOU BETTER NOT HAVE TOLD MUM I FELL OVER IN HER DRESS!
ITALIA
MAYBE I DID, MAYBE I DIDN'T!
Salumi
FESTA!
POSTE

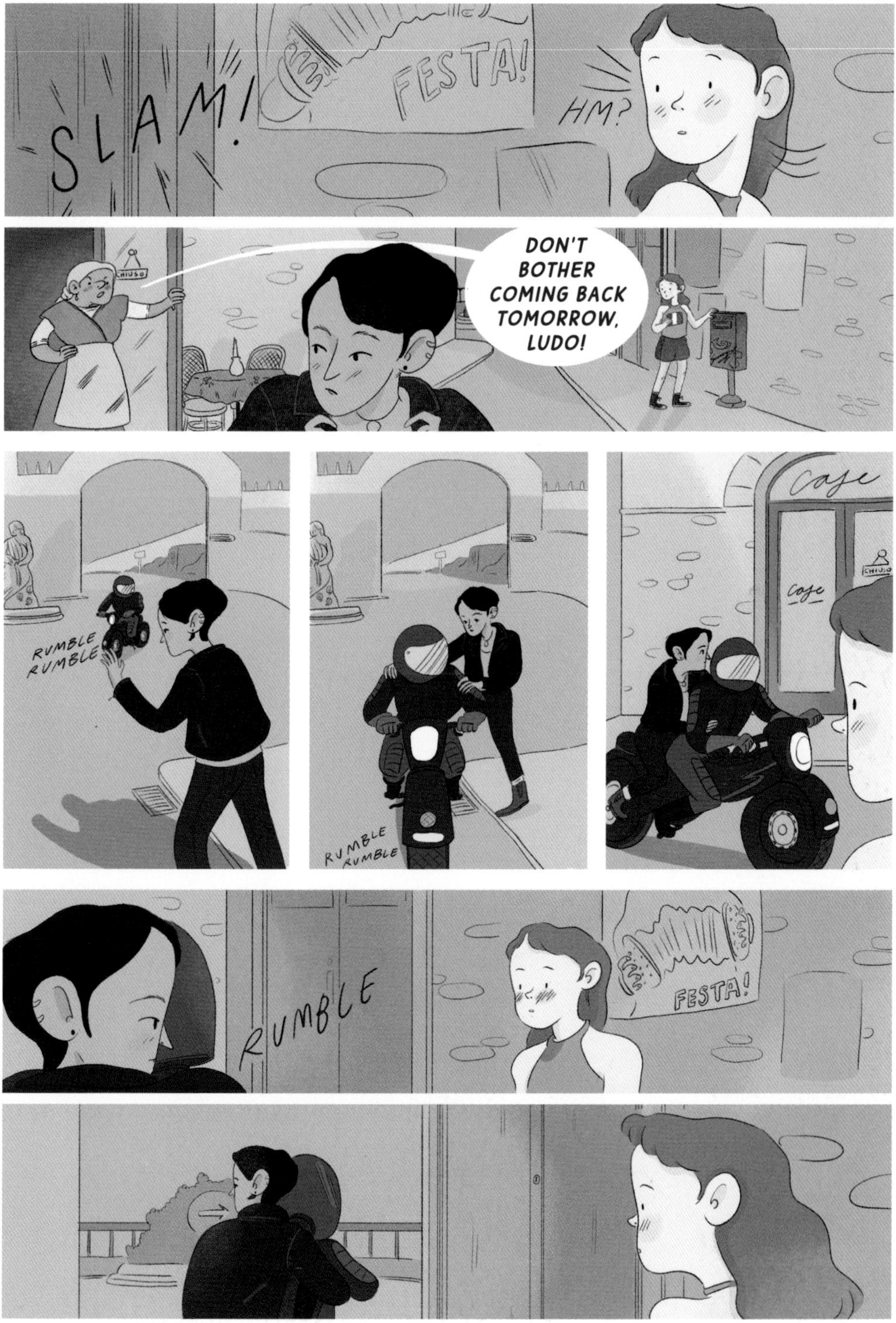
SLAM!
FESTA!
HM?
CHIUSO
DON'T BOTHER COMING BACK TOMORROW, LUDO!
RUMBLE RUMBLE
RUMBLE RUMBLE
CAFE
CAFE
CHIUSO
RUMBLE
FESTA!

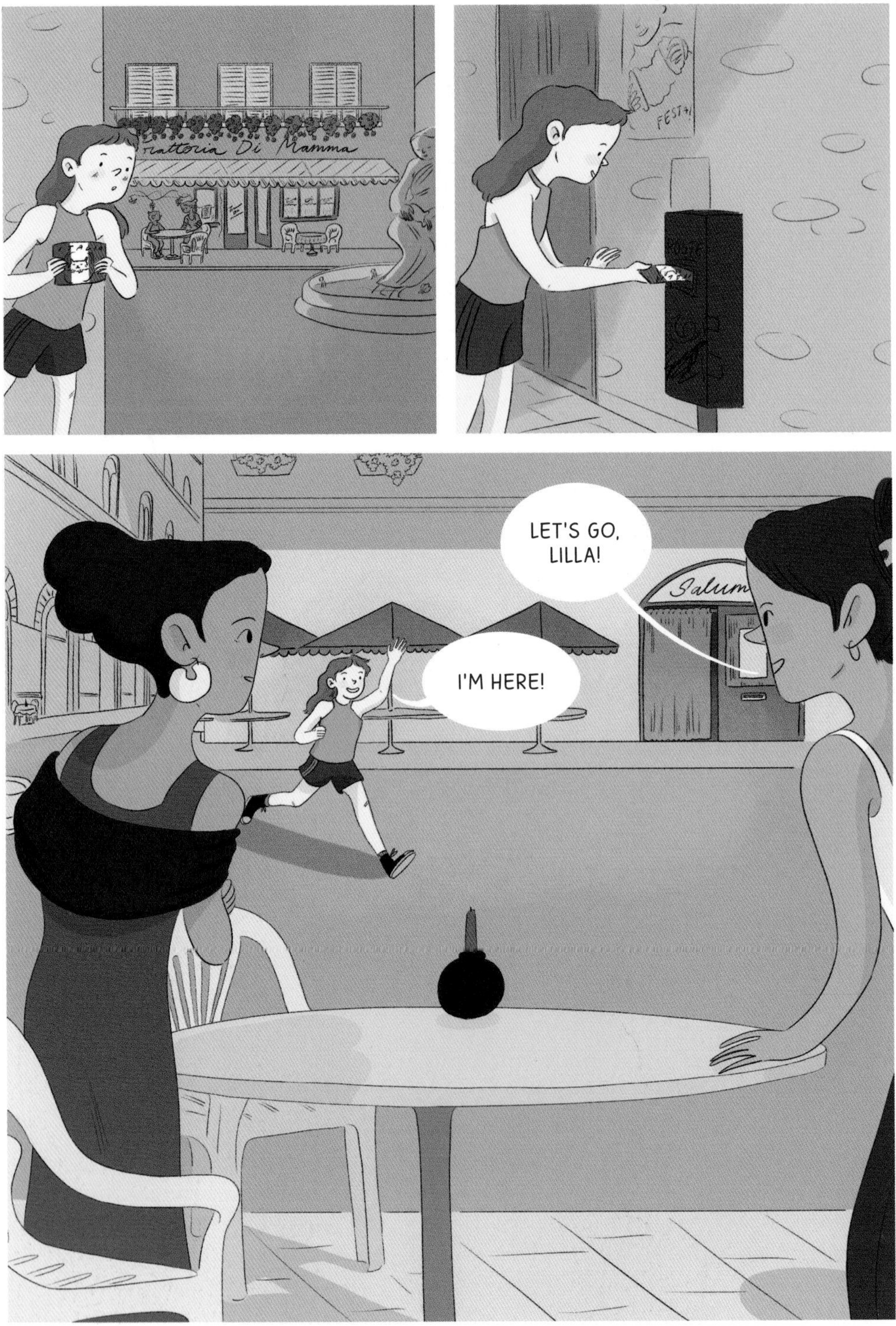
LET'S GO, LILLA!
I'M HERE!

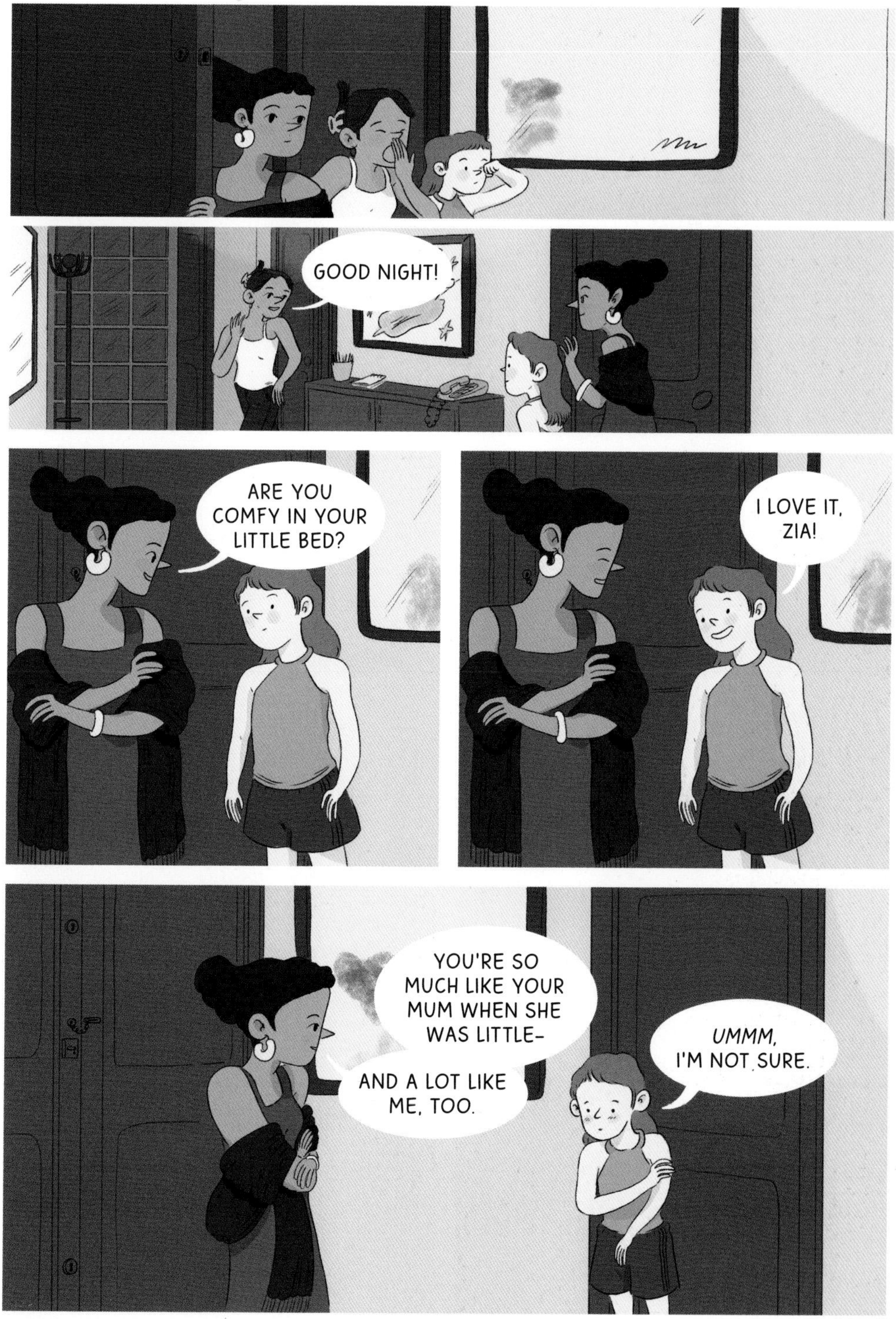
GOOD NIGHT!
ARE YOU COMFY IN YOUR LITTLE BED?
I LOVE IT, ZIA!
YOU'RE SO MUCH LIKE YOUR MUM WHEN SHE WAS LITTLE-
AND A LOT LIKE ME, TOO.
UMMM, I'M NOT SURE.

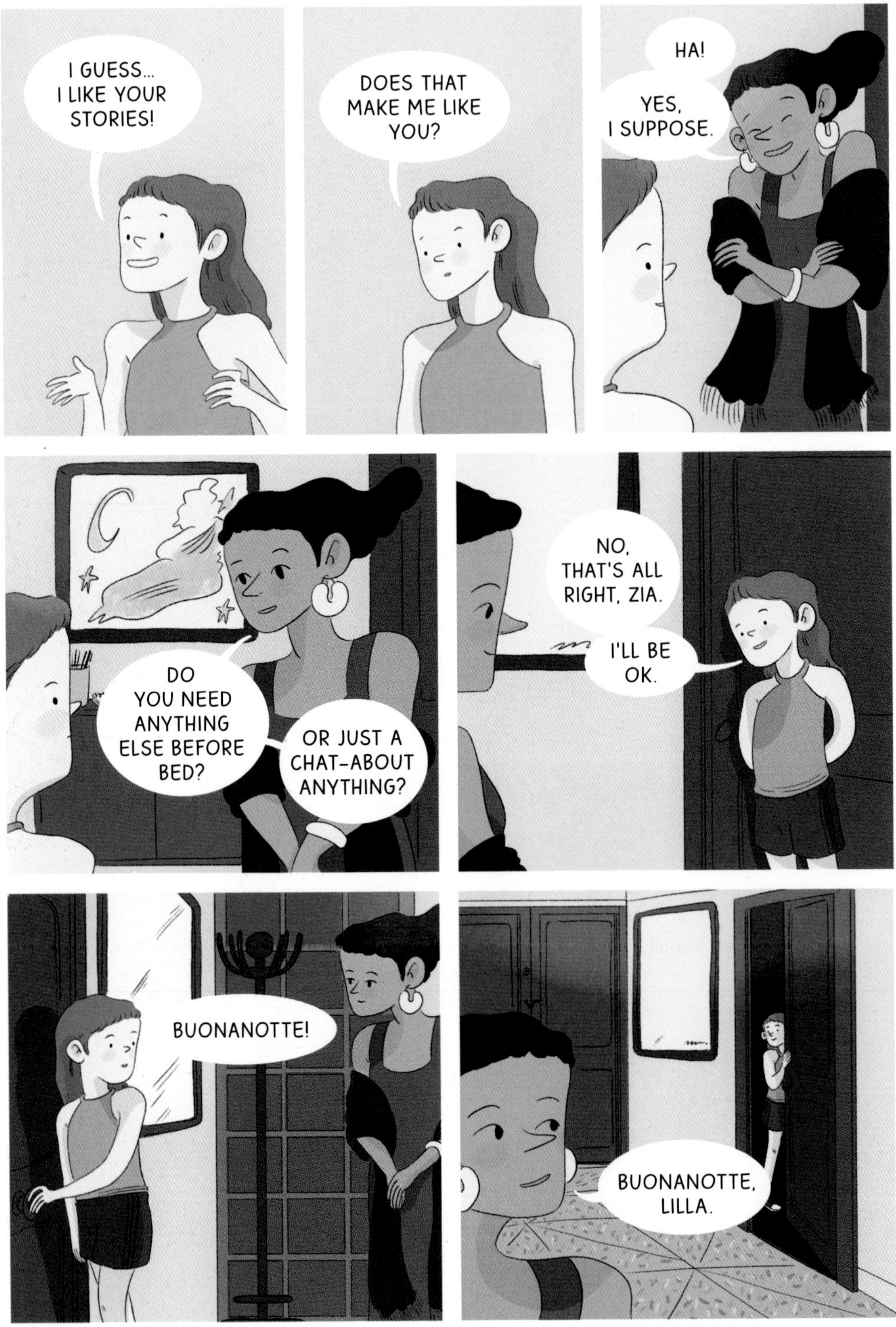
I GUESS...
I LIKE YOUR STORIES!
DOES THAT MAKE ME LIKE YOU?
HA!
YES, I SUPPOSE.
DO YOU NEED ANYTHING ELSE BEFORE BED?
OR JUST A CHAT-ABOUT ANYTHING?
NO, THAT'S ALL RIGHT, ZIA.
I'LL BE OK.
BUONANOTTE!
BUONANOTTE, LILLA.

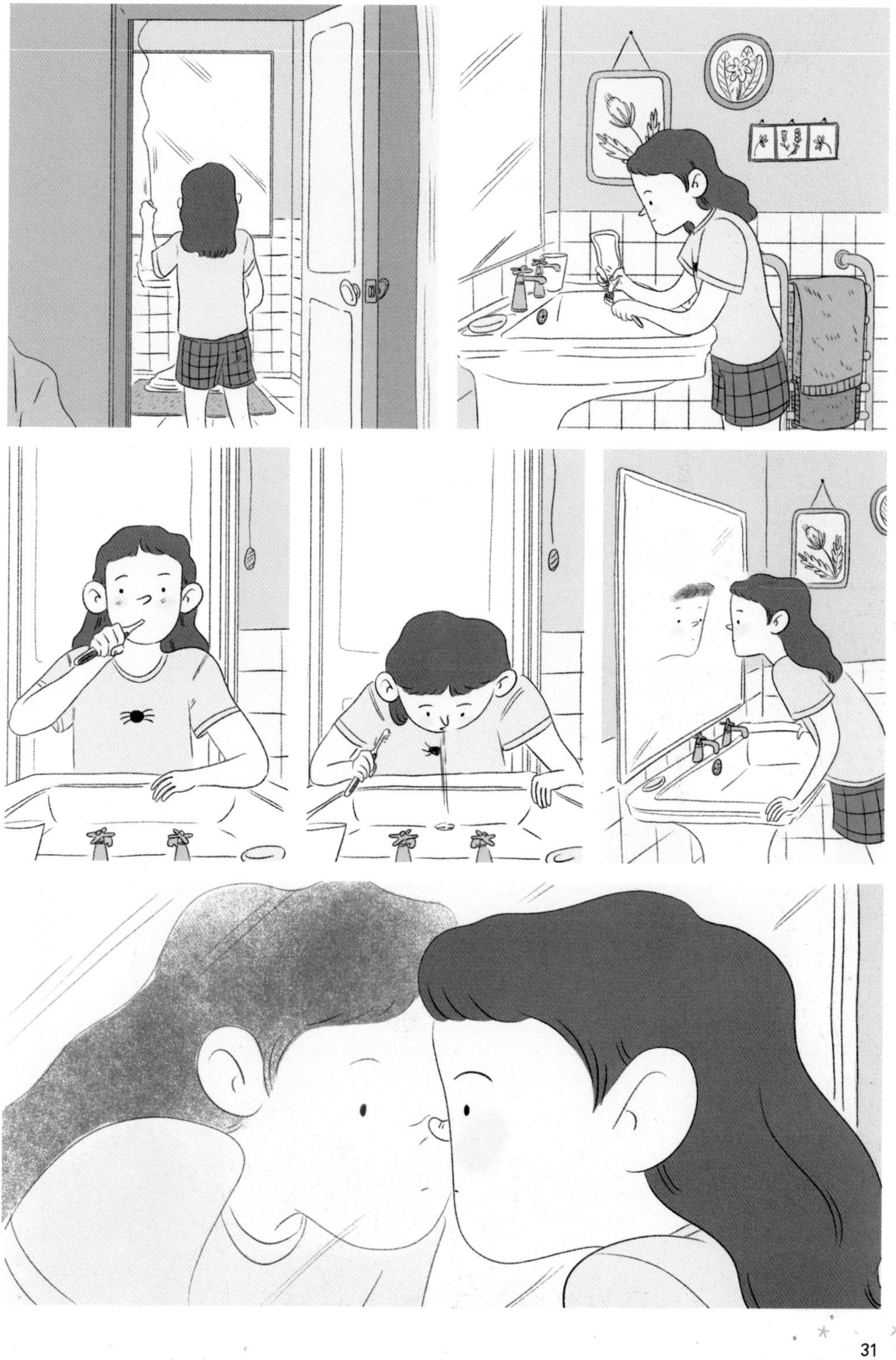

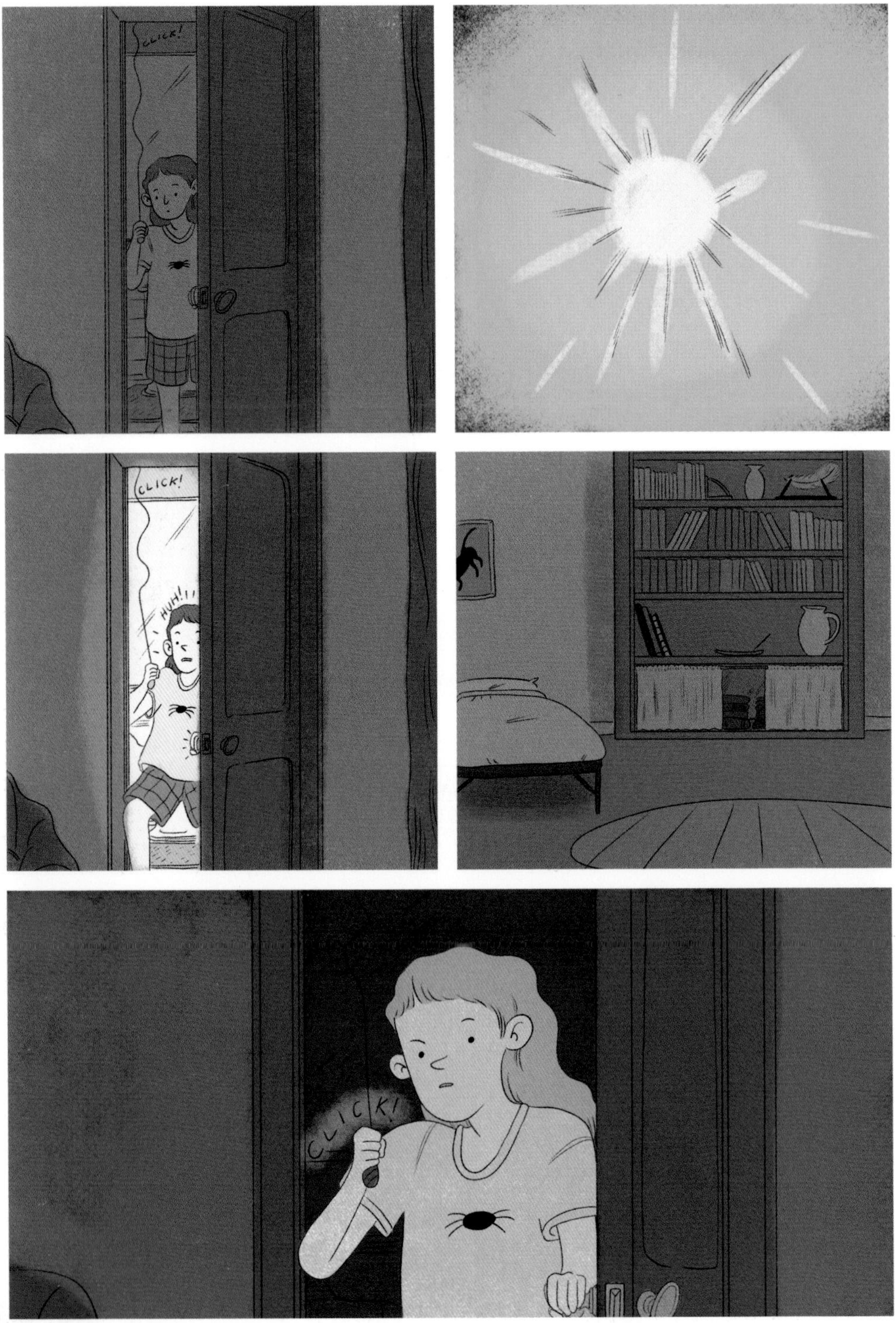
CLICK!
CLICK!
HUH!!!
CLICK!

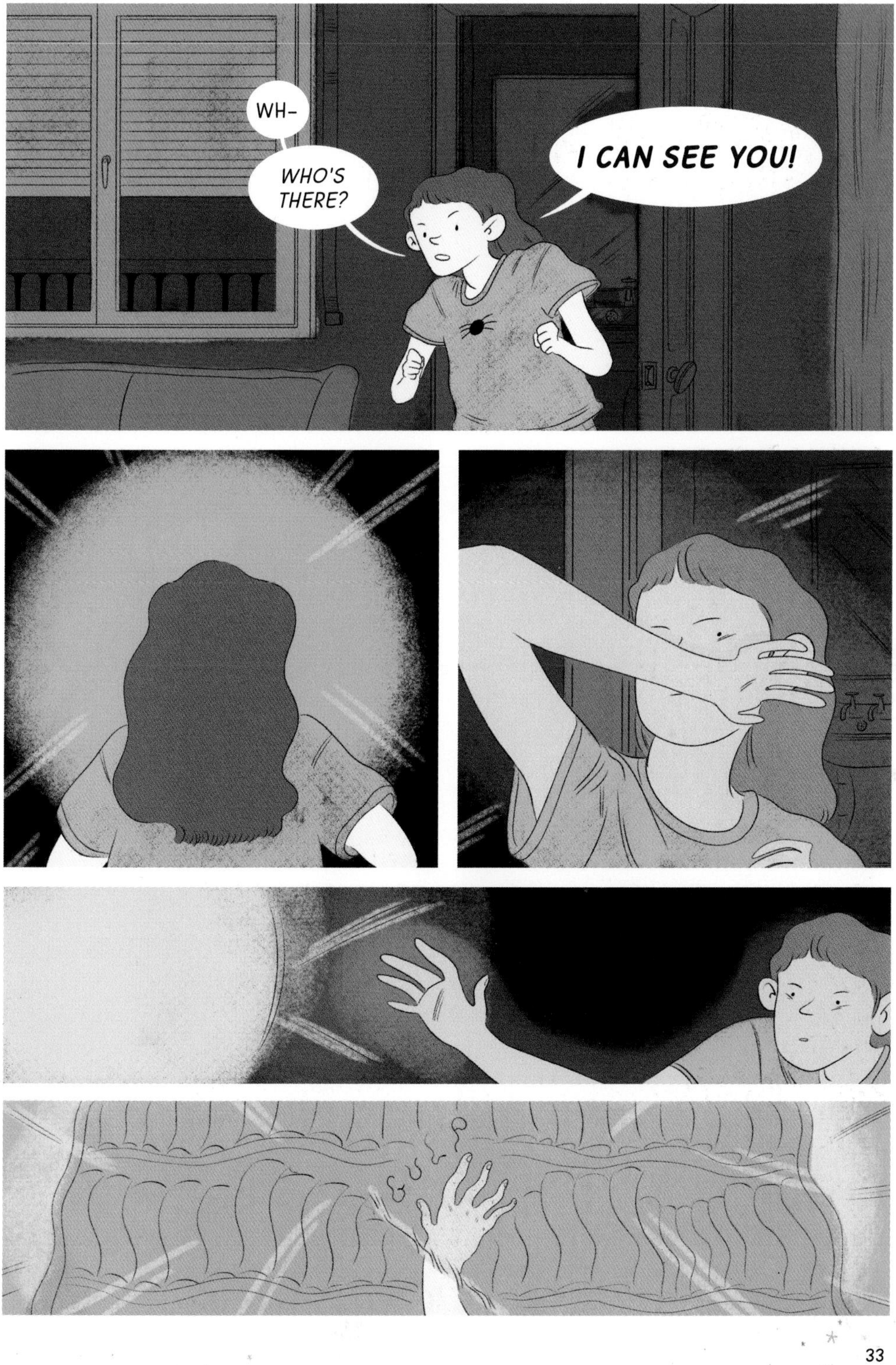
WH-
WHO'S THERE?
I CAN SEE YOU!

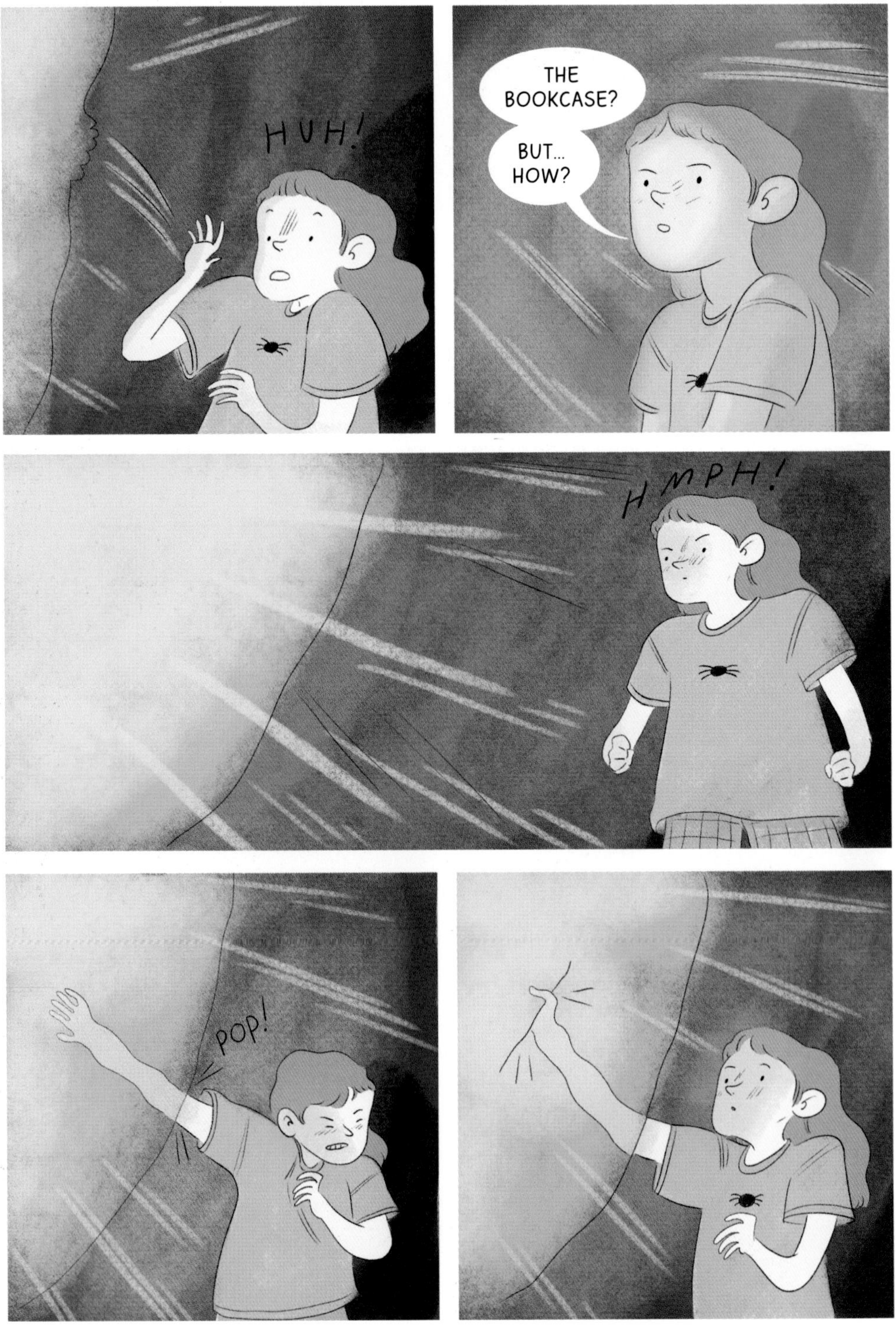
HUH!
THE BOOKCASE?
BUT... HOW?
HMPH!
POP!

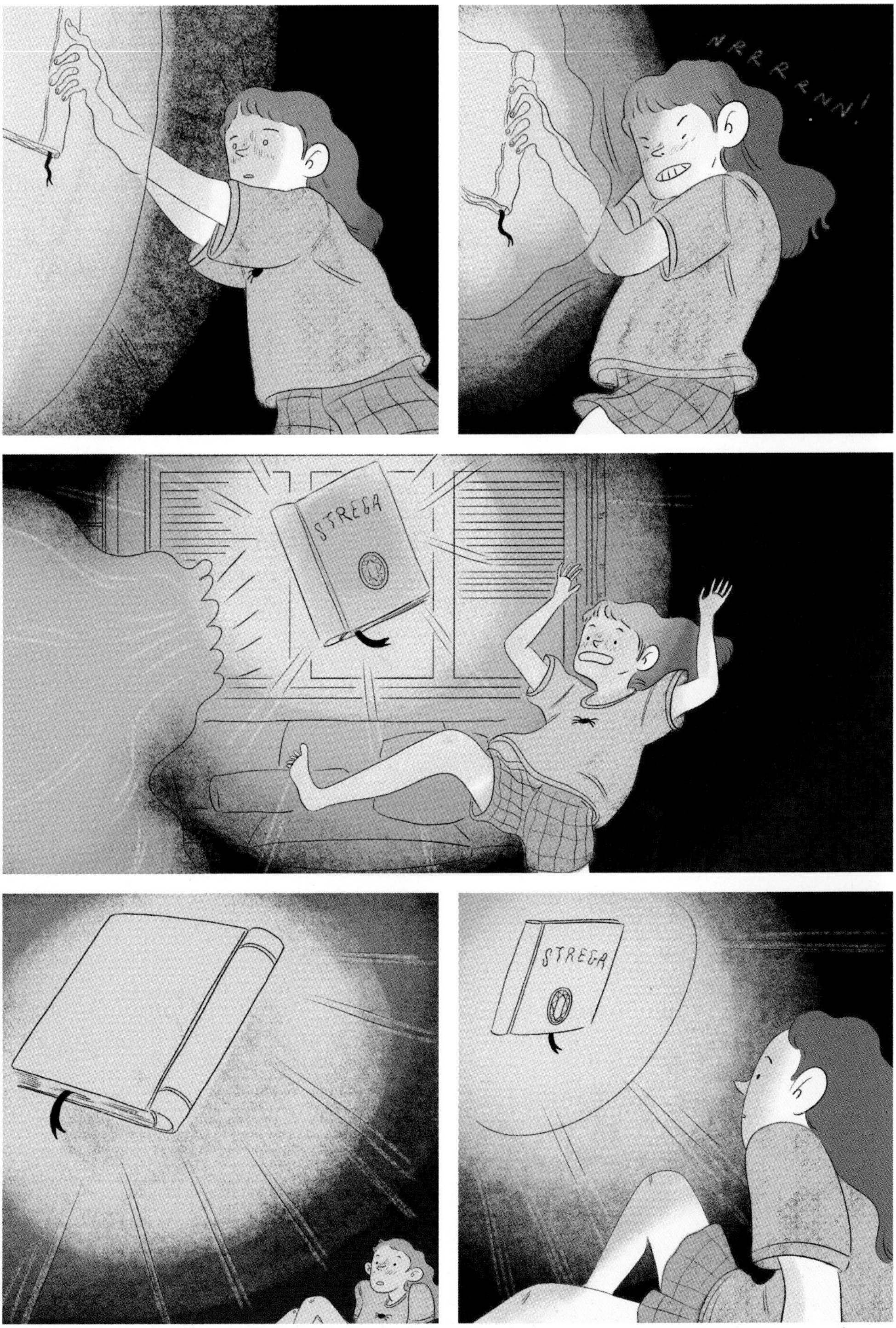
NRRRRNN!
STREGA
STREGA

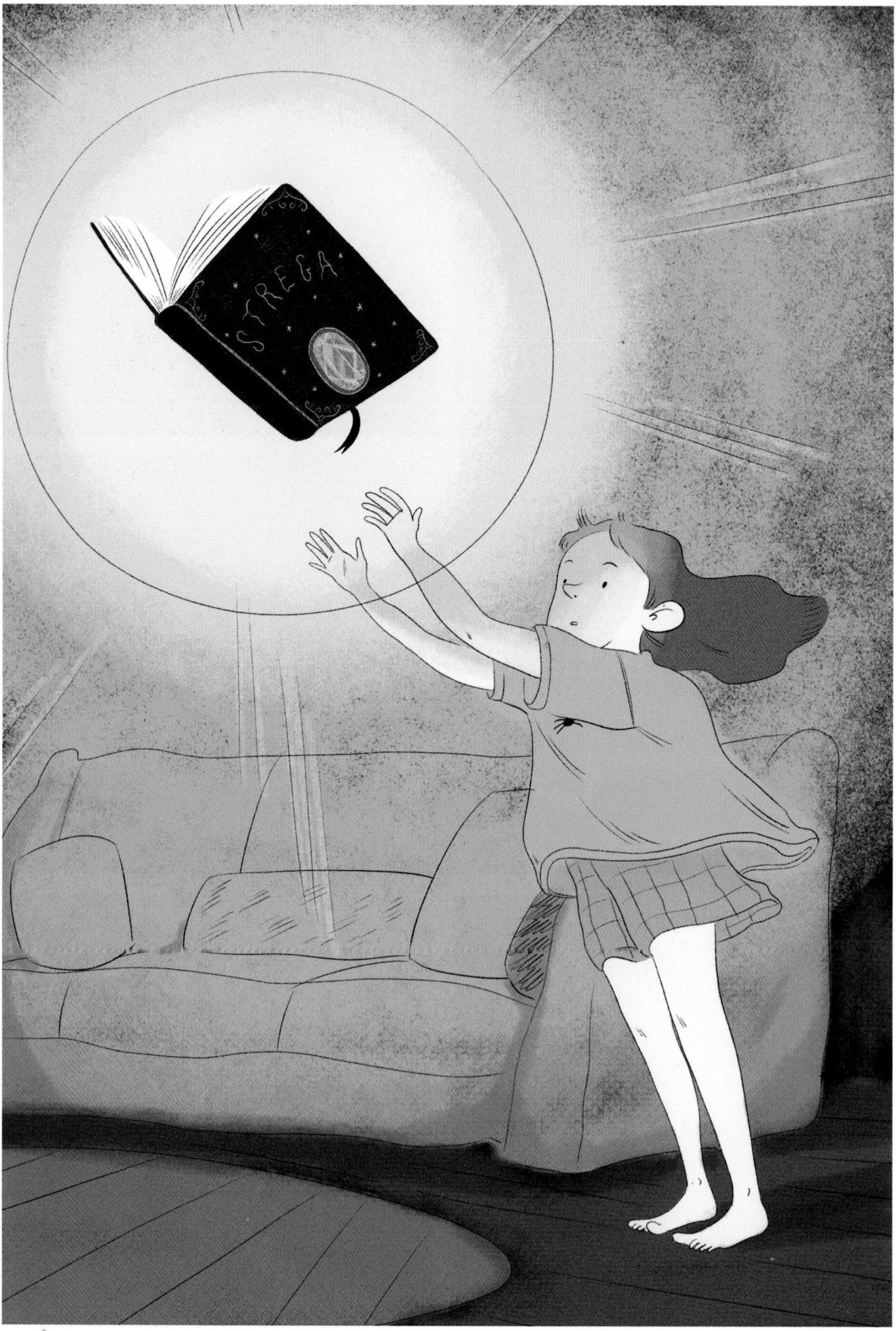
STREGA

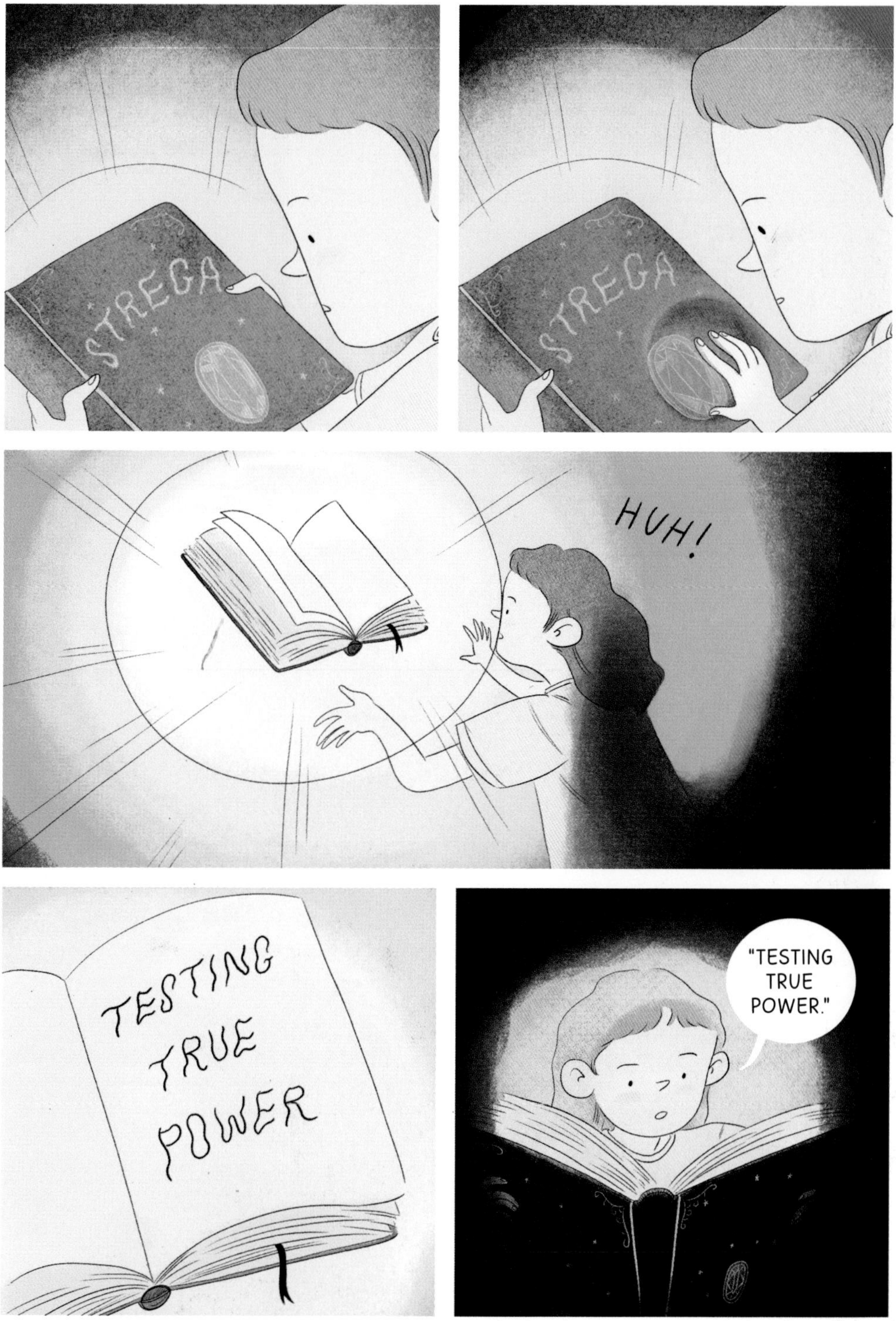
STREGA
STREGA
HUH!
TESTING TRUE POWER
"TESTING TRUE POWER."

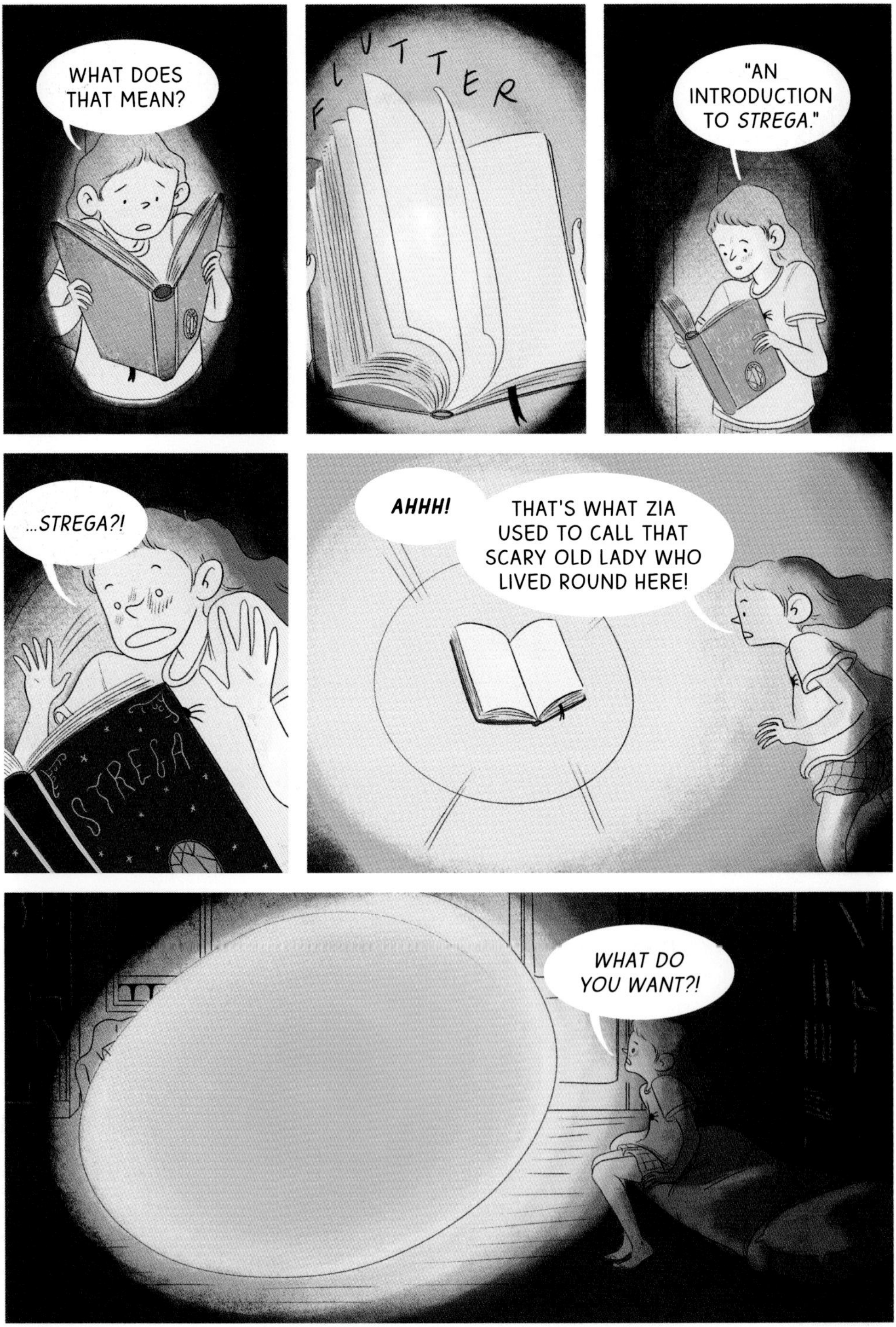
WHAT DOES THAT MEAN?
FLUTTER
"AN INTRODUCTION TO *STREGA*."
...*STREGA*?!
STREGA
AHHH!
THAT'S WHAT ZIA USED TO CALL THAT SCARY OLD LADY WHO LIVED ROUND HERE!
WHAT DO YOU WANT?!

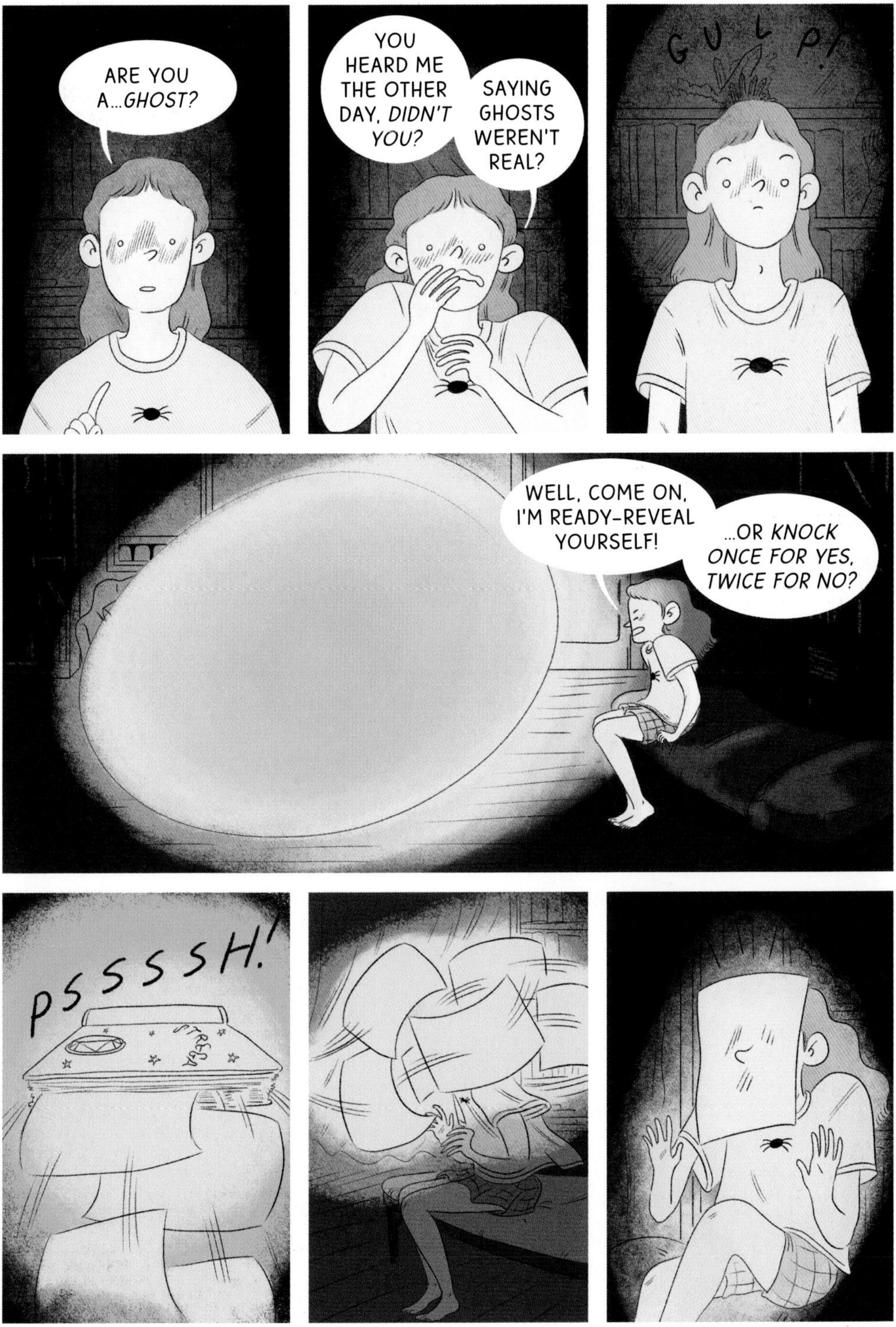
ARE YOU A...*GHOST?*
YOU HEARD ME THE OTHER DAY, *DIDN'T YOU?*
SAYING GHOSTS WEREN'T REAL?
GULP!
WELL, COME ON, I'M READY–REVEAL YOURSELF!
...OR *KNOCK* ONCE FOR YES, TWICE FOR NO?
PSSSSH!
STREGA

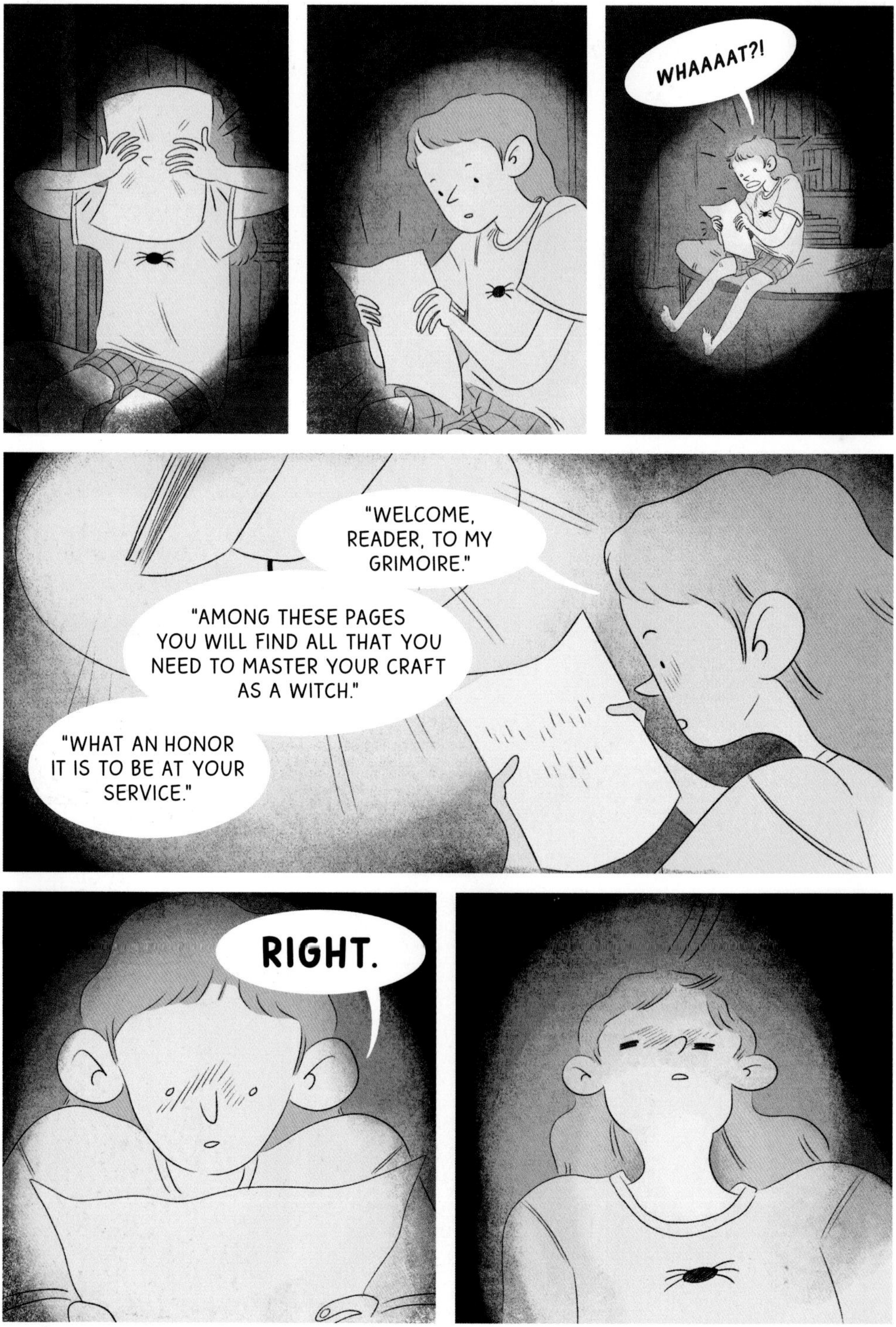
WHAAAAT?!
"WELCOME, READER, TO MY GRIMOIRE."
"AMONG THESE PAGES YOU WILL FIND ALL THAT YOU NEED TO MASTER YOUR CRAFT AS A WITCH."
"WHAT AN HONOR IT IS TO BE AT YOUR SERVICE."
RIGHT.

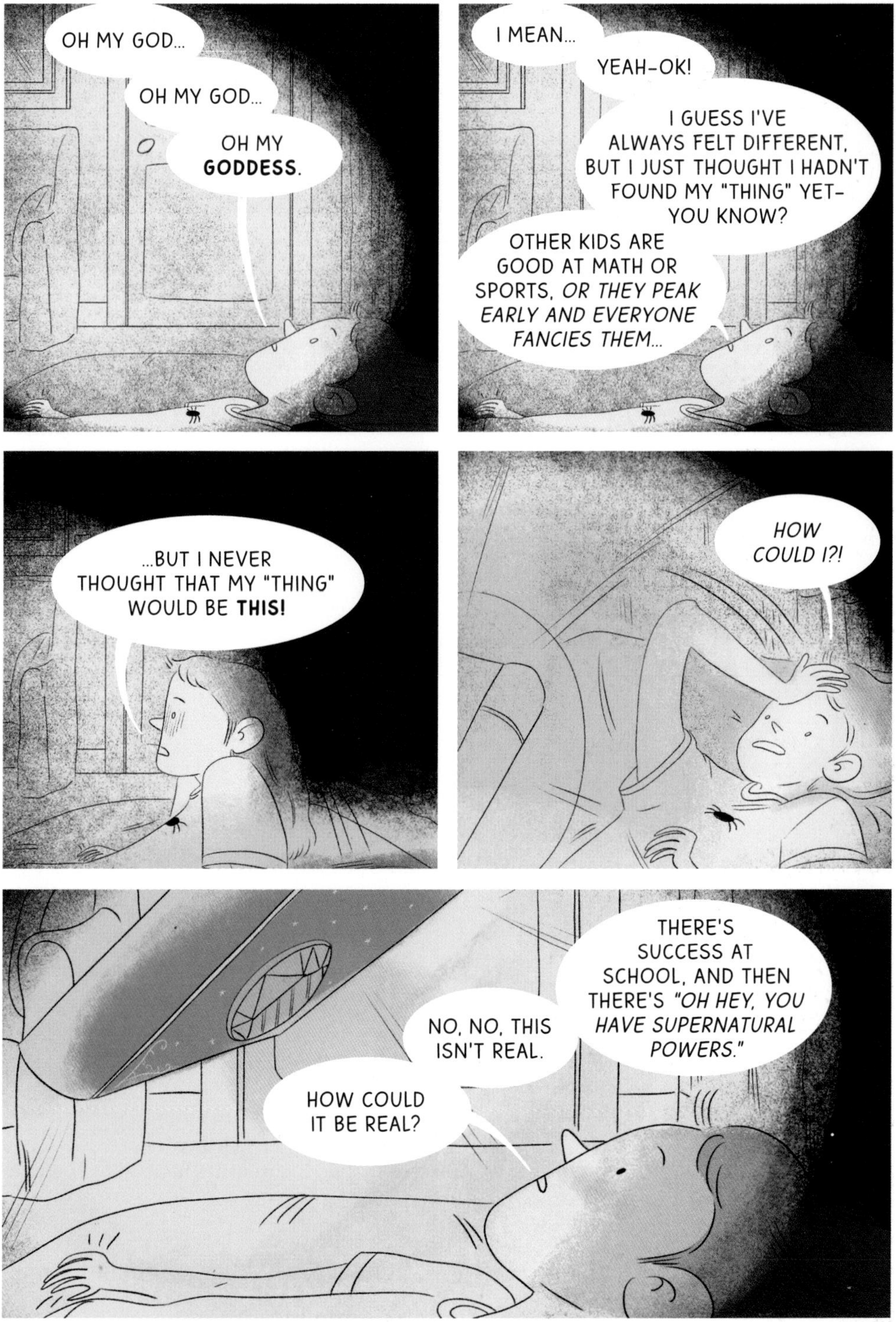
OH MY GOD...
OH MY GOD...
OH MY **GODDESS**.
I MEAN...
YEAH-OK!
I GUESS I'VE ALWAYS FELT DIFFERENT, BUT I JUST THOUGHT I HADN'T FOUND MY "THING" YET- YOU KNOW?
OTHER KIDS ARE GOOD AT MATH OR SPORTS, *OR THEY PEAK EARLY AND EVERYONE FANCIES THEM...*
...BUT I NEVER THOUGHT THAT MY "THING" WOULD BE **THIS!**
HOW COULD I?!
THERE'S SUCCESS AT SCHOOL, AND THEN THERE'S *"OH HEY, YOU HAVE SUPERNATURAL POWERS."*
NO, NO, THIS ISN'T REAL.
HOW COULD IT BE REAL?

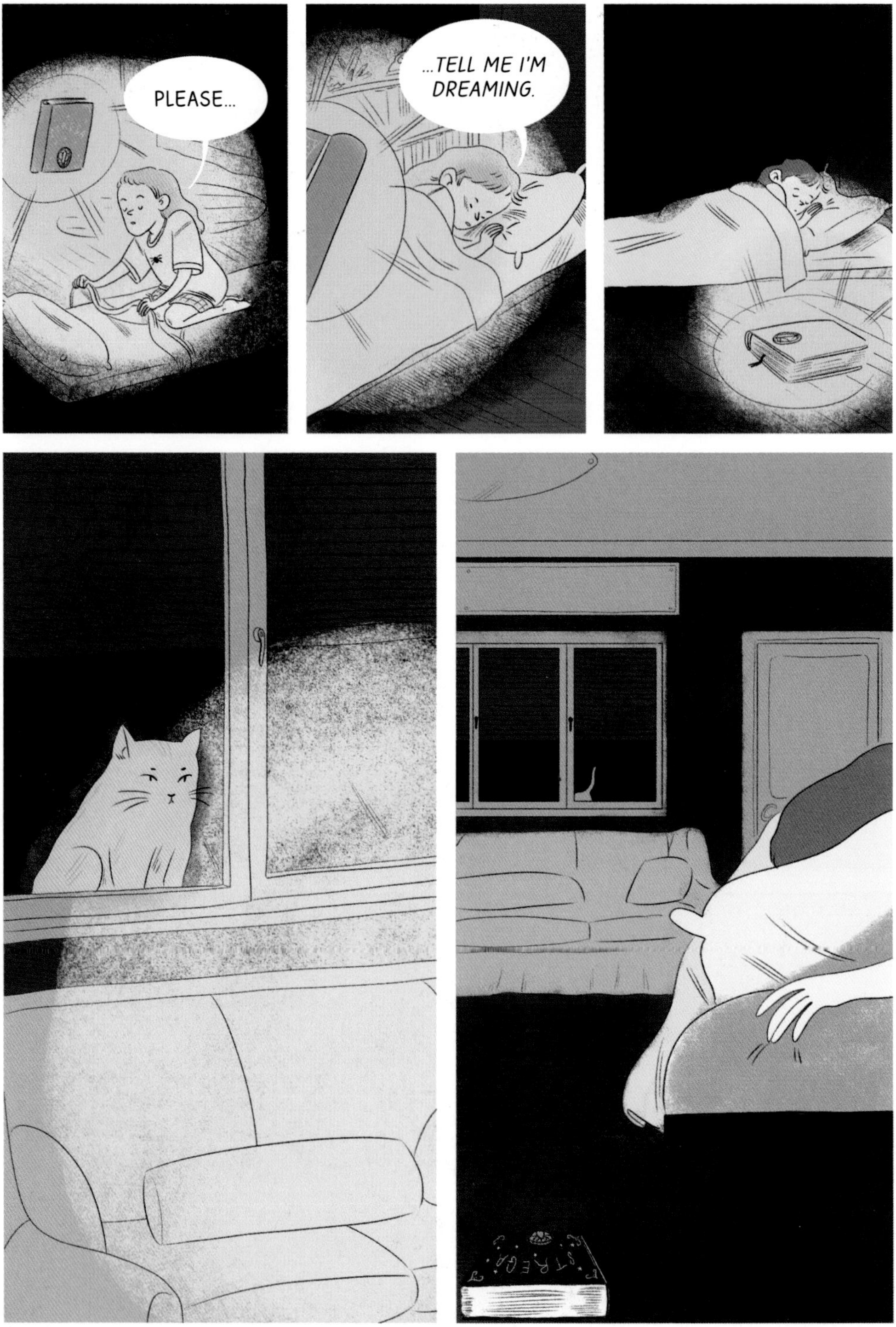
PLEASE...
...TELL ME I'M DREAMING.

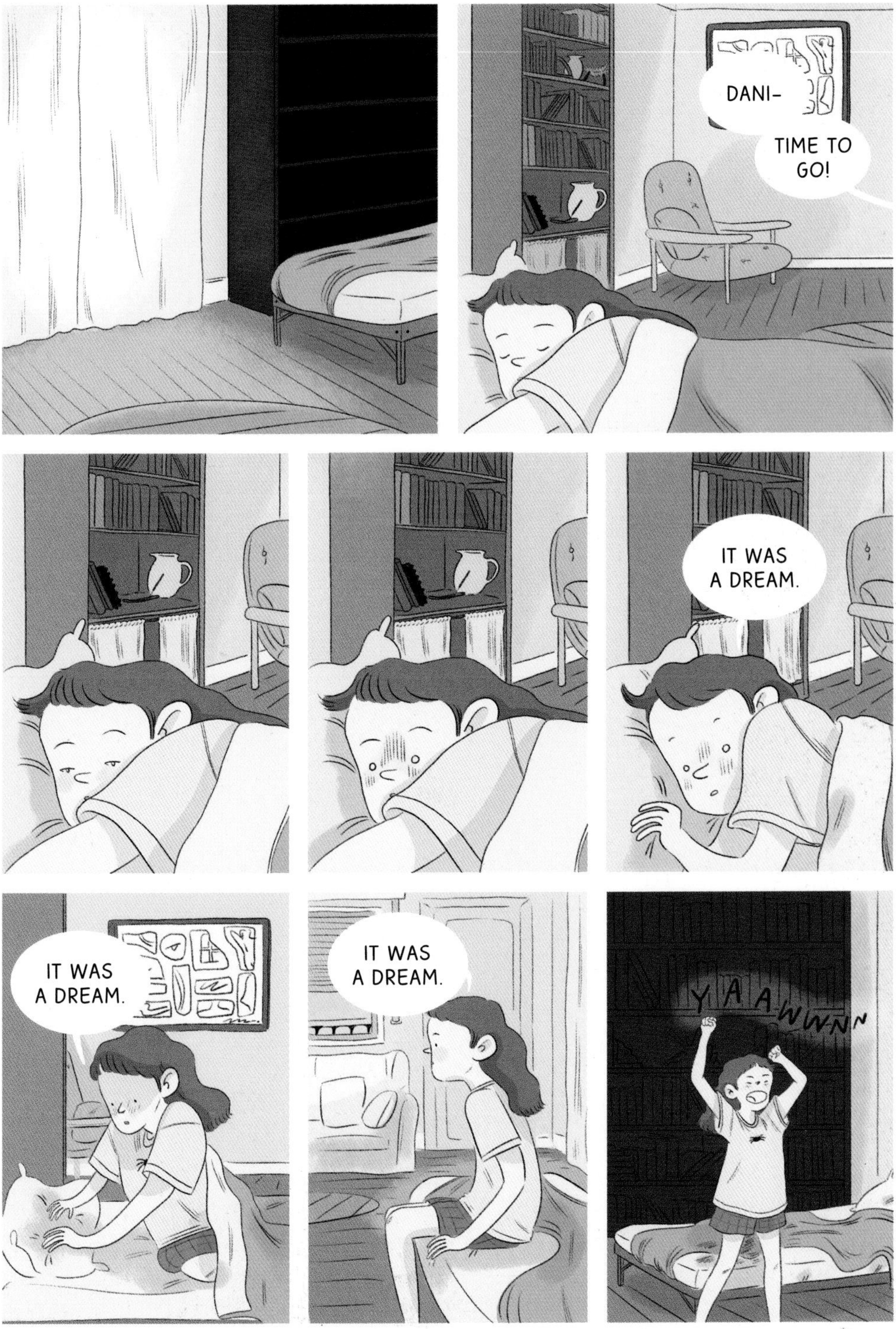
DANI-
TIME TO GO!
IT WAS A DREAM.
IT WAS A DREAM.
IT WAS A DREAM.
YAAWWNN

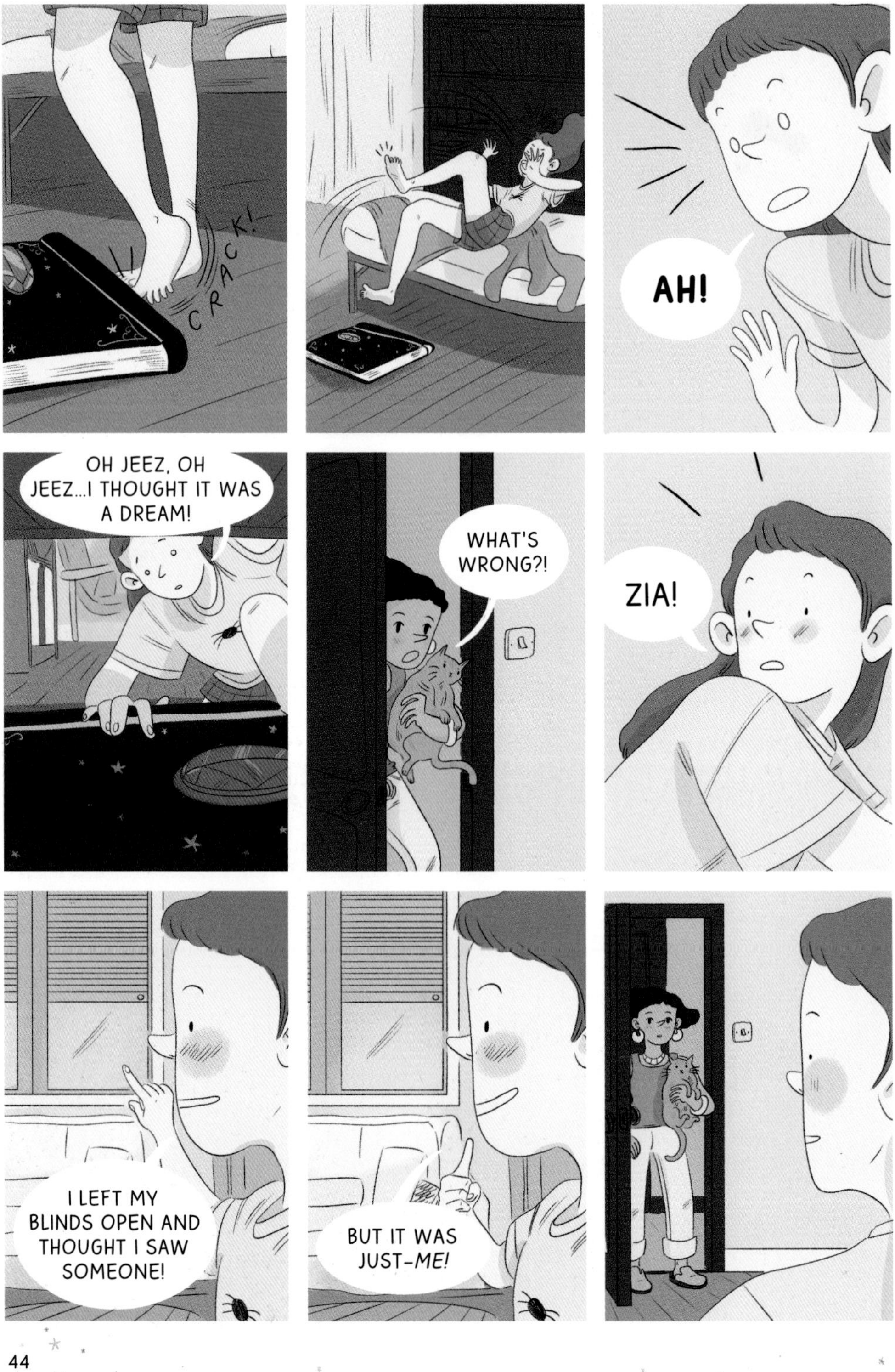
CRACK!
AH!
OH JEEZ, OH JEEZ...I THOUGHT IT WAS A DREAM!
WHAT'S WRONG?!
ZIA!
I LEFT MY BLINDS OPEN AND THOUGHT I SAW SOMEONE!
BUT IT WAS JUST-*ME!*

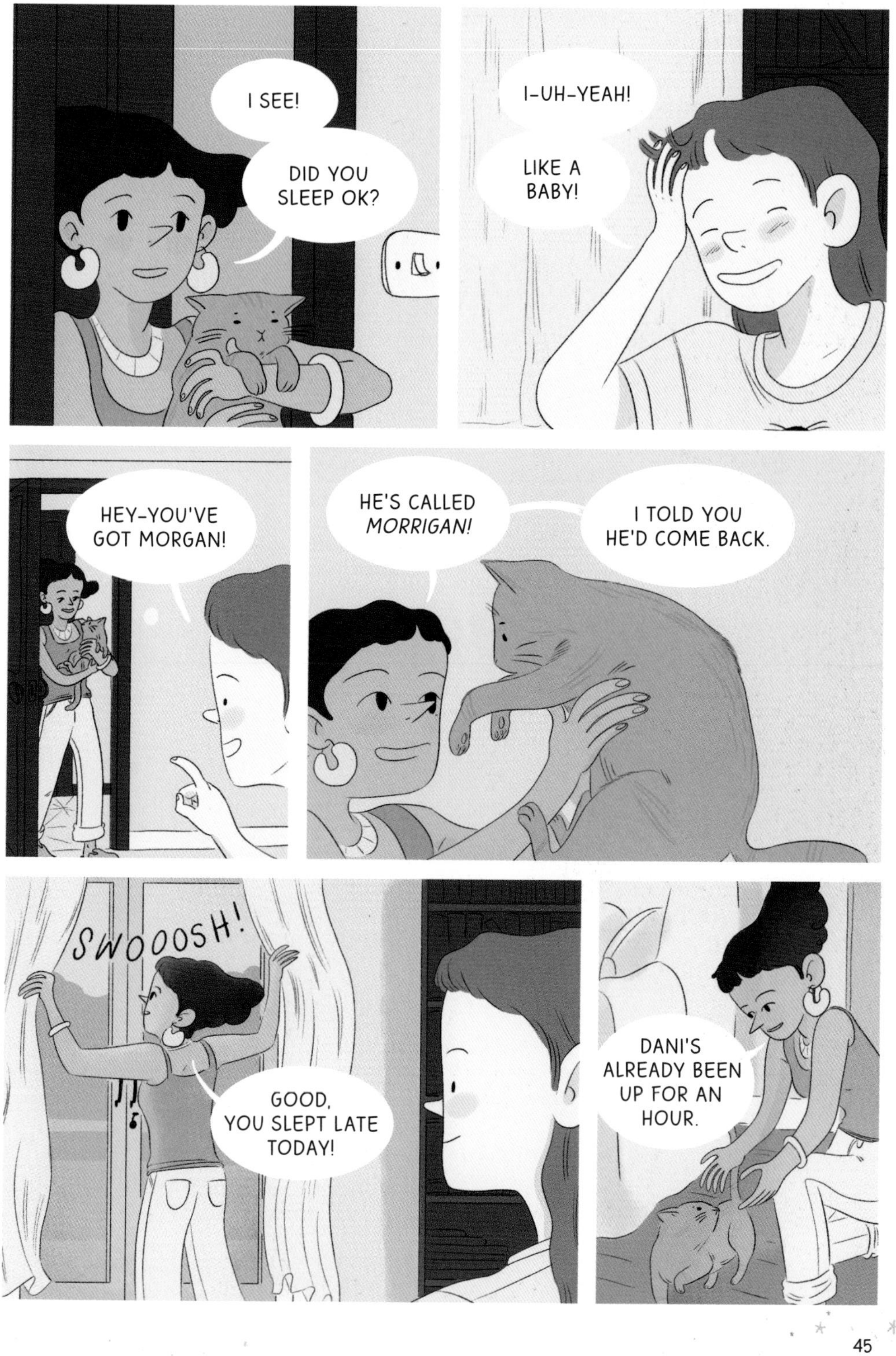
I SEE!
DID YOU SLEEP OK?
I-UH-YEAH!
LIKE A BABY!
HEY-YOU'VE GOT MORGAN!
HE'S CALLED *MORRIGAN!*
I TOLD YOU HE'D COME BACK.
SWOOOSH!
GOOD, YOU SLEPT LATE TODAY!
DANI'S ALREADY BEEN UP FOR AN HOUR.

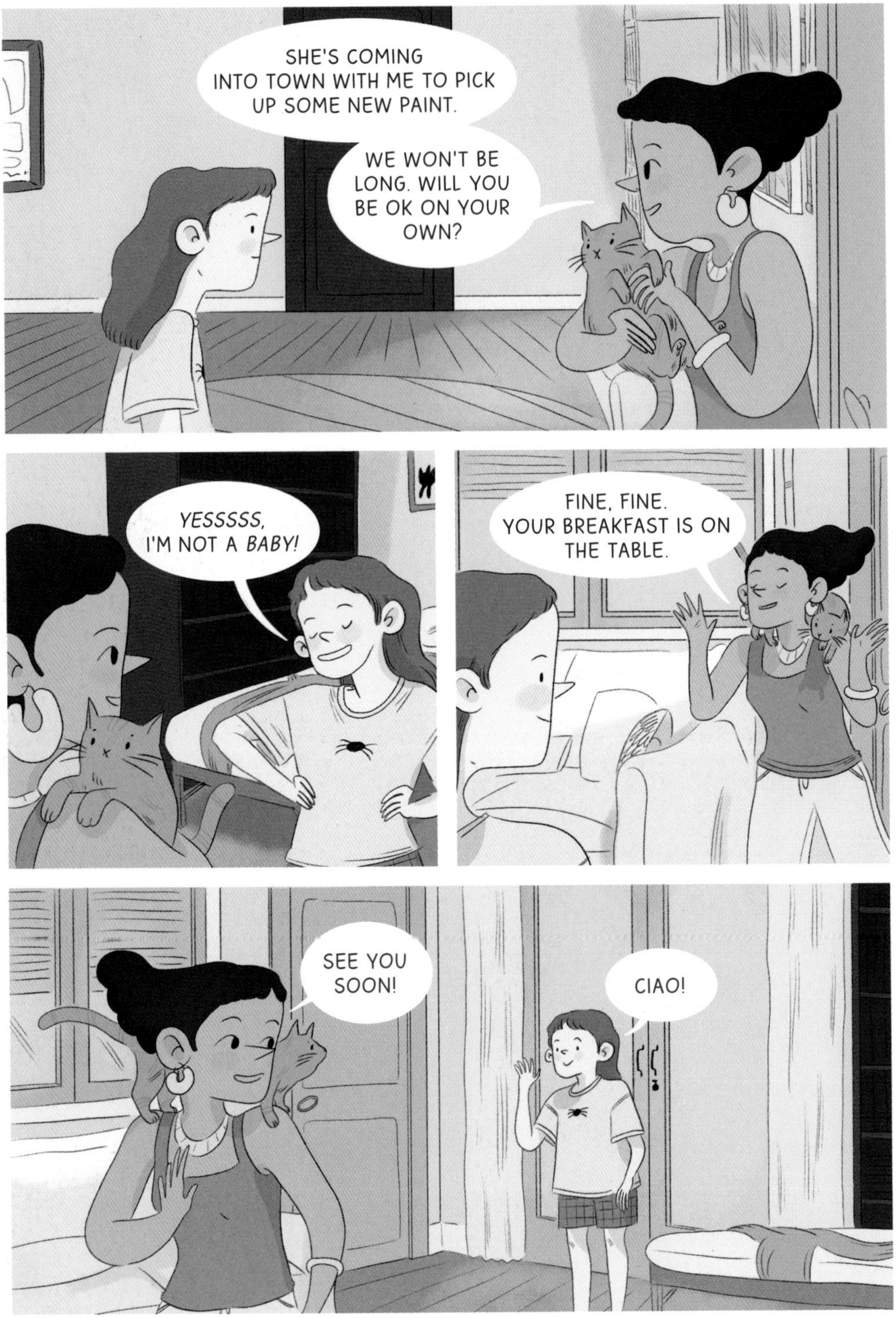
SHE'S COMING INTO TOWN WITH ME TO PICK UP SOME NEW PAINT.
WE WON'T BE LONG. WILL YOU BE OK ON YOUR OWN?
YESSSSS, I'M NOT A *BABY!*
FINE, FINE. YOUR BREAKFAST IS ON THE TABLE.
SEE YOU SOON!
CIAO!

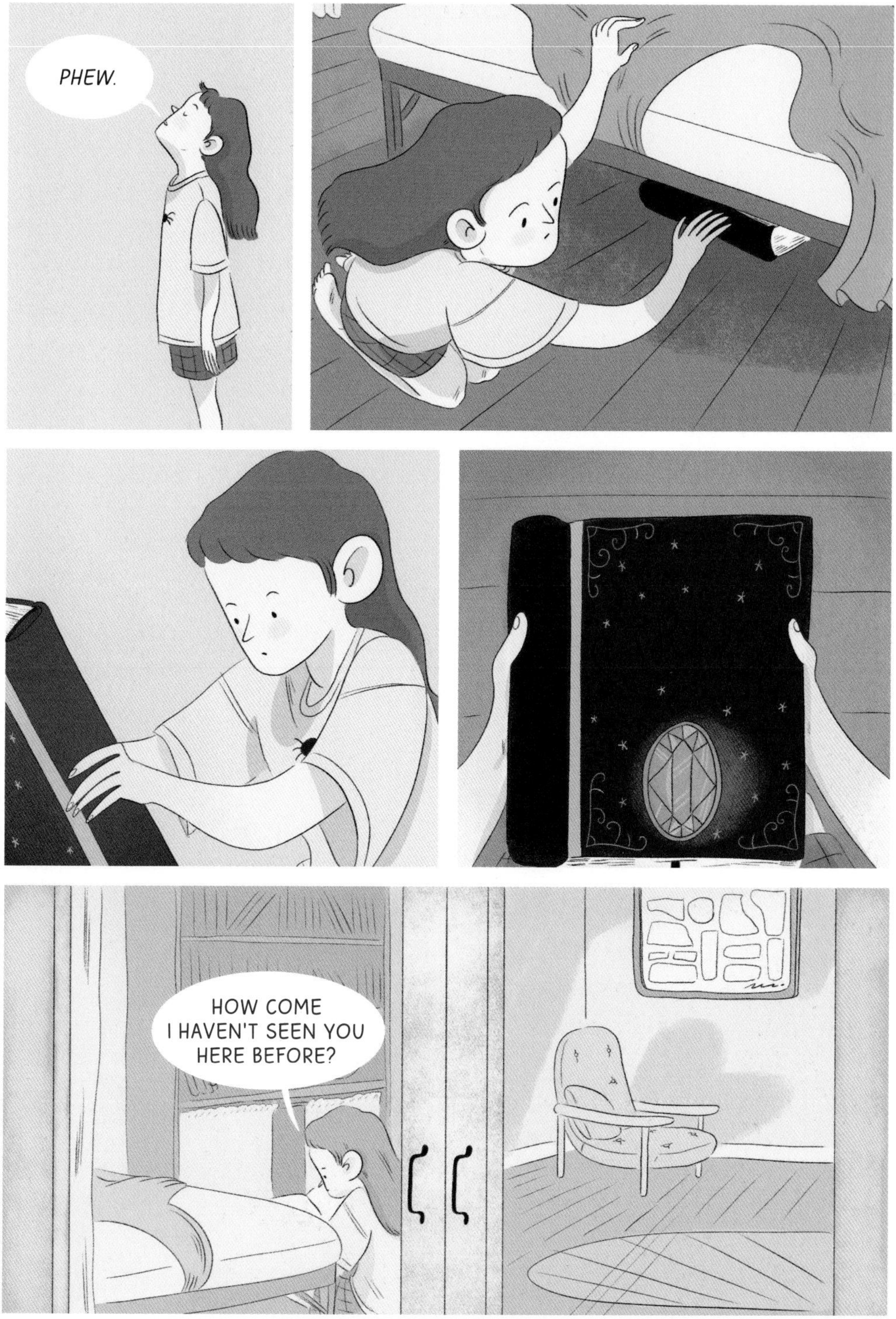
PHEW.
HOW COME I HAVEN'T SEEN YOU HERE BEFORE?

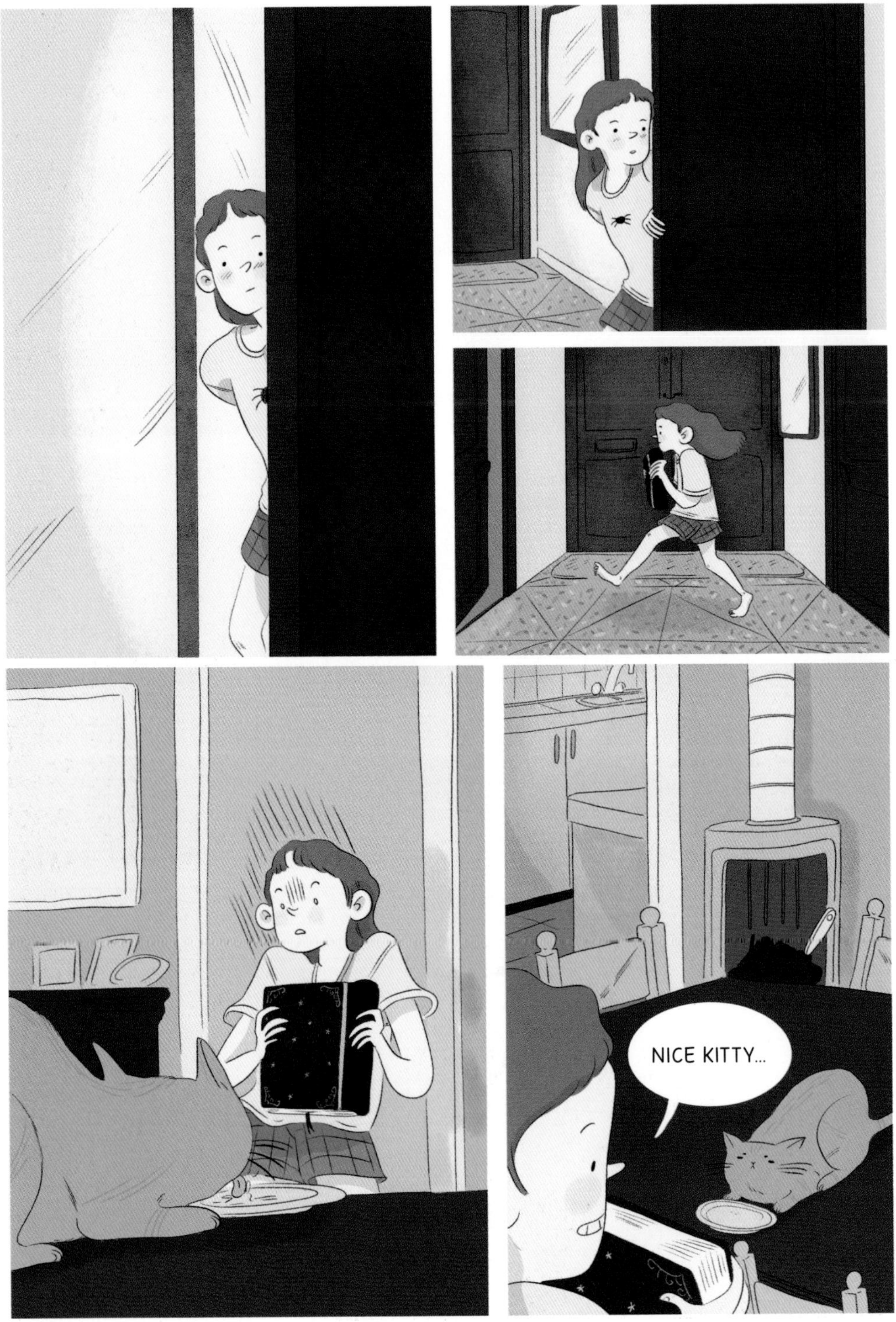
NICE KITTY...

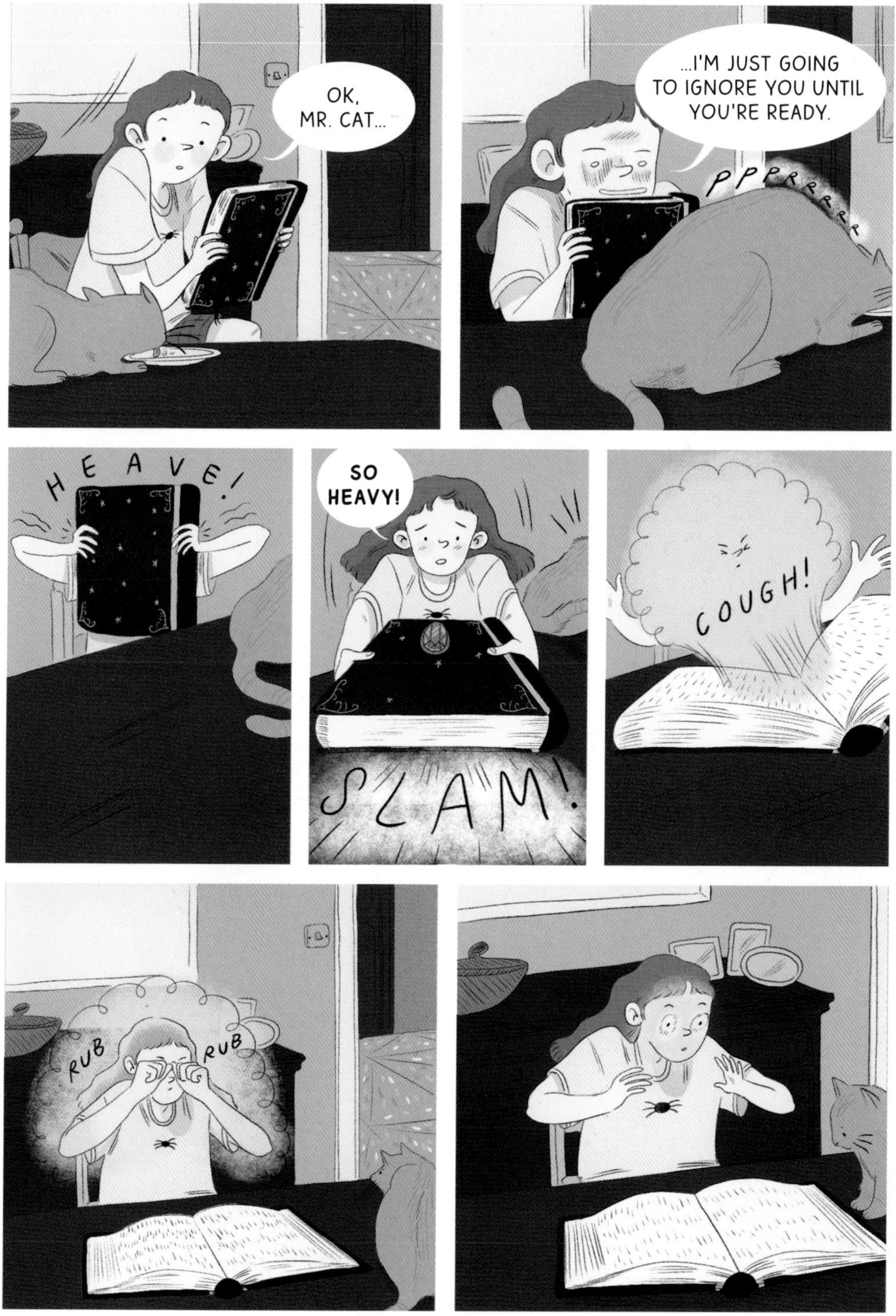
OK,
MR. CAT...
...I'M JUST GOING
TO IGNORE YOU UNTIL
YOU'RE READY.
PPPRRRRRR
HEAVE!
SO
HEAVY!
SLAM!
COUGH!
RUB
RUB

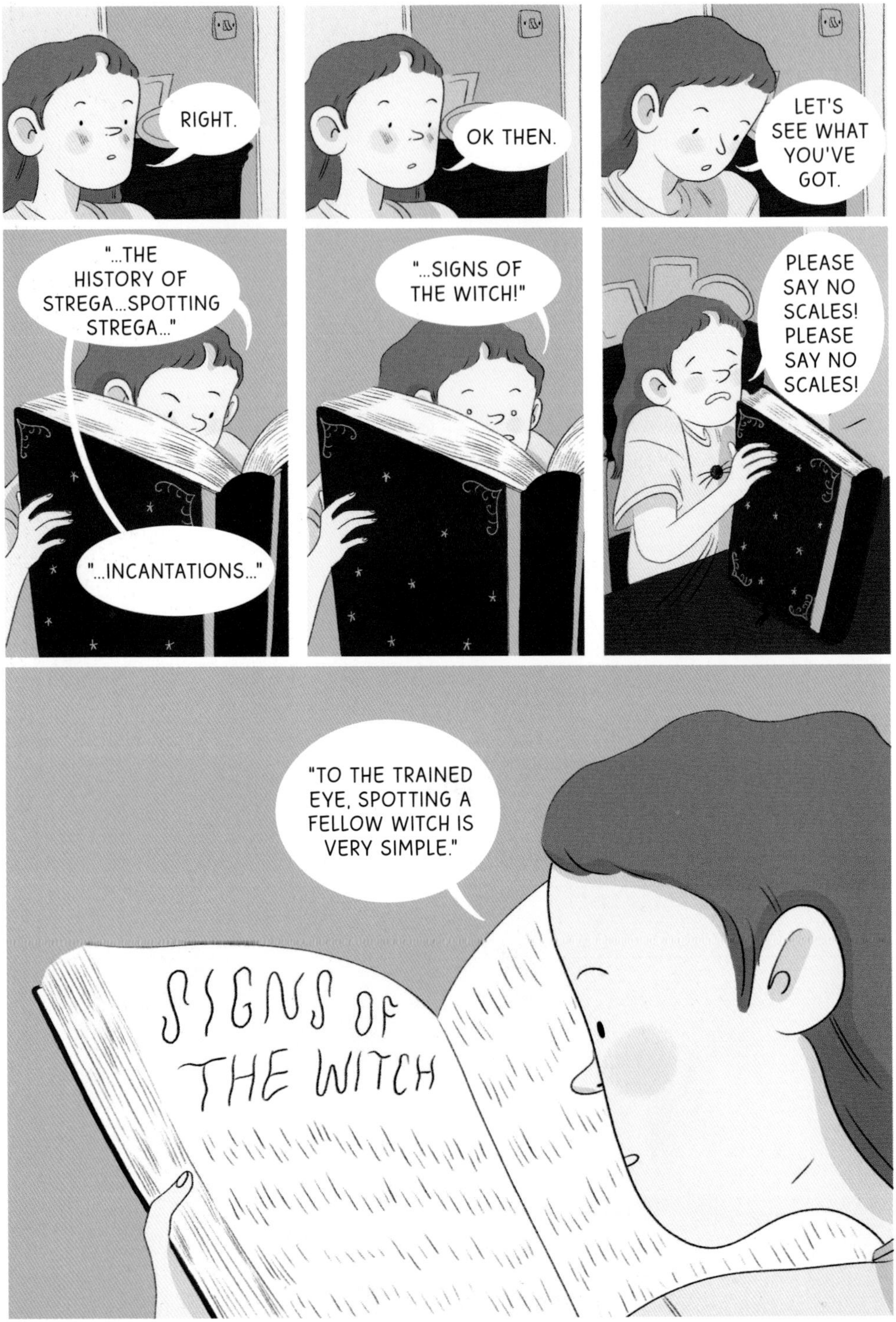
RIGHT.
OK THEN.
LET'S SEE WHAT YOU'VE GOT.
"...THE HISTORY OF STREGA...SPOTTING STREGA..."
"...INCANTATIONS..."
"...SIGNS OF THE WITCH!"
PLEASE SAY NO SCALES! PLEASE SAY NO SCALES!
"TO THE TRAINED EYE, SPOTTING A FELLOW WITCH IS VERY SIMPLE."
SIGNS OF THE WITCH

"HOWEVER–"

"TO THOSE IN THE EARLY STAGES OF UNCOVERING THEIR POWERS, HERE ARE A FEW TIPS...."

FIRST, NO WITCH HAS EVER BEEN SEEN WITHOUT A 'TOUCH OF THE SORCERESS.' THIS COULD BE A BEAUTY SPOT UNDER THEIR RIGHT EYE, A THREE-PRONGED BIRTHMARK APPEARING ON THEIR BODY, OR RED HAIR."

"OTHER, LESS DOCUMENTED FORMS HAVE BEEN NOTED, SUCH AS A DOUBLE-JOINTED THUMB, A HAND WITH A SIXTH FINGER, AND IN SOME VERY RARE CASES, A FORKED TONGUE."

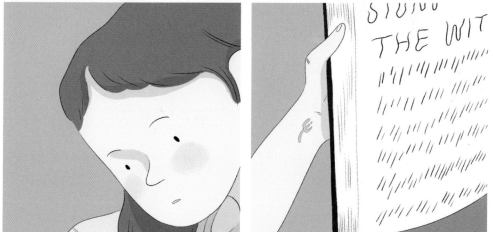

THE WIT

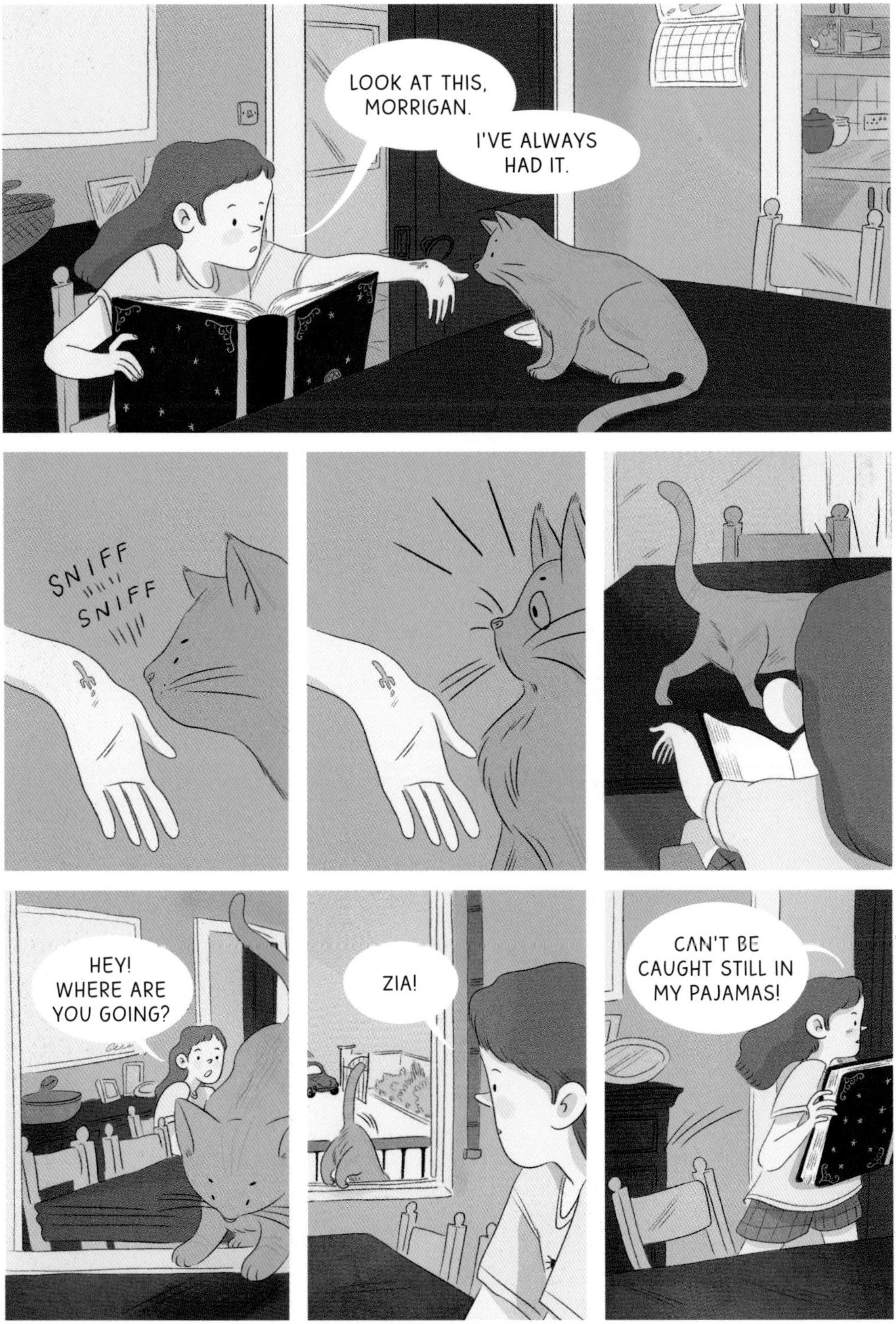
LOOK AT THIS, MORRIGAN.
I'VE ALWAYS HAD IT.
SNIFF SNIFF
HEY! WHERE ARE YOU GOING?
ZIA!
CAN'T BE CAUGHT STILL IN MY PAJAMAS!

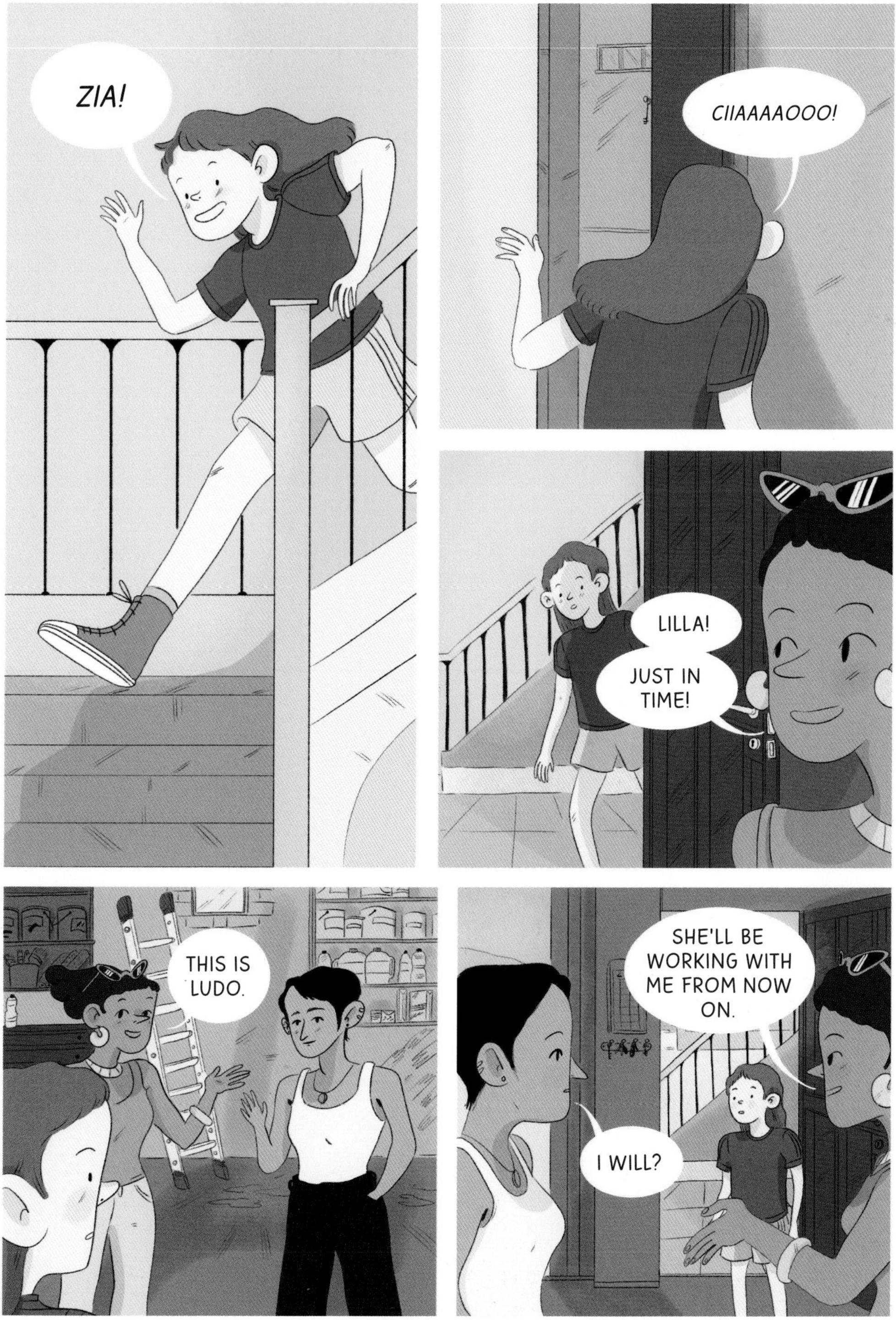
ZIA!
CIIAAAAOOO!
LILLA!
JUST IN TIME!
THIS IS LUDO.
SHE'LL BE WORKING WITH ME FROM NOW ON.
I WILL?

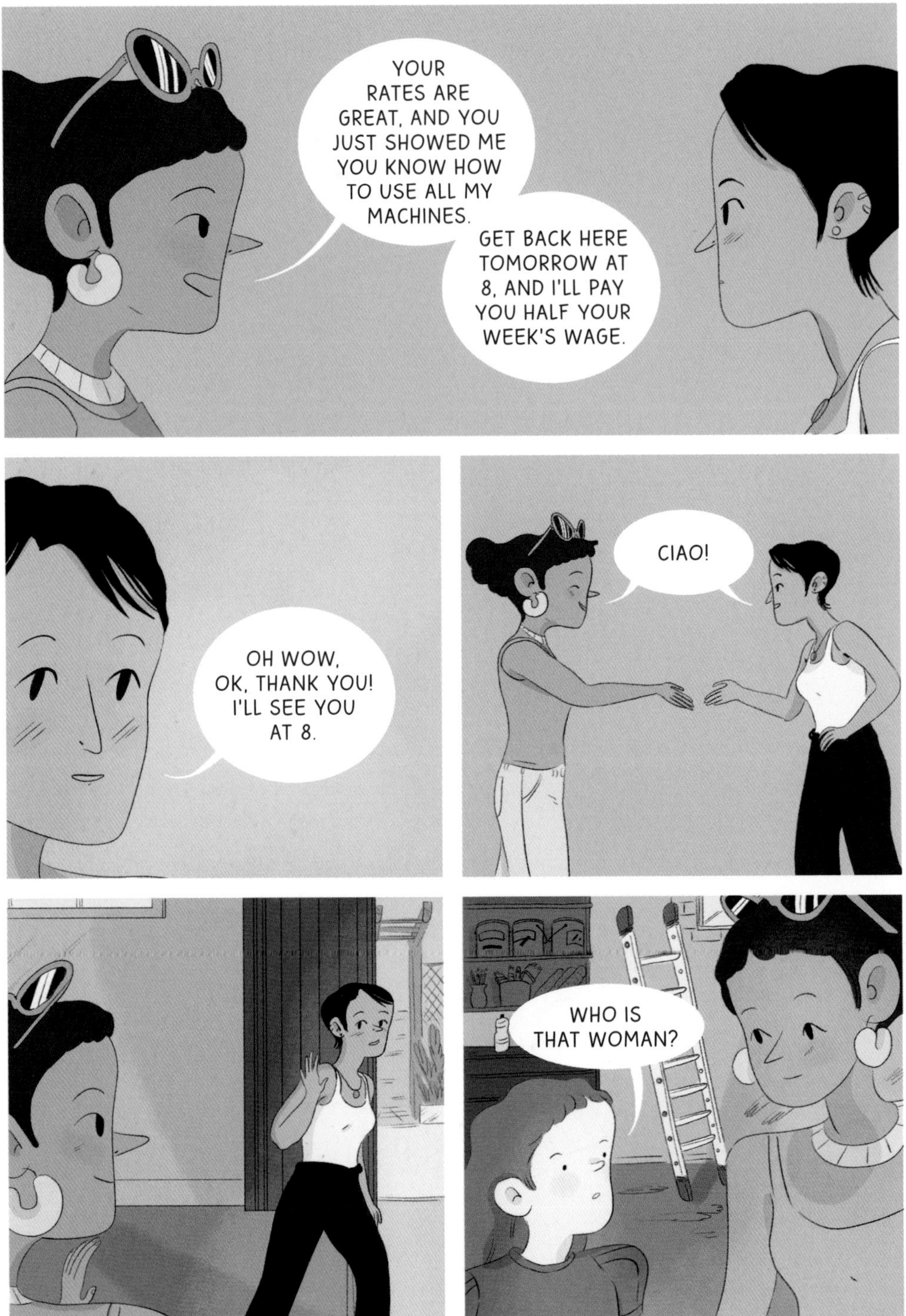
YOUR RATES ARE GREAT, AND YOU JUST SHOWED ME YOU KNOW HOW TO USE ALL MY MACHINES.
GET BACK HERE TOMORROW AT 8, AND I'LL PAY YOU HALF YOUR WEEK'S WAGE.
OH WOW, OK, THANK YOU! I'LL SEE YOU AT 8.
CIAO!
WHO IS THAT WOMAN?

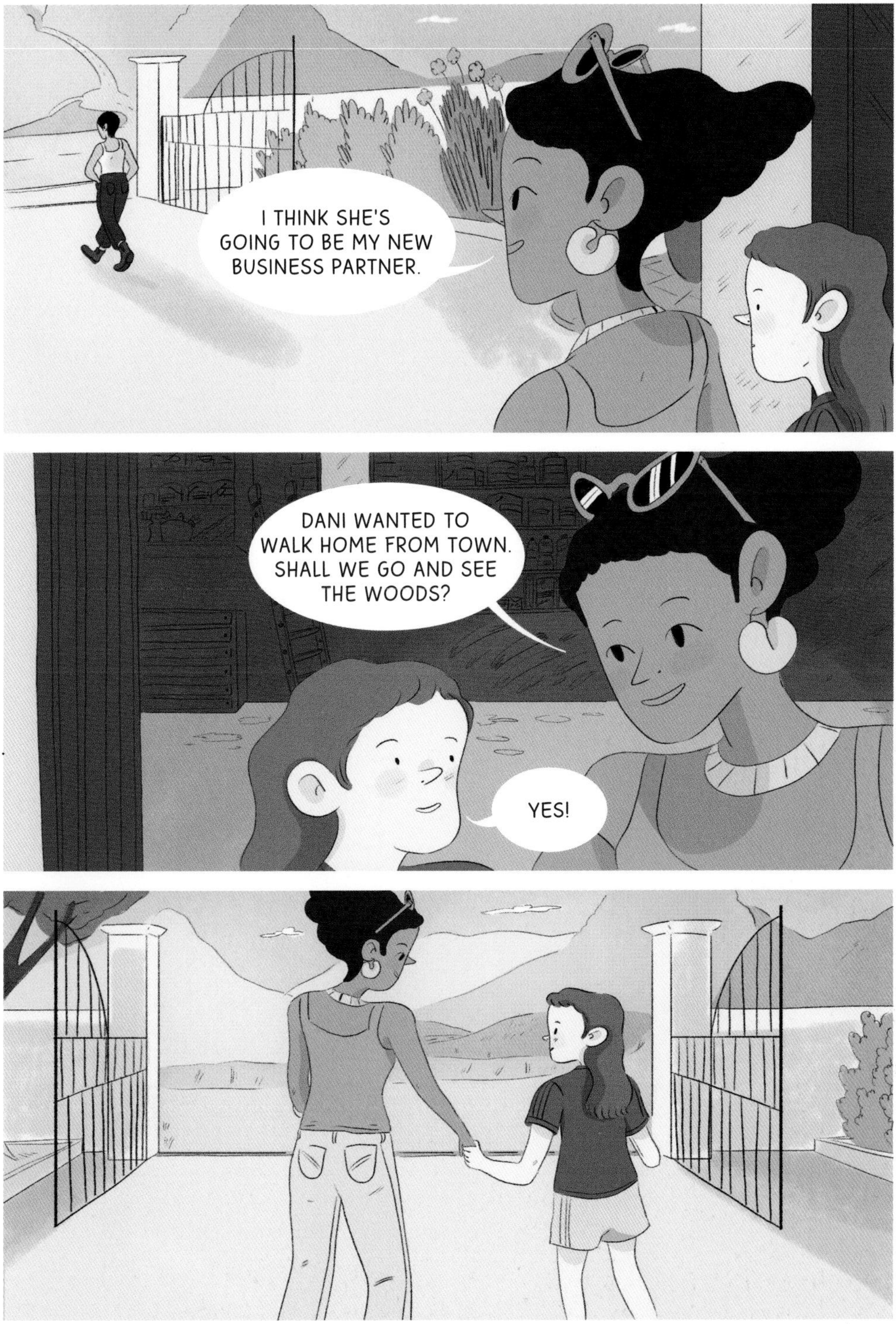
I THINK SHE'S GOING TO BE MY NEW BUSINESS PARTNER.
DANI WANTED TO WALK HOME FROM TOWN. SHALL WE GO AND SEE THE WOODS?
YES!

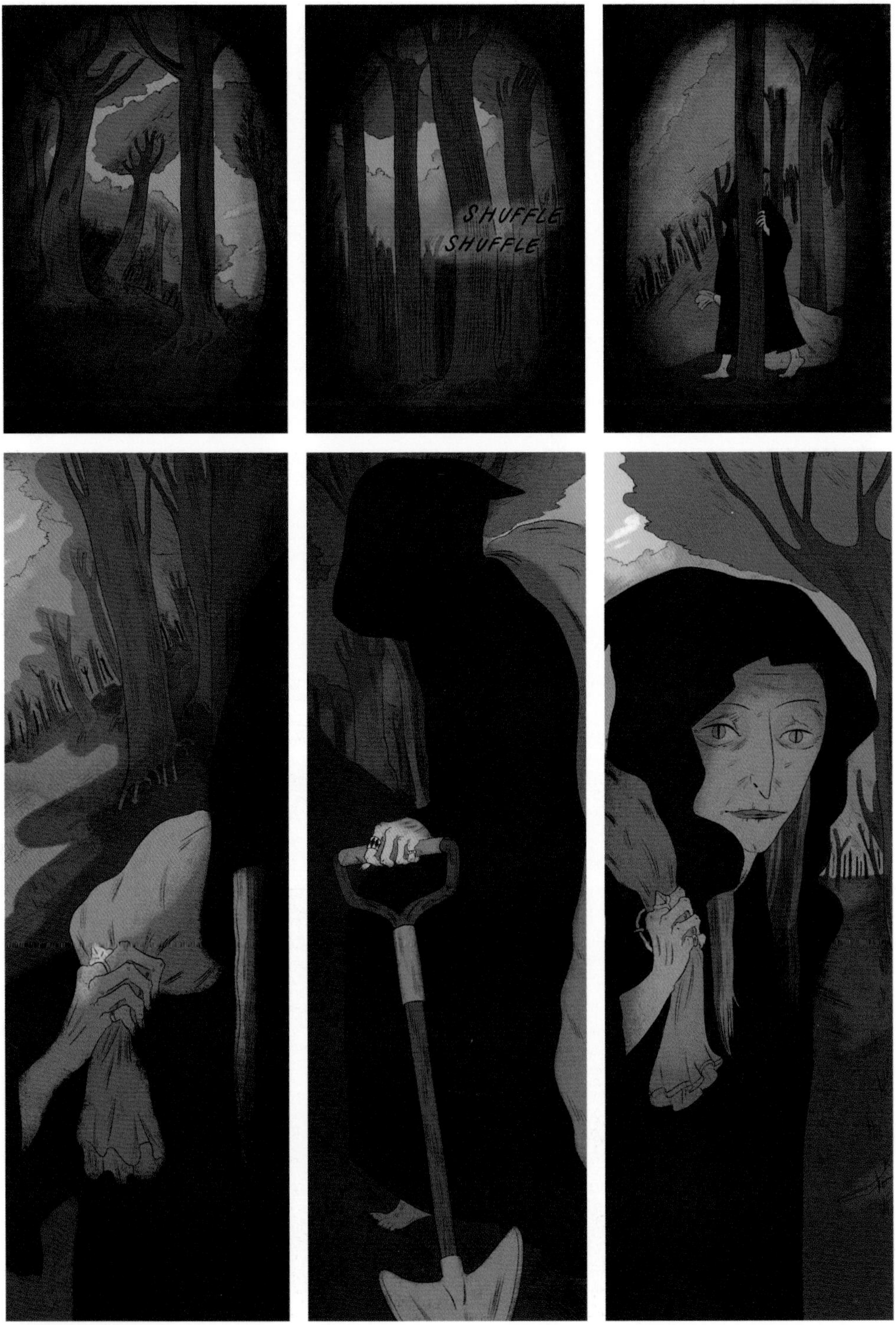
SHUFFLE
SHUFFLE

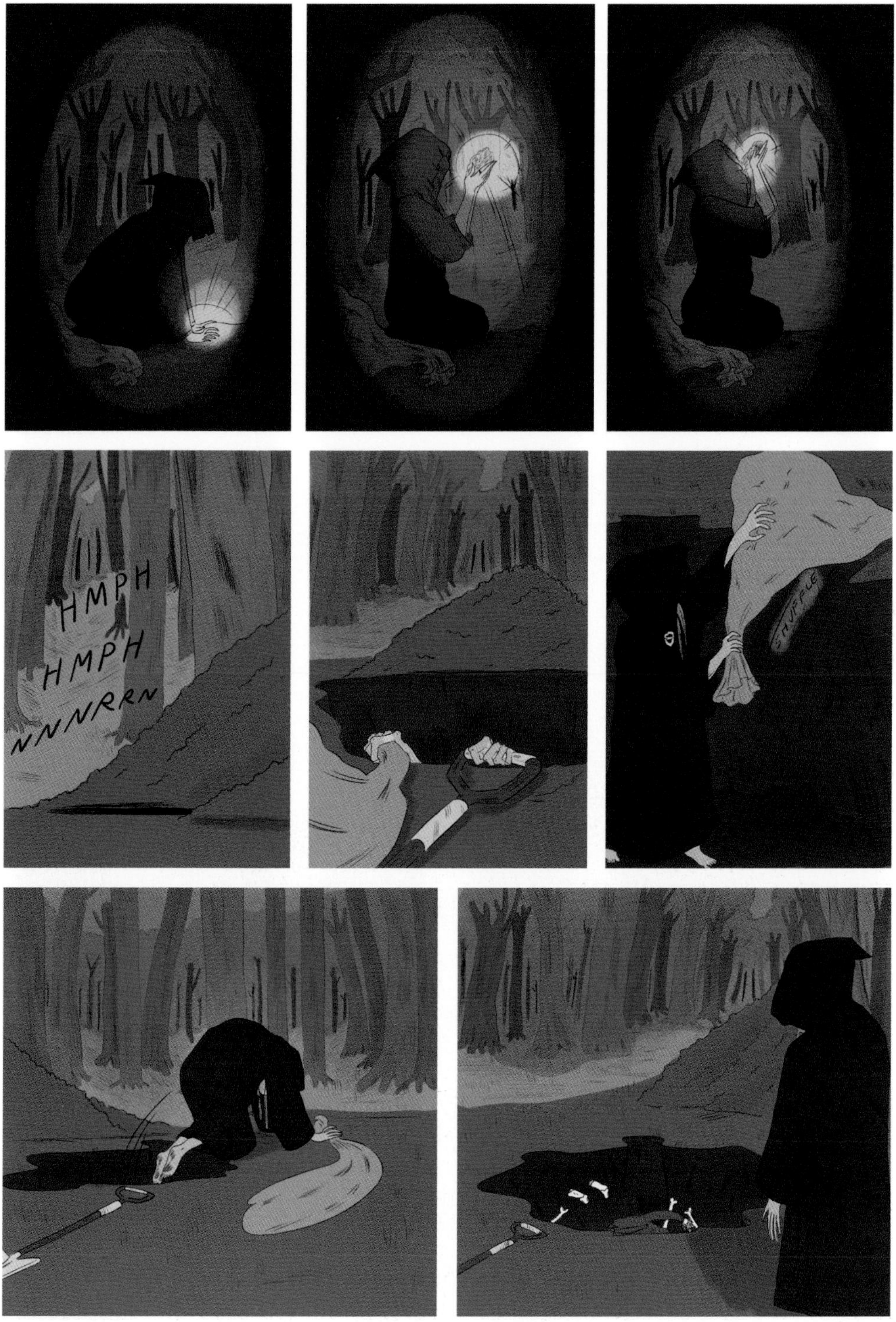
HMPH
HMPH
NNNRRN
SHUFFLE

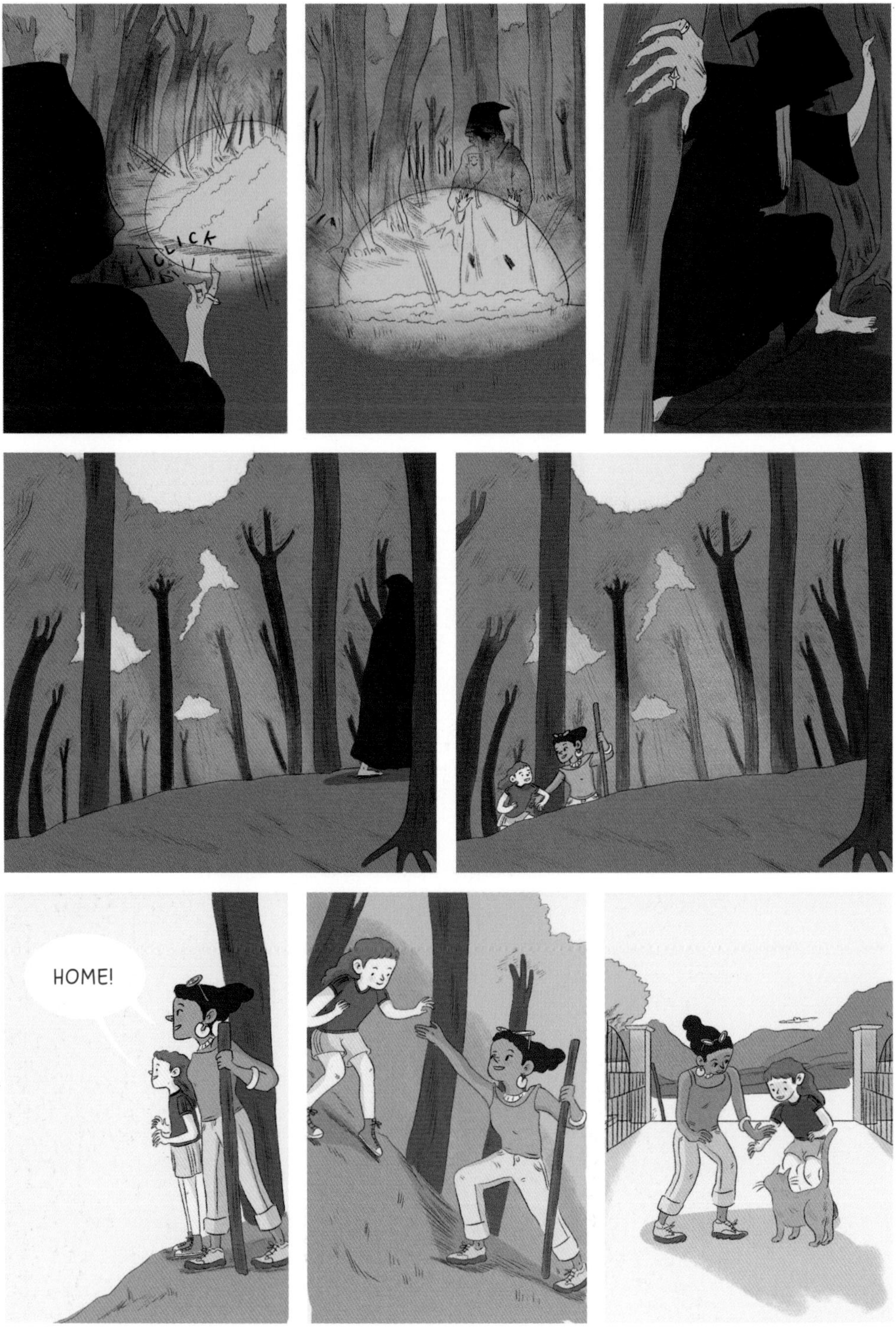
CLICK
HOME!

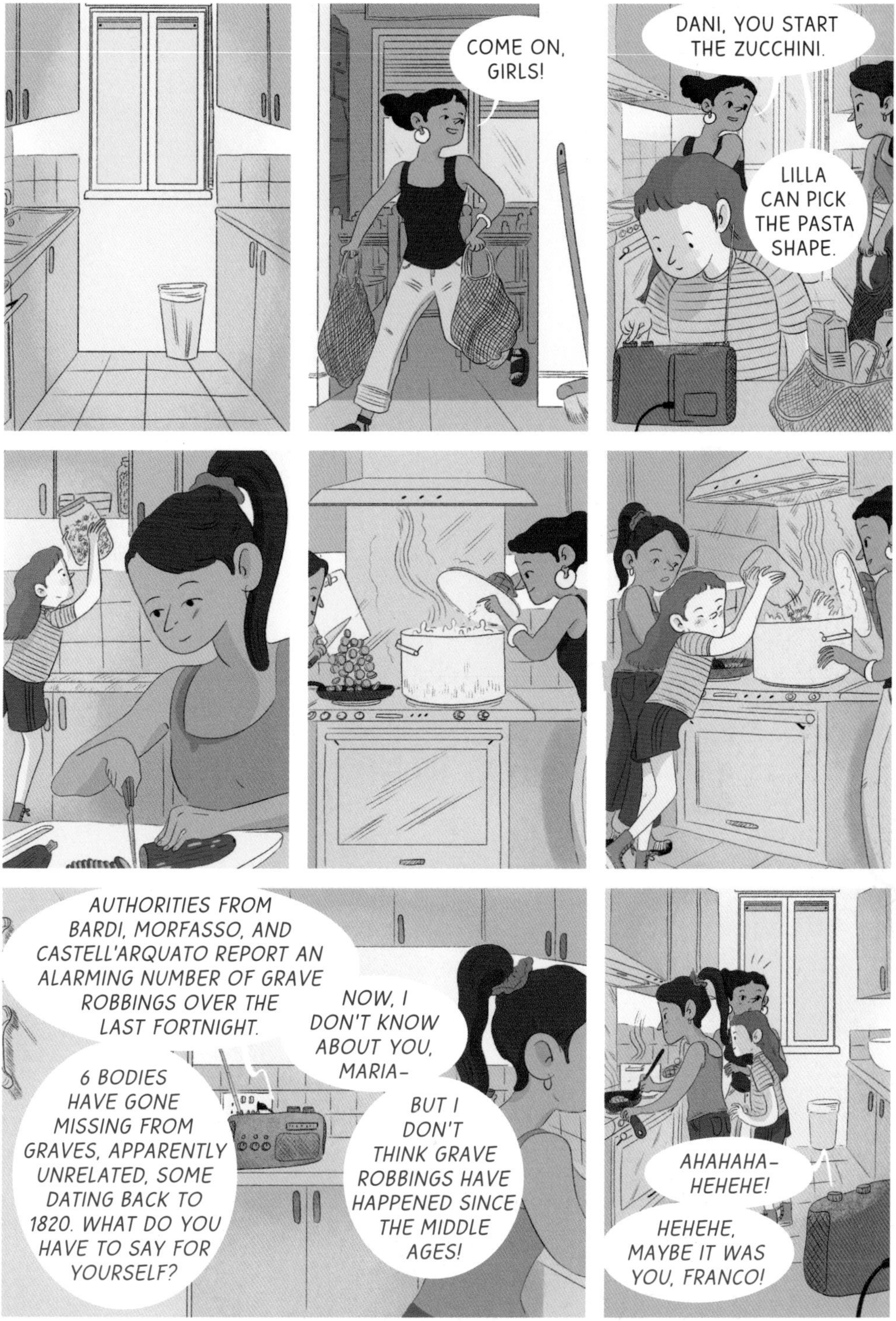
COME ON, GIRLS!
DANI, YOU START THE ZUCCHINI.
LILLA CAN PICK THE PASTA SHAPE.
AUTHORITIES FROM BARDI, MORFASSO, AND CASTELL'ARQUATO REPORT AN ALARMING NUMBER OF GRAVE ROBBINGS OVER THE LAST FORTNIGHT.
6 BODIES HAVE GONE MISSING FROM GRAVES, APPARENTLY UNRELATED, SOME DATING BACK TO 1820. WHAT DO YOU HAVE TO SAY FOR YOURSELF?
NOW, I DON'T KNOW ABOUT YOU, MARIA-
BUT I DON'T THINK GRAVE ROBBINGS HAVE HAPPENED SINCE THE MIDDLE AGES!
AHAHAHA-HEHEHE!
HEHEHE, MAYBE IT WAS YOU, FRANCO!

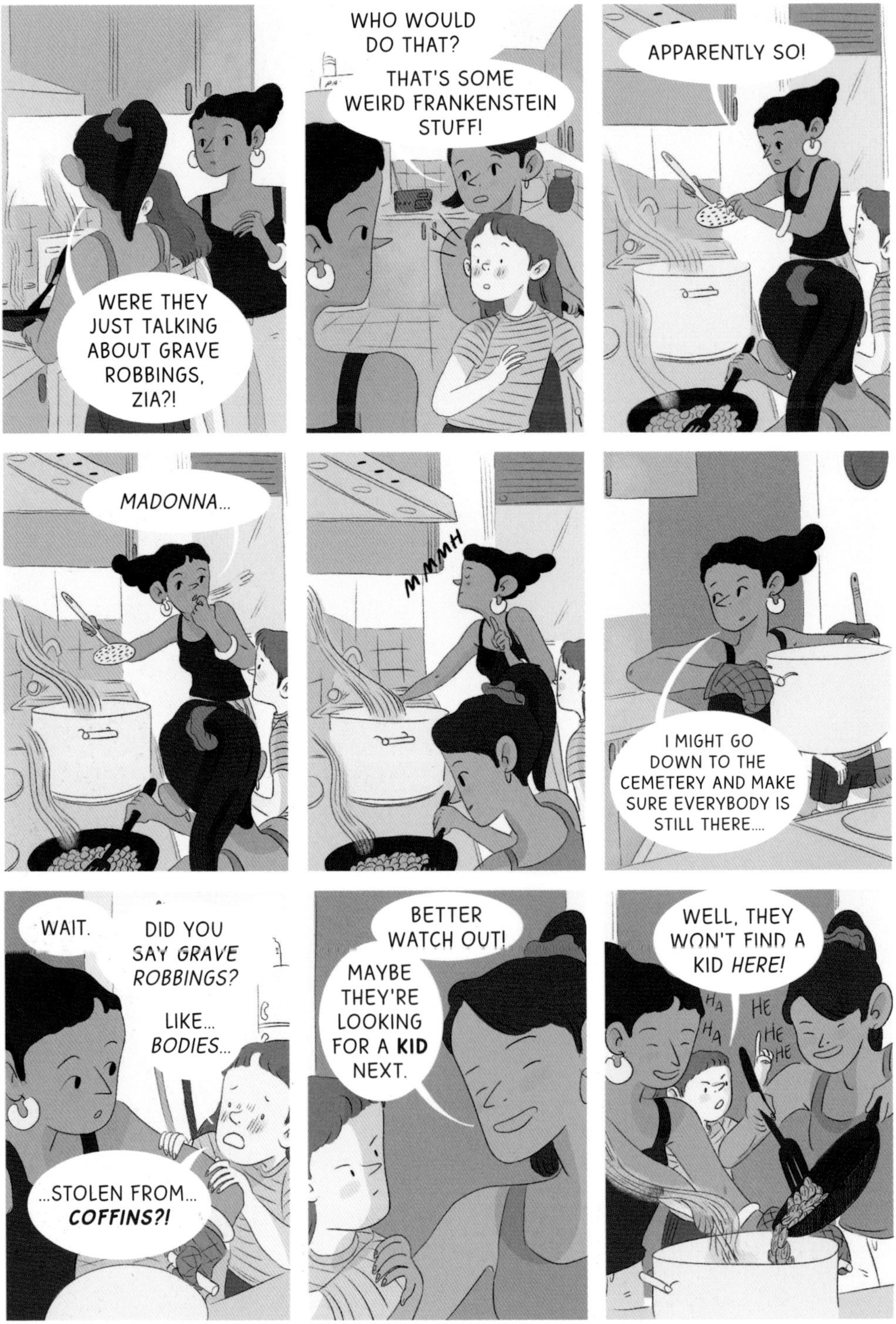
WERE THEY JUST TALKING ABOUT GRAVE ROBBINGS, ZIA?!
WHO WOULD DO THAT?
THAT'S SOME WEIRD FRANKENSTEIN STUFF!
APPARENTLY SO!
MADONNA...
MMMH
I MIGHT GO DOWN TO THE CEMETERY AND MAKE SURE EVERYBODY IS STILL THERE....
WAIT.
DID YOU SAY GRAVE ROBBINGS?
LIKE... BODIES...
...STOLEN FROM... COFFINS?!
BETTER WATCH OUT!
MAYBE THEY'RE LOOKING FOR A KID NEXT.
WELL, THEY WON'T FIND A KID HERE!
HA HA
HE HE HE

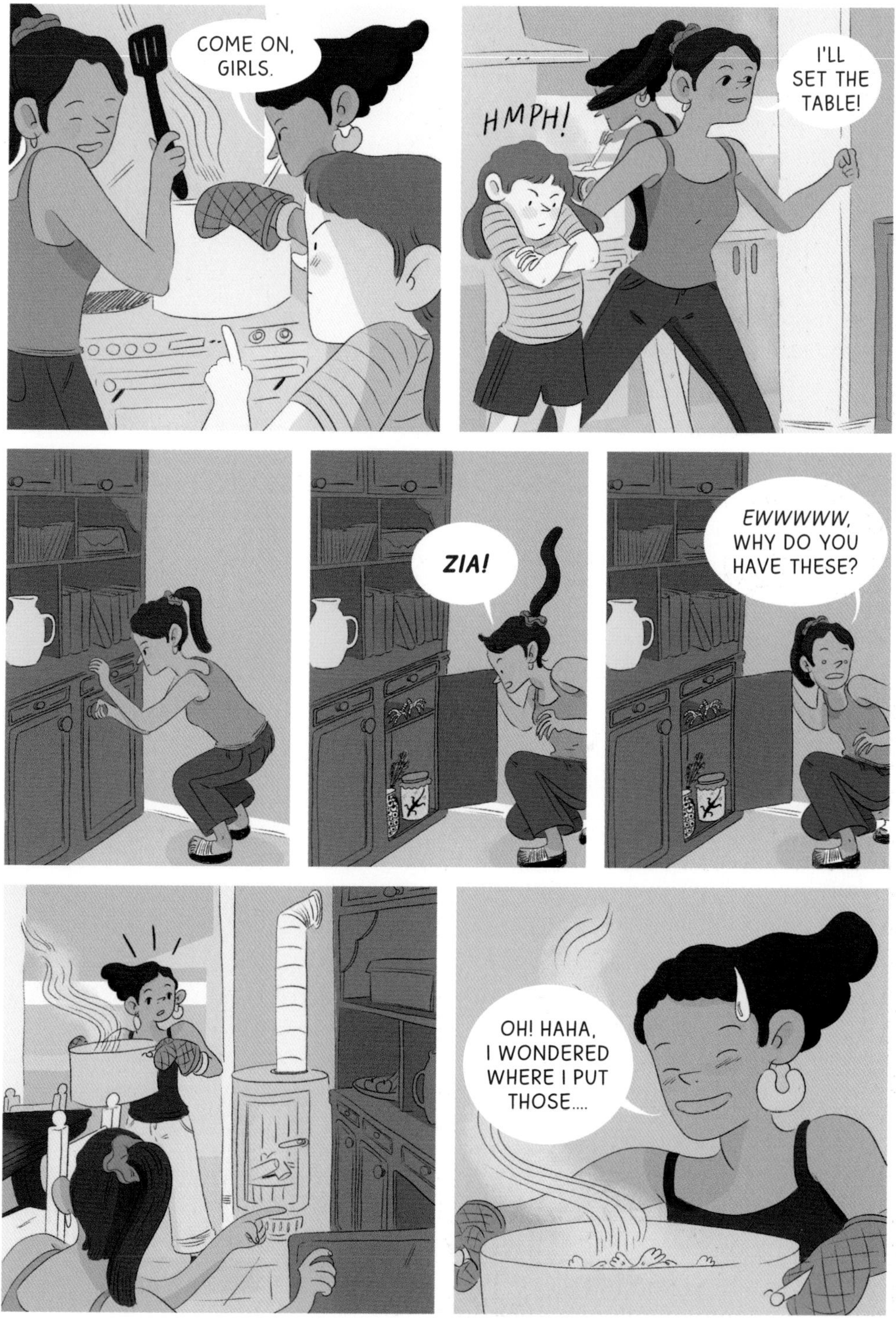
COME ON, GIRLS.
HMPH!
I'LL SET THE TABLE!
ZIA!
EWWWWW, WHY DO YOU HAVE THESE?
OH! HAHA, I WONDERED WHERE I PUT THOSE....

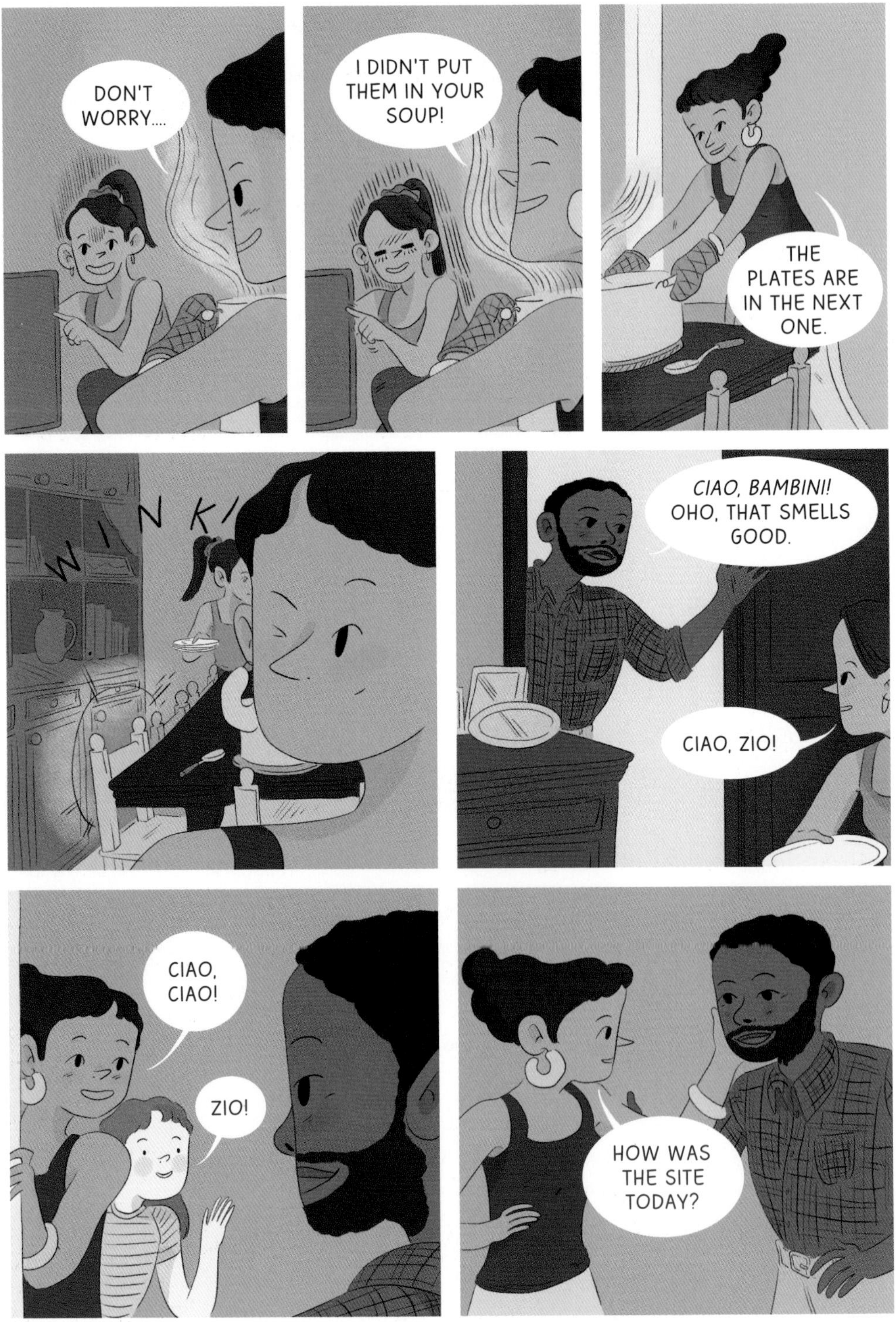
DON'T WORRY....
I DIDN'T PUT THEM IN YOUR SOUP!
THE PLATES ARE IN THE NEXT ONE.
WINK!
CIAO, BAMBINI! OHO, THAT SMELLS GOOD.
CIAO, ZIO!
CIAO, CIAO!
ZIO!
HOW WAS THE SITE TODAY?

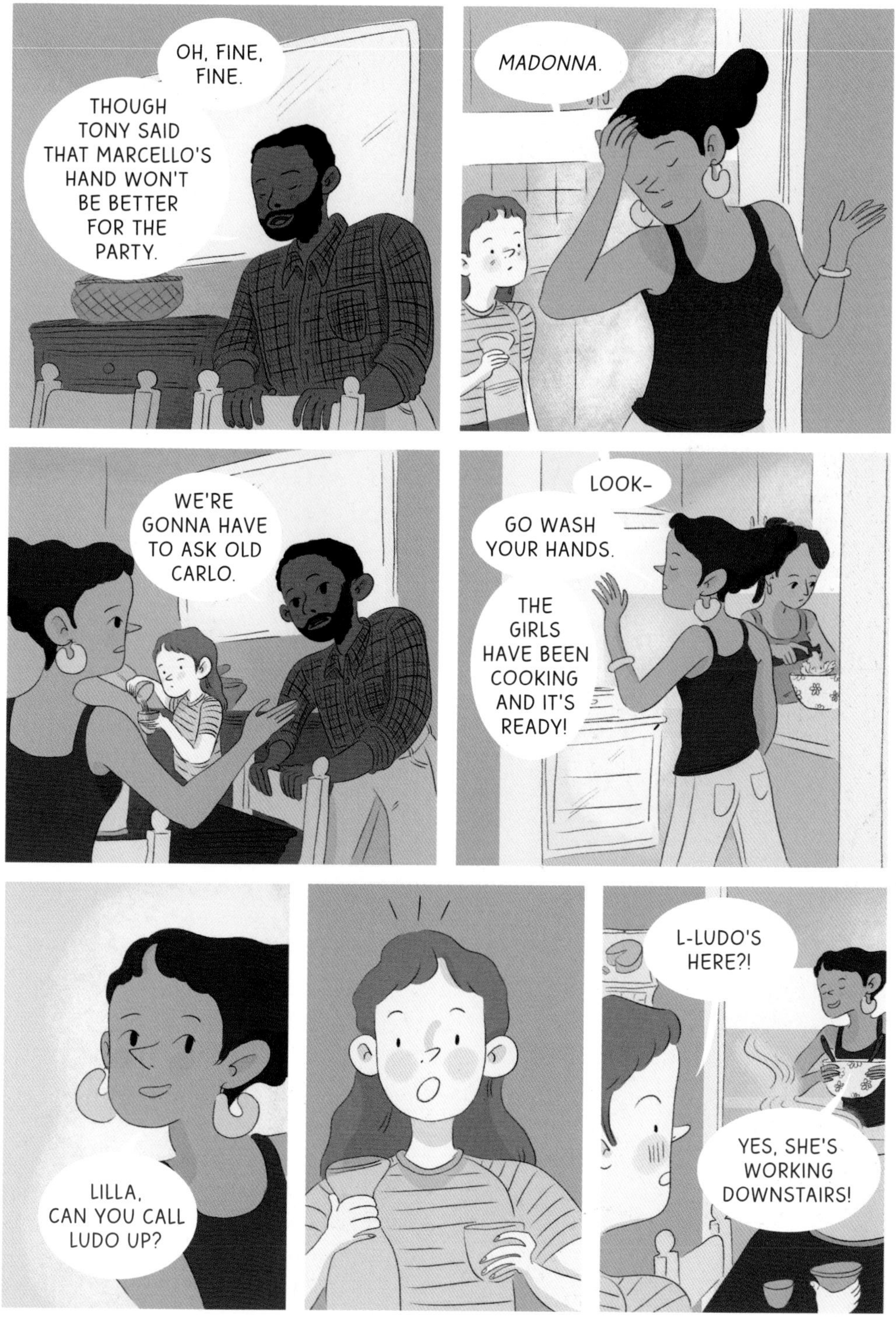
OH, FINE, FINE.
THOUGH TONY SAID THAT MARCELLO'S HAND WON'T BE BETTER FOR THE PARTY.
MADONNA.
WE'RE GONNA HAVE TO ASK OLD CARLO.
LOOK-
GO WASH YOUR HANDS.
THE GIRLS HAVE BEEN COOKING AND IT'S READY!
LILLA, CAN YOU CALL LUDO UP?
L-LUDO'S HERE?!
YES, SHE'S WORKING DOWNSTAIRS!

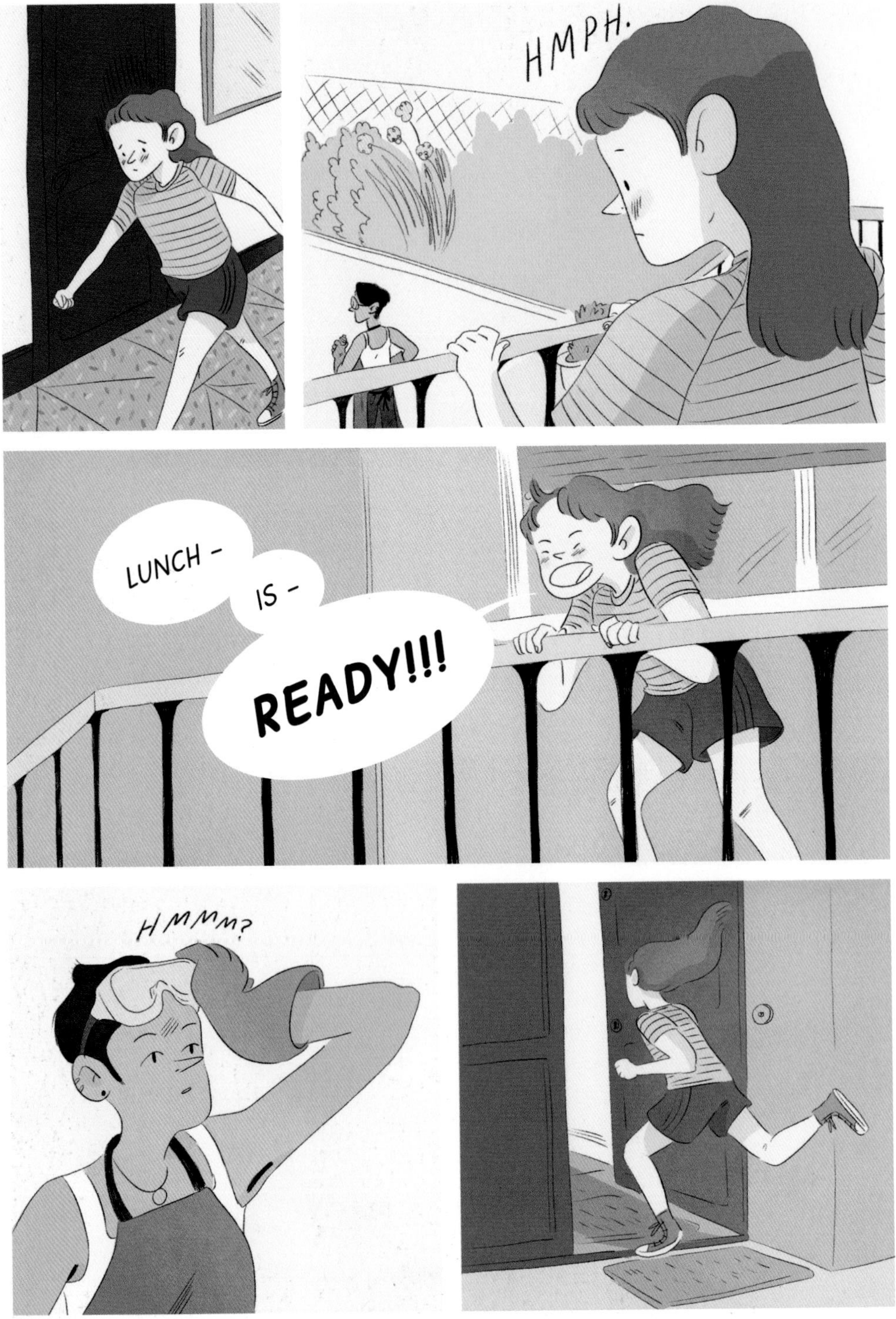
HMPH.
LUNCH -
IS -
READY!!!
HMMM?

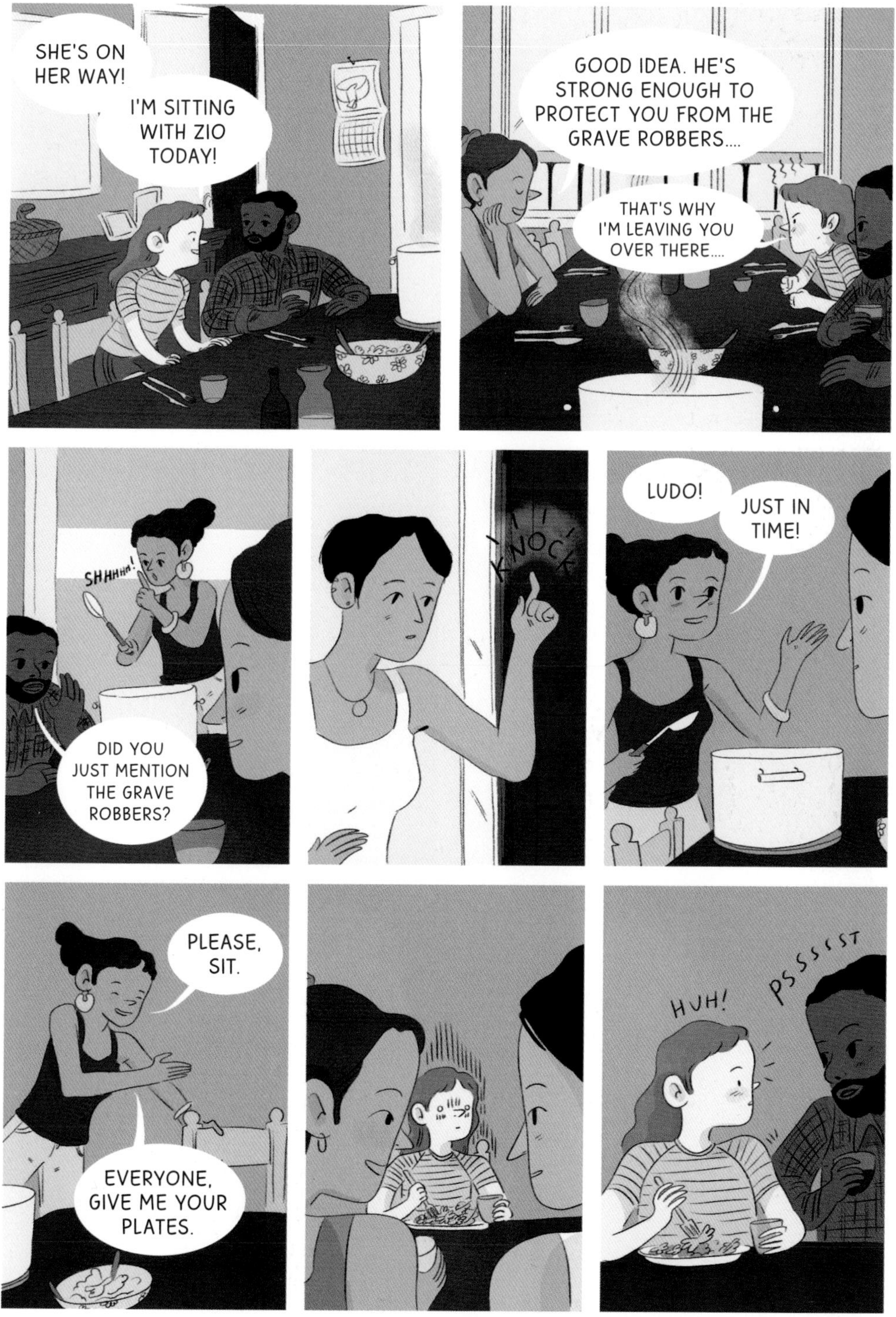
SHE'S ON HER WAY!
I'M SITTING WITH ZIO TODAY!
GOOD IDEA. HE'S STRONG ENOUGH TO PROTECT YOU FROM THE GRAVE ROBBERS....
THAT'S WHY I'M LEAVING YOU OVER THERE....
SHHHHH!
DID YOU JUST MENTION THE GRAVE ROBBERS?
KNOCK
LUDO!
JUST IN TIME!
PLEASE, SIT.
EVERYONE, GIVE ME YOUR PLATES.
HUH!
PSSSSST

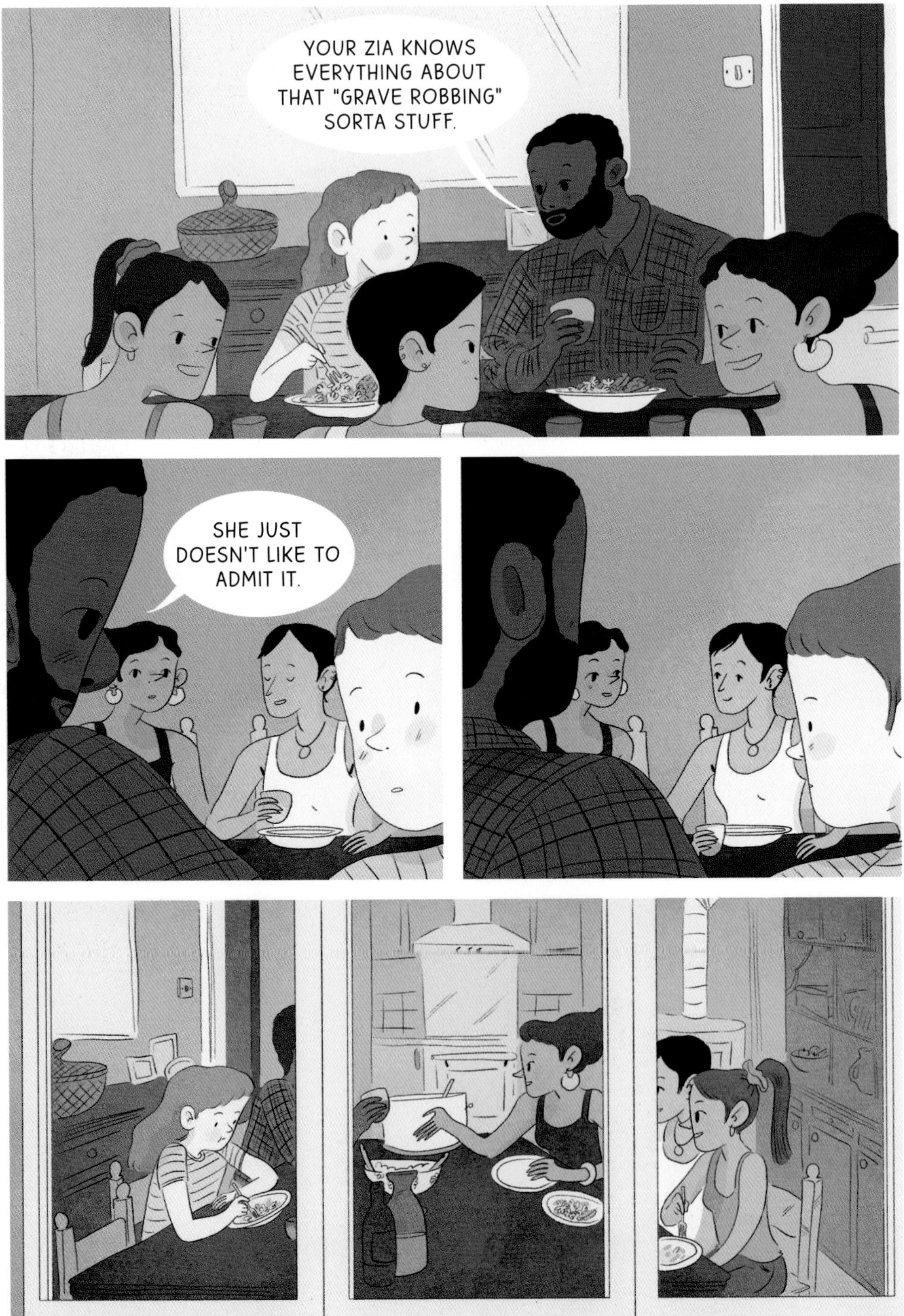
YOUR ZIA KNOWS EVERYTHING ABOUT THAT "GRAVE ROBBING" SORTA STUFF.
SHE JUST DOESN'T LIKE TO ADMIT IT.

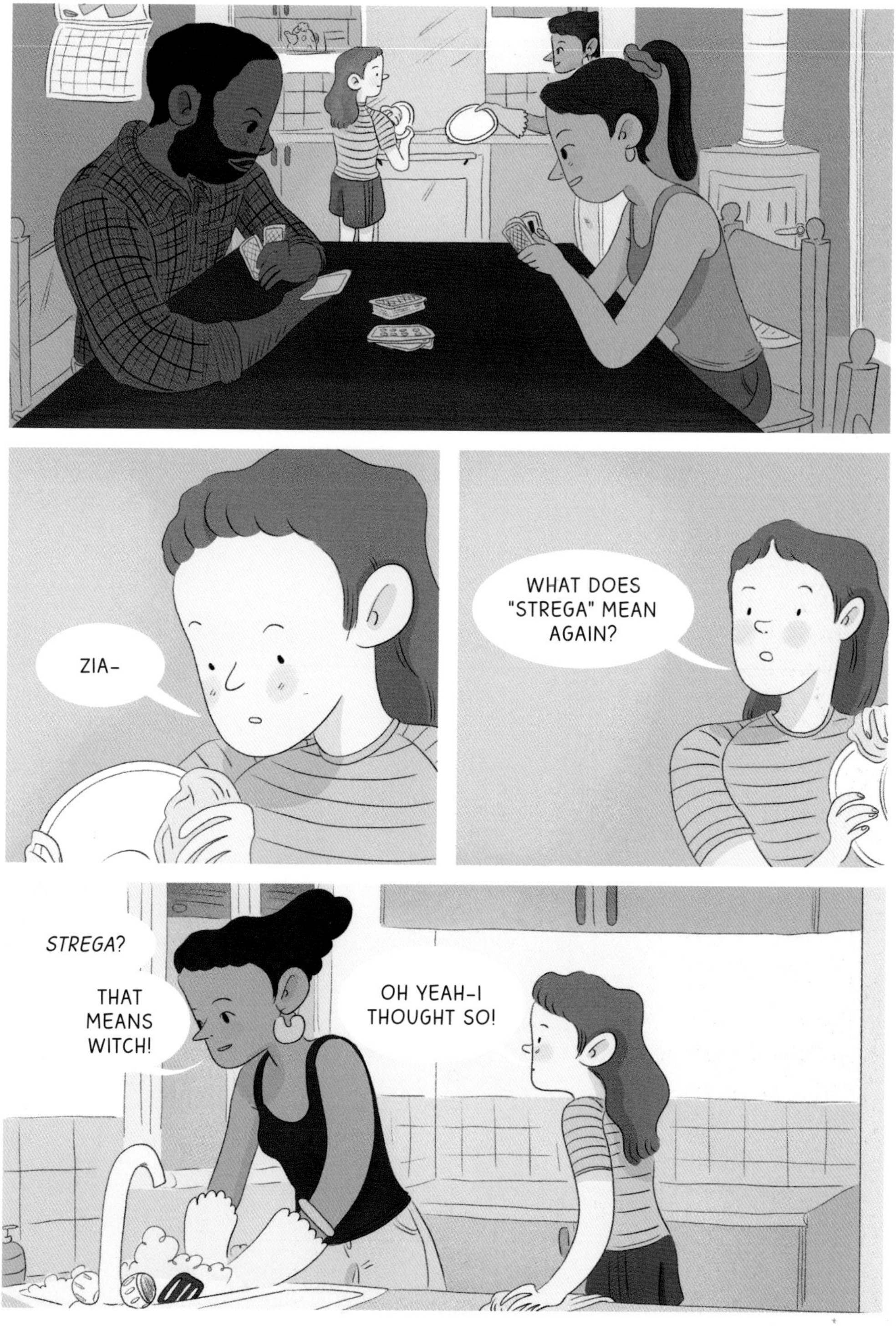
ZIA-
WHAT DOES "STREGA" MEAN AGAIN?
STREGA?
THAT MEANS WITCH!
OH YEAH-I THOUGHT SO!

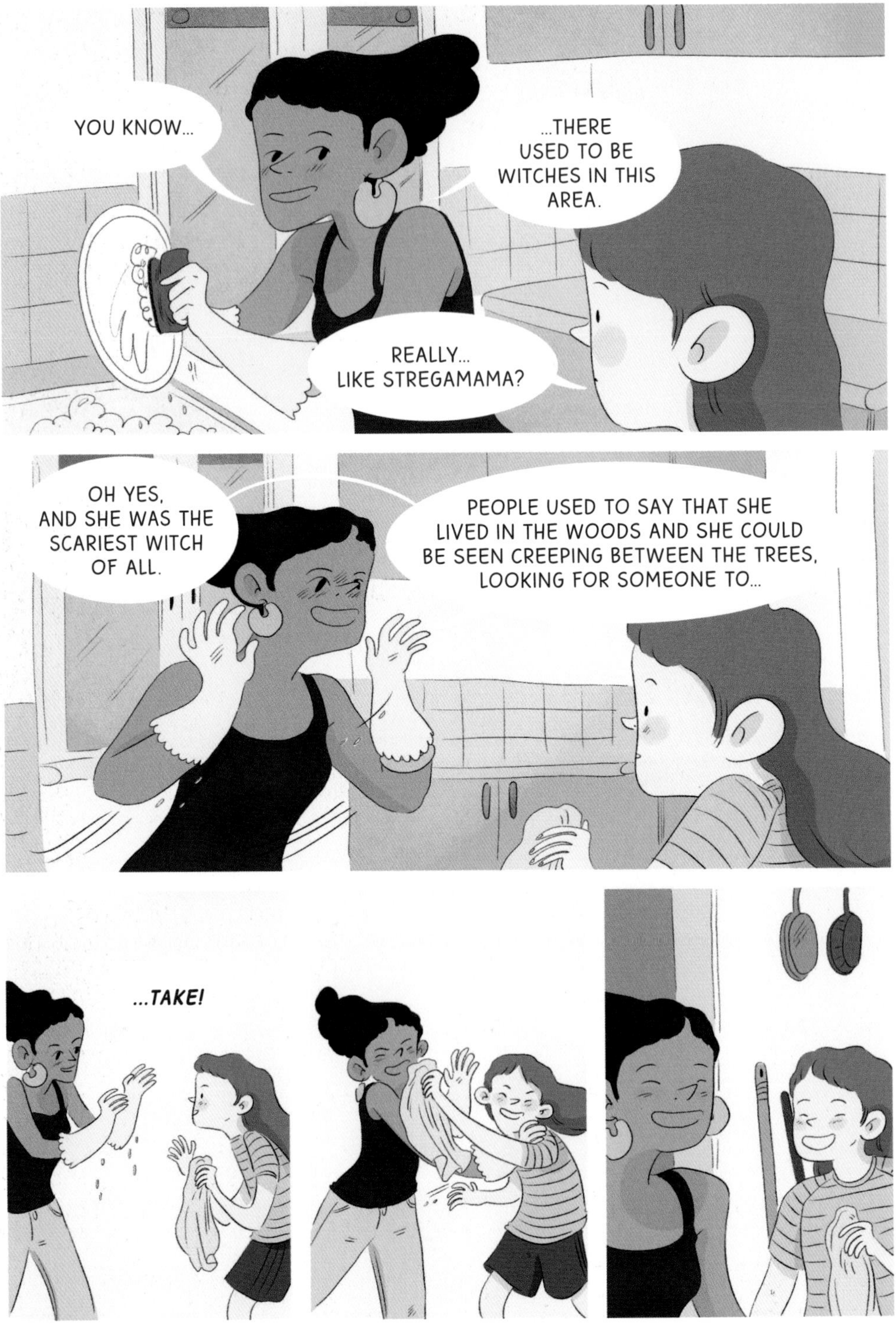

YOU KNOW...
...THERE USED TO BE WITCHES IN THIS AREA.
REALLY... LIKE STREGAMAMA?
OH YES, AND SHE WAS THE SCARIEST WITCH OF ALL.
PEOPLE USED TO SAY THAT SHE LIVED IN THE WOODS AND SHE COULD BE SEEN CREEPING BETWEEN THE TREES, LOOKING FOR SOMEONE TO...
...TAKE!

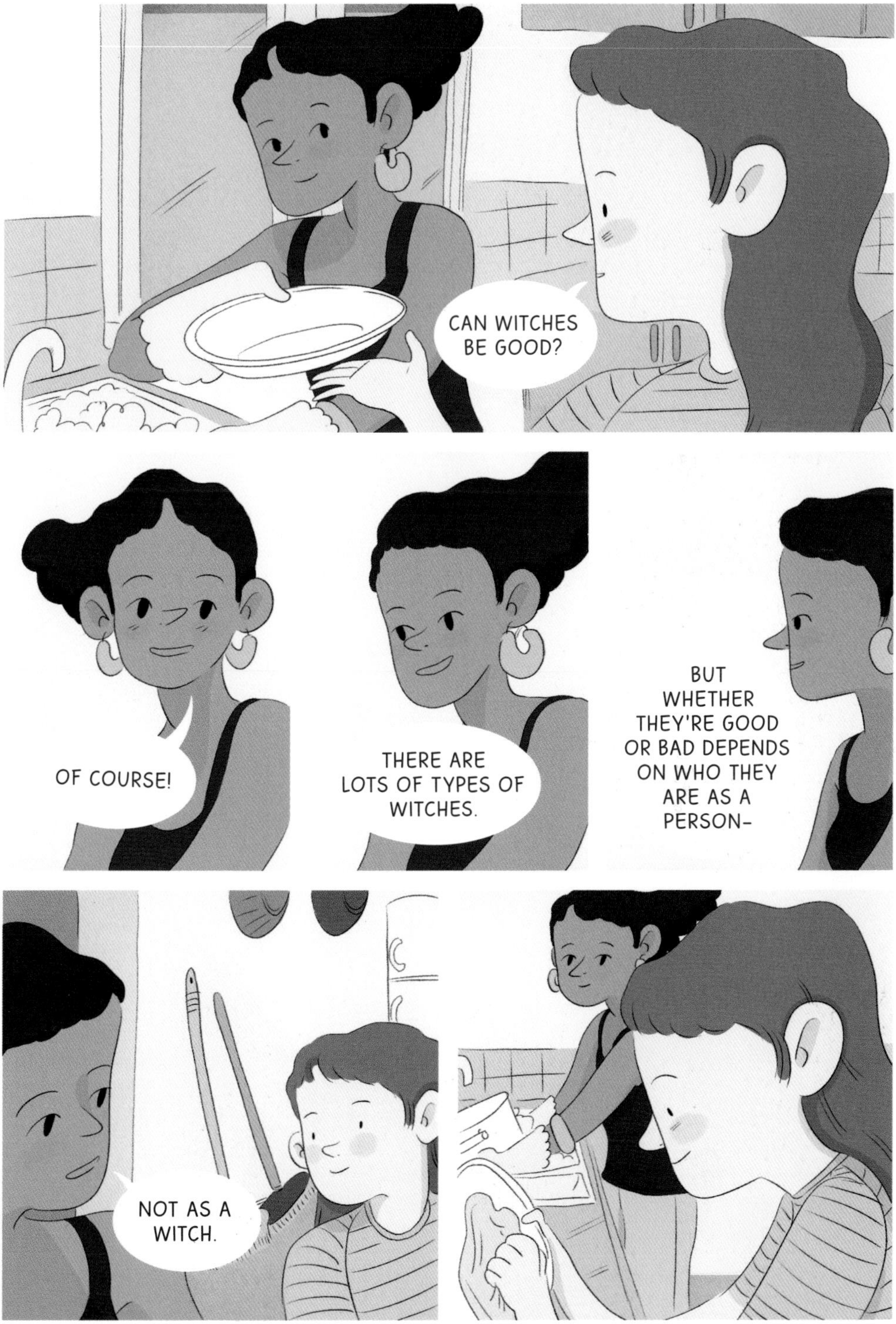
CAN WITCHES BE GOOD?
OF COURSE!
THERE ARE LOTS OF TYPES OF WITCHES.
BUT WHETHER THEY'RE GOOD OR BAD DEPENDS ON WHO THEY ARE AS A PERSON-
NOT AS A WITCH.

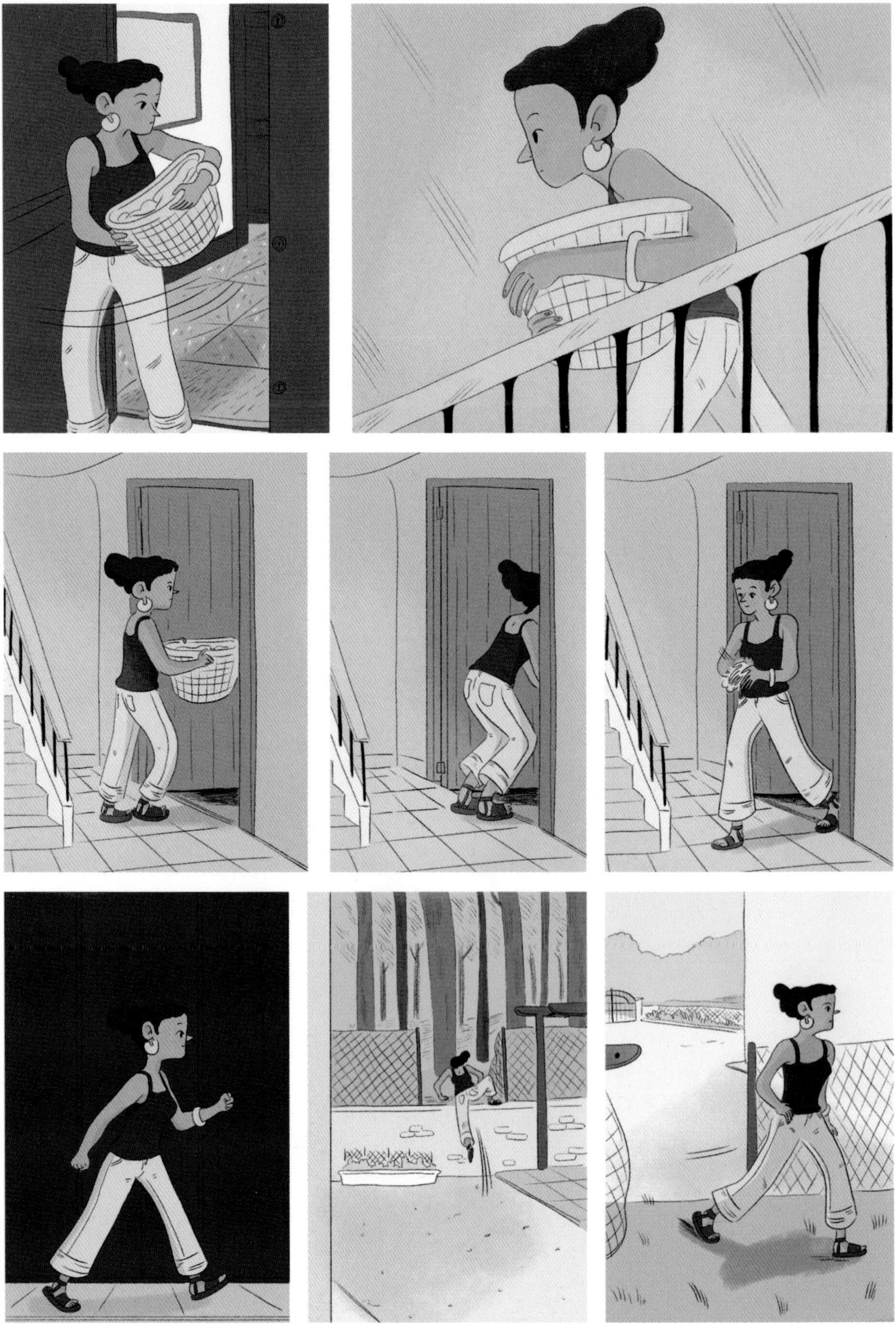

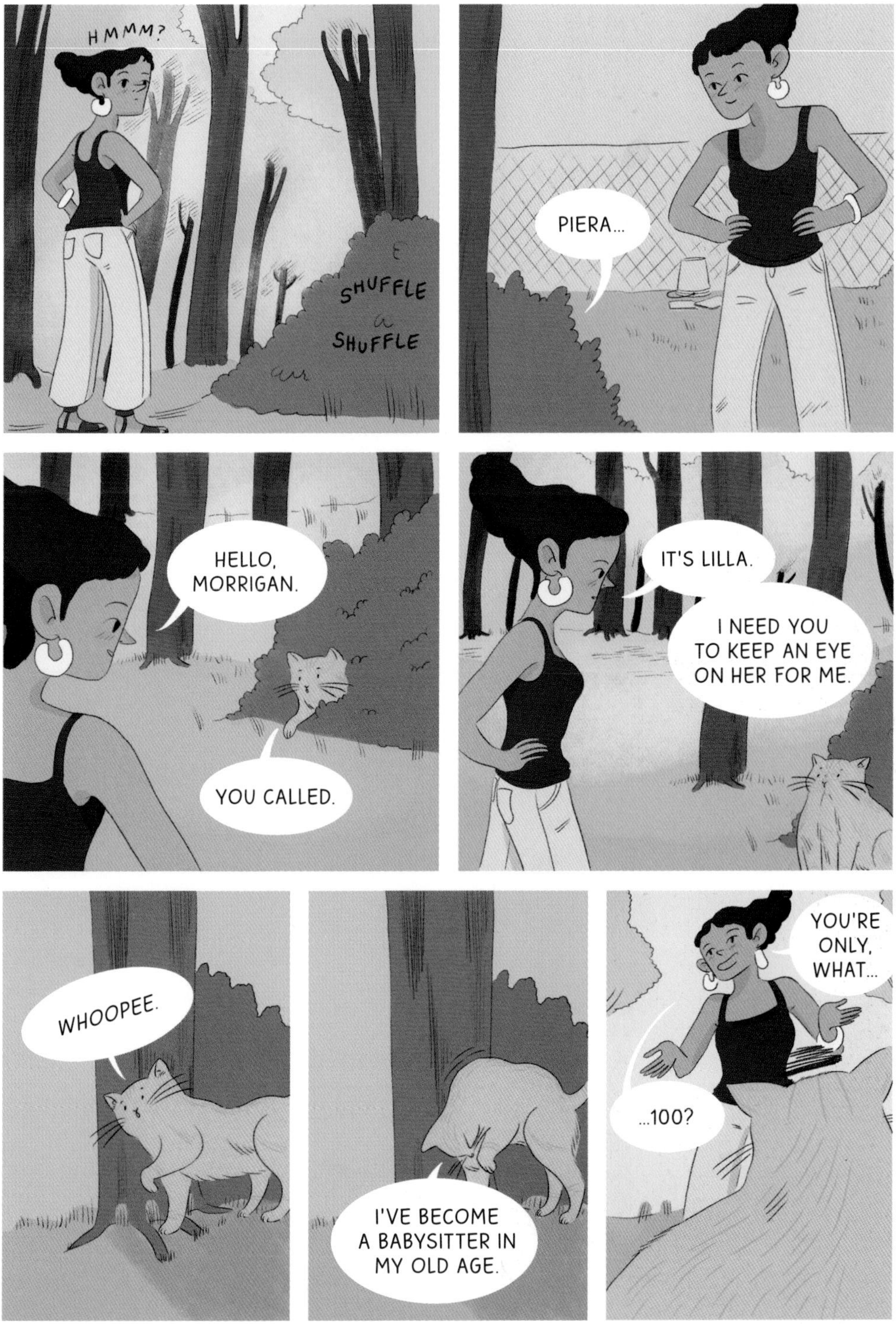
HMMM?
SHUFFLE
SHUFFLE
PIERA...
HELLO, MORRIGAN.
YOU CALLED.
IT'S LILLA.
I NEED YOU TO KEEP AN EYE ON HER FOR ME.
WHOOPEE.
I'VE BECOME A BABYSITTER IN MY OLD AGE.
YOU'RE ONLY, WHAT...
...100?

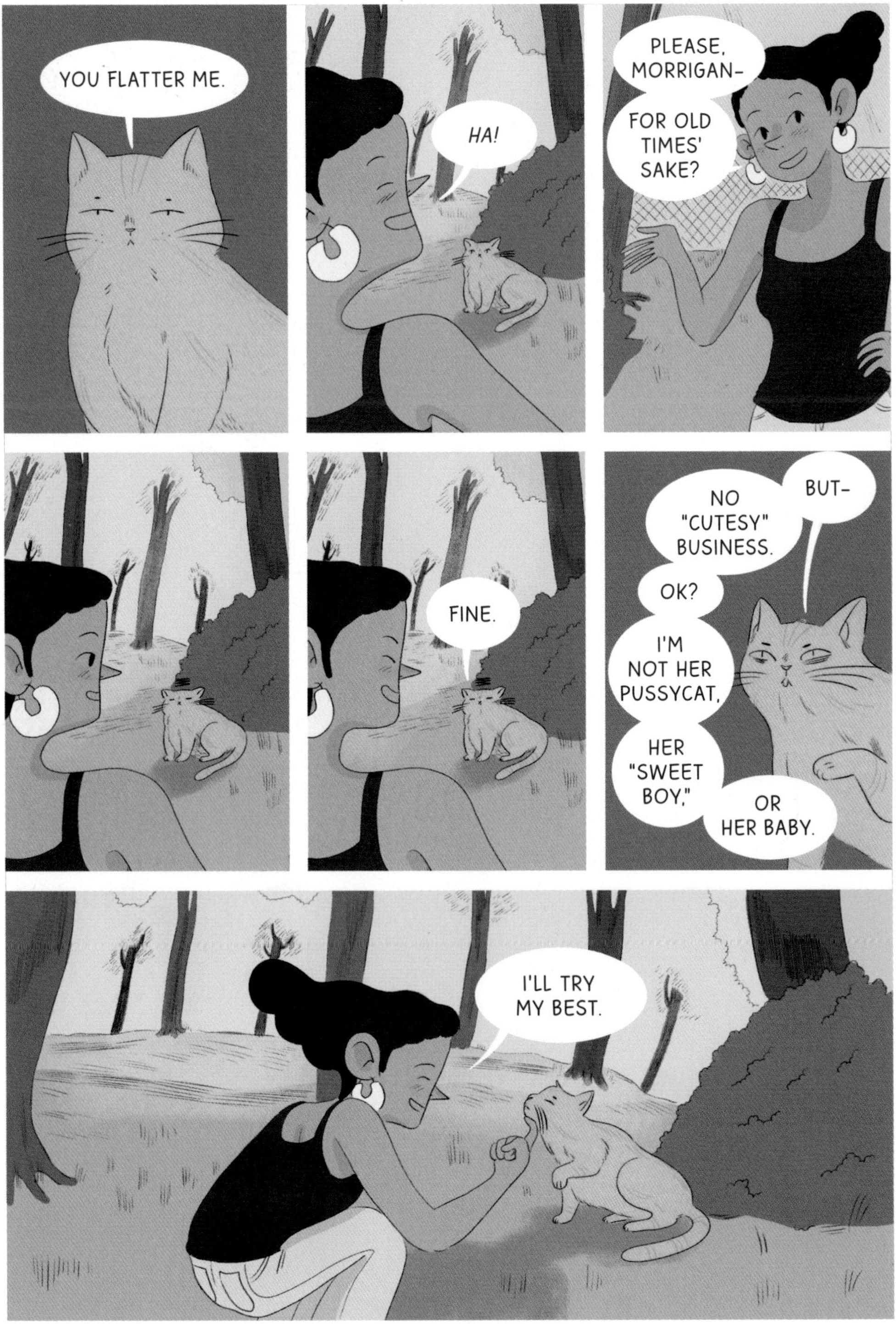
YOU FLATTER ME.
HA!
PLEASE, MORRIGAN-
FOR OLD TIMES' SAKE?
FINE.
NO "CUTESY" BUSINESS.
OK?
BUT-
I'M NOT HER PUSSYCAT,
HER "SWEET BOY,"
OR HER BABY.
I'LL TRY MY BEST.

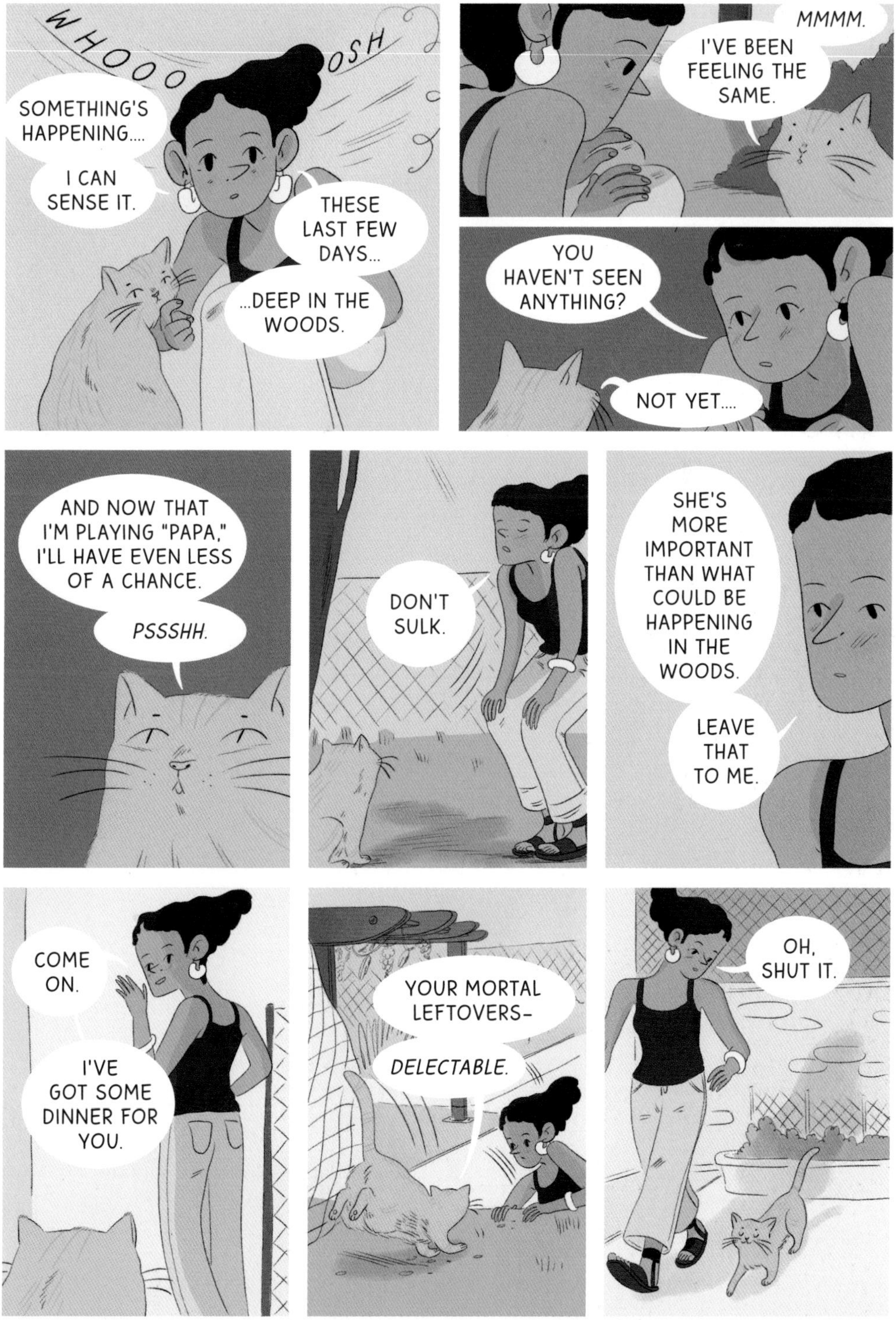
WHOOOOSH
SOMETHING'S HAPPENING....
I CAN SENSE IT.
THESE LAST FEW DAYS...
...DEEP IN THE WOODS.
MMMM.
I'VE BEEN FEELING THE SAME.
YOU HAVEN'T SEEN ANYTHING?
NOT YET....
AND NOW THAT I'M PLAYING "PAPA," I'LL HAVE EVEN LESS OF A CHANCE.
PSSSHH.
DON'T SULK.
SHE'S MORE IMPORTANT THAN WHAT COULD BE HAPPENING IN THE WOODS.
LEAVE THAT TO ME.
COME ON.
I'VE GOT SOME DINNER FOR YOU.
YOUR MORTAL LEFTOVERS–
DELECTABLE.
OH, SHUT IT.

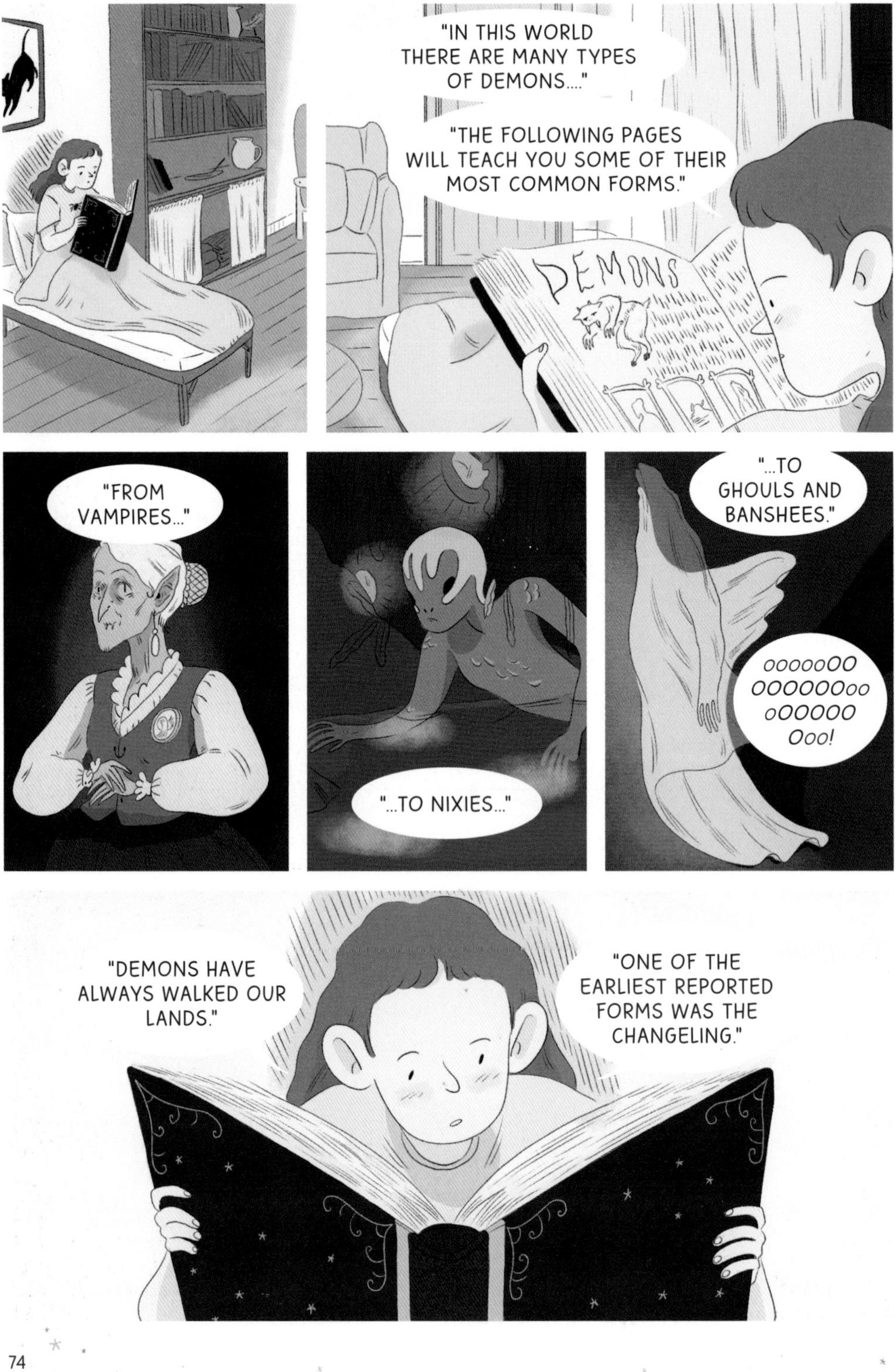
"IN THIS WORLD THERE ARE MANY TYPES OF DEMONS...."
"THE FOLLOWING PAGES WILL TEACH YOU SOME OF THEIR MOST COMMON FORMS."
DEMONS
"FROM VAMPIRES..."
"...TO NIXIES..."
"...TO GHOULS AND BANSHEES."
oooooOO OOOOOOoo oOOOOO Ooo!
"DEMONS HAVE ALWAYS WALKED OUR LANDS."
"ONE OF THE EARLIEST REPORTED FORMS WAS THE CHANGELING."

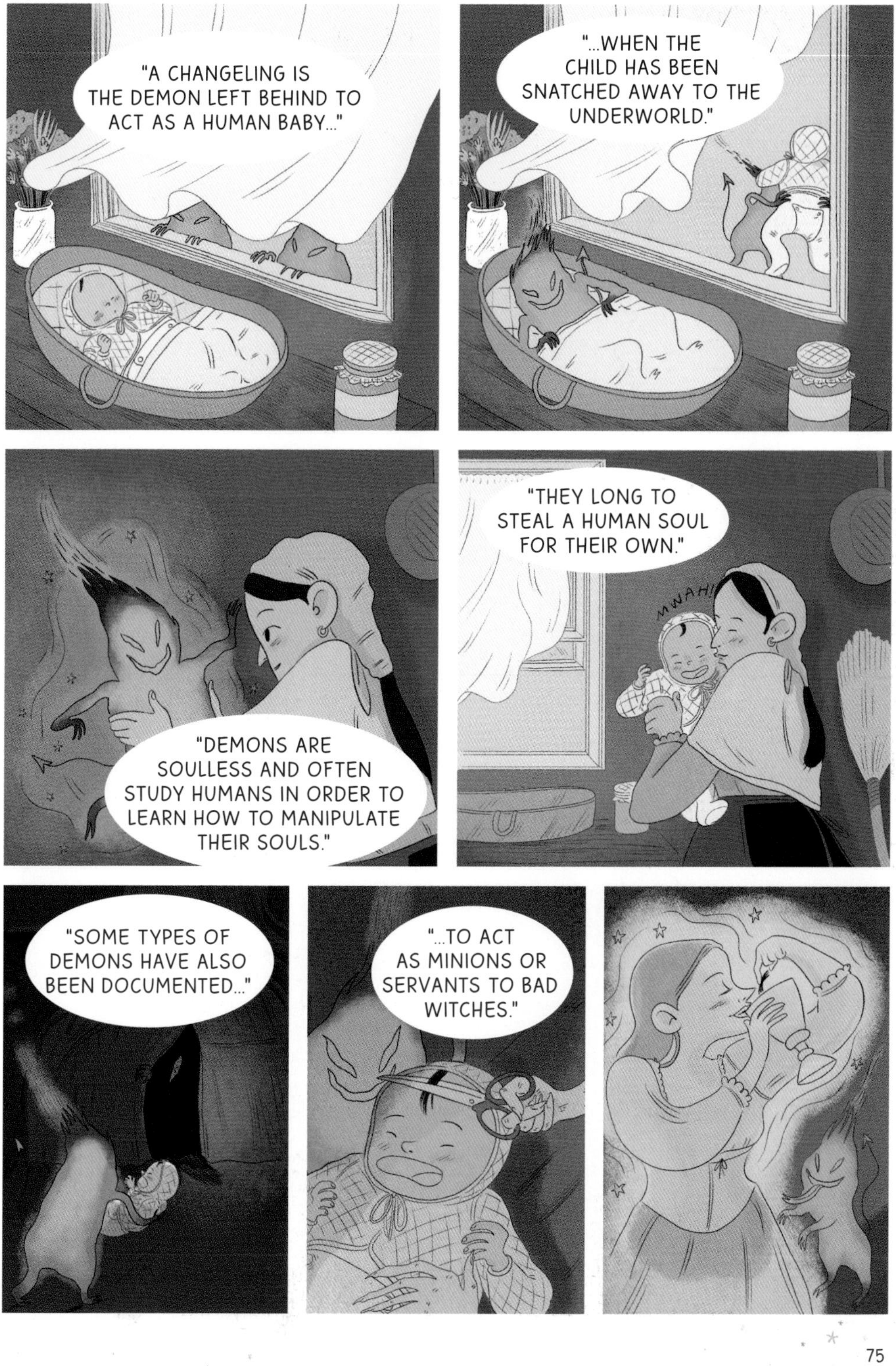
"A CHANGELING IS THE DEMON LEFT BEHIND TO ACT AS A HUMAN BABY..."
"...WHEN THE CHILD HAS BEEN SNATCHED AWAY TO THE UNDERWORLD."
"DEMONS ARE SOULLESS AND OFTEN STUDY HUMANS IN ORDER TO LEARN HOW TO MANIPULATE THEIR SOULS."
"THEY LONG TO STEAL A HUMAN SOUL FOR THEIR OWN."
MWAH!
"SOME TYPES OF DEMONS HAVE ALSO BEEN DOCUMENTED..."
"...TO ACT AS MINIONS OR SERVANTS TO BAD WITCHES."

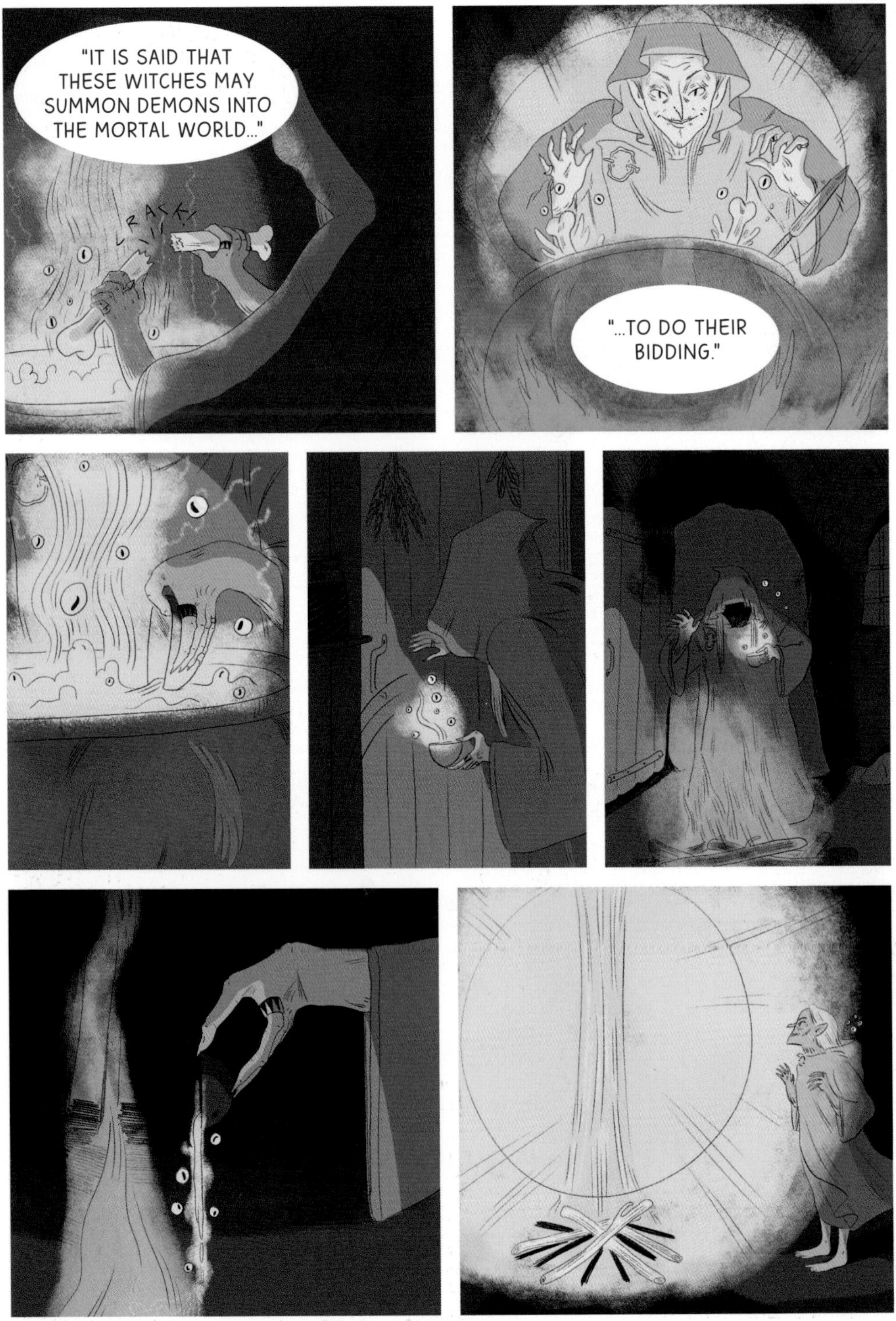
"IT IS SAID THAT THESE WITCHES MAY SUMMON DEMONS INTO THE MORTAL WORLD..."
CRACK!
"...TO DO THEIR BIDDING."

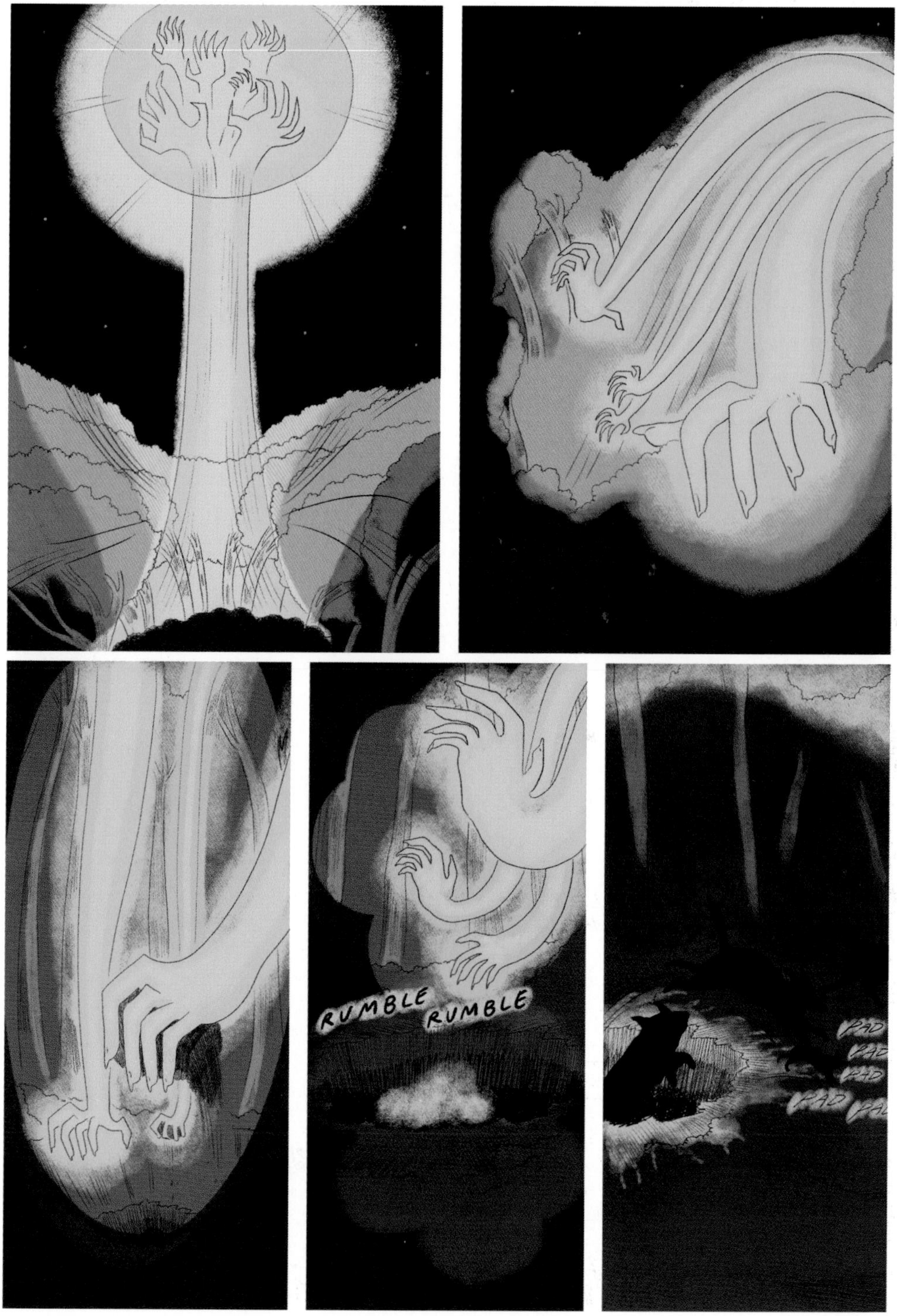
RUMBLE
RUMBLE
PAD
PAD
PAD
PAD

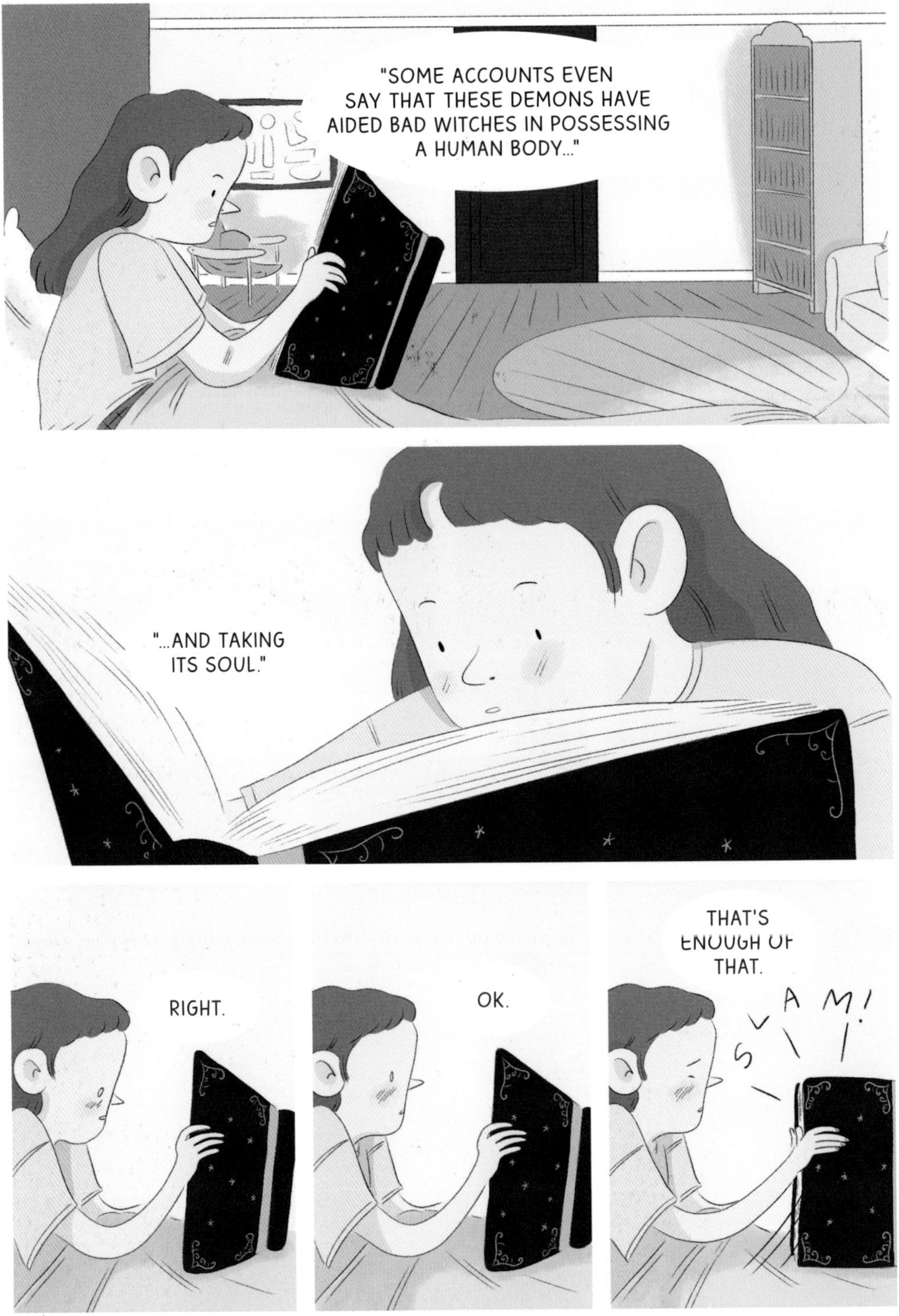
"SOME ACCOUNTS EVEN SAY THAT THESE DEMONS HAVE AIDED BAD WITCHES IN POSSESSING A HUMAN BODY..."
"...AND TAKING ITS SOUL."
RIGHT.
OK.
THAT'S ENOUGH OF THAT.
SLAM!

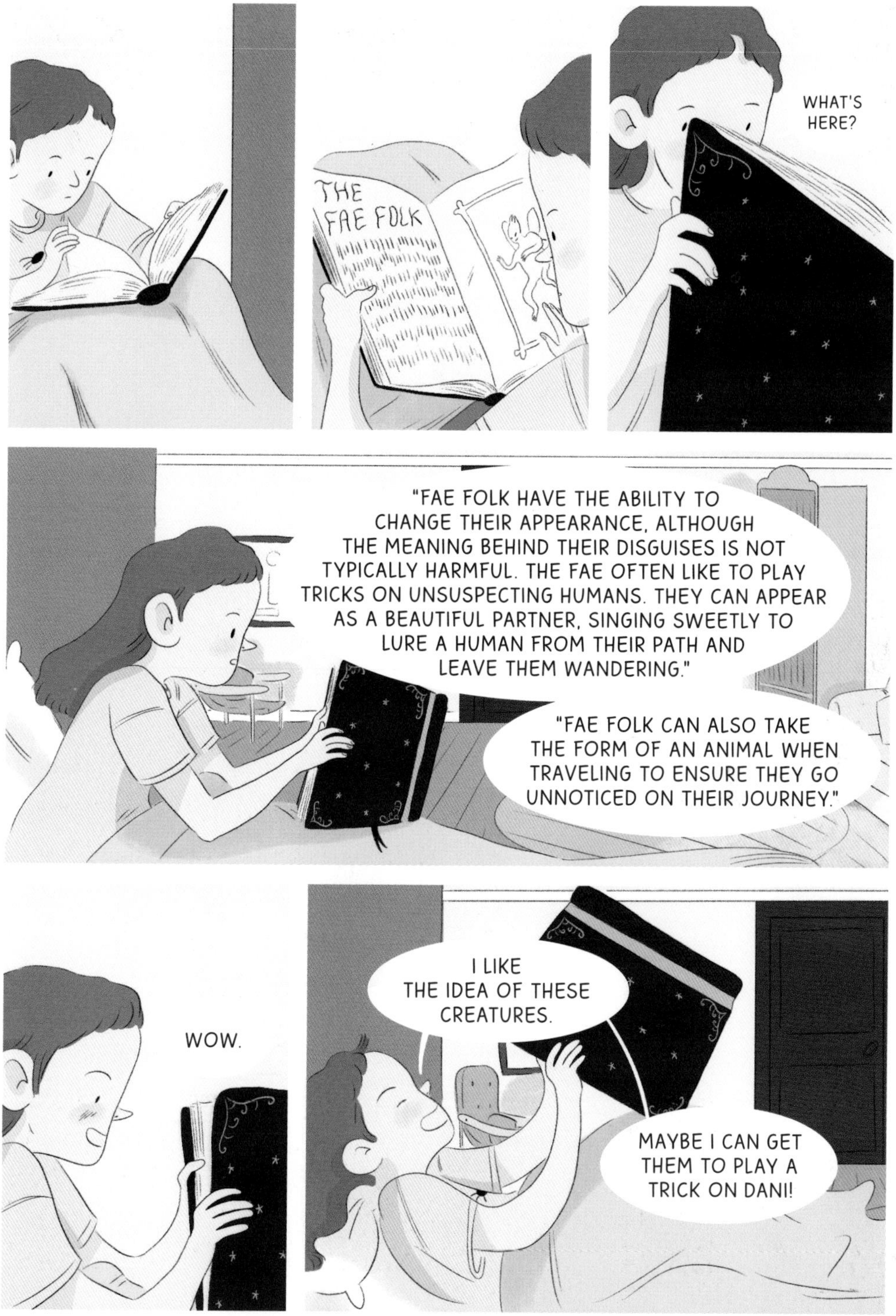
THE FAE FOLK
WHAT'S HERE?
"FAE FOLK HAVE THE ABILITY TO CHANGE THEIR APPEARANCE, ALTHOUGH THE MEANING BEHIND THEIR DISGUISES IS NOT TYPICALLY HARMFUL. THE FAE OFTEN LIKE TO PLAY TRICKS ON UNSUSPECTING HUMANS. THEY CAN APPEAR AS A BEAUTIFUL PARTNER, SINGING SWEETLY TO LURE A HUMAN FROM THEIR PATH AND LEAVE THEM WANDERING."
"FAE FOLK CAN ALSO TAKE THE FORM OF AN ANIMAL WHEN TRAVELING TO ENSURE THEY GO UNNOTICED ON THEIR JOURNEY."
WOW.
I LIKE THE IDEA OF THESE CREATURES.
MAYBE I CAN GET THEM TO PLAY A TRICK ON DANI!

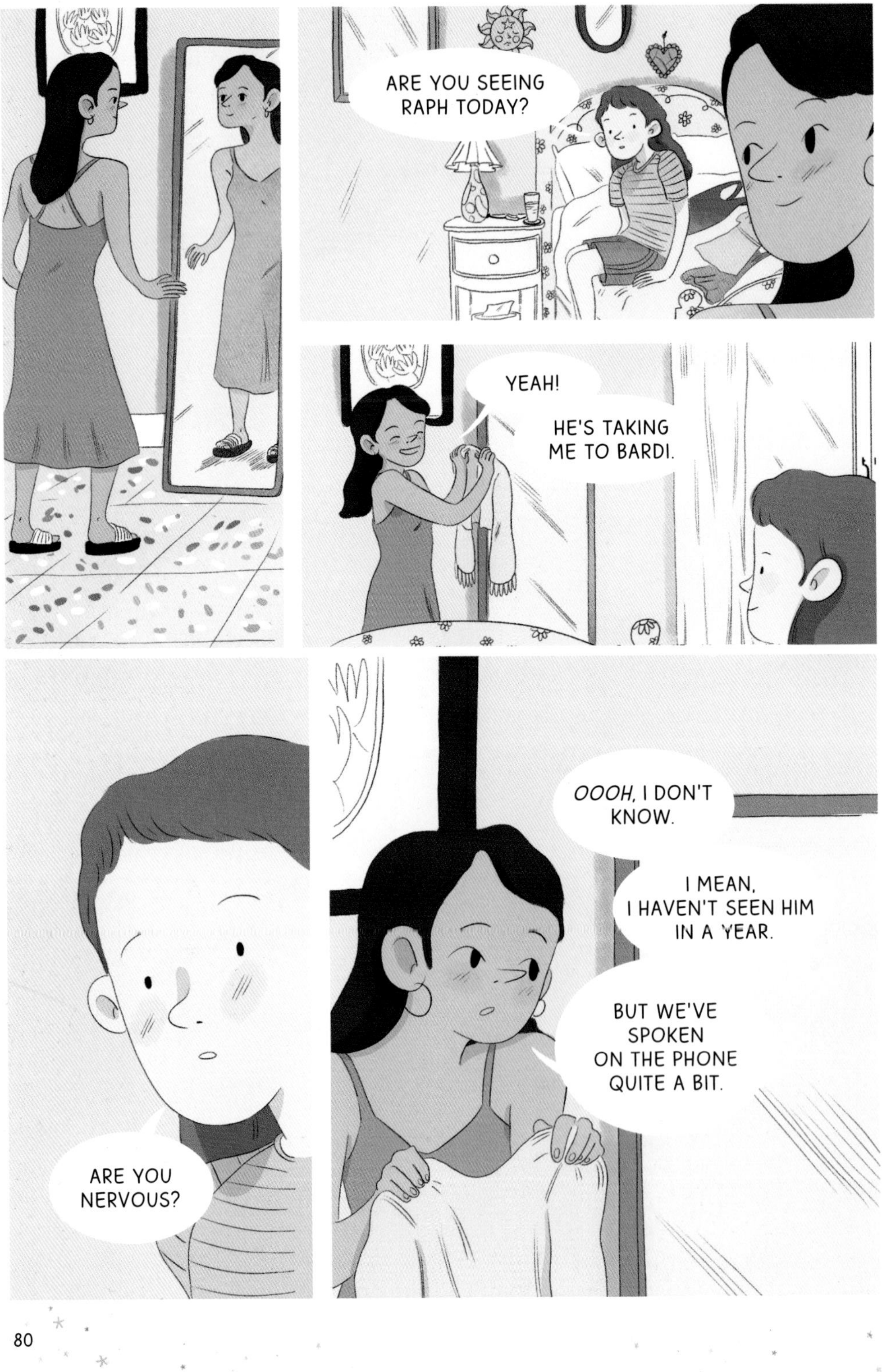
ARE YOU SEEING RAPH TODAY?
YEAH!
HE'S TAKING ME TO BARDI.
ARE YOU NERVOUS?
OOOH, I DON'T KNOW.
I MEAN, I HAVEN'T SEEN HIM IN A YEAR.
BUT WE'VE SPOKEN ON THE PHONE QUITE A BIT.

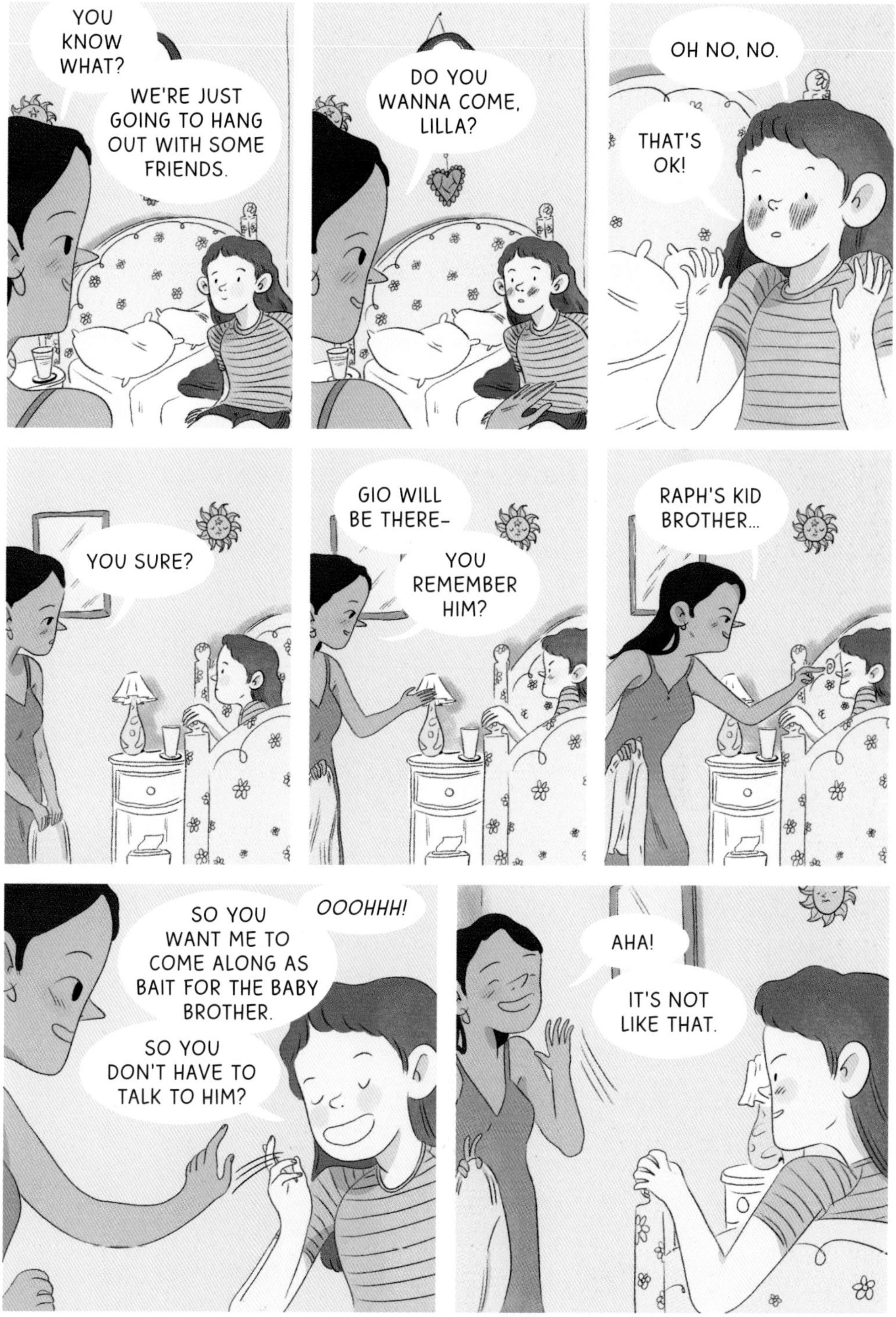
YOU KNOW WHAT?
WE'RE JUST GOING TO HANG OUT WITH SOME FRIENDS.
DO YOU WANNA COME, LILLA?
OH NO, NO.
THAT'S OK!
YOU SURE?
GIO WILL BE THERE-
YOU REMEMBER HIM?
RAPH'S KID BROTHER...
SO YOU WANT ME TO COME ALONG AS BAIT FOR THE BABY BROTHER.
OOOHHH!
SO YOU DON'T HAVE TO TALK TO HIM?
AHA!
IT'S NOT LIKE THAT.

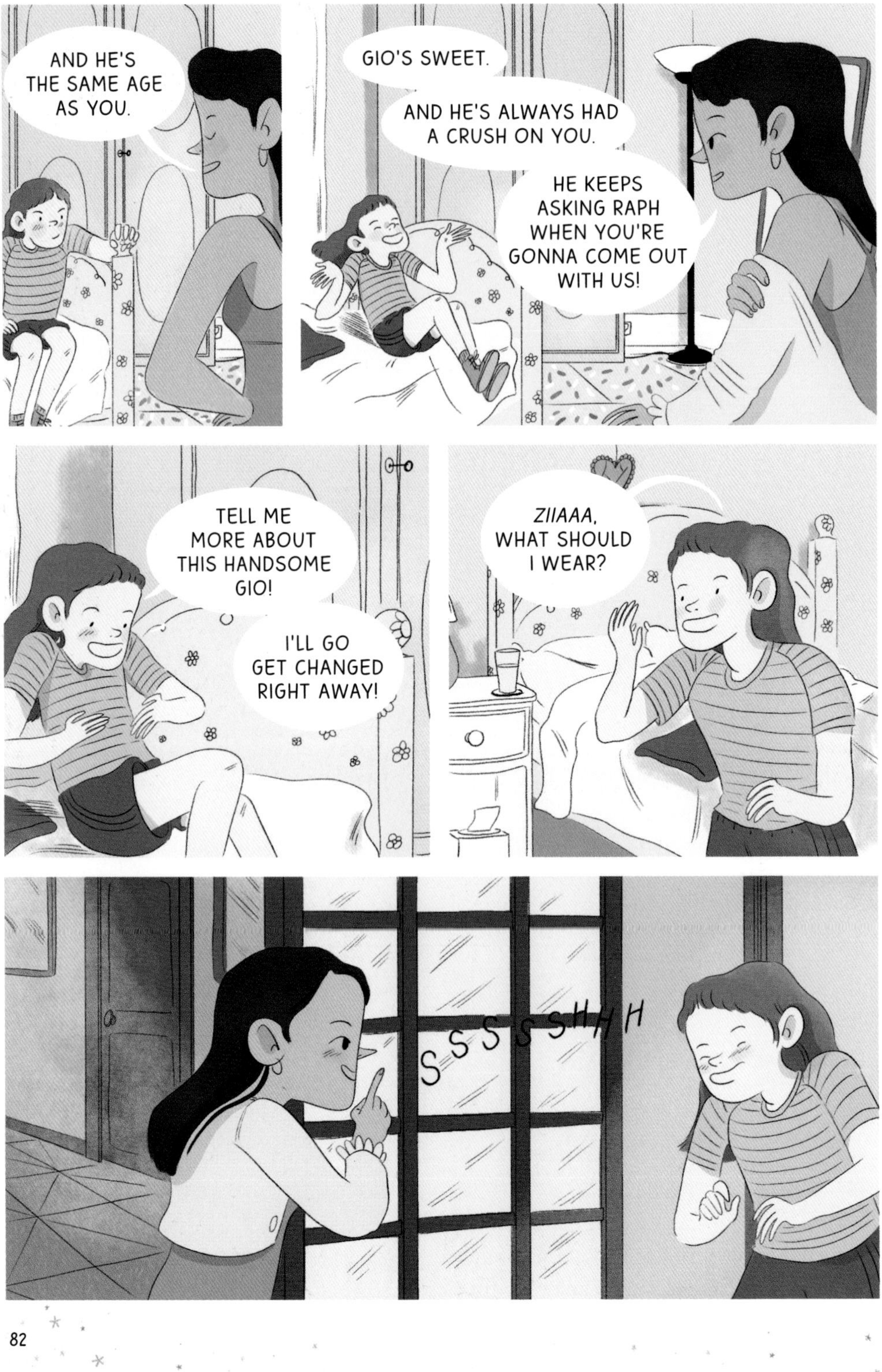
AND HE'S THE SAME AGE AS YOU.
GIO'S SWEET.
AND HE'S ALWAYS HAD A CRUSH ON YOU.
HE KEEPS ASKING RAPH WHEN YOU'RE GONNA COME OUT WITH US!
TELL ME MORE ABOUT THIS HANDSOME GIO!
I'LL GO GET CHANGED RIGHT AWAY!
ZIIAAA, WHAT SHOULD I WEAR?
SSSSSHHH

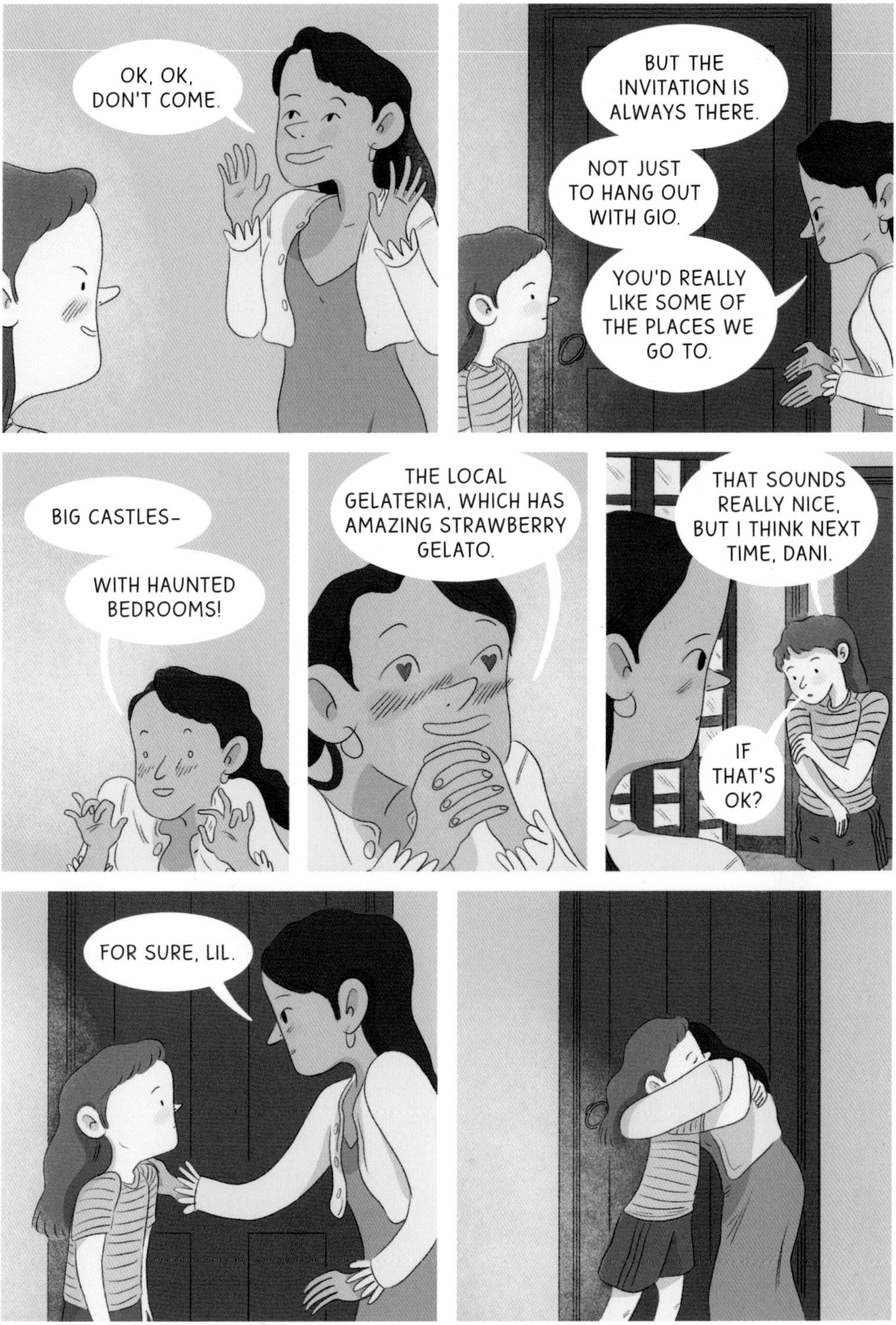
OK, OK, DON'T COME.
BUT THE INVITATION IS ALWAYS THERE.
NOT JUST TO HANG OUT WITH GIO.
YOU'D REALLY LIKE SOME OF THE PLACES WE GO TO.
BIG CASTLES-
WITH HAUNTED BEDROOMS!
THE LOCAL GELATERIA, WHICH HAS AMAZING STRAWBERRY GELATO.
THAT SOUNDS REALLY NICE, BUT I THINK NEXT TIME, DANI.
IF THAT'S OK?
FOR SURE, LIL.

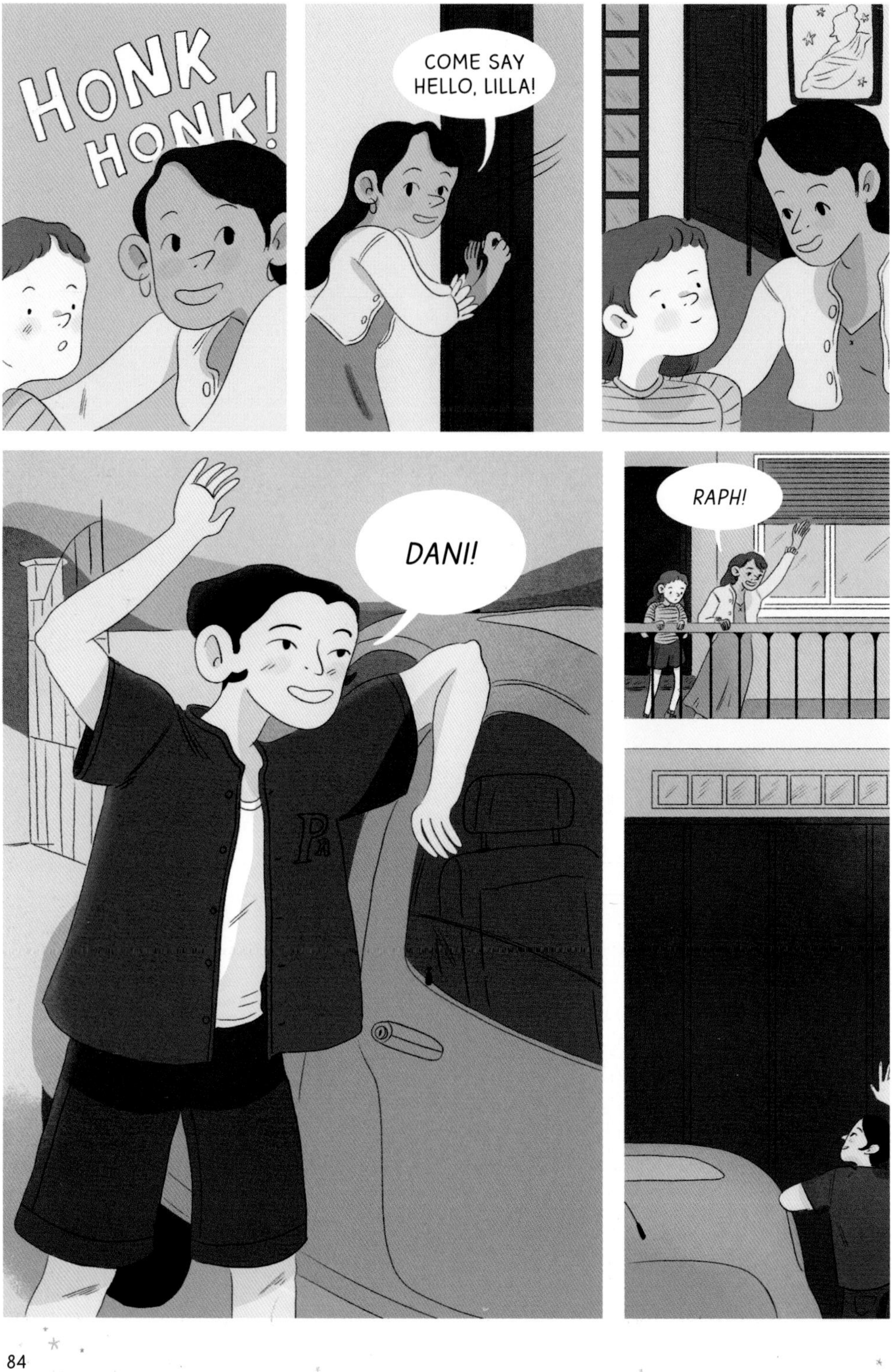
HONK HONK!
COME SAY HELLO, LILLA!
DANI!
RAPH!

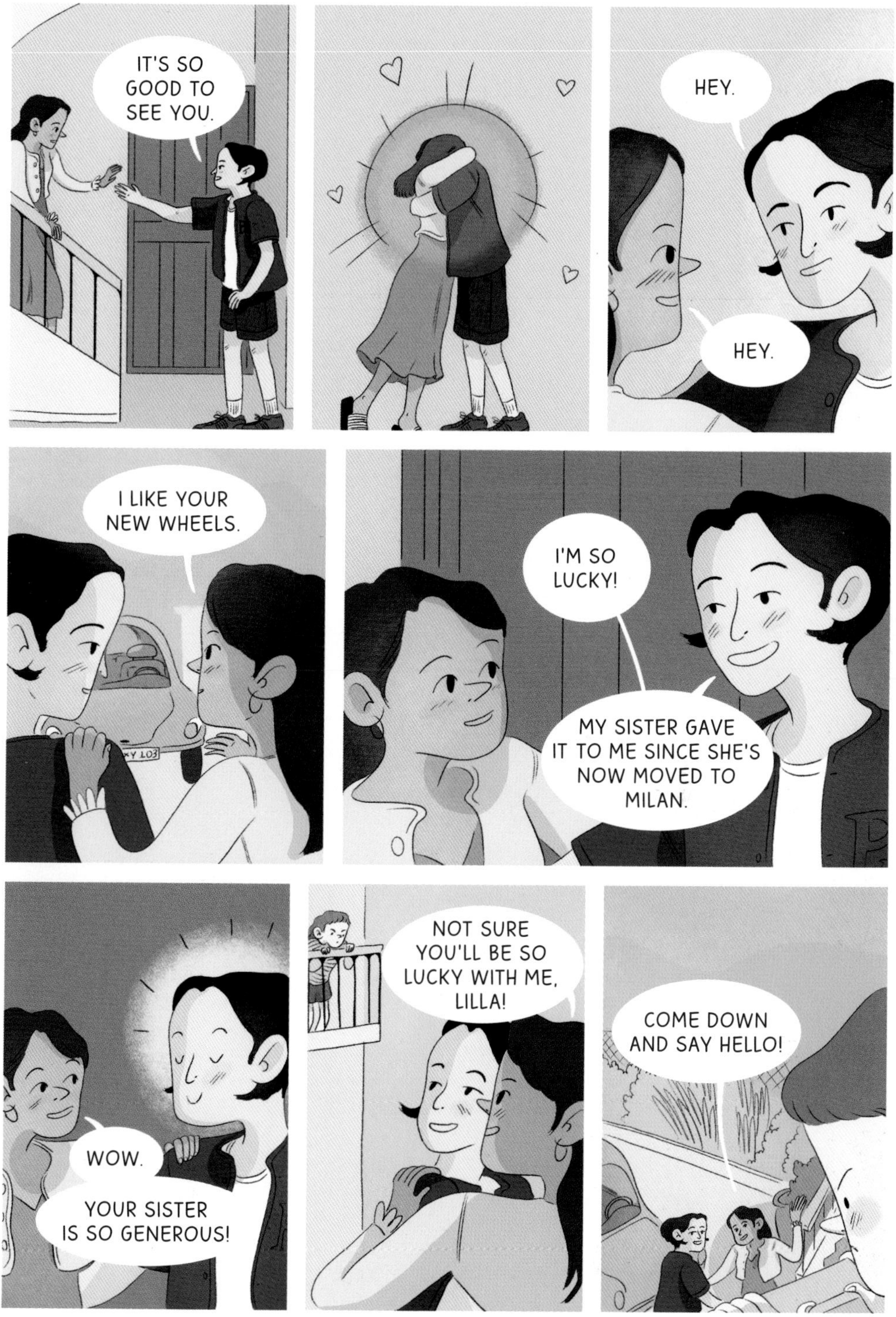
IT'S SO GOOD TO SEE YOU.
HEY.
HEY.
I LIKE YOUR NEW WHEELS.
I'M SO LUCKY!
MY SISTER GAVE IT TO ME SINCE SHE'S NOW MOVED TO MILAN.
WOW.
YOUR SISTER IS SO GENEROUS!
NOT SURE YOU'LL BE SO LUCKY WITH ME, LILLA!
COME DOWN AND SAY HELLO!

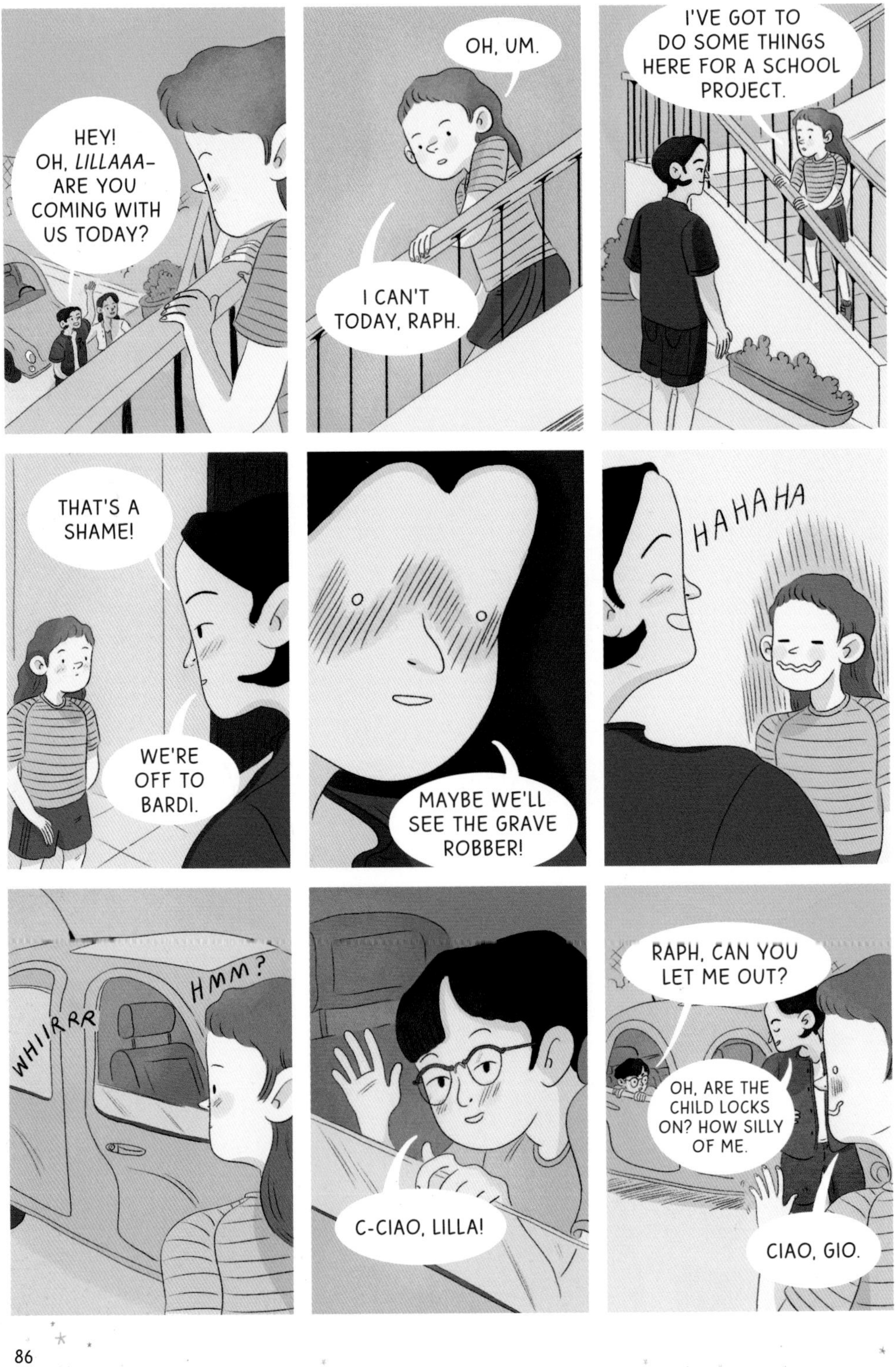
HEY!
OH, *LILLAAA*- ARE YOU COMING WITH US TODAY?
OH, UM.
I CAN'T TODAY, RAPH.
I'VE GOT TO DO SOME THINGS HERE FOR A SCHOOL PROJECT.
THAT'S A SHAME!
WE'RE OFF TO BARDI.
MAYBE WE'LL SEE THE GRAVE ROBBER!
HAHAHA
WHIIRRR
HMM?
C-CIAO, LILLA!
RAPH, CAN YOU LET ME OUT?
OH, ARE THE CHILD LOCKS ON? HOW SILLY OF ME.
CIAO, GIO.

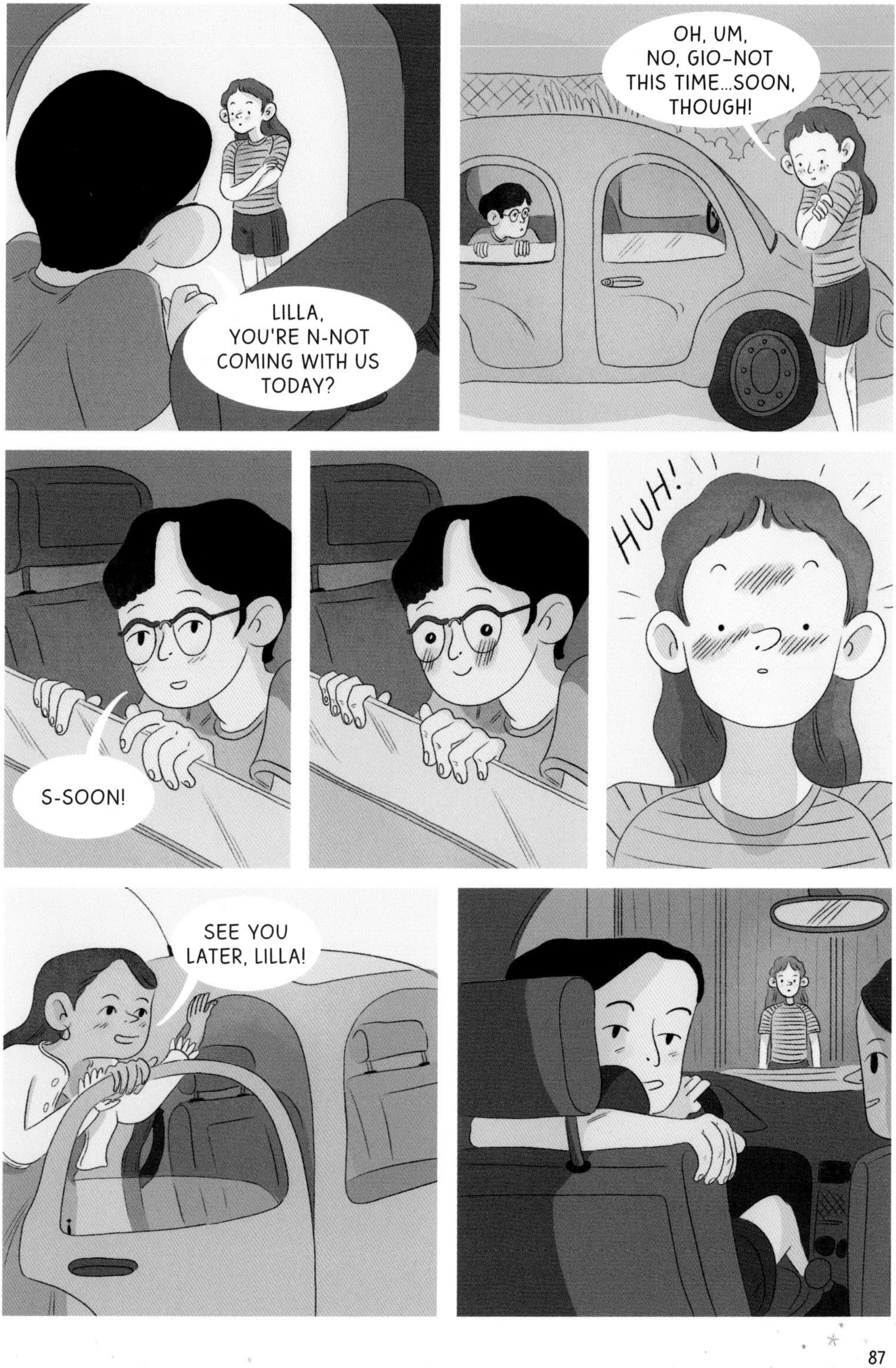
LILLA, YOU'RE N-NOT COMING WITH US TODAY?
OH, UM, NO, GIO–NOT THIS TIME...SOON, THOUGH!
S-SOON!
HUH!
SEE YOU LATER, LILLA!

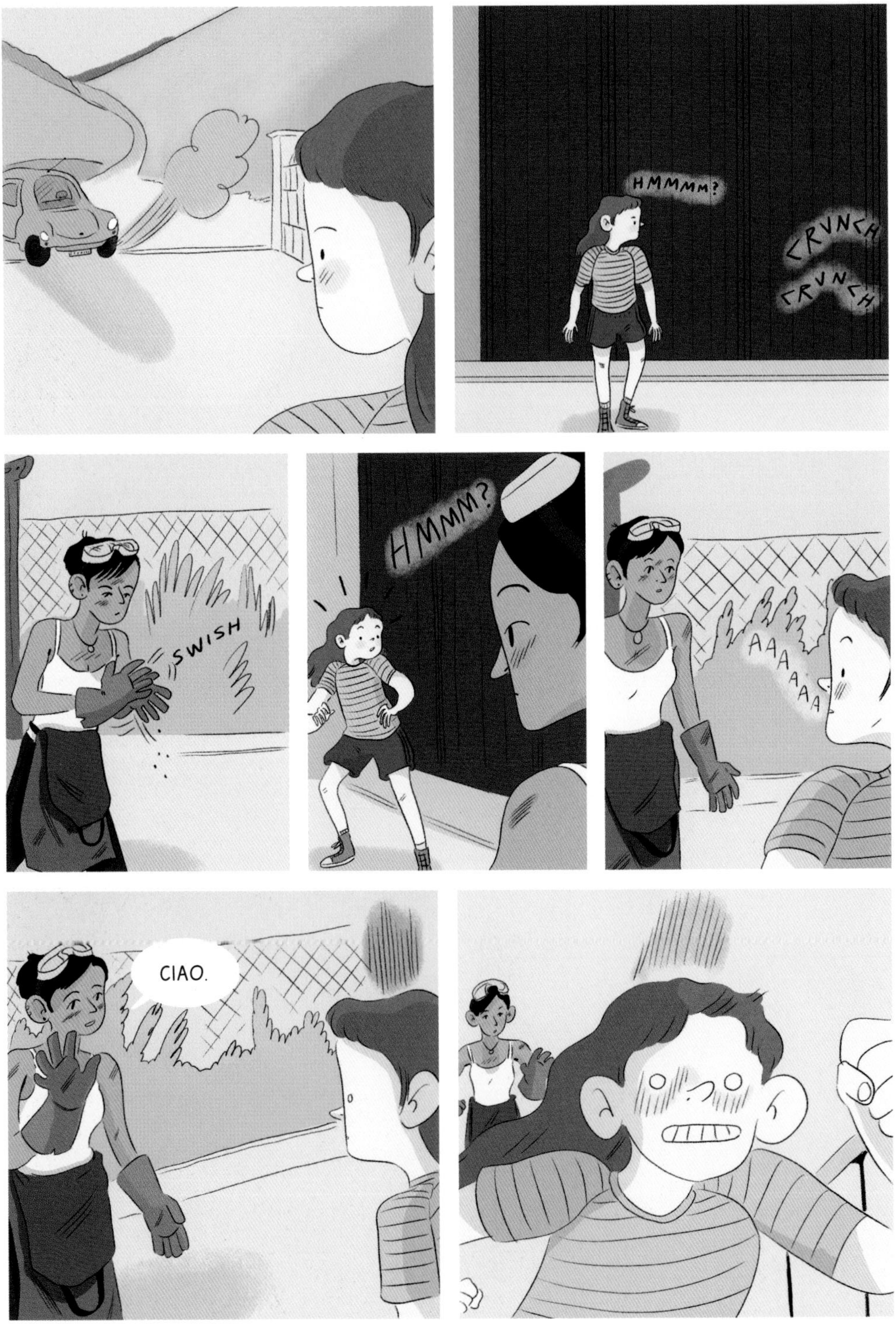
HMMMM?
CRUNCH
CRUNCH
SWISH
HMMM?
AAAAAA
CIAO.

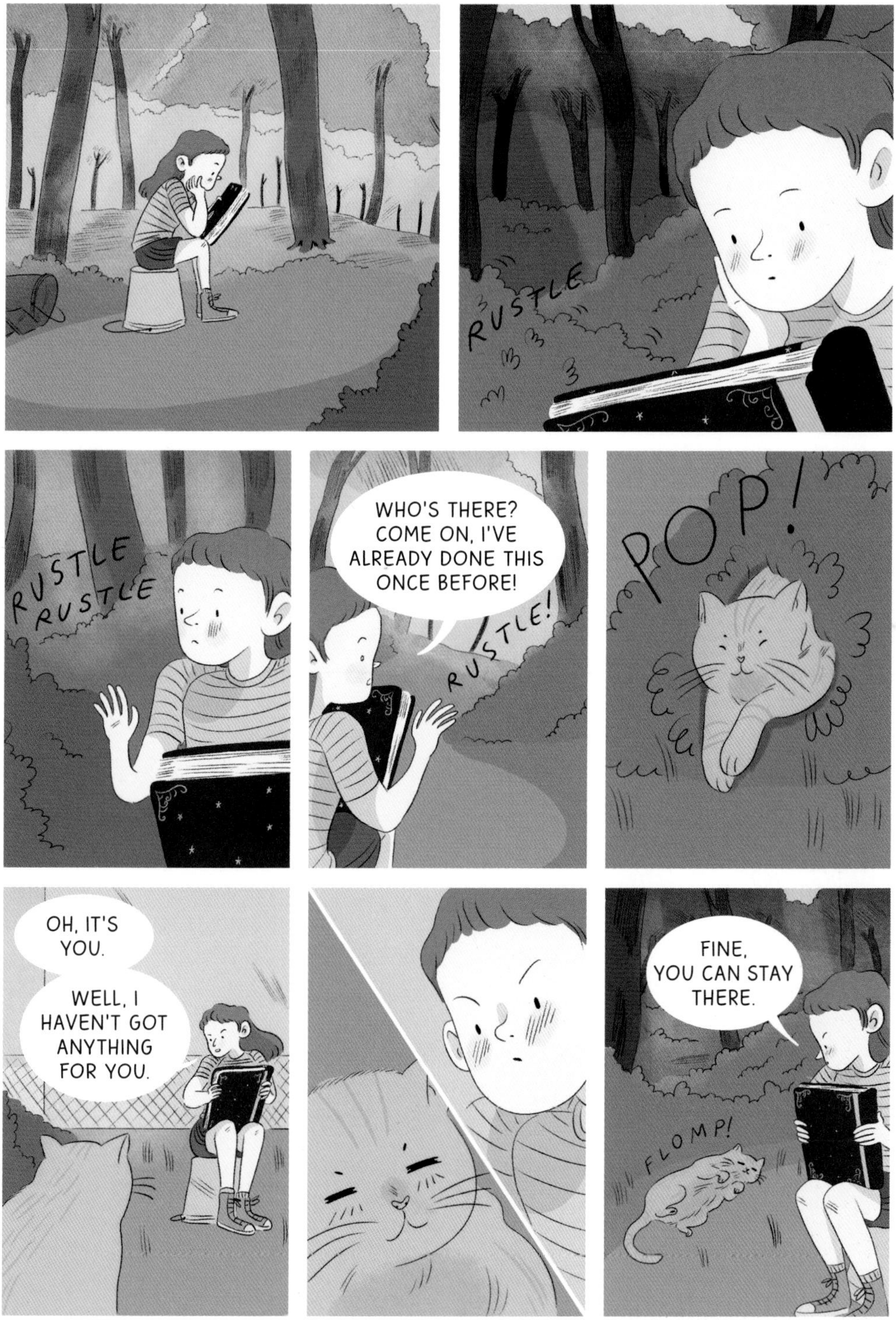
RUSTLE
RUSTLE
RUSTLE
WHO'S THERE? COME ON, I'VE ALREADY DONE THIS ONCE BEFORE!
RUSTLE!
POP!
OH, IT'S YOU.
WELL, I HAVEN'T GOT ANYTHING FOR YOU.
FINE, YOU CAN STAY THERE.
FLOMP!

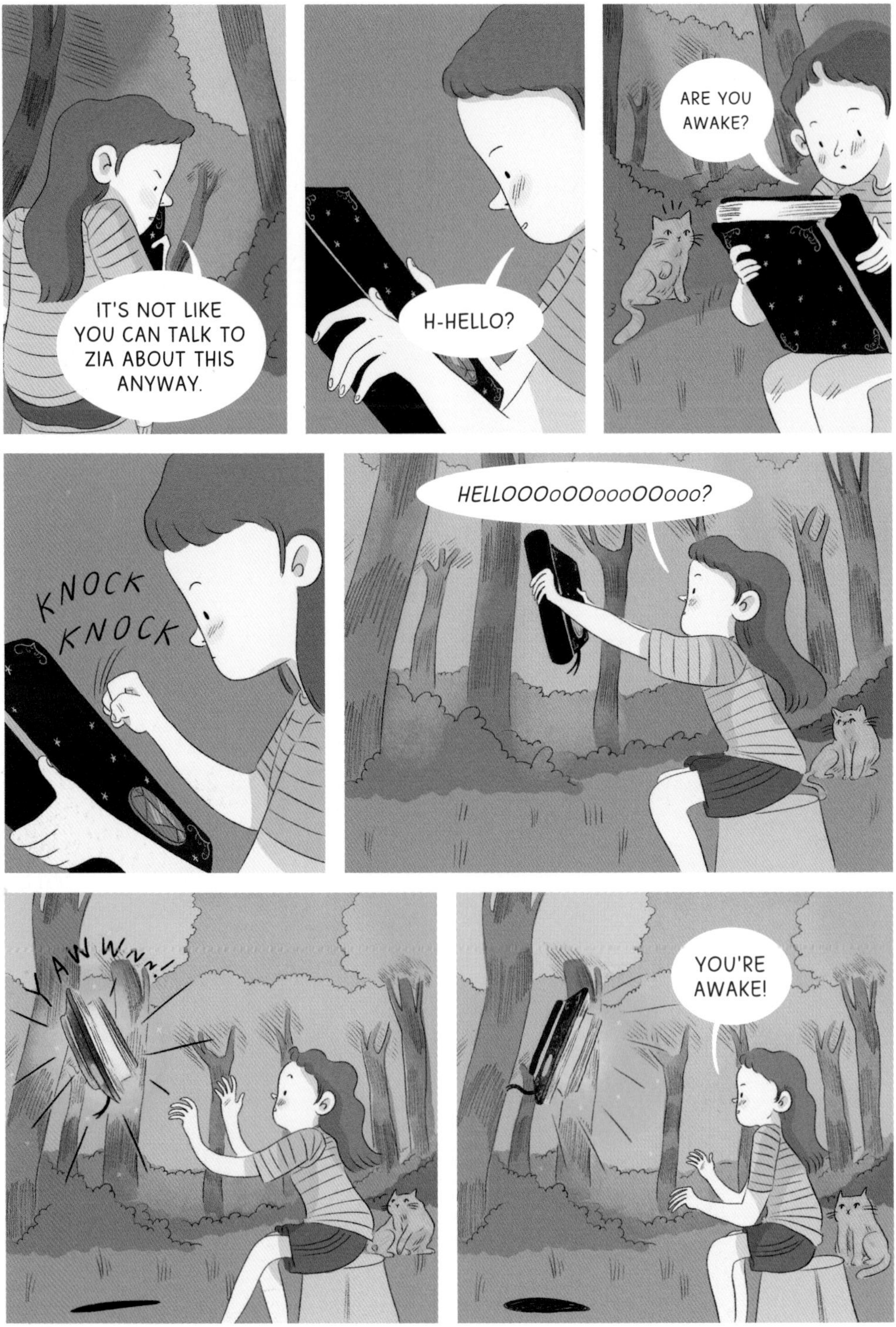
IT'S NOT LIKE YOU CAN TALK TO ZIA ABOUT THIS ANYWAY.
H-HELLO?
ARE YOU AWAKE?
KNOCK KNOCK
HELLOOOoOOoooOOooo?
YAWWNN!
YOU'RE AWAKE!

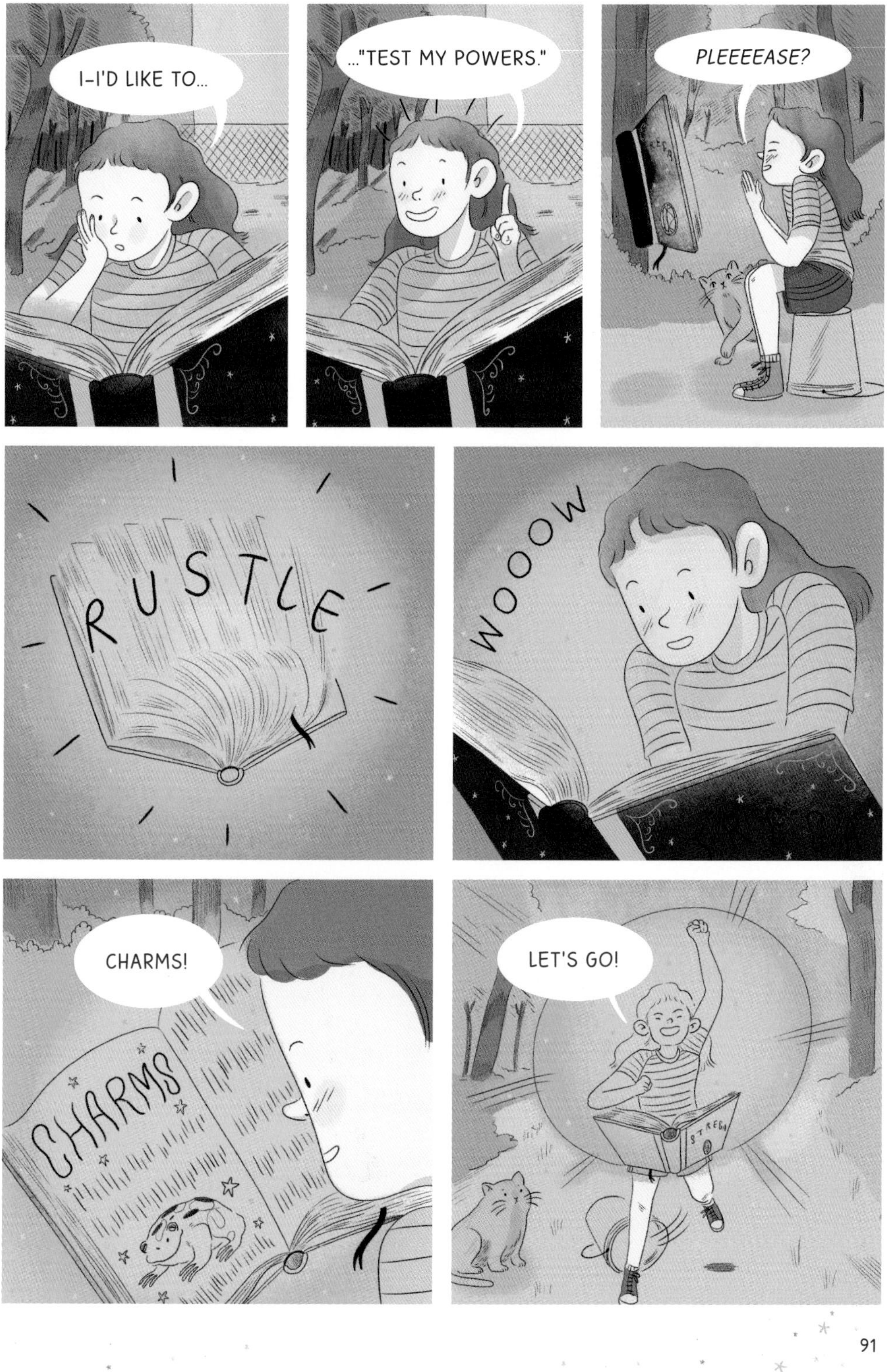
I-I'D LIKE TO...
..."TEST MY POWERS."
PLEEEEASE?
RUSTLE
WOOOW
CHARMS!
CHARMS
LET'S GO!
STREGA

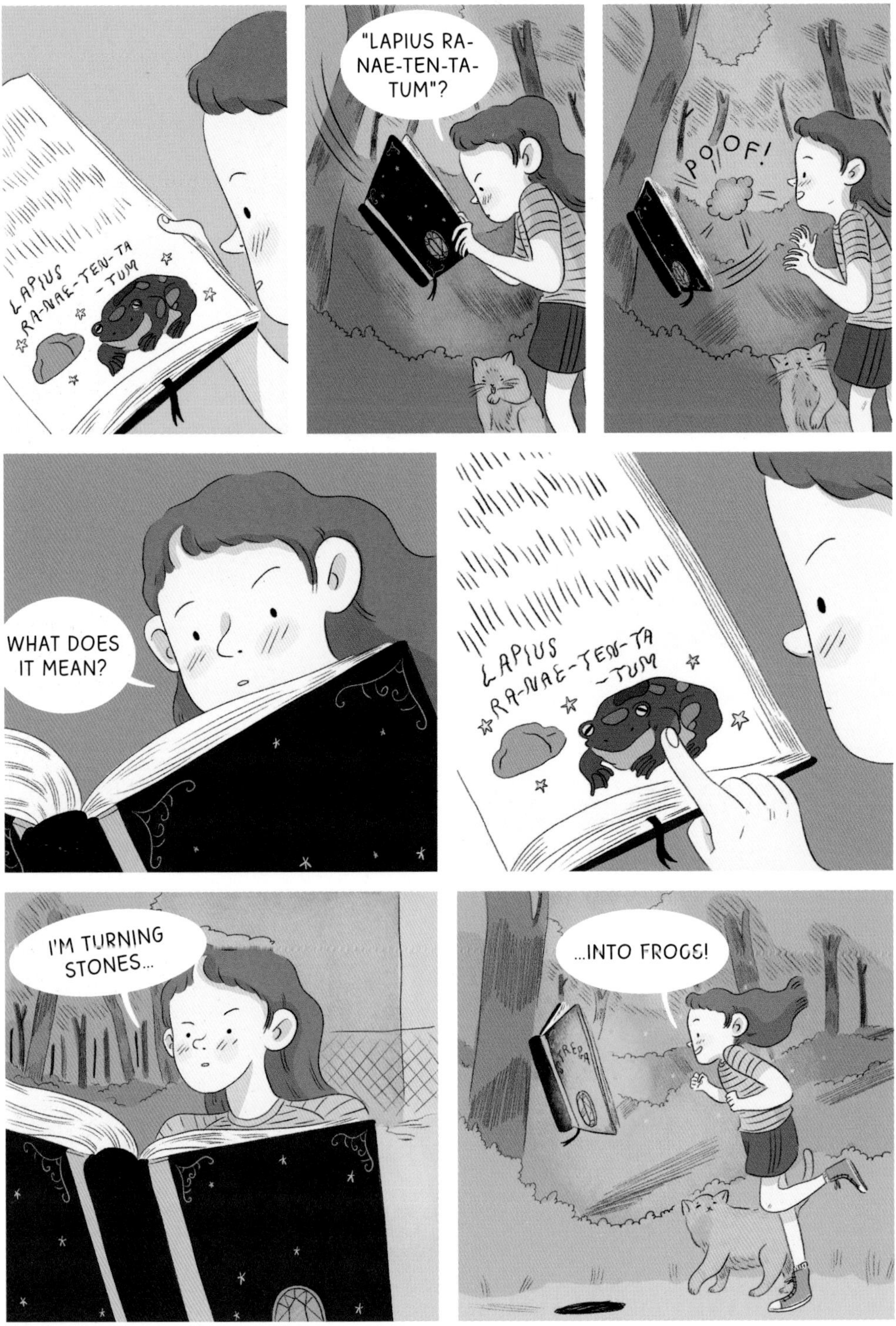
LAPIUS RA-NAE-TEN-TA-TUM
"LAPIUS RA-NAE-TEN-TA-TUM"?
POOF!
WHAT DOES IT MEAN?
LAPIUS RA-NAE-TEN-TA-TUM
I'M TURNING STONES...
...INTO FROGS!
STREGA

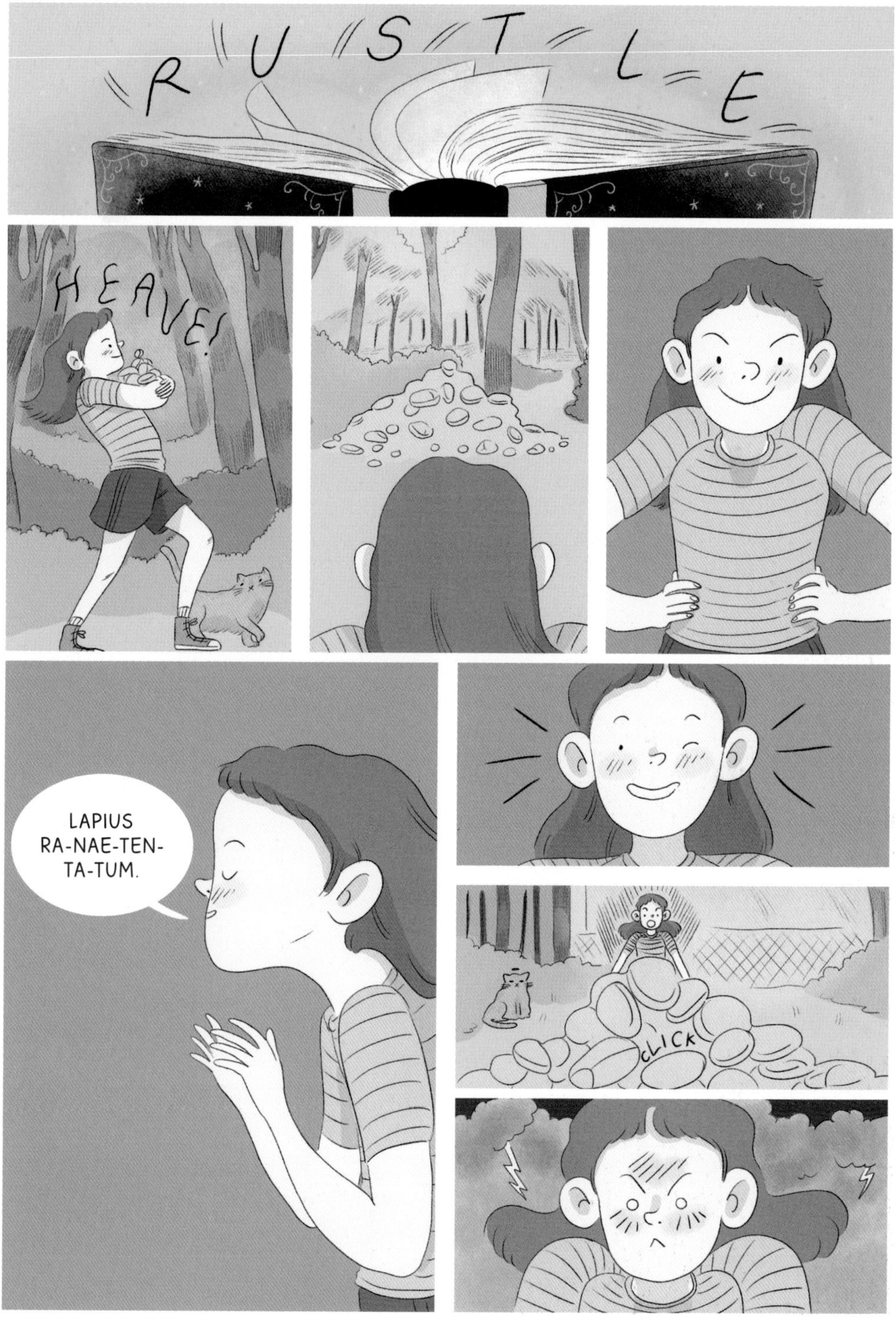
RUSTLE
HEAVE!
LAPIUS RA-NAE-TEN-TA-TUM.
CLICK

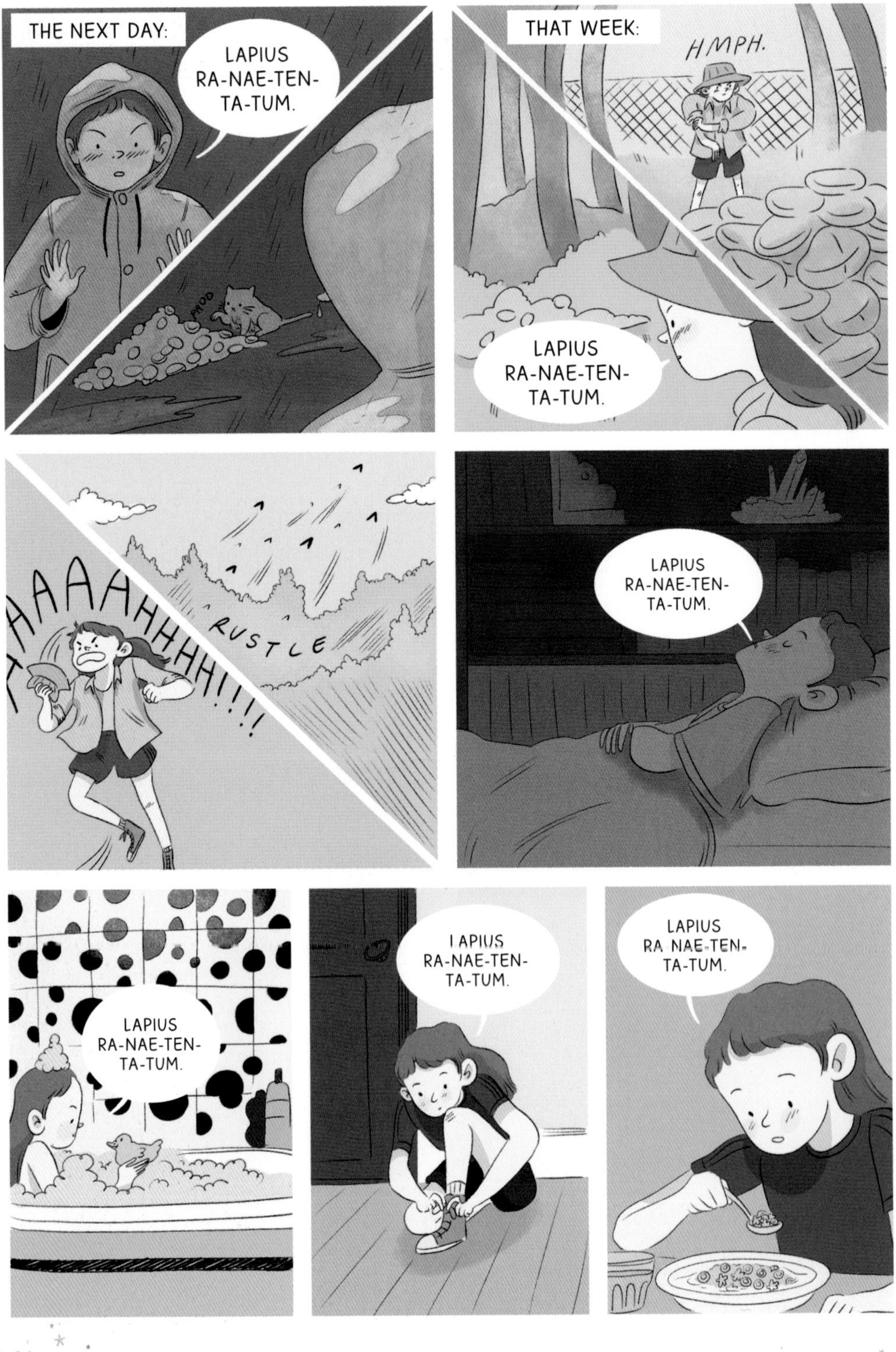
THE NEXT DAY:
LAPIUS RA-NAE-TEN-TA-TUM.
PROD
THAT WEEK:
HMPH.
LAPIUS RA-NAE-TEN-TA-TUM.
AAAAAHHHHH!!!!
RUSTLE
LAPIUS RA-NAE-TEN-TA-TUM.
LAPIUS RA-NAE-TEN-TA-TUM.
LAPIUS RA-NAE-TEN-TA-TUM.
LAPIUS RA-NAE-TEN-TA-TUM.

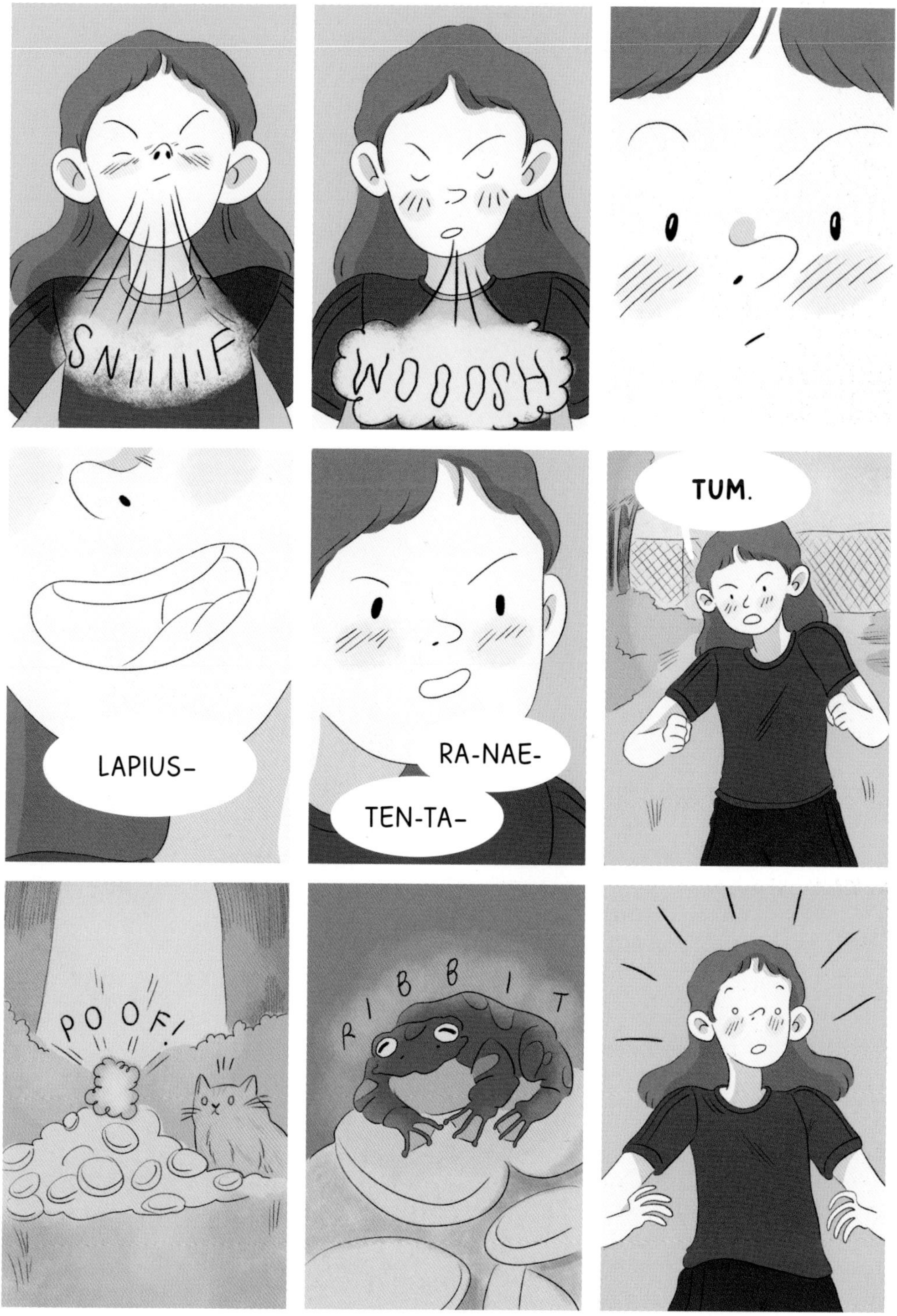
SNIIIIIF
WOOOSH
LAPIUS-
RA-NAE-
TEN-TA-
TUM.
POOF!
RIBBIT

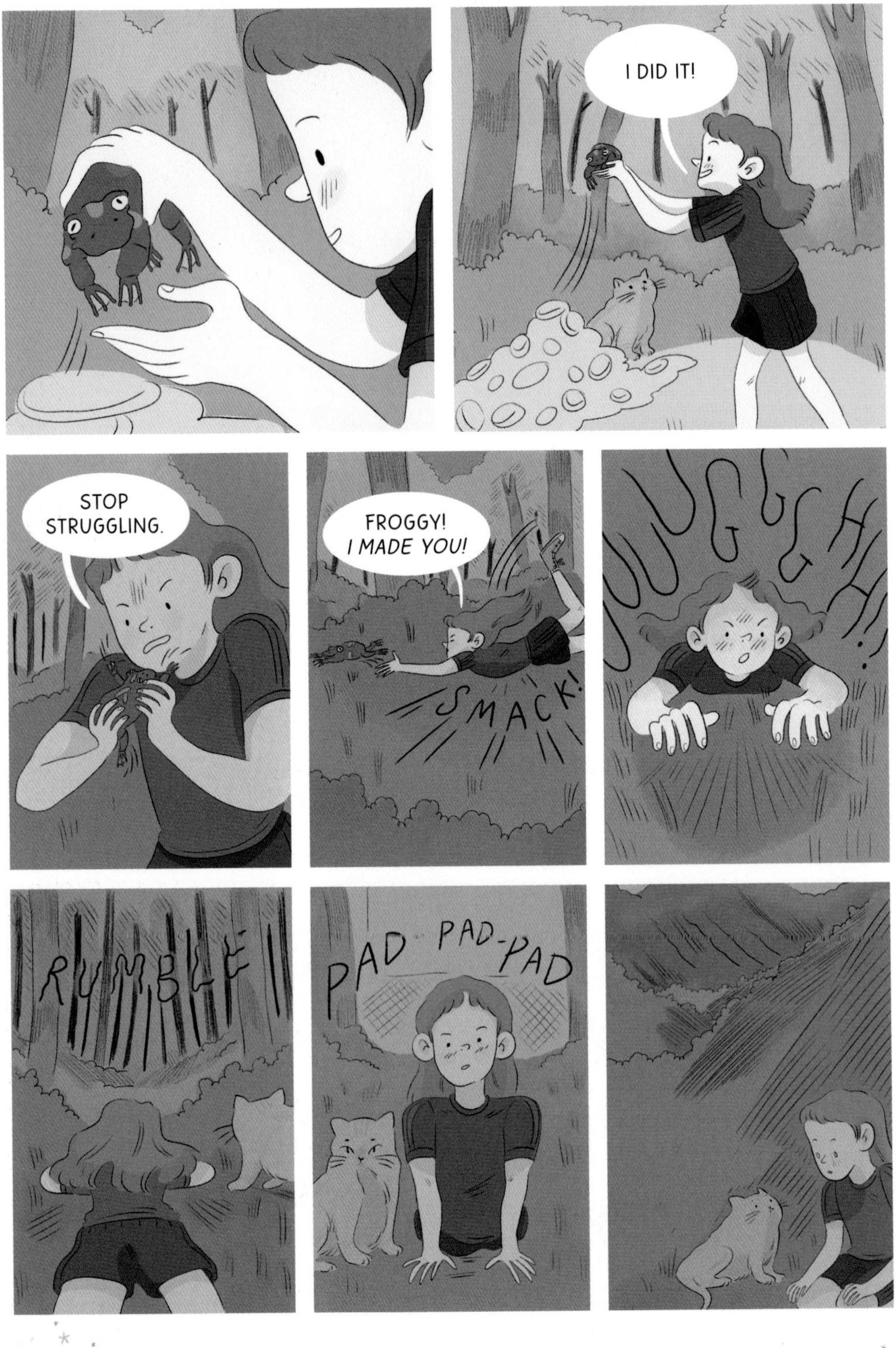
I DID IT!
STOP STRUGGLING.
FROGGY! I MADE YOU!
SMACK!
RUMBLE
PAD PAD-PAD

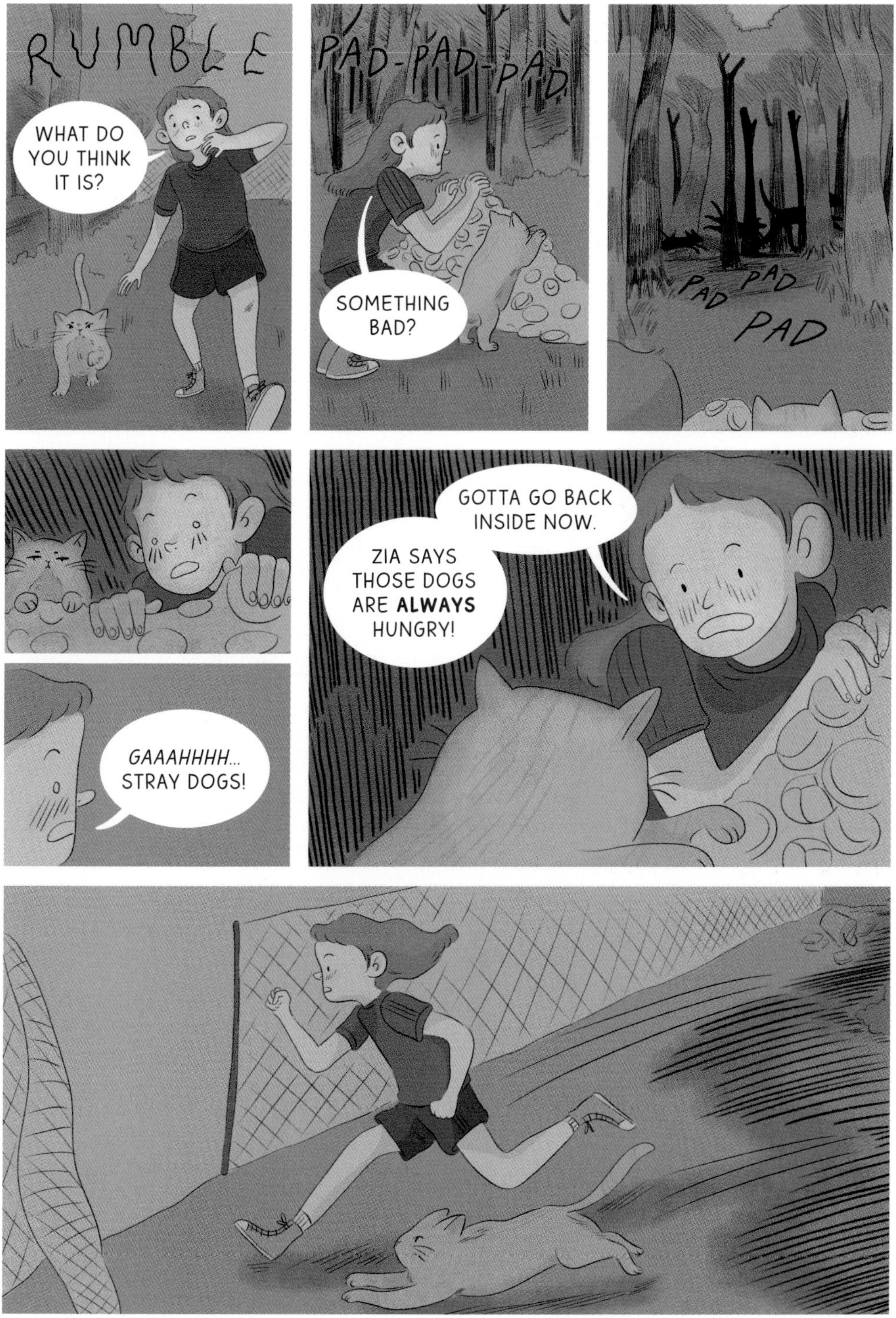
RUMBLE
WHAT DO YOU THINK IT IS?
PAD-PAD-PAD
SOMETHING BAD?
PAD PAD
PAD
GAAAHHHH... STRAY DOGS!
GOTTA GO BACK INSIDE NOW.
ZIA SAYS THOSE DOGS ARE **ALWAYS** HUNGRY!

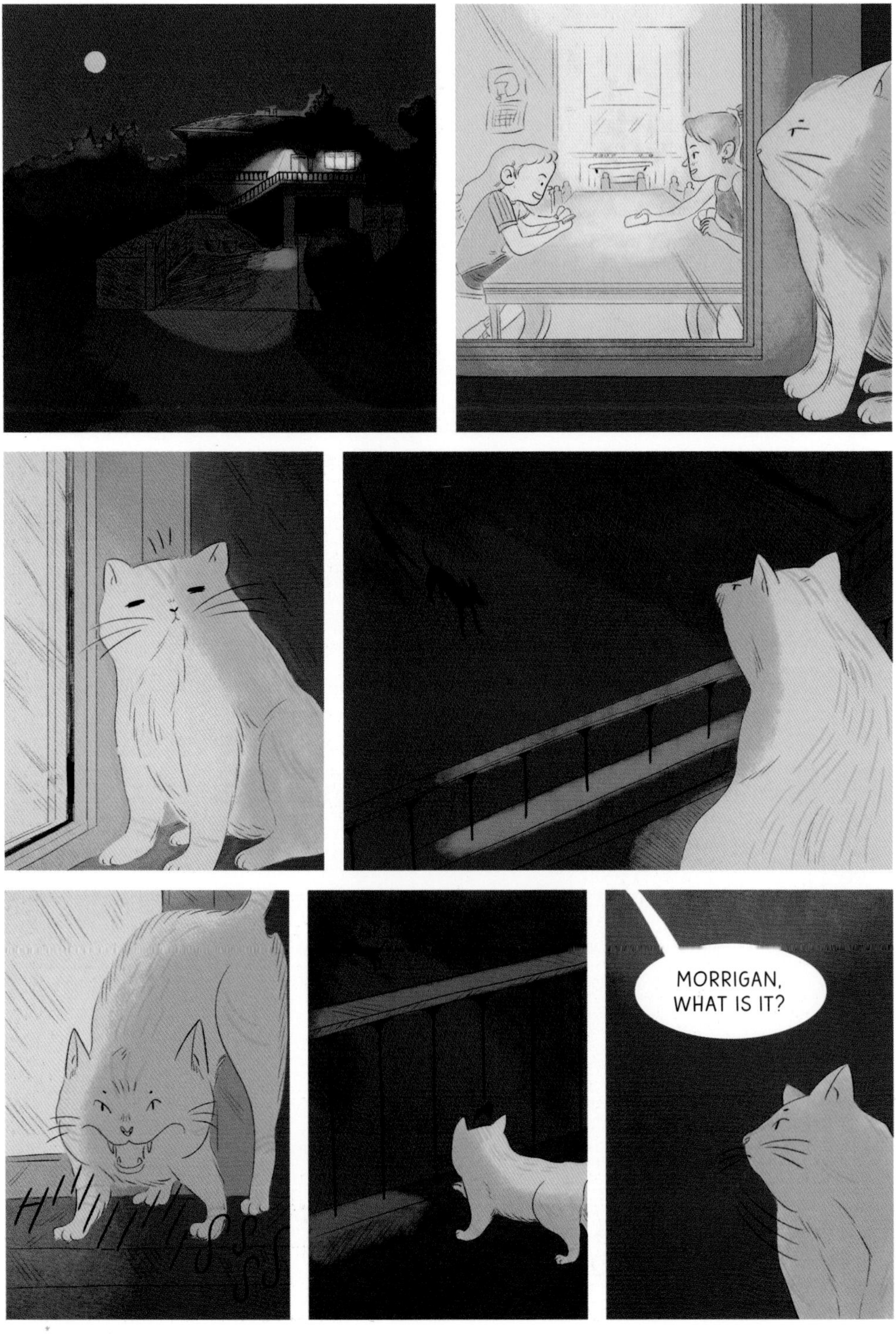
HIIIIIISSS
MORRIGAN, WHAT IS IT?

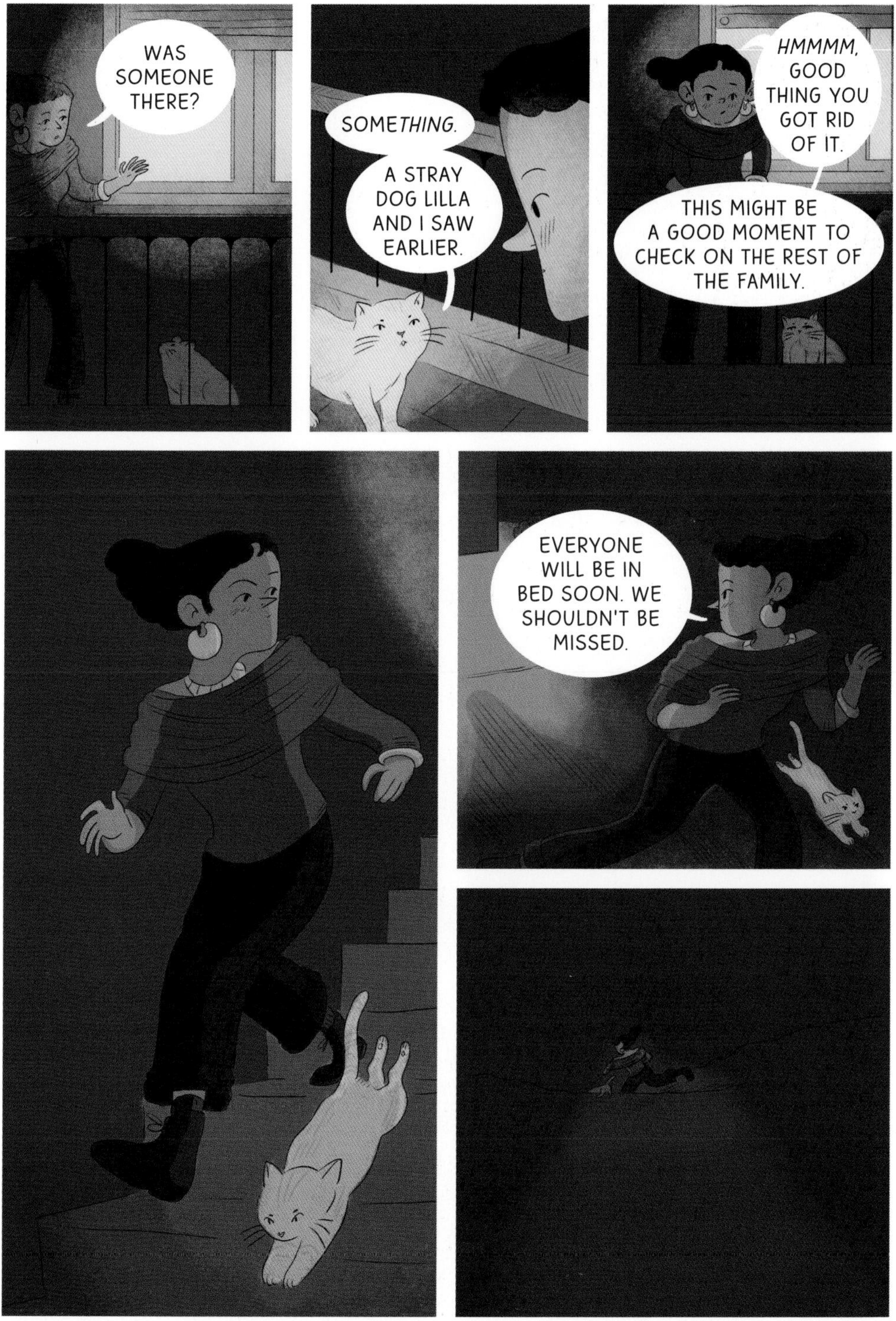
WAS SOMEONE THERE?
SOME*THING.*
A STRAY DOG LILLA AND I SAW EARLIER.
HMMMM, GOOD THING YOU GOT RID OF IT.
THIS MIGHT BE A GOOD MOMENT TO CHECK ON THE REST OF THE FAMILY.
EVERYONE WILL BE IN BED SOON. WE SHOULDN'T BE MISSED.

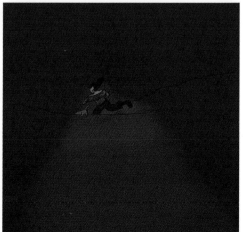

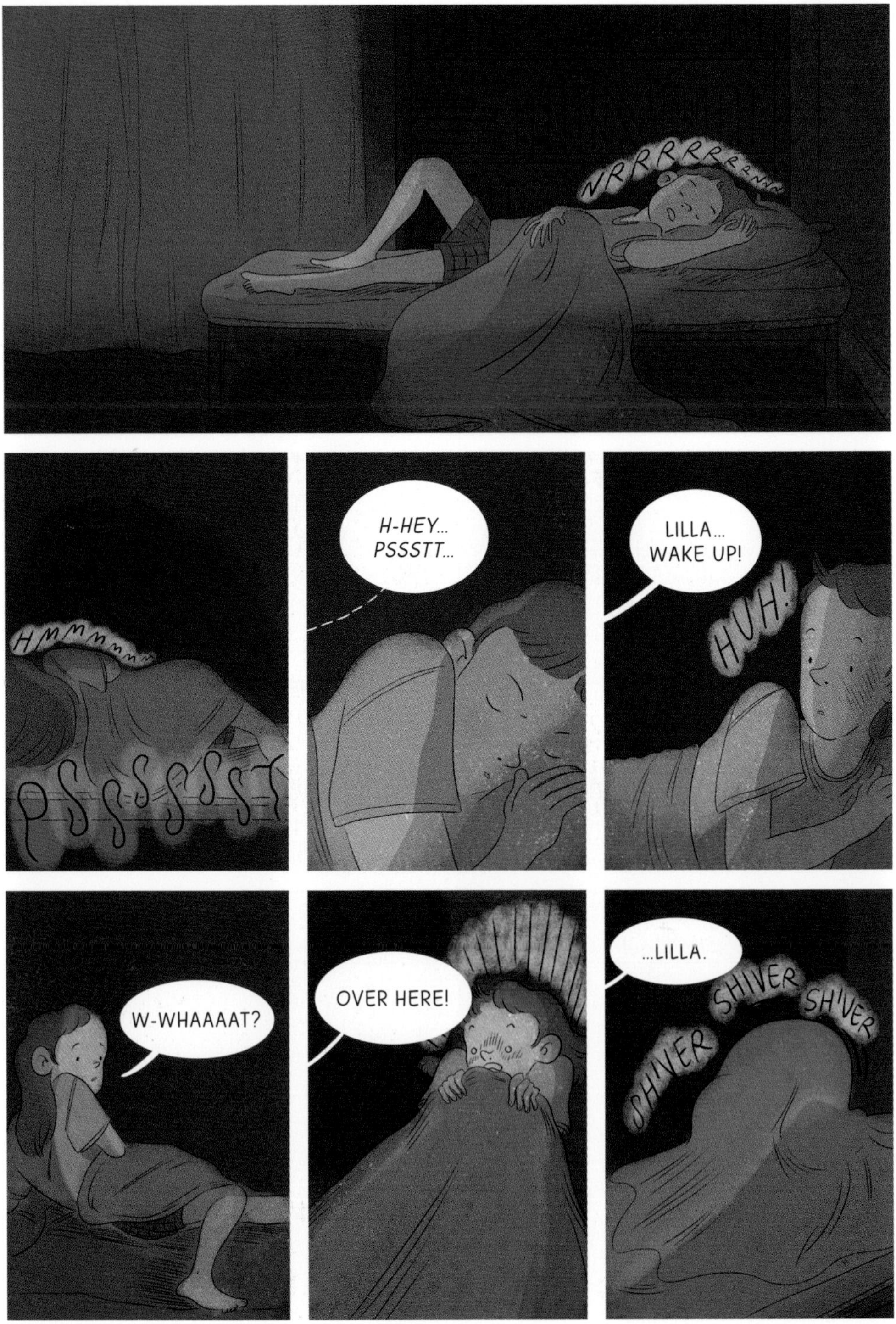
NRRRRRRRRnnn
HMMMmmmm
PSSSSSST
H-HEY... PSSSTT...
LILLA... WAKE UP!
HUH!
W-WHAAAAT?
OVER HERE!
...LILLA.
SHIVER
SHIVER
SHIVER

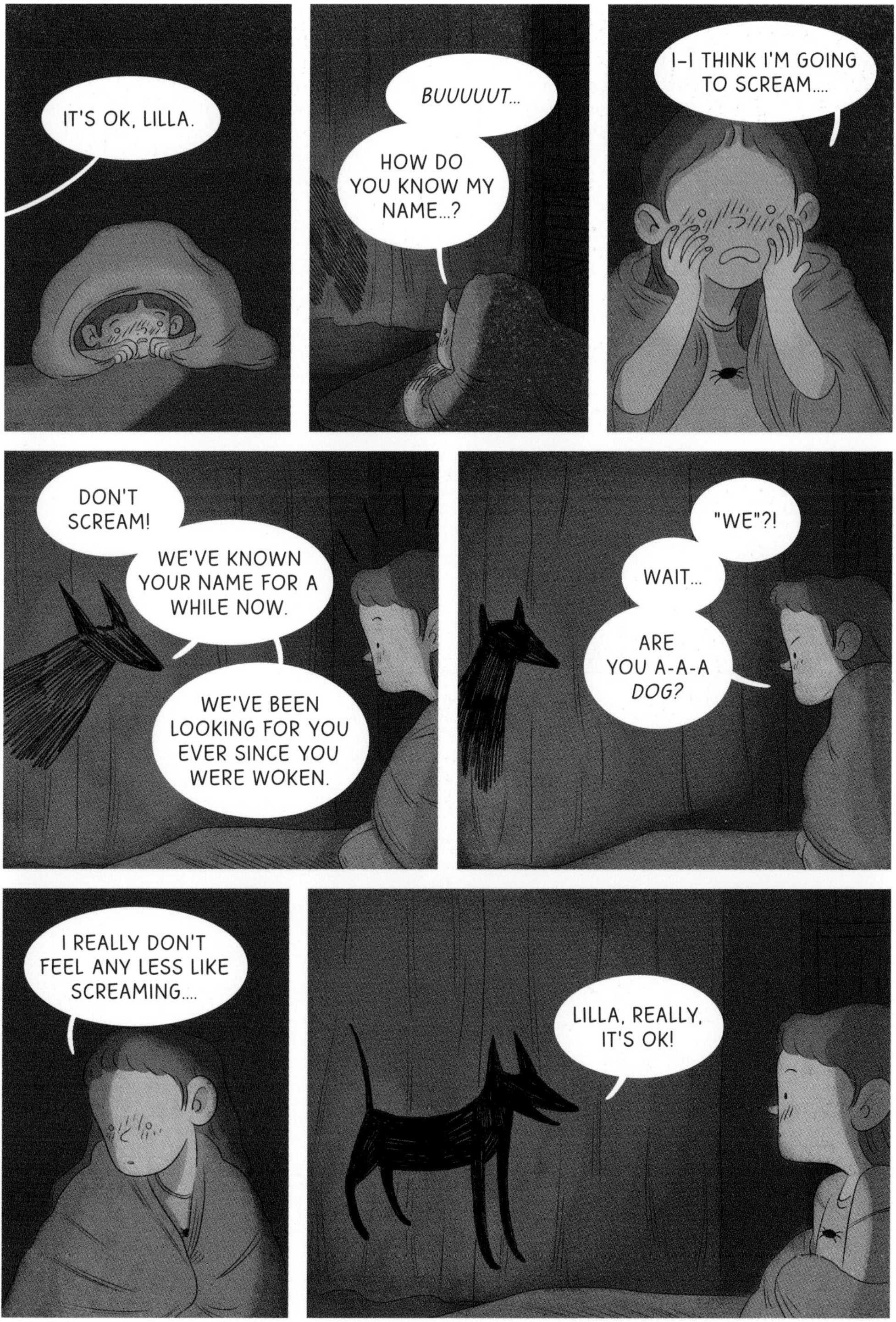
IT'S OK, LILLA.
BUUUUUT...
HOW DO YOU KNOW MY NAME...?
I–I THINK I'M GOING TO SCREAM....
DON'T SCREAM!
WE'VE KNOWN YOUR NAME FOR A WHILE NOW.
WE'VE BEEN LOOKING FOR YOU EVER SINCE YOU WERE WOKEN.
"WE"?!
WAIT...
ARE YOU A-A-A DOG?
I REALLY DON'T FEEL ANY LESS LIKE SCREAMING....
LILLA, REALLY, IT'S OK!

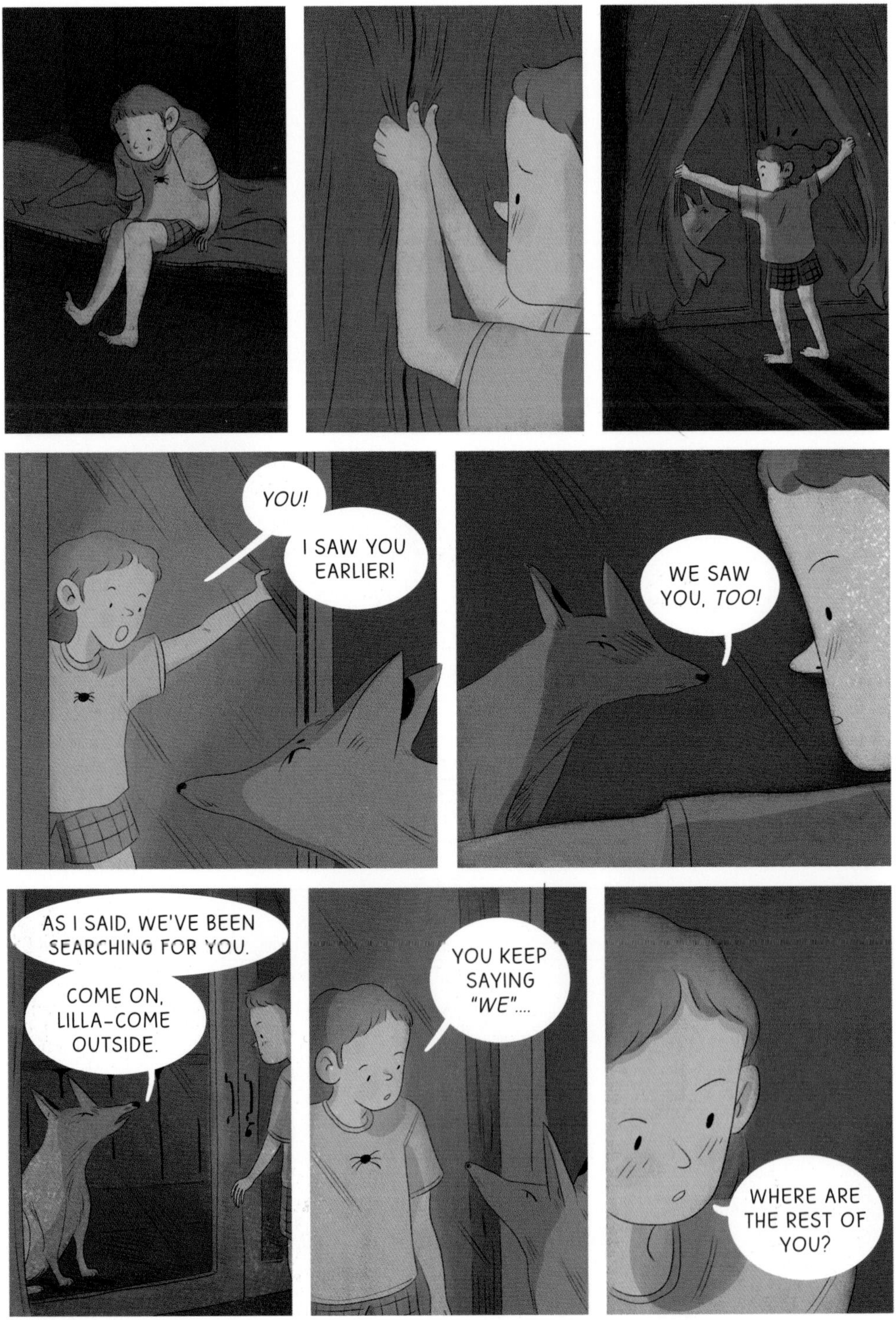
YOU!
I SAW YOU EARLIER!
WE SAW YOU, *TOO!*
AS I SAID, WE'VE BEEN SEARCHING FOR YOU.
COME ON, LILLA–COME OUTSIDE.
YOU KEEP SAYING *"WE"*....
WHERE ARE THE REST OF YOU?

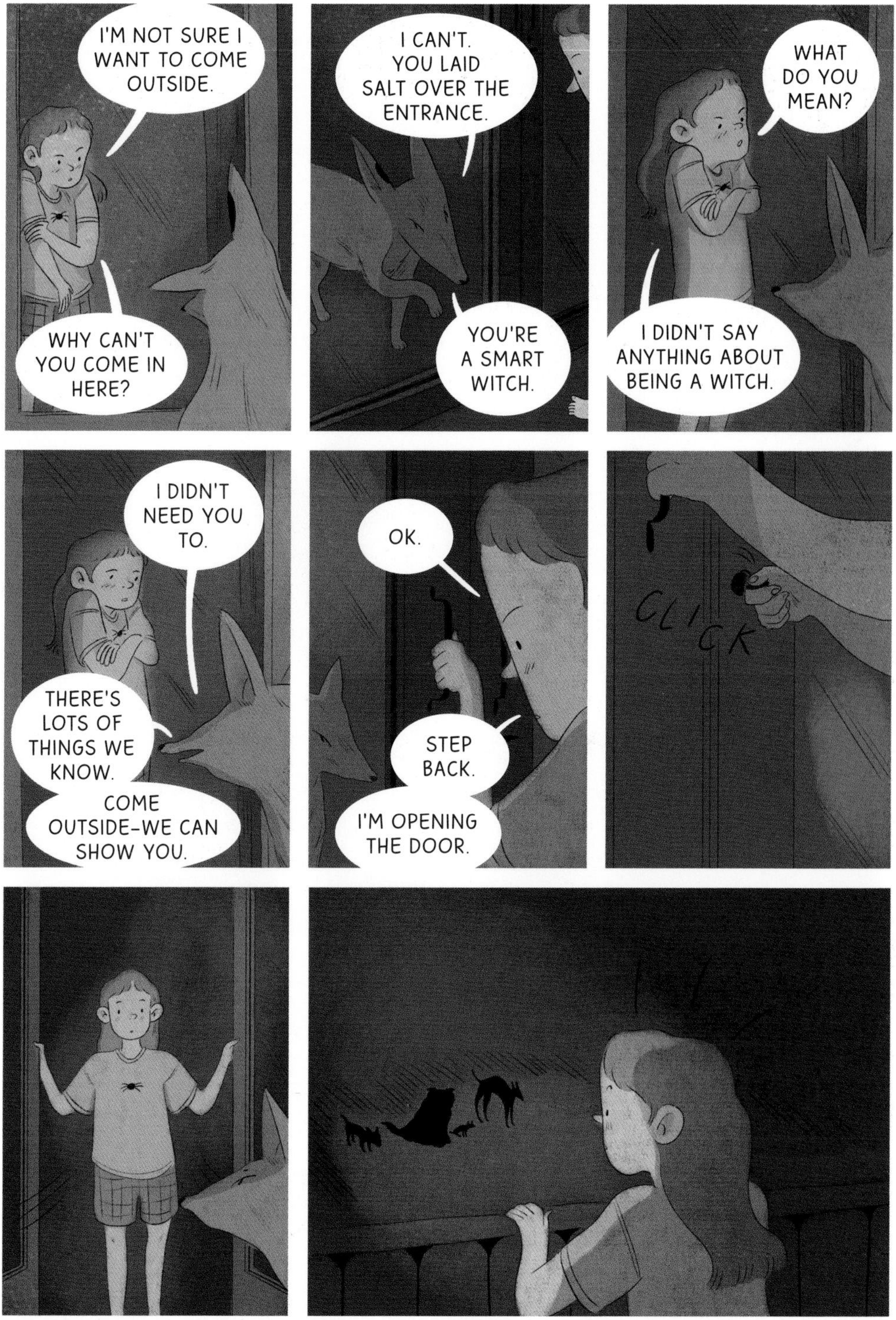
I'M NOT SURE I WANT TO COME OUTSIDE.
WHY CAN'T YOU COME IN HERE?
I CAN'T. YOU LAID SALT OVER THE ENTRANCE.
YOU'RE A SMART WITCH.
WHAT DO YOU MEAN?
I DIDN'T SAY ANYTHING ABOUT BEING A WITCH.
I DIDN'T NEED YOU TO.
THERE'S LOTS OF THINGS WE KNOW.
COME OUTSIDE–WE CAN SHOW YOU.
OK.
STEP BACK.
I'M OPENING THE DOOR.
CLICK

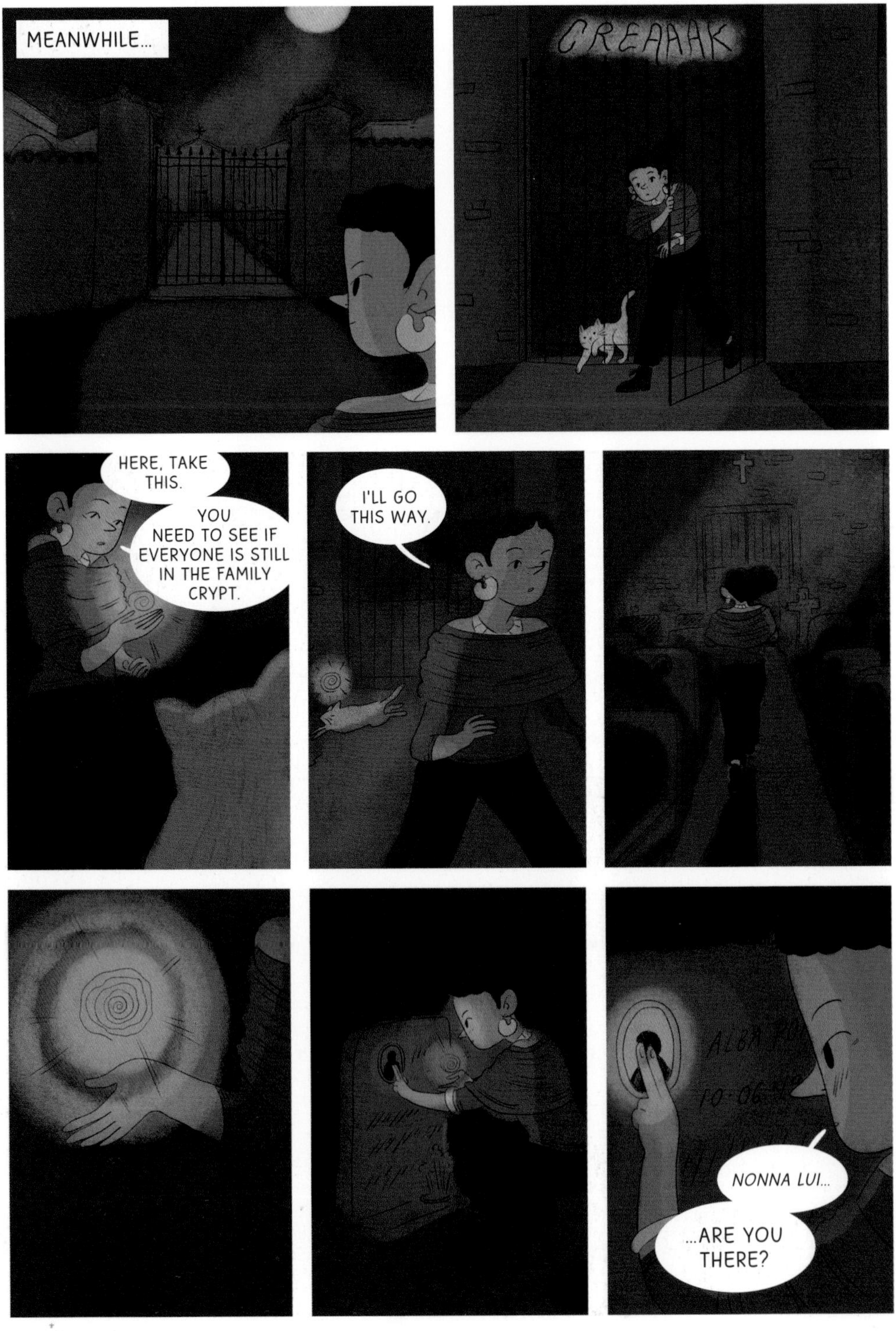
MEANWHILE...
CREAAAK
HERE, TAKE THIS.
YOU NEED TO SEE IF EVERYONE IS STILL IN THE FAMILY CRYPT.
I'LL GO THIS WAY.
NONNA LUI...
...ARE YOU THERE?

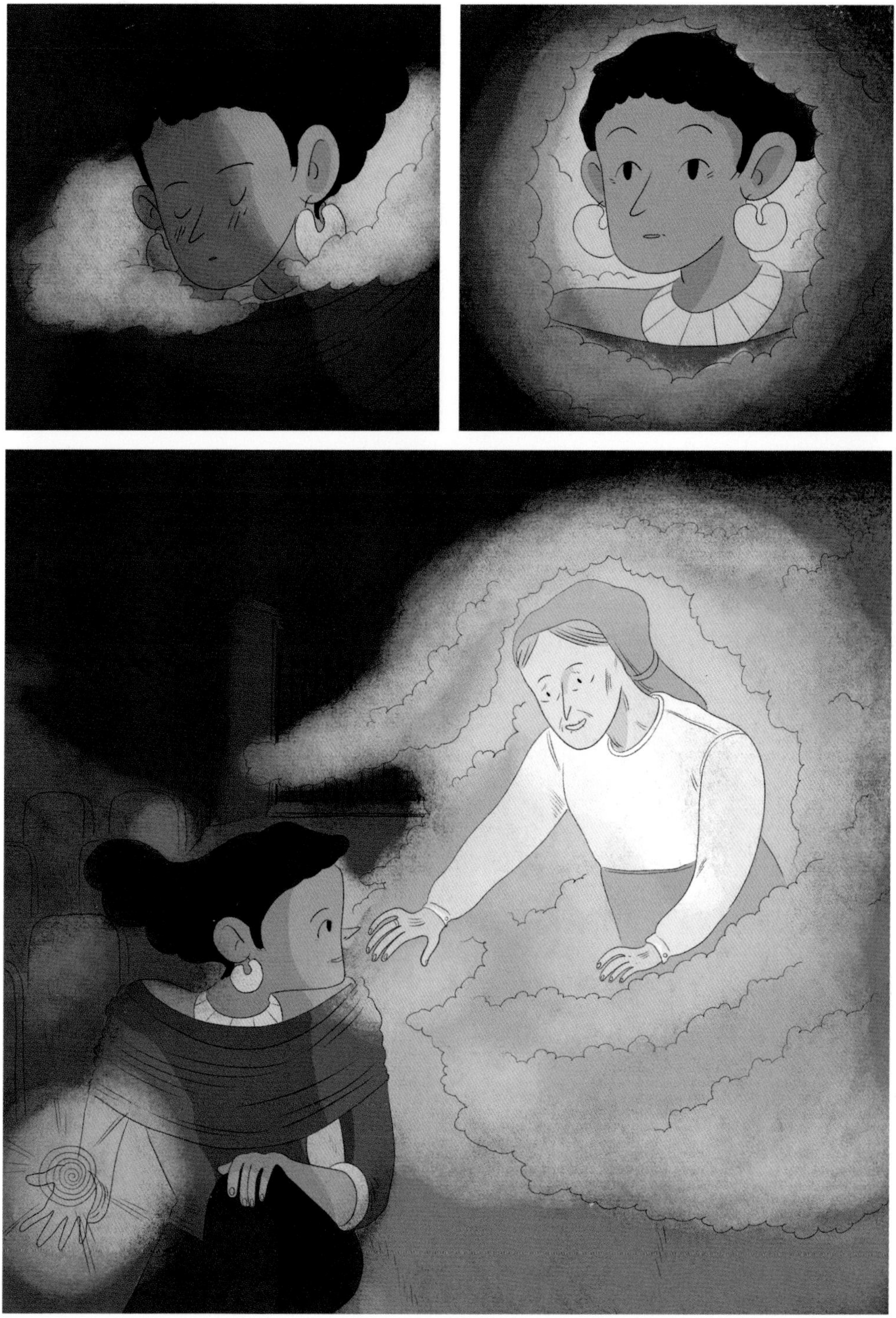

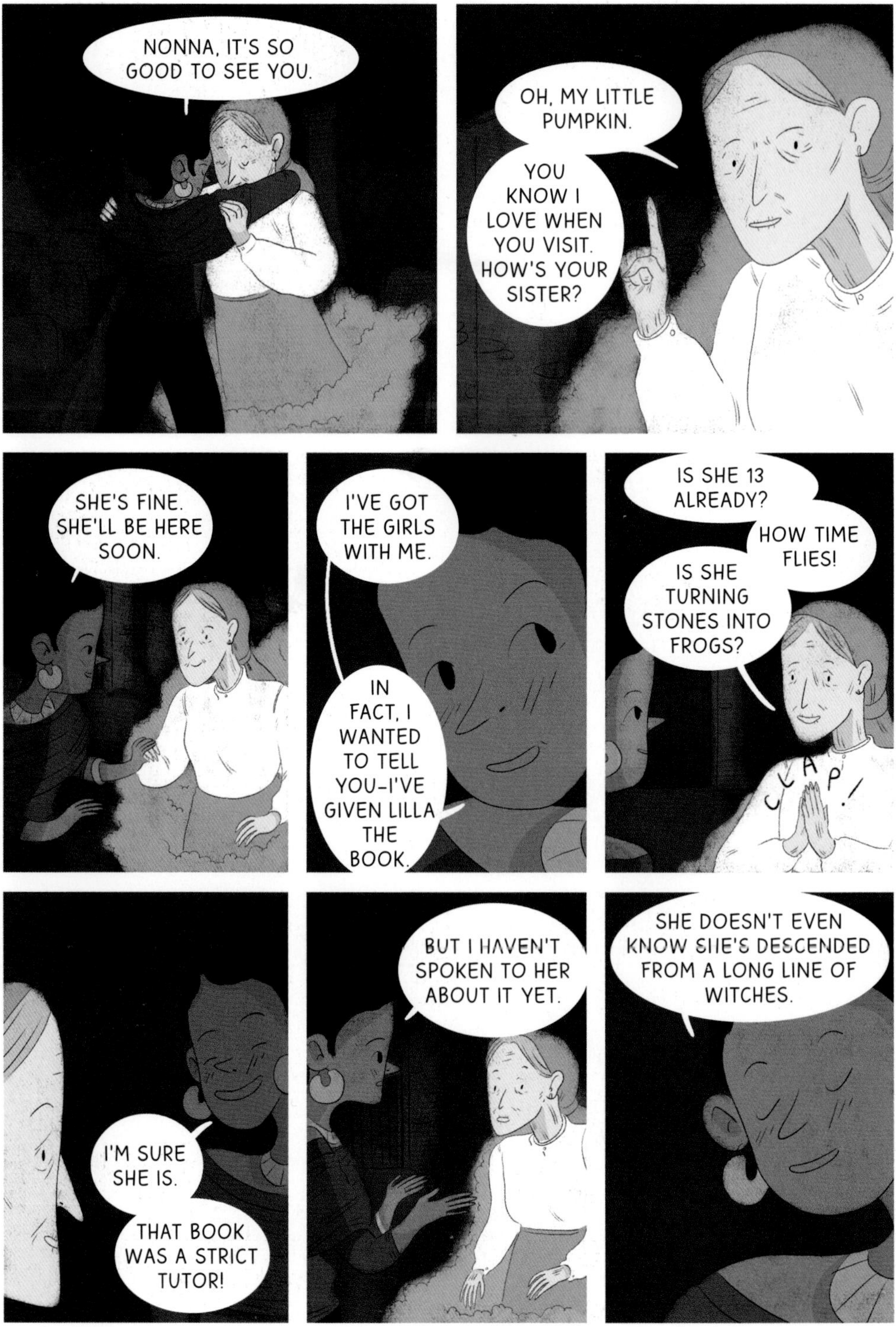
NONNA, IT'S SO GOOD TO SEE YOU.
OH, MY LITTLE PUMPKIN.
YOU KNOW I LOVE WHEN YOU VISIT. HOW'S YOUR SISTER?
SHE'S FINE. SHE'LL BE HERE SOON.
I'VE GOT THE GIRLS WITH ME.
IN FACT, I WANTED TO TELL YOU-I'VE GIVEN LILLA THE BOOK.
IS SHE 13 ALREADY?
HOW TIME FLIES!
IS SHE TURNING STONES INTO FROGS?
CLAP!
I'M SURE SHE IS.
THAT BOOK WAS A STRICT TUTOR!
BUT I HAVEN'T SPOKEN TO HER ABOUT IT YET.
SHE DOESN'T EVEN KNOW SHE'S DESCENDED FROM A LONG LINE OF WITCHES.

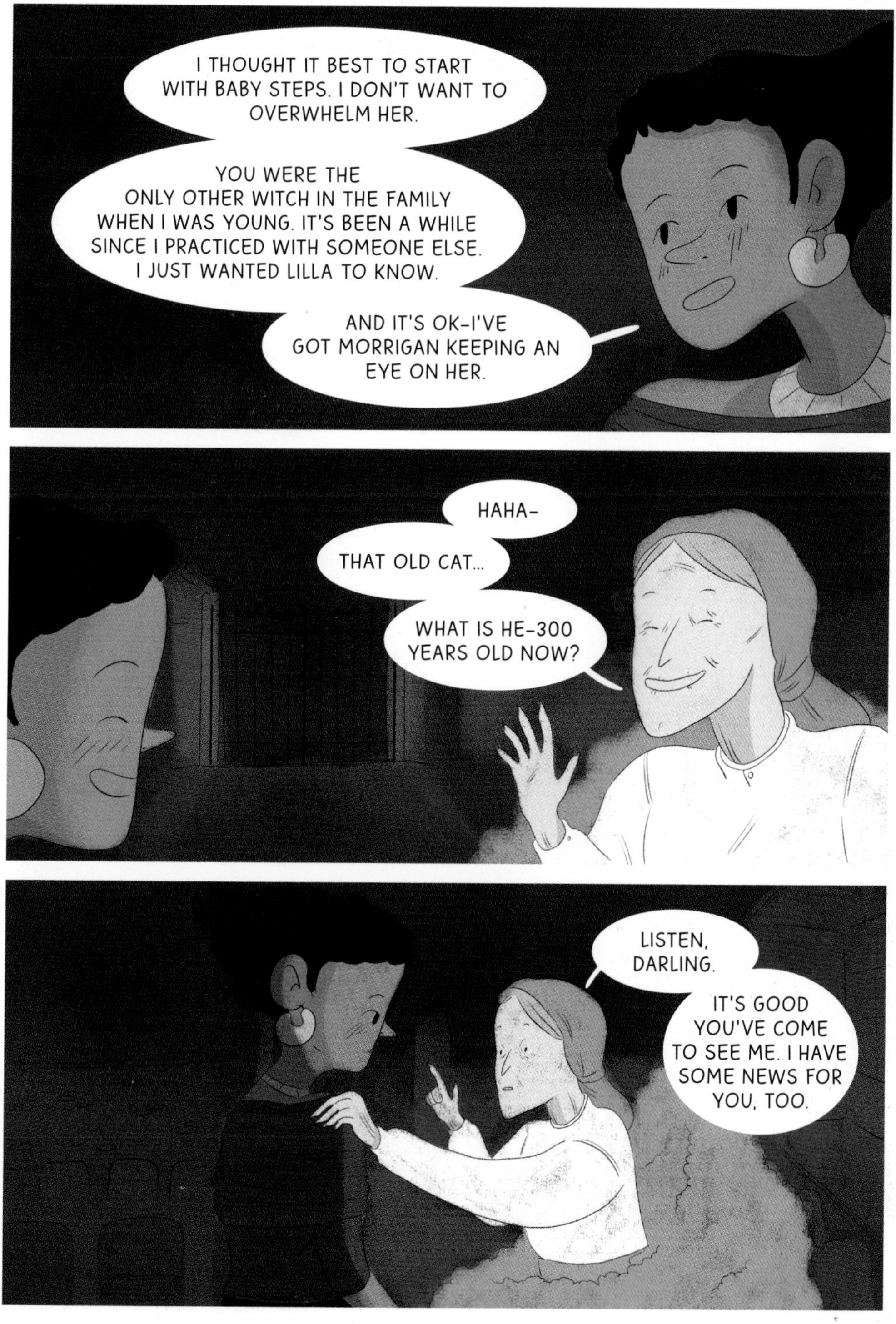
I THOUGHT IT BEST TO START WITH BABY STEPS. I DON'T WANT TO OVERWHELM HER.
YOU WERE THE ONLY OTHER WITCH IN THE FAMILY WHEN I WAS YOUNG. IT'S BEEN A WHILE SINCE I PRACTICED WITH SOMEONE ELSE. I JUST WANTED LILLA TO KNOW.
AND IT'S OK-I'VE GOT MORRIGAN KEEPING AN EYE ON HER.
HAHA-
THAT OLD CAT...
WHAT IS HE-300 YEARS OLD NOW?
LISTEN, DARLING.
IT'S GOOD YOU'VE COME TO SEE ME. I HAVE SOME NEWS FOR YOU, TOO.

EVERYONE'S BEEN TALKING ABOUT THE GRAVE ROBBINGS.

EVERYONE?

YOU KNOW–

ALL OF US ON THE *OTHER SIDE.*

"BEYOND THE GRAVE."

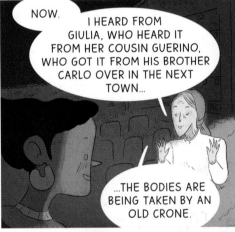

NOW.

I HEARD FROM GIULIA, WHO HEARD IT FROM HER COUSIN GUERINO, WHO GOT IT FROM HIS BROTHER CARLO OVER IN THE NEXT TOWN...

...THE BODIES ARE BEING TAKEN BY AN OLD CRONE.

WE THINK IT'S *STREGAMAMA.*

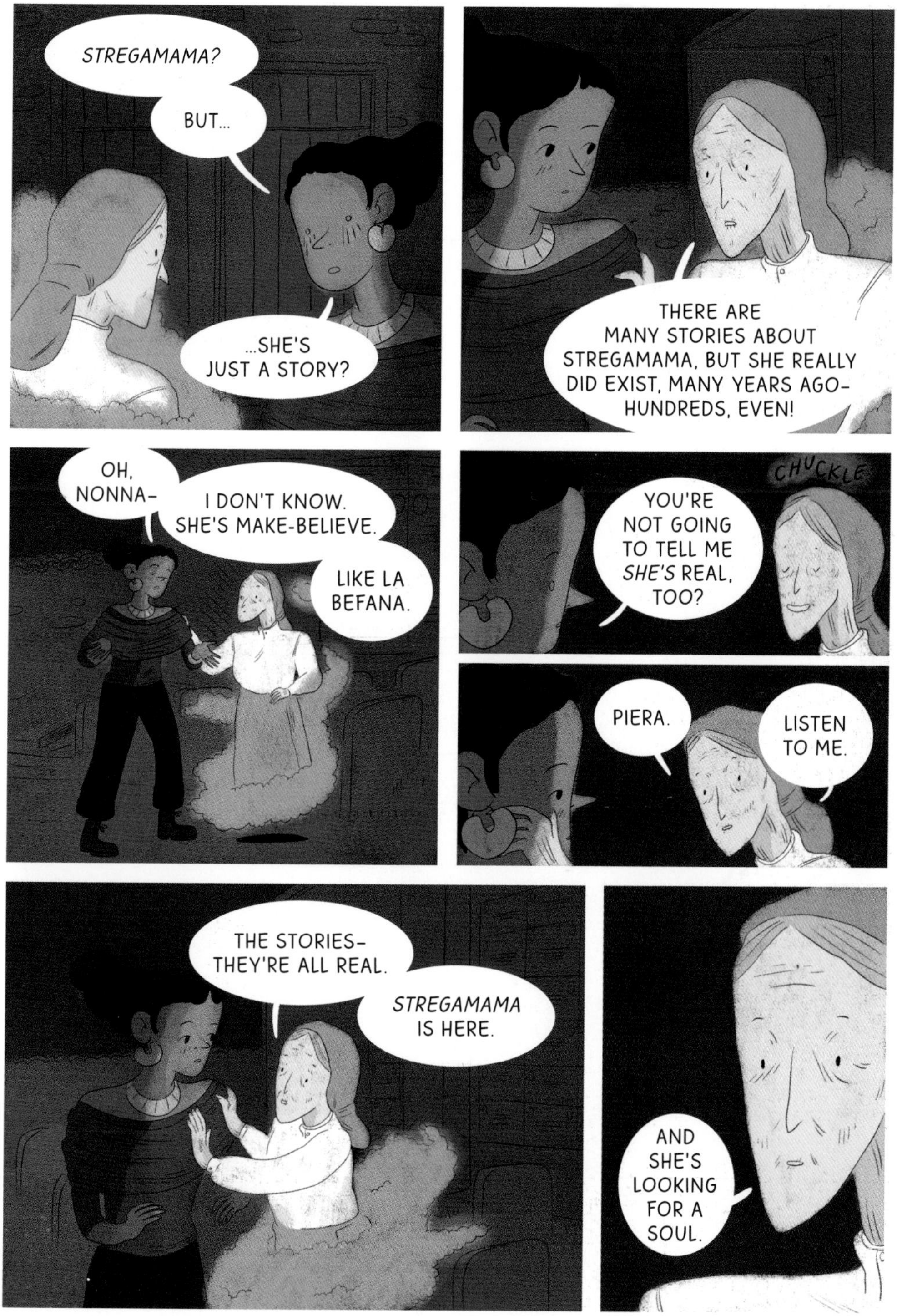
STREGAMAMA?
BUT...
...SHE'S JUST A STORY?
THERE ARE MANY STORIES ABOUT STREGAMAMA, BUT SHE REALLY DID EXIST, MANY YEARS AGO–HUNDREDS, EVEN!
OH, NONNA–
I DON'T KNOW. SHE'S MAKE-BELIEVE.
LIKE LA BEFANA.
CHUCKLE
YOU'RE NOT GOING TO TELL ME *SHE'S* REAL, TOO?
PIERA.
LISTEN TO ME.
THE STORIES–THEY'RE ALL REAL.
STREGAMAMA IS HERE.
AND SHE'S LOOKING FOR A SOUL.

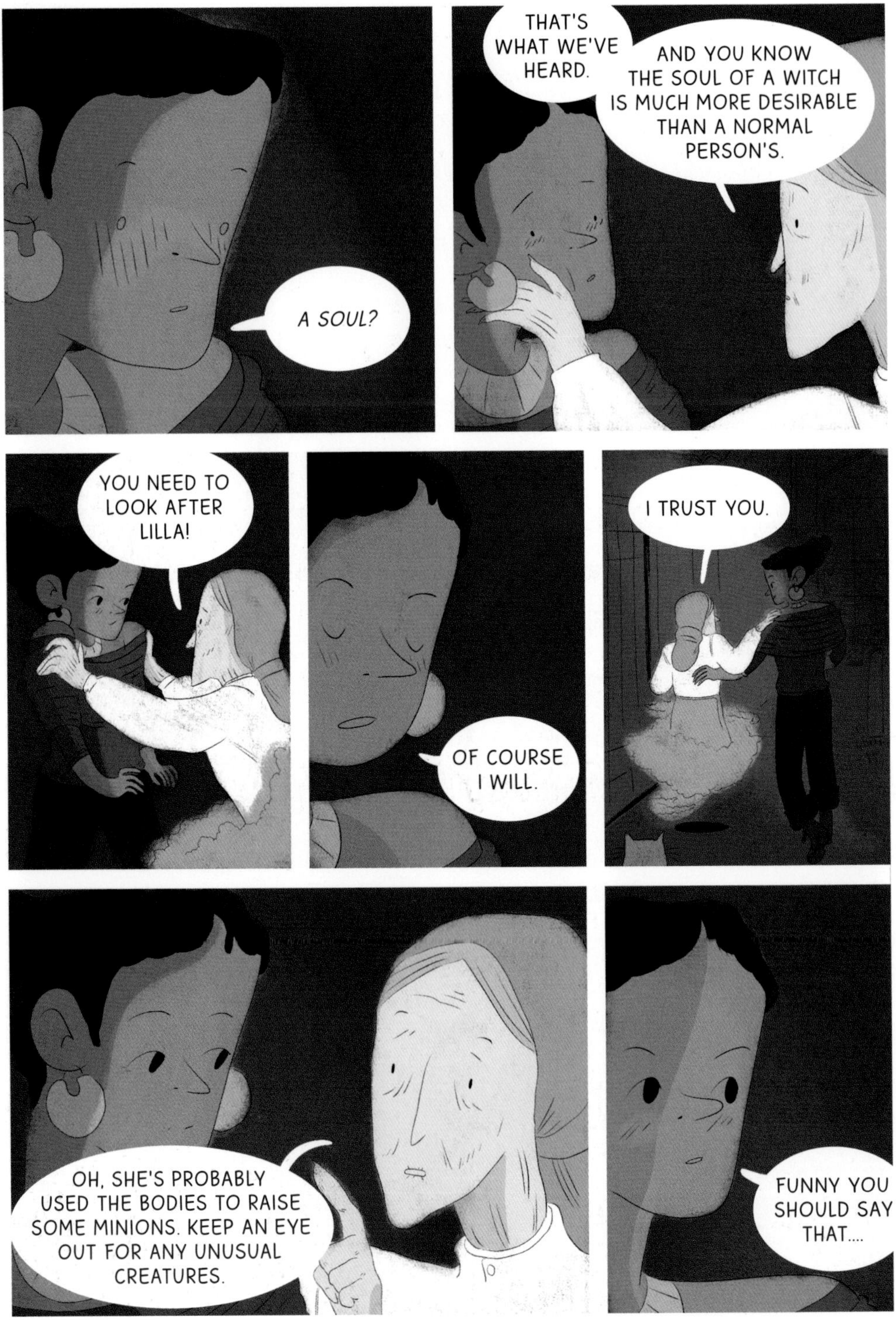

A SOUL?
THAT'S WHAT WE'VE HEARD.
AND YOU KNOW THE SOUL OF A WITCH IS MUCH MORE DESIRABLE THAN A NORMAL PERSON'S.
YOU NEED TO LOOK AFTER LILLA!
OF COURSE I WILL.
I TRUST YOU.
OH, SHE'S PROBABLY USED THE BODIES TO RAISE SOME MINIONS. KEEP AN EYE OUT FOR ANY UNUSUAL CREATURES.
FUNNY YOU SHOULD SAY THAT....

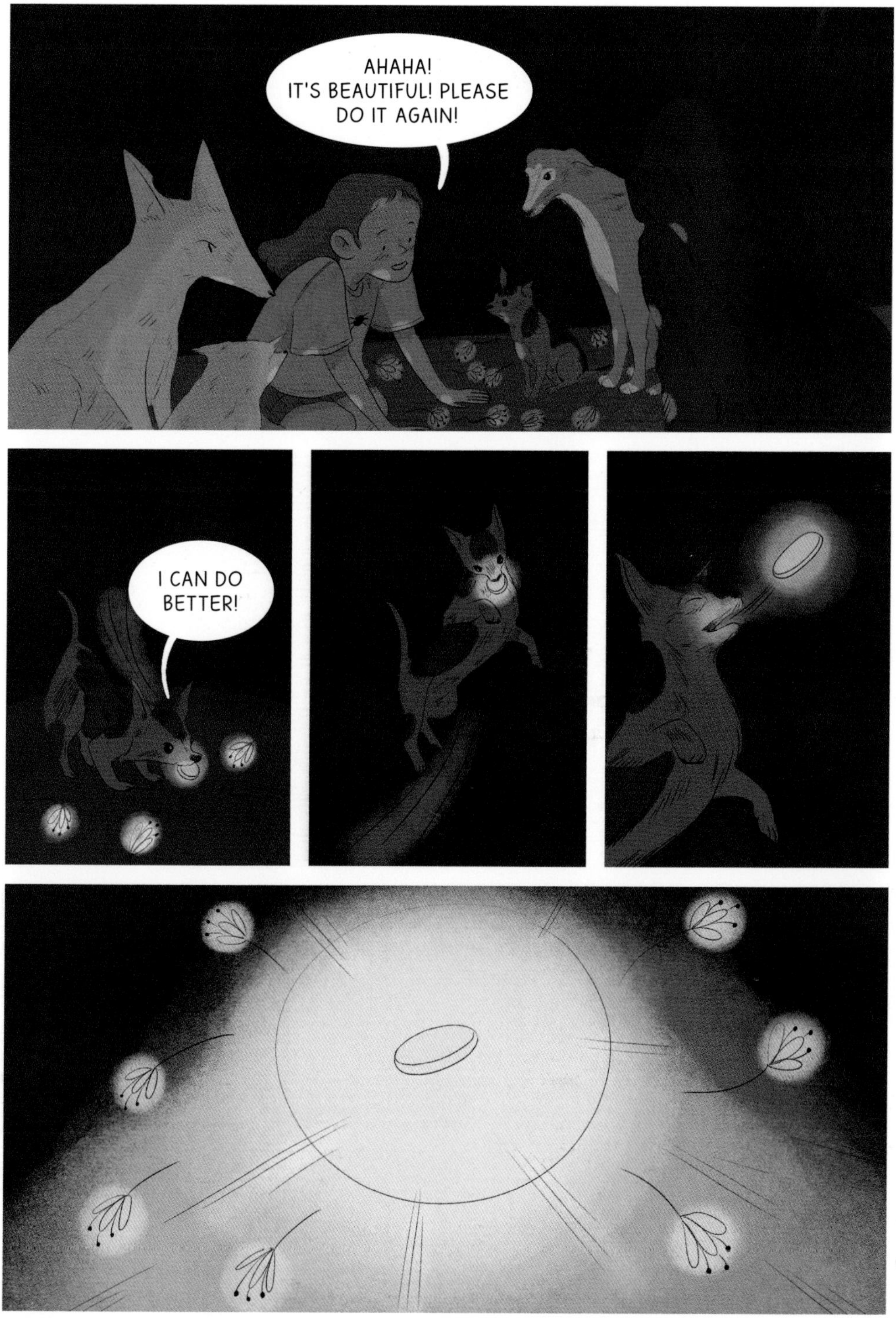
AHAHA! IT'S BEAUTIFUL! PLEASE DO IT AGAIN!
I CAN DO BETTER!

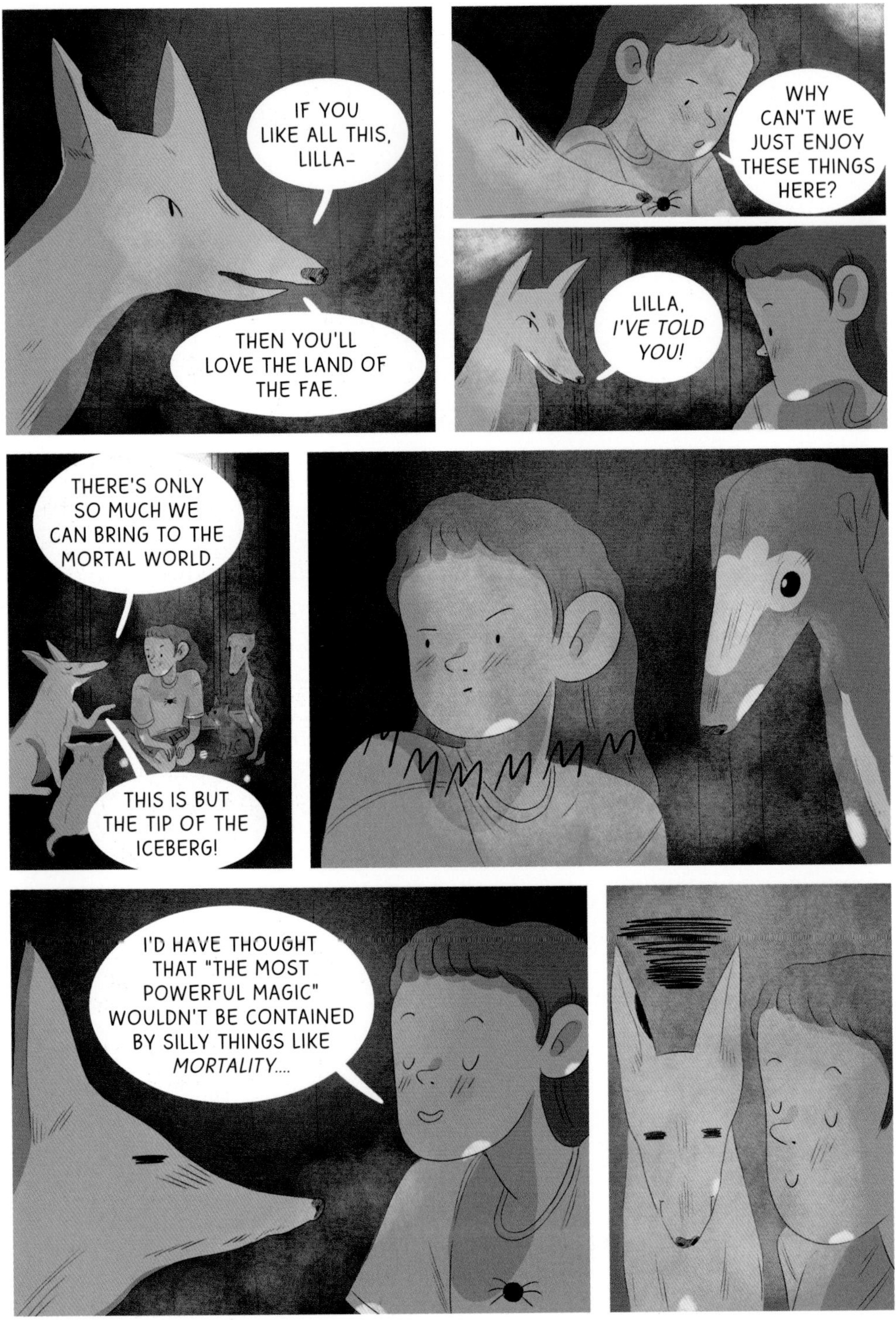
IF YOU LIKE ALL THIS, LILLA-
THEN YOU'LL LOVE THE LAND OF THE FAE.
WHY CAN'T WE JUST ENJOY THESE THINGS HERE?
LILLA, *I'VE TOLD YOU!*
THERE'S ONLY SO MUCH WE CAN BRING TO THE MORTAL WORLD.
THIS IS BUT THE TIP OF THE ICEBERG!
MMMMMMM
I'D HAVE THOUGHT THAT "THE MOST POWERFUL MAGIC" WOULDN'T BE CONTAINED BY SILLY THINGS LIKE *MORTALITY*....

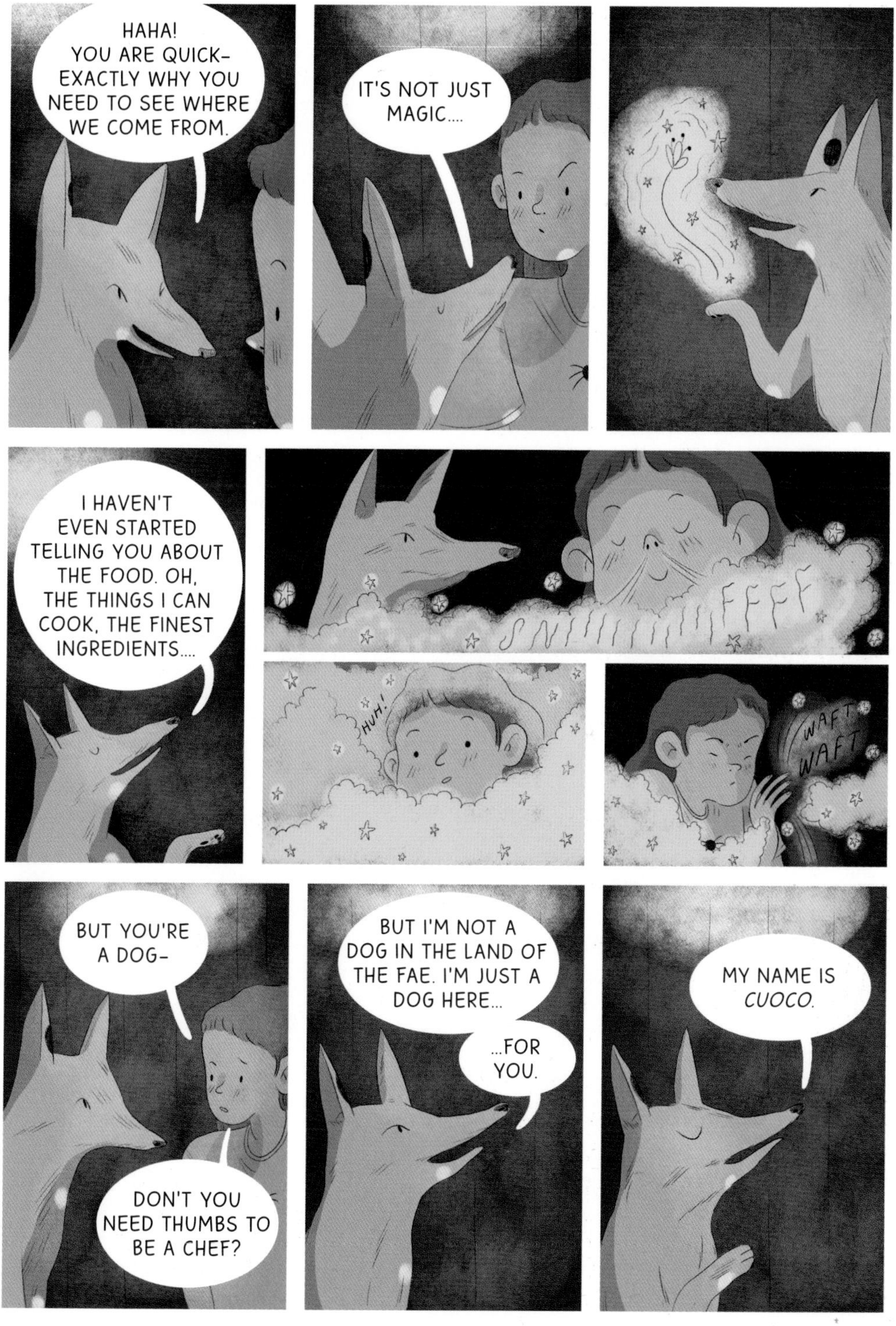
HAHA! YOU ARE QUICK– EXACTLY WHY YOU NEED TO SEE WHERE WE COME FROM.
IT'S NOT JUST MAGIC....
I HAVEN'T EVEN STARTED TELLING YOU ABOUT THE FOOD. OH, THE THINGS I CAN COOK, THE FINEST INGREDIENTS....
SNIIIIIIIIIFFFF
HUH!
WAFT WAFT
BUT YOU'RE A DOG–
DON'T YOU NEED THUMBS TO BE A CHEF?
BUT I'M NOT A DOG IN THE LAND OF THE FAE. I'M JUST A DOG HERE...
...FOR YOU.
MY NAME IS *CUOCO.*

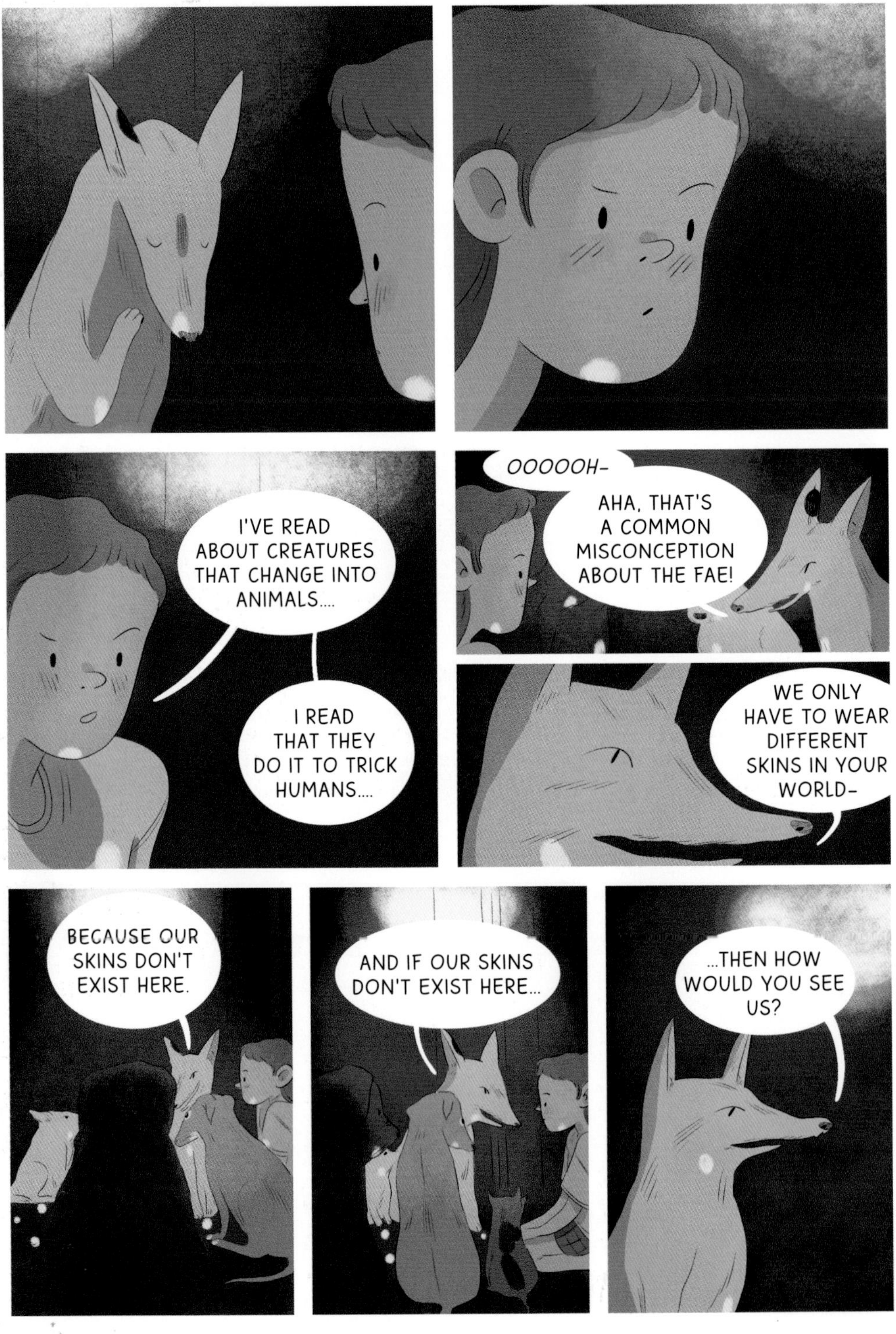
I'VE READ ABOUT CREATURES THAT CHANGE INTO ANIMALS....
I READ THAT THEY DO IT TO TRICK HUMANS....
OOOOOH-
AHA, THAT'S A COMMON MISCONCEPTION ABOUT THE FAE!
WE ONLY HAVE TO WEAR DIFFERENT SKINS IN YOUR WORLD-
BECAUSE OUR SKINS DON'T EXIST HERE.
AND IF OUR SKINS DON'T EXIST HERE...
...THEN HOW WOULD YOU SEE US?

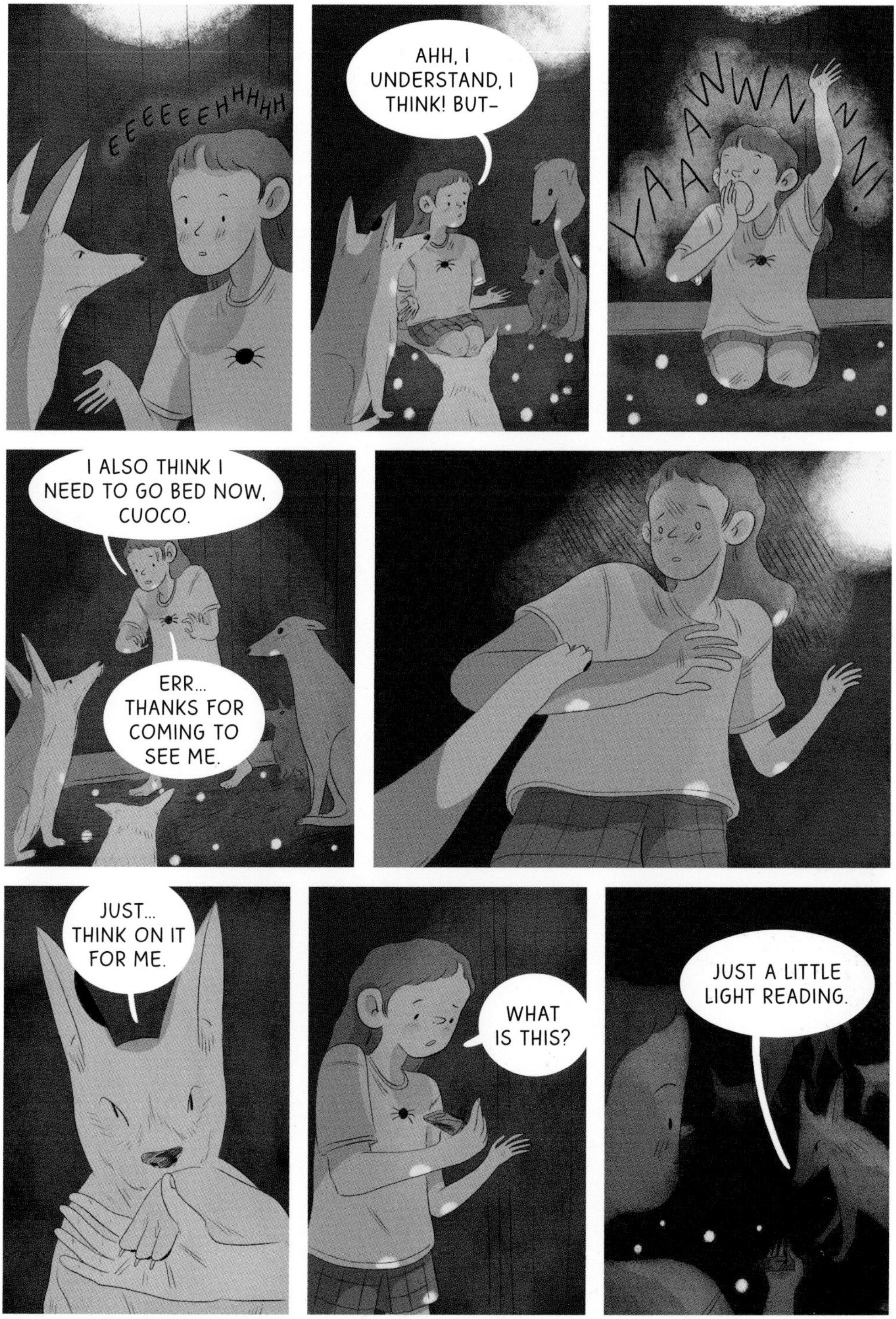

EEEEEEEHHHHH
AHH, I UNDERSTAND, I THINK! BUT–
YAAAWWNNN!
I ALSO THINK I NEED TO GO BED NOW, CUOCO.
ERR... THANKS FOR COMING TO SEE ME.
JUST... THINK ON IT FOR ME.
WHAT IS THIS?
JUST A LITTLE LIGHT READING.

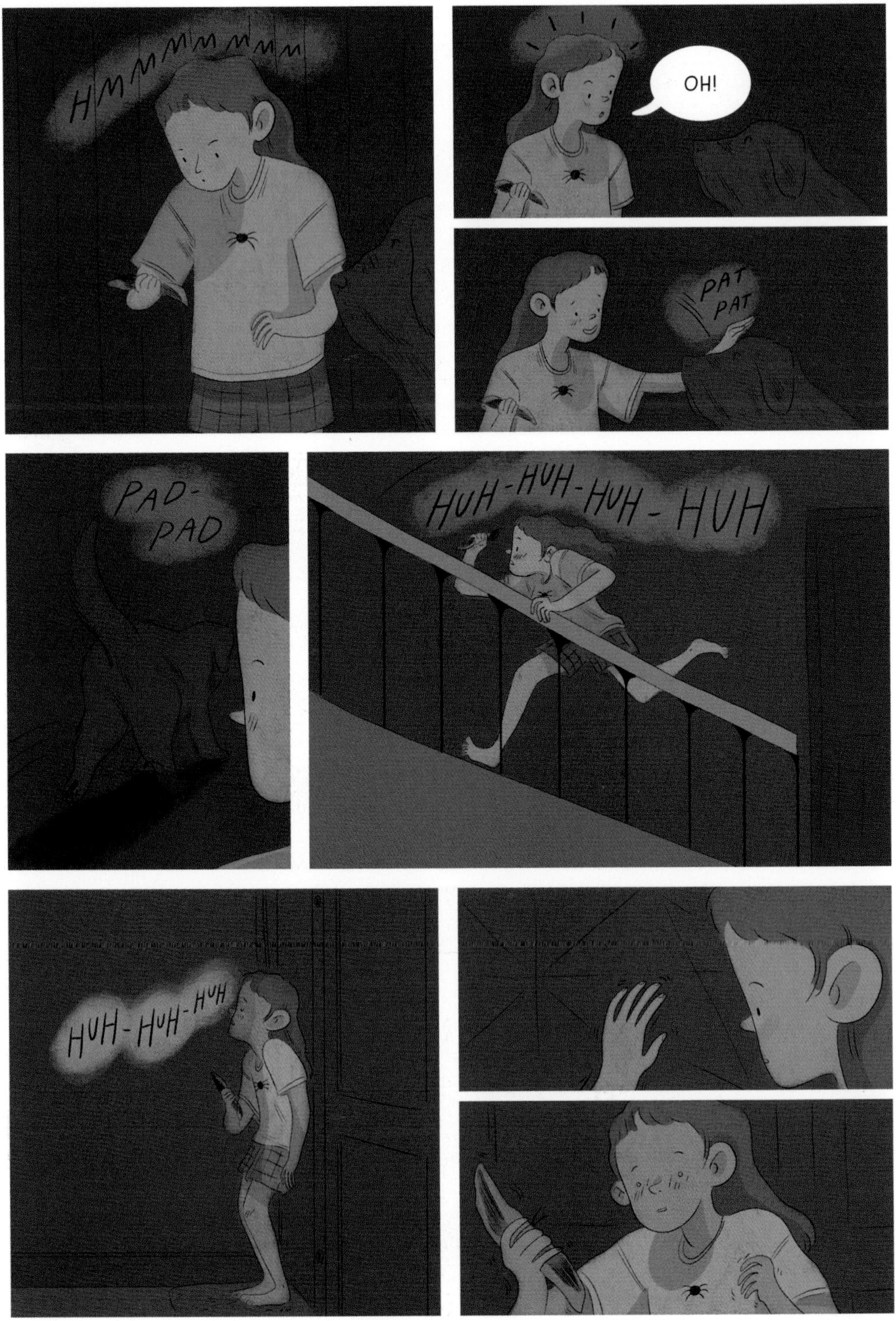
HMMMMMMMMM
OH!
PAT PAT
PAD-PAD
HUH-HUH-HUH-HUH
HUH-HUH-HUH

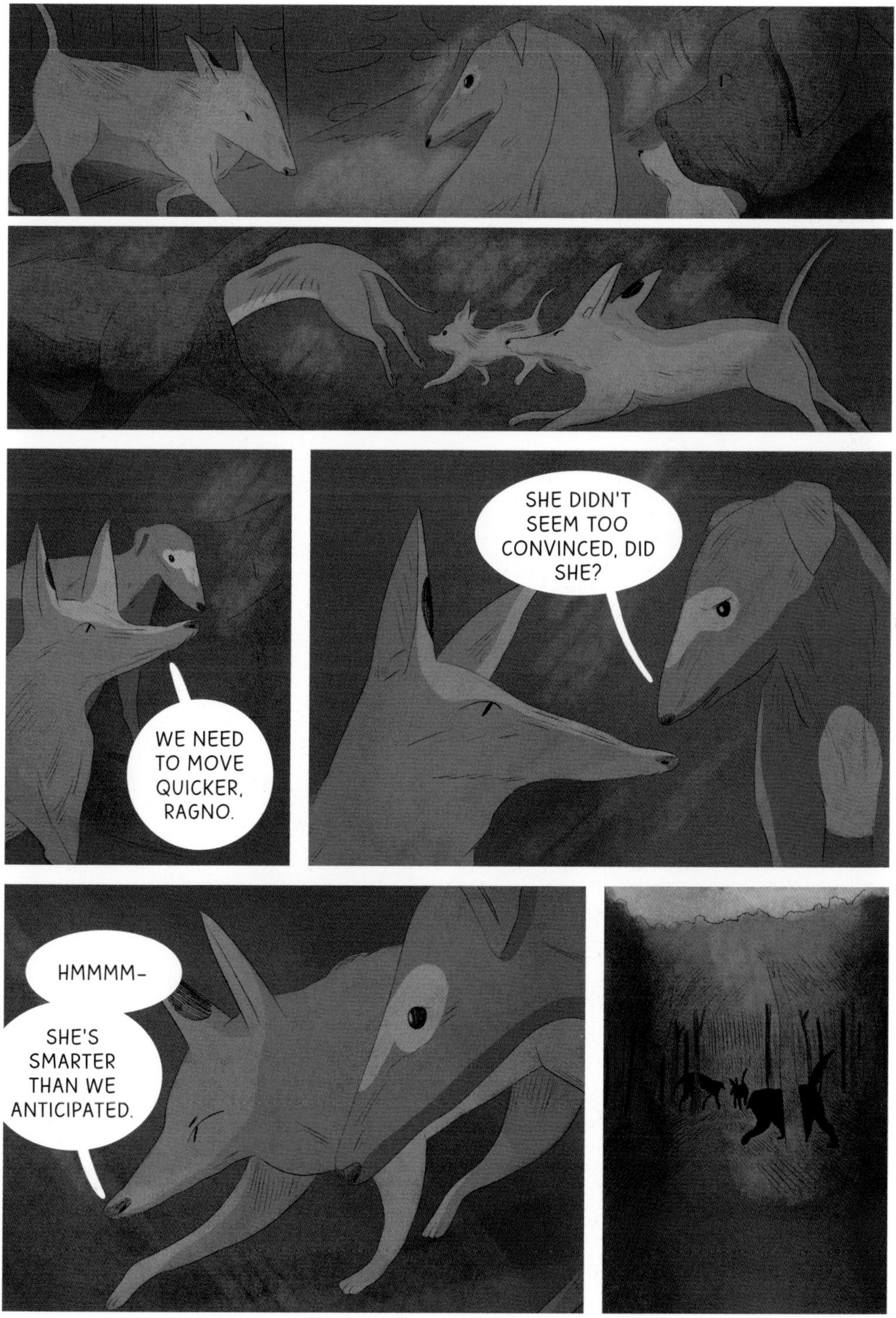
WE NEED TO MOVE QUICKER, RAGNO.
SHE DIDN'T SEEM TOO CONVINCED, DID SHE?
HMMMM-
SHE'S SMARTER THAN WE ANTICIPATED.

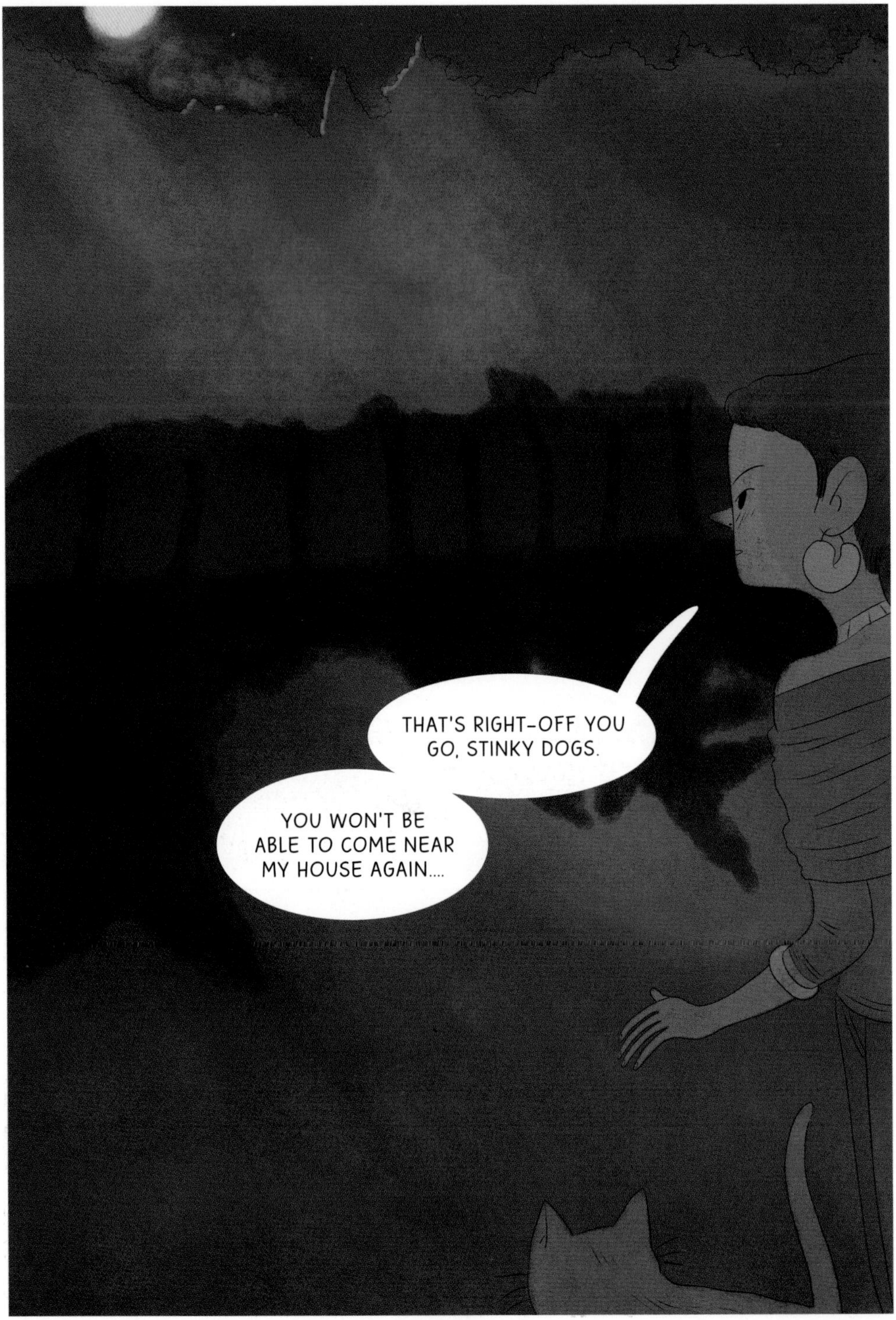
THAT'S RIGHT–OFF YOU GO, STINKY DOGS.
YOU WON'T BE ABLE TO COME NEAR MY HOUSE AGAIN....

ROOT FROM HOME...

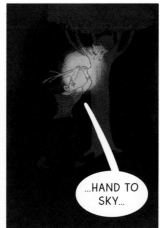

...HAND TO SKY...

...ANOINT MY FAMILY WHERE THEY LIE.

MUMBLE BUMBLE RUMBLE

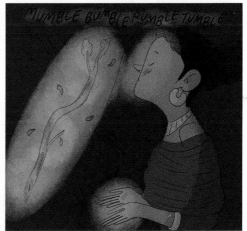

MUMBLE BUMBLE RUMBLE TUMBLE

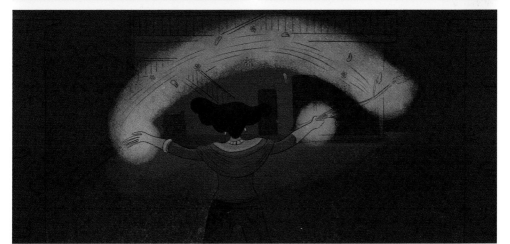

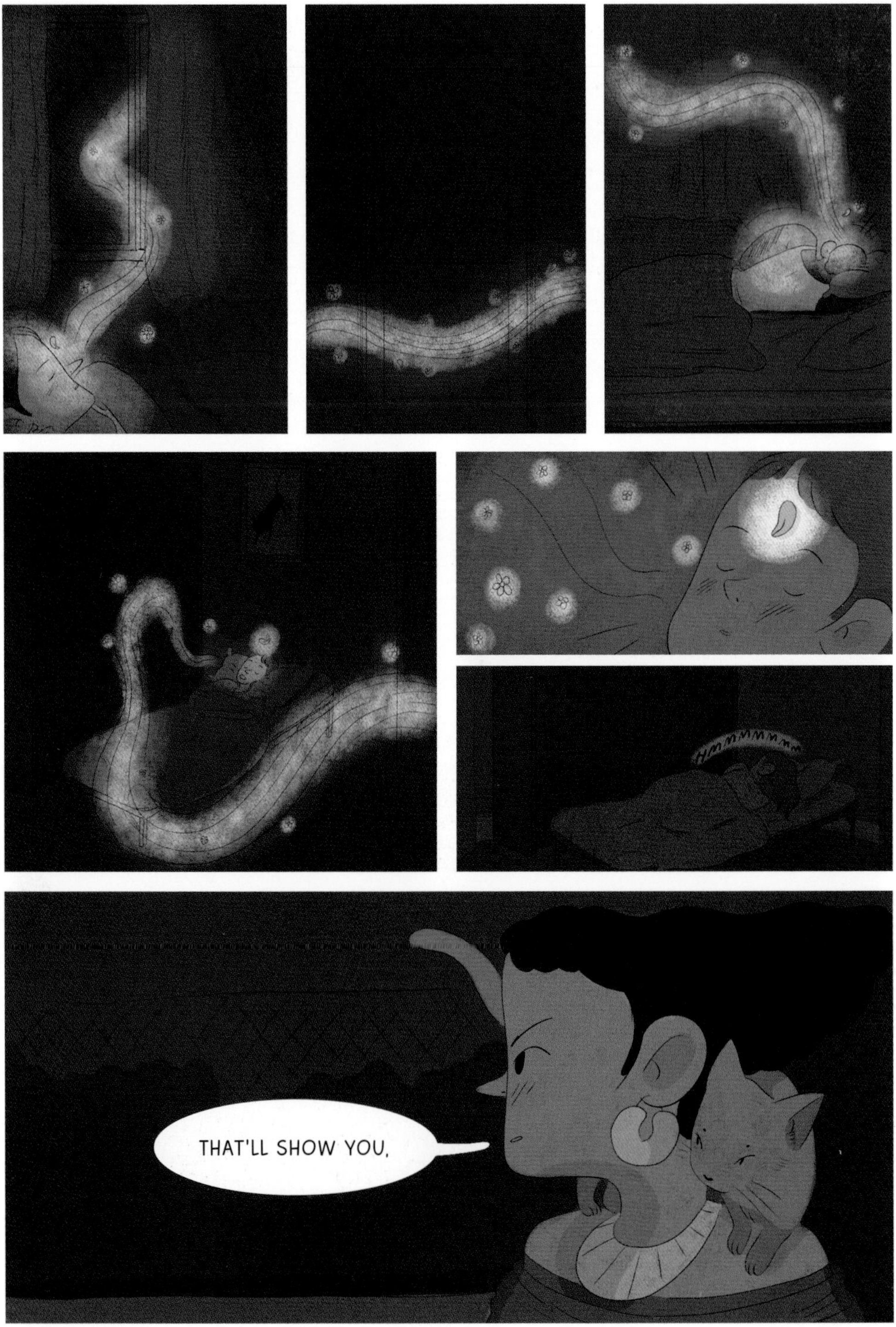
HMMMMMMM
THAT'LL SHOW YOU,

KNOCK
KNOCK

COME ON—

I'VE GOT BREAKFAST.

OH, COME ON, DON'T START ACTING LIKE A REAL PUSSYCAT NOW.

I'M HERE, I'M HERE.

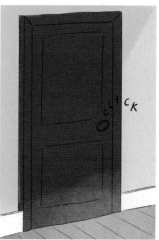

CLICK

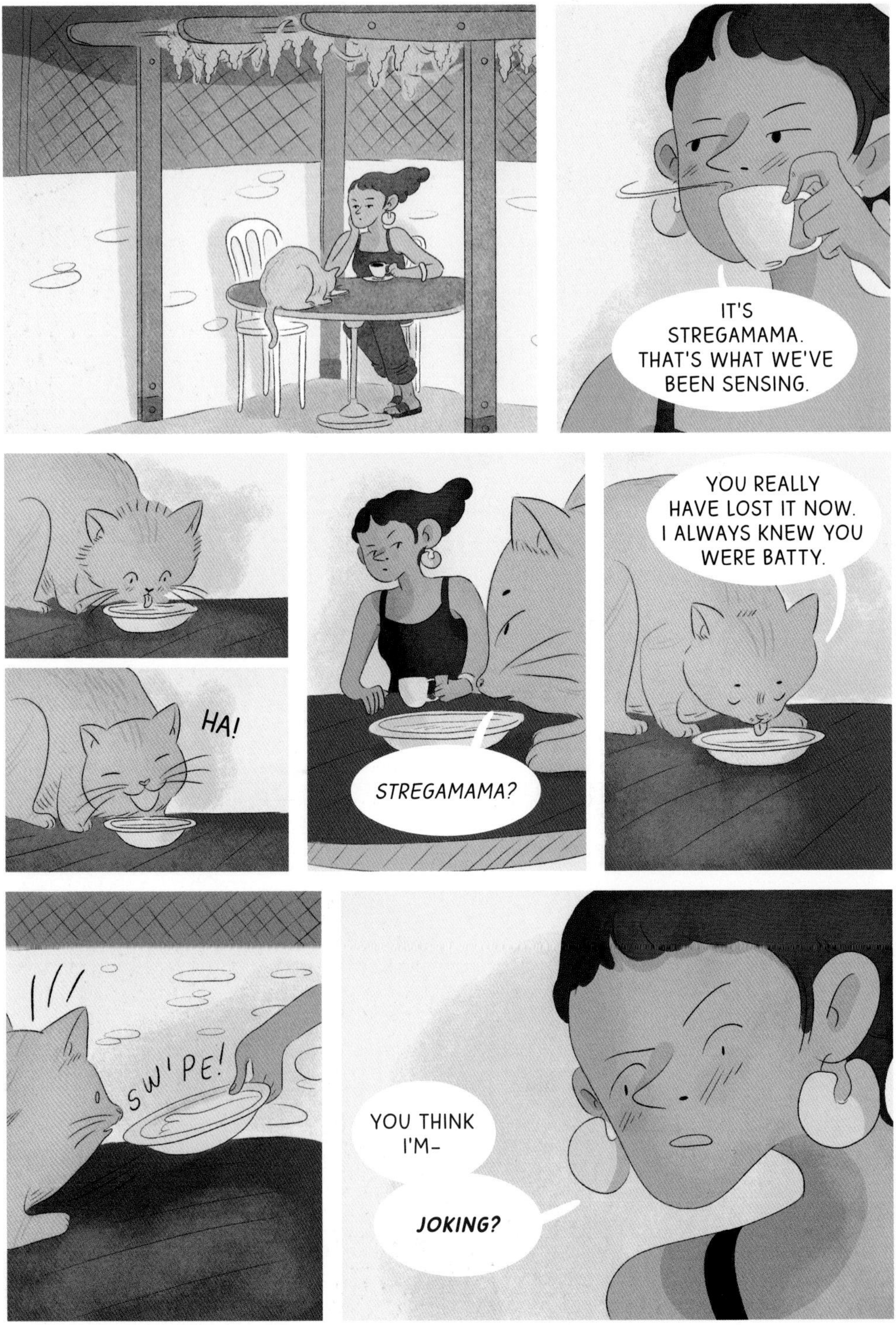
IT'S STREGAMAMA. THAT'S WHAT WE'VE BEEN SENSING.
HA!
STREGAMAMA?
YOU REALLY HAVE LOST IT NOW. I ALWAYS KNEW YOU WERE BATTY.
SWIPE!
YOU THINK I'M–
JOKING?

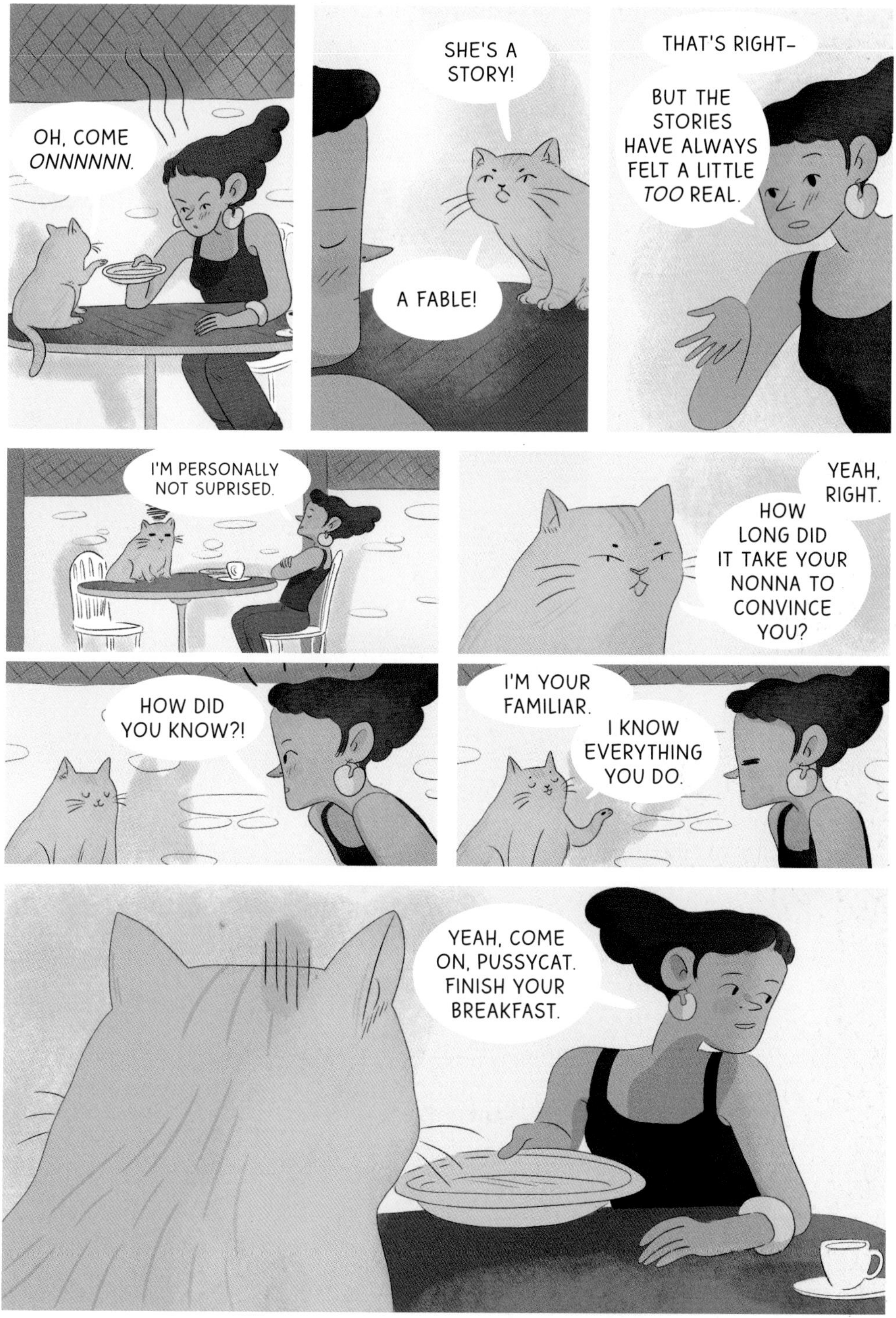
OH, COME *ONNNNNN.*
SHE'S A STORY!
A FABLE!
THAT'S RIGHT–
BUT THE STORIES HAVE ALWAYS FELT A LITTLE *TOO* REAL.
I'M PERSONALLY NOT SUPRISED.
YEAH, RIGHT.
HOW LONG DID IT TAKE YOUR NONNA TO CONVINCE YOU?
HOW DID YOU KNOW?!
I'M YOUR FAMILIAR.
I KNOW EVERYTHING YOU DO.
YEAH, COME ON, PUSSYCAT. FINISH YOUR BREAKFAST.

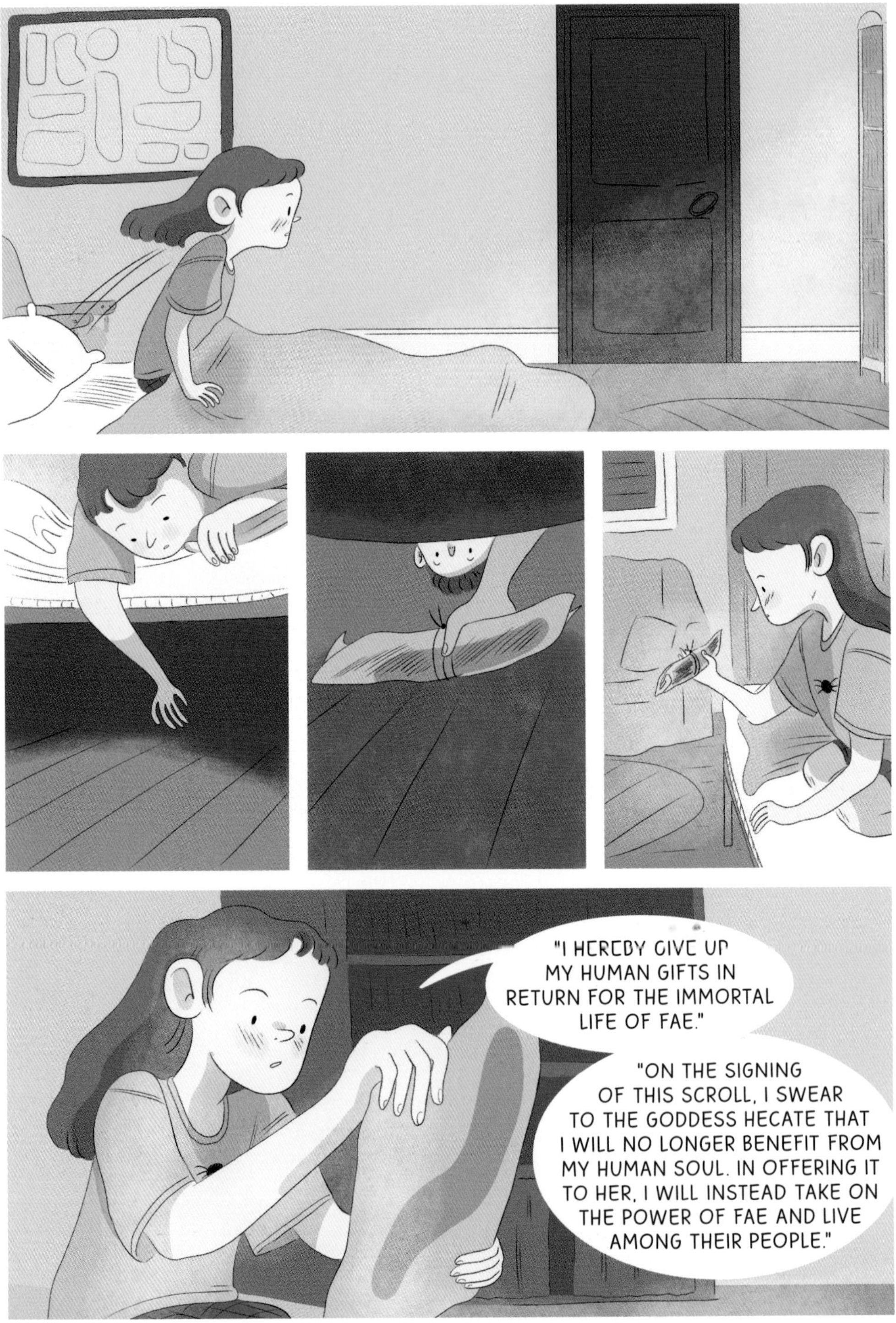
"I HEREBY GIVE UP MY HUMAN GIFTS IN RETURN FOR THE IMMORTAL LIFE OF FAE."
"ON THE SIGNING OF THIS SCROLL, I SWEAR TO THE GODDESS HECATE THAT I WILL NO LONGER BENEFIT FROM MY HUMAN SOUL. IN OFFERING IT TO HER, I WILL INSTEAD TAKE ON THE POWER OF FAE AND LIVE AMONG THEIR PEOPLE."

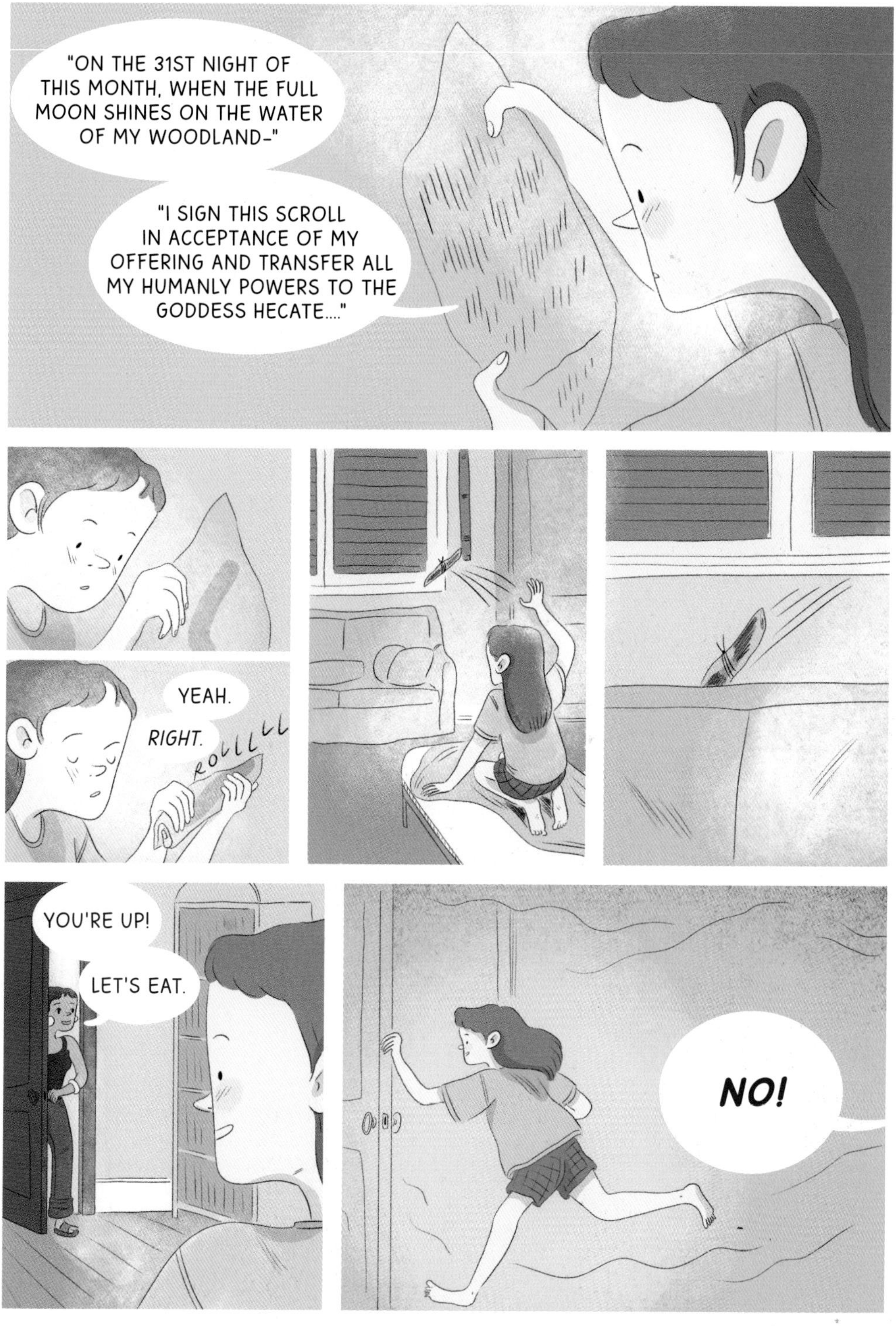

"ON THE 31ST NIGHT OF THIS MONTH, WHEN THE FULL MOON SHINES ON THE WATER OF MY WOODLAND-"
"I SIGN THIS SCROLL IN ACCEPTANCE OF MY OFFERING AND TRANSFER ALL MY HUMANLY POWERS TO THE GODDESS HECATE...."
YEAH.
RIGHT.
ROLLLLLL
YOU'RE UP!
LET'S EAT.
NO!

SHE'S THROWN IT ASIDE—

CUOCO!

YOU SAID IT WAS DONE—

BUT YOU'VE FAILED ME.

I'M SORRY, MAMA.

WE WILL TRY AGAIN.

TRY HARDER!

GO! NOW!

IF I'M GOING TO HAVE ANY CHANCE OF SURVIVING HERE, YOU'LL HAVE TO GET HER TO SIGN IT.

NO USE CHARMING HER AGAIN. HIT HER WHERE SHE'S WEAKEST.

YES, MAMA, OF COURSE!

I WON'T FAIL YOU THIS TIME.

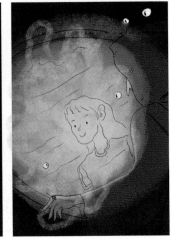

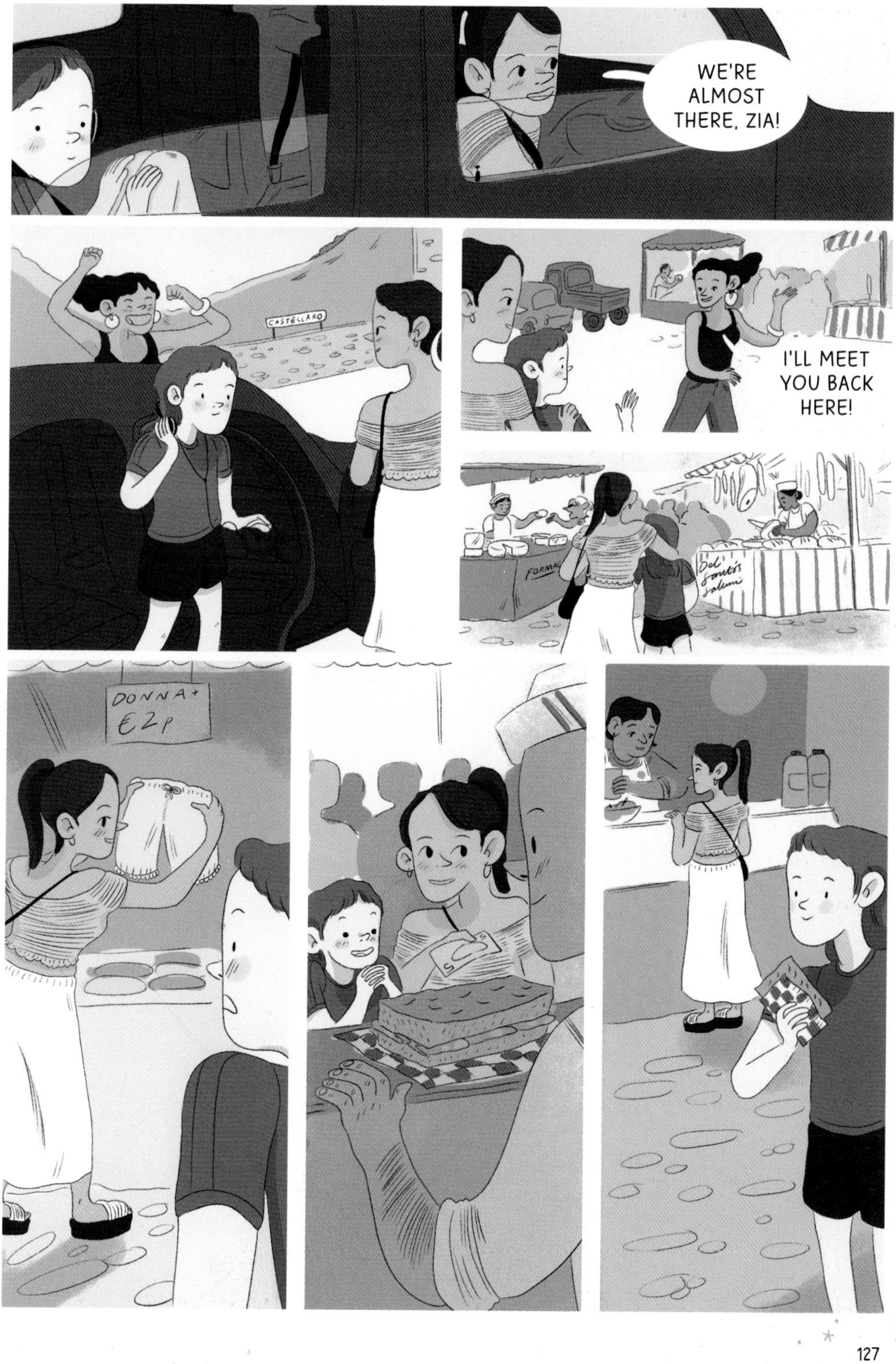
WE'RE ALMOST THERE, ZIA!
CASTELLARO
I'LL MEET YOU BACK HERE!

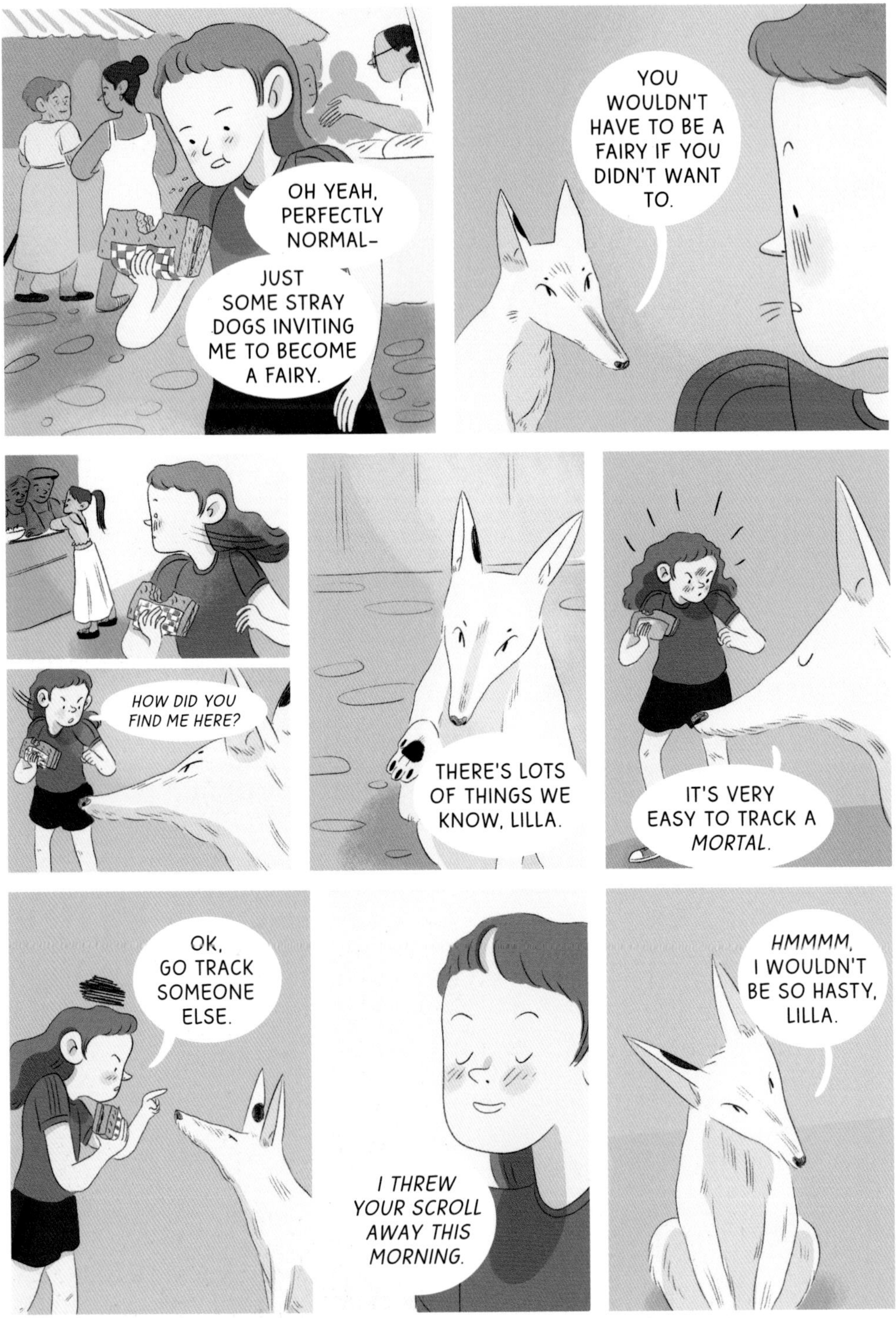
OH YEAH, PERFECTLY NORMAL-
JUST SOME STRAY DOGS INVITING ME TO BECOME A FAIRY.
YOU WOULDN'T HAVE TO BE A FAIRY IF YOU DIDN'T WANT TO.
HOW DID YOU FIND ME HERE?
THERE'S LOTS OF THINGS WE KNOW, LILLA.
IT'S VERY EASY TO TRACK A *MORTAL*.
OK, GO TRACK SOMEONE ELSE.
I THREW YOUR SCROLL AWAY THIS MORNING.
HMMMM, I WOULDN'T BE SO HASTY, LILLA.

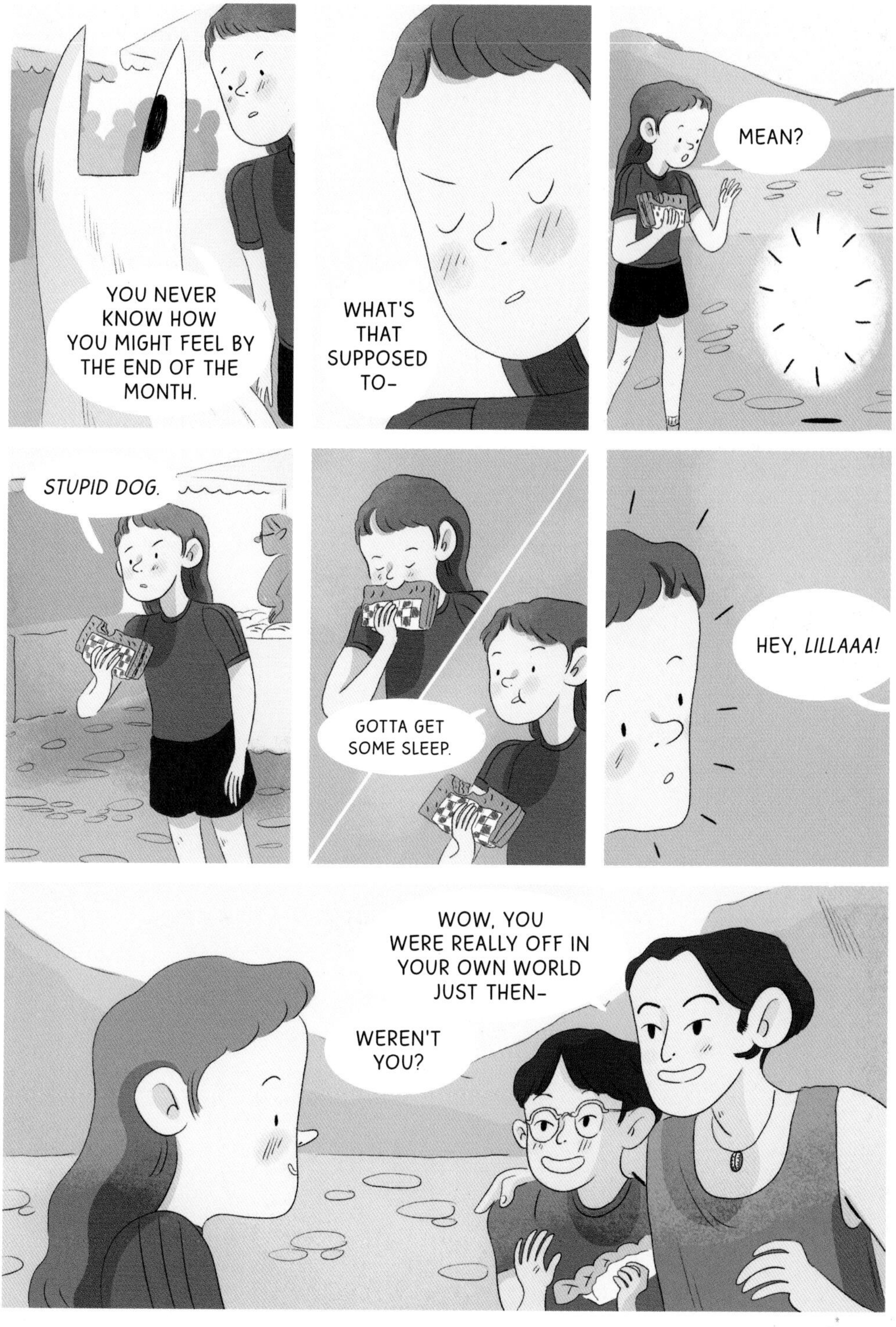
YOU NEVER KNOW HOW YOU MIGHT FEEL BY THE END OF THE MONTH.
WHAT'S THAT SUPPOSED TO-
MEAN?
STUPID DOG.
GOTTA GET SOME SLEEP.
HEY, *LILLAAA!*
WOW, YOU WERE REALLY OFF IN YOUR OWN WORLD JUST THEN-
WEREN'T YOU?

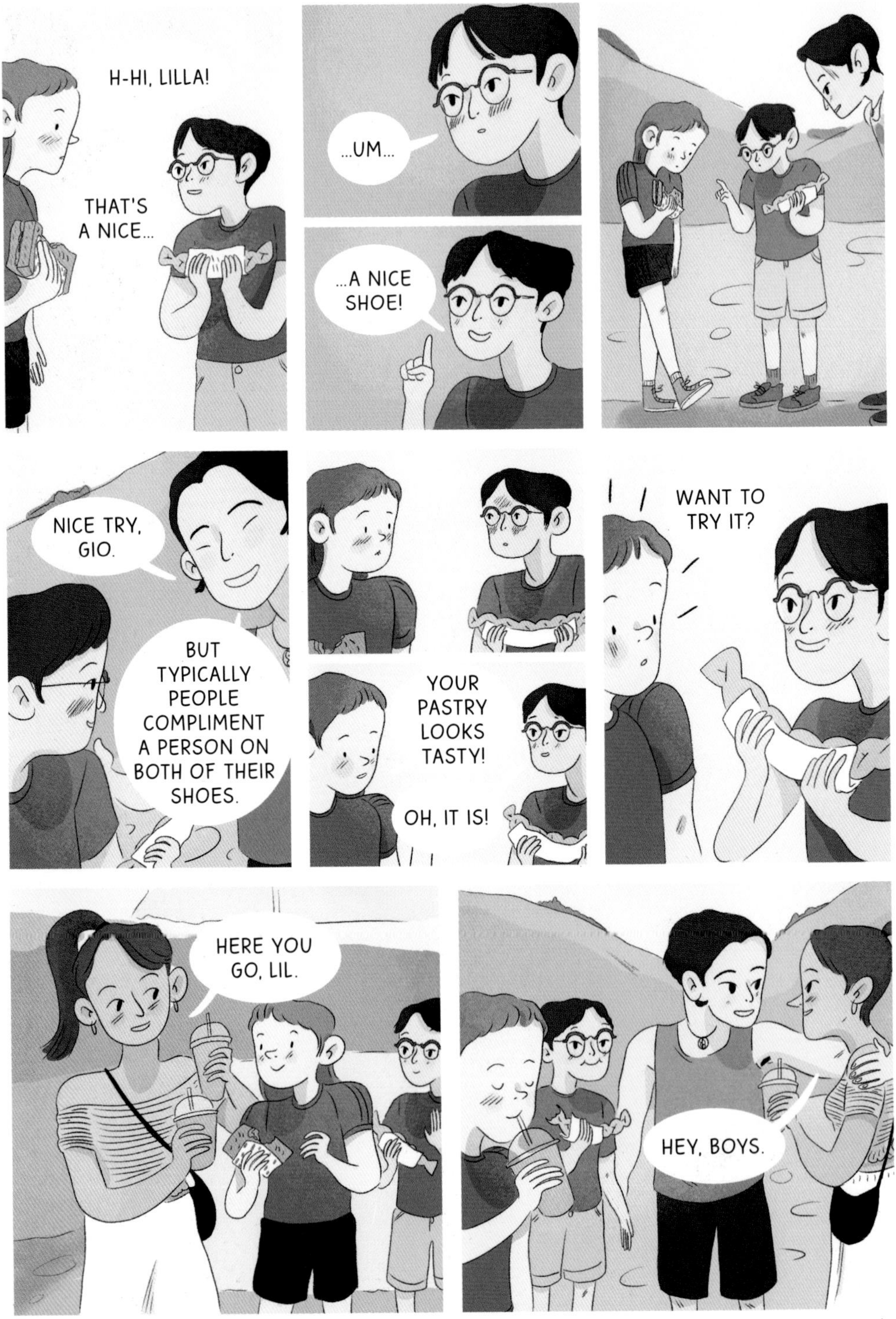
H-HI, LILLA!
THAT'S A NICE...
...UM...
...A NICE SHOE!
NICE TRY, GIO.
BUT TYPICALLY PEOPLE COMPLIMENT A PERSON ON BOTH OF THEIR SHOES.
YOUR PASTRY LOOKS TASTY!
OH, IT IS!
WANT TO TRY IT?
HERE YOU GO, LIL.
HEY, BOYS.

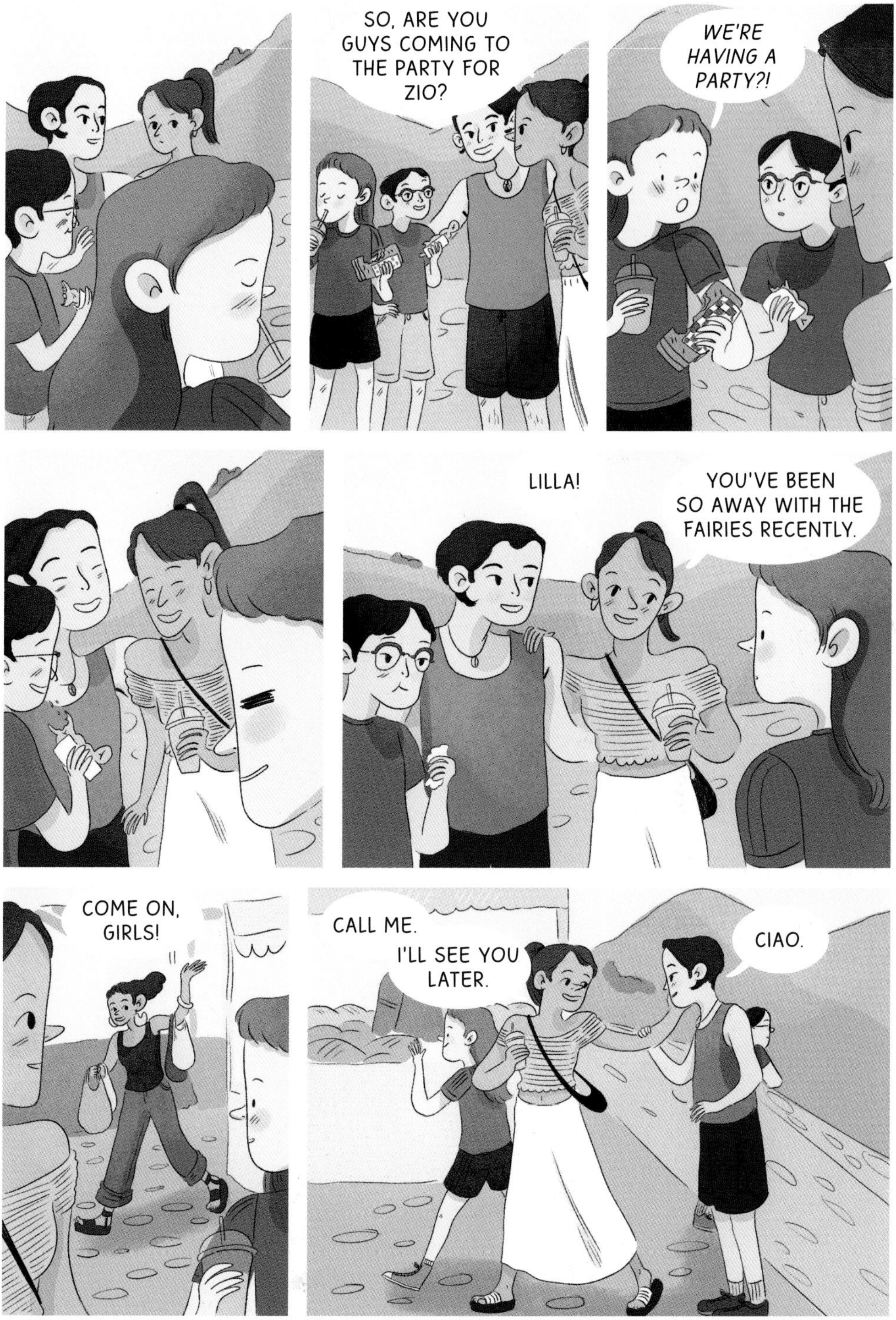
SO, ARE YOU GUYS COMING TO THE PARTY FOR ZIO?
WE'RE HAVING A PARTY?!
LILLA!
YOU'VE BEEN SO AWAY WITH THE FAIRIES RECENTLY.
COME ON, GIRLS!
CALL ME.
I'LL SEE YOU LATER.
CIAO.

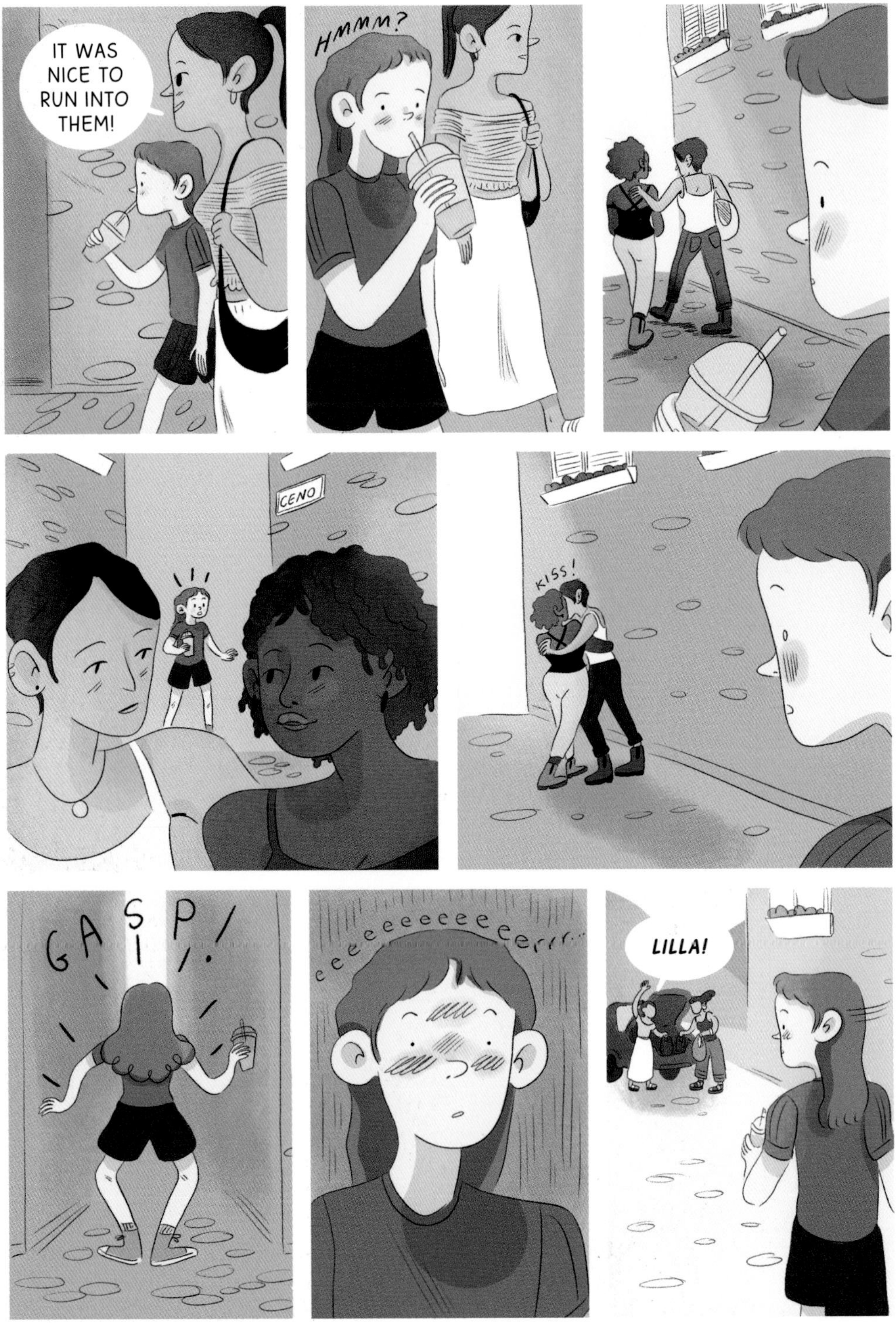
IT WAS NICE TO RUN INTO THEM!
HMMM?
CENO
KISS!
GASP!
eeeeeeeeeeeeerrr...
LILLA!

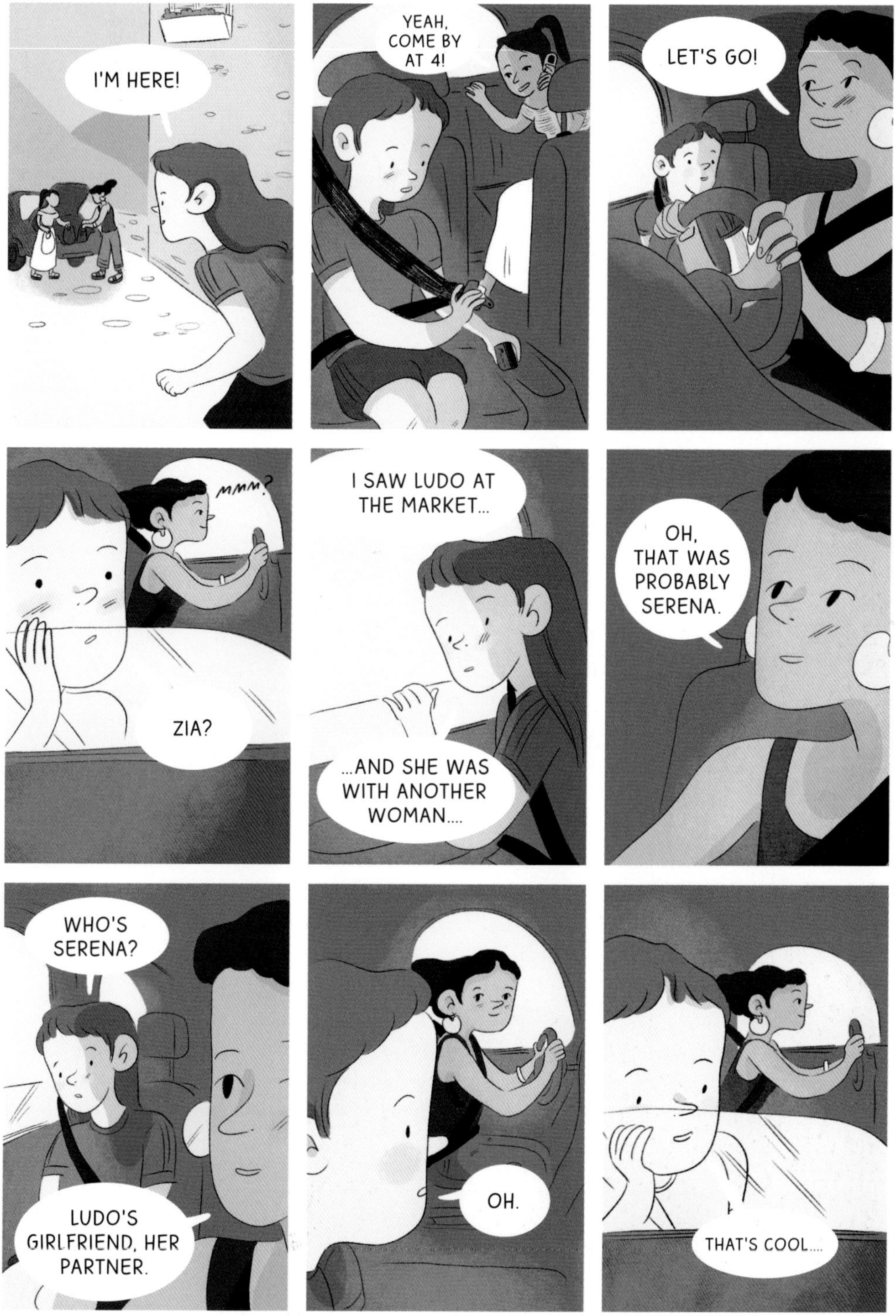
I'M HERE!
YEAH, COME BY AT 4!
LET'S GO!
MMM?
ZIA?
I SAW LUDO AT THE MARKET...
...AND SHE WAS WITH ANOTHER WOMAN....
OH, THAT WAS PROBABLY SERENA.
WHO'S SERENA?
LUDO'S GIRLFRIEND, HER PARTNER.
OH.
THAT'S COOL....

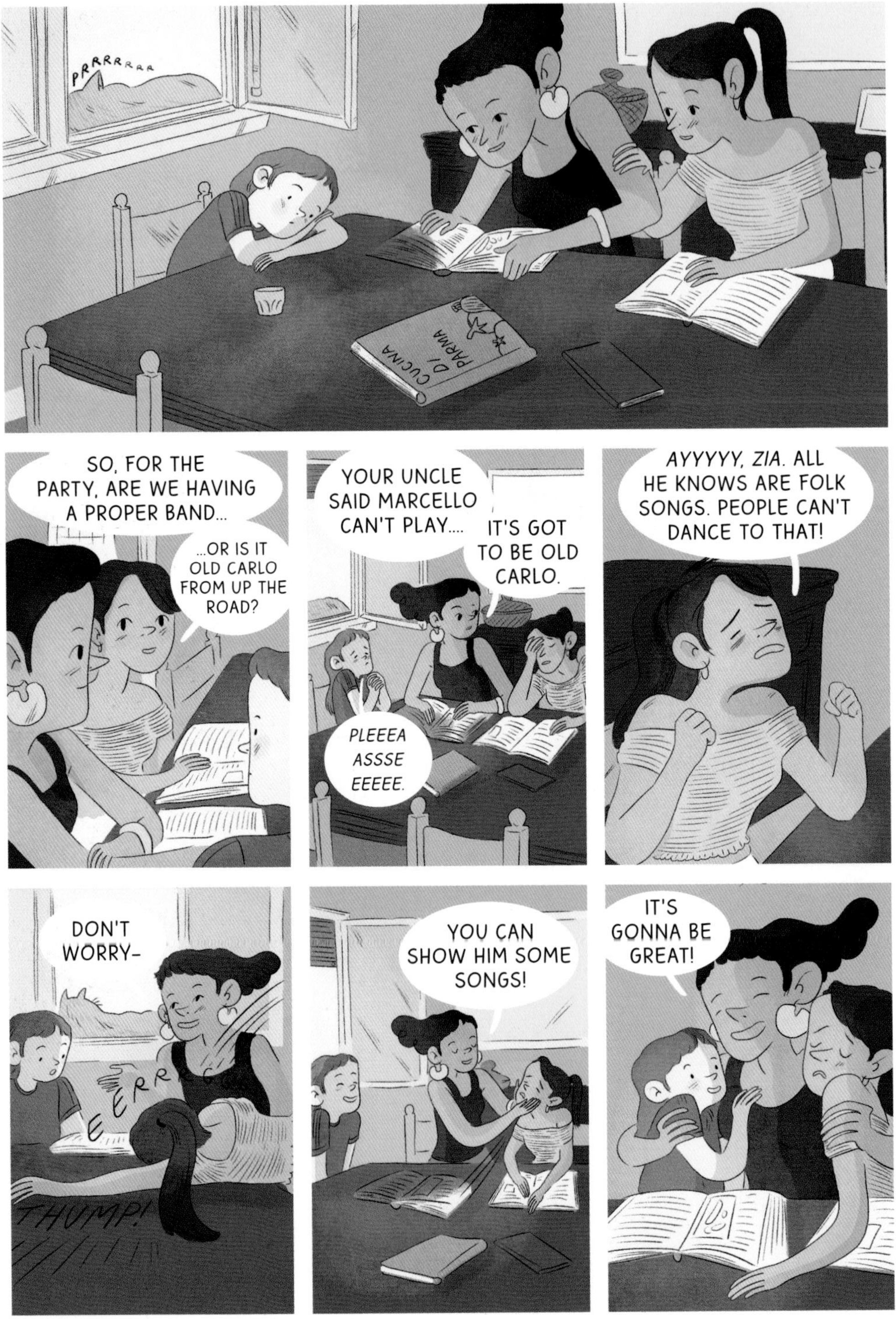
PRRRRRRR
CUCINA DI PARMA
SO, FOR THE PARTY, ARE WE HAVING A PROPER BAND...
...OR IS IT OLD CARLO FROM UP THE ROAD?
YOUR UNCLE SAID MARCELLO CAN'T PLAY....
IT'S GOT TO BE OLD CARLO.
PLEEEA ASSSE EEEEE.
AYYYYY, ZIA. ALL HE KNOWS ARE FOLK SONGS. PEOPLE CAN'T DANCE TO THAT!
DON'T WORRY-
EERR
THUMP!
YOU CAN SHOW HIM SOME SONGS!
IT'S GONNA BE GREAT!

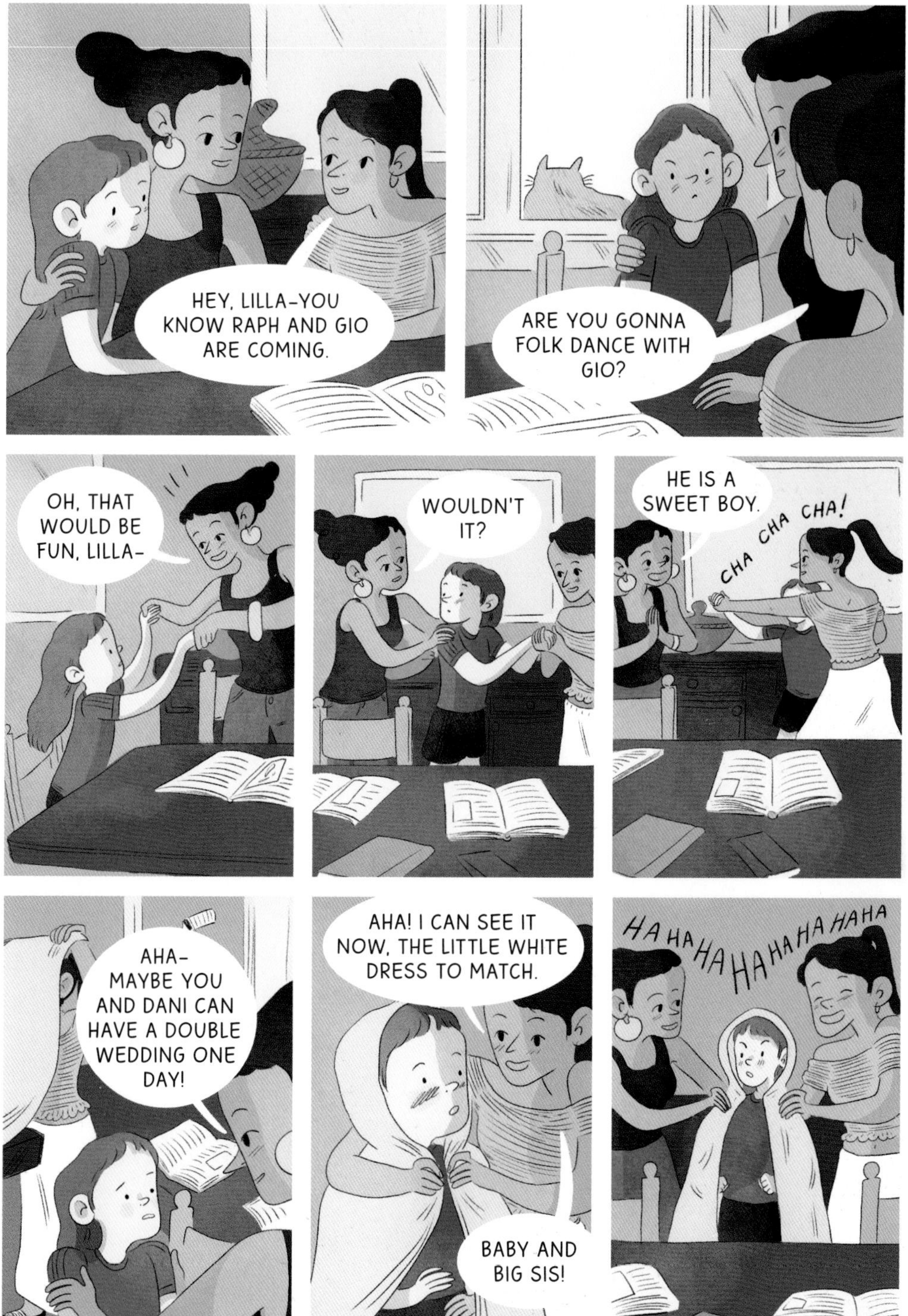
HEY, LILLA-YOU KNOW RAPH AND GIO ARE COMING.
ARE YOU GONNA FOLK DANCE WITH GIO?
OH, THAT WOULD BE FUN, LILLA-
WOULDN'T IT?
HE IS A SWEET BOY.
CHA CHA CHA!
AHA- MAYBE YOU AND DANI CAN HAVE A DOUBLE WEDDING ONE DAY!
AHA! I CAN SEE IT NOW, THE LITTLE WHITE DRESS TO MATCH.
BABY AND BIG SIS!
HA HA HA HA HA HA HA HA HA HA

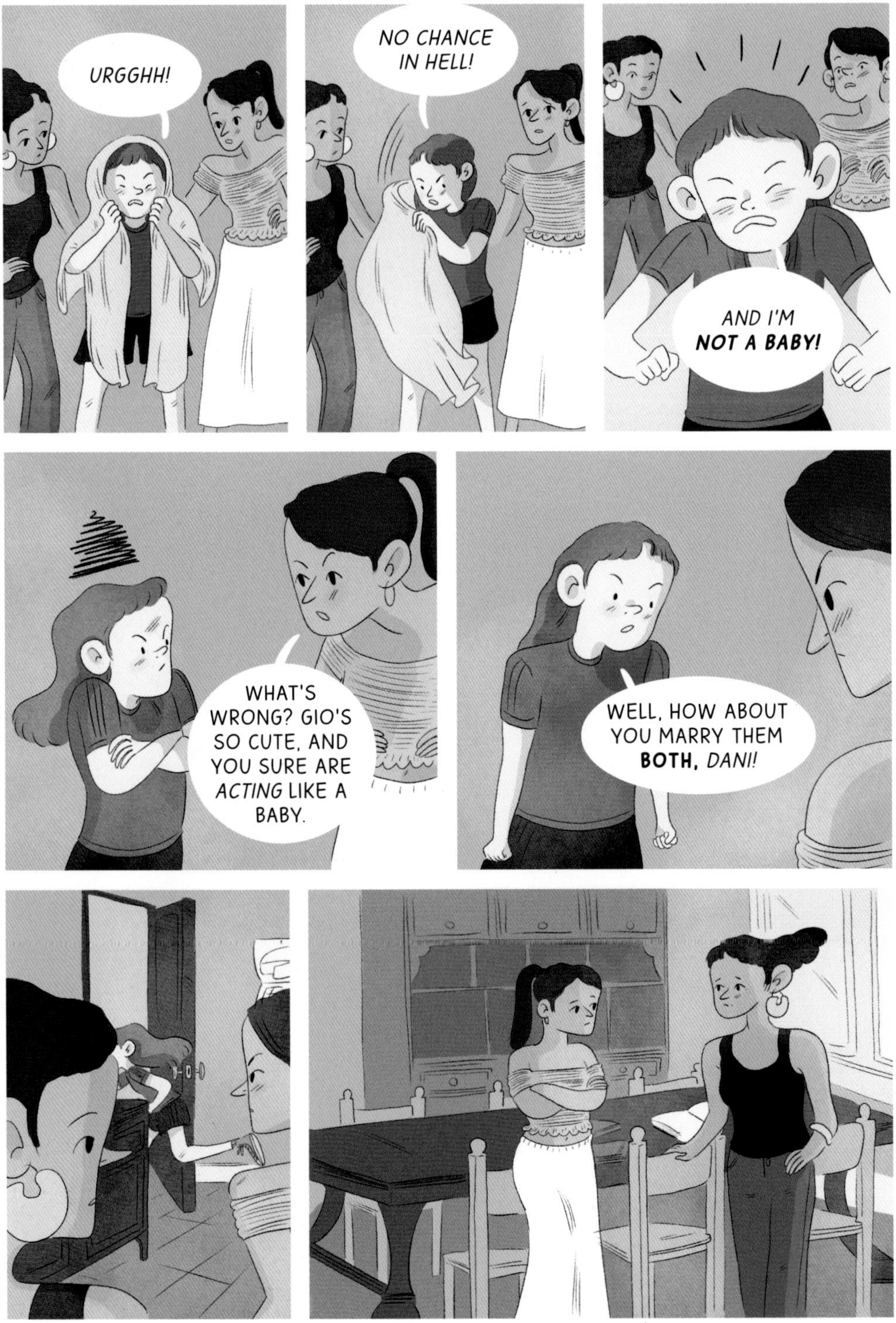
URGGHH!
NO CHANCE IN HELL!
AND I'M **NOT A BABY!**
WHAT'S WRONG? GIO'S SO CUTE, AND YOU SURE ARE *ACTING* LIKE A BABY.
WELL, HOW ABOUT YOU MARRY THEM **BOTH,** *DANI!*

FLAP
FLAP
HMPH!

SOMETIMES I REALLY **HATE** HER!

NNNRRRRRNN

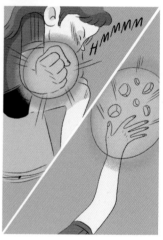

HMMMM

WHAT?

SCATTER

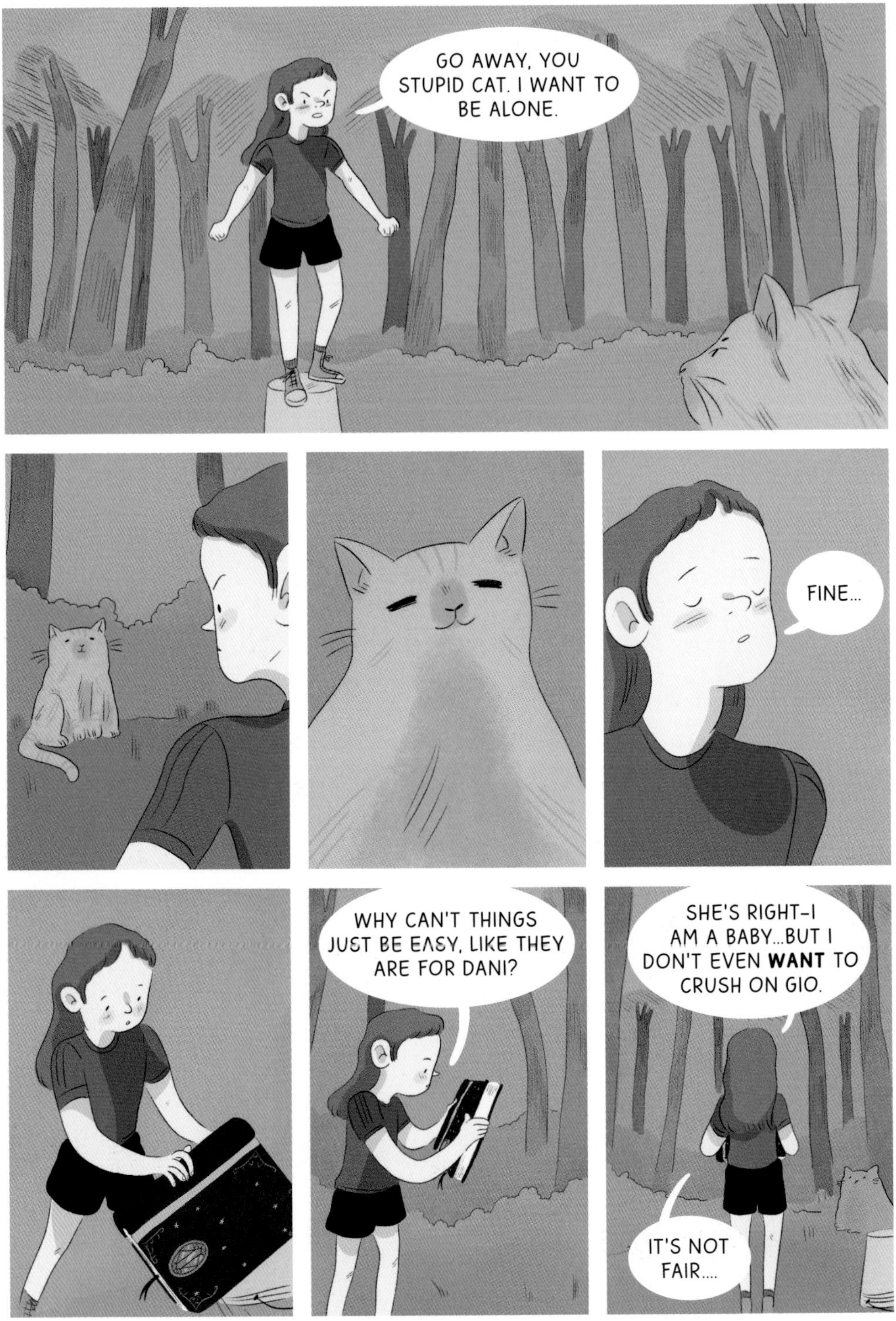
GO AWAY, YOU STUPID CAT. I WANT TO BE ALONE.
FINE...
WHY CAN'T THINGS JUST BE EASY, LIKE THEY ARE FOR DANI?
SHE'S RIGHT—I AM A BABY...BUT I DON'T EVEN **WANT** TO CRUSH ON GIO.
IT'S NOT FAIR....

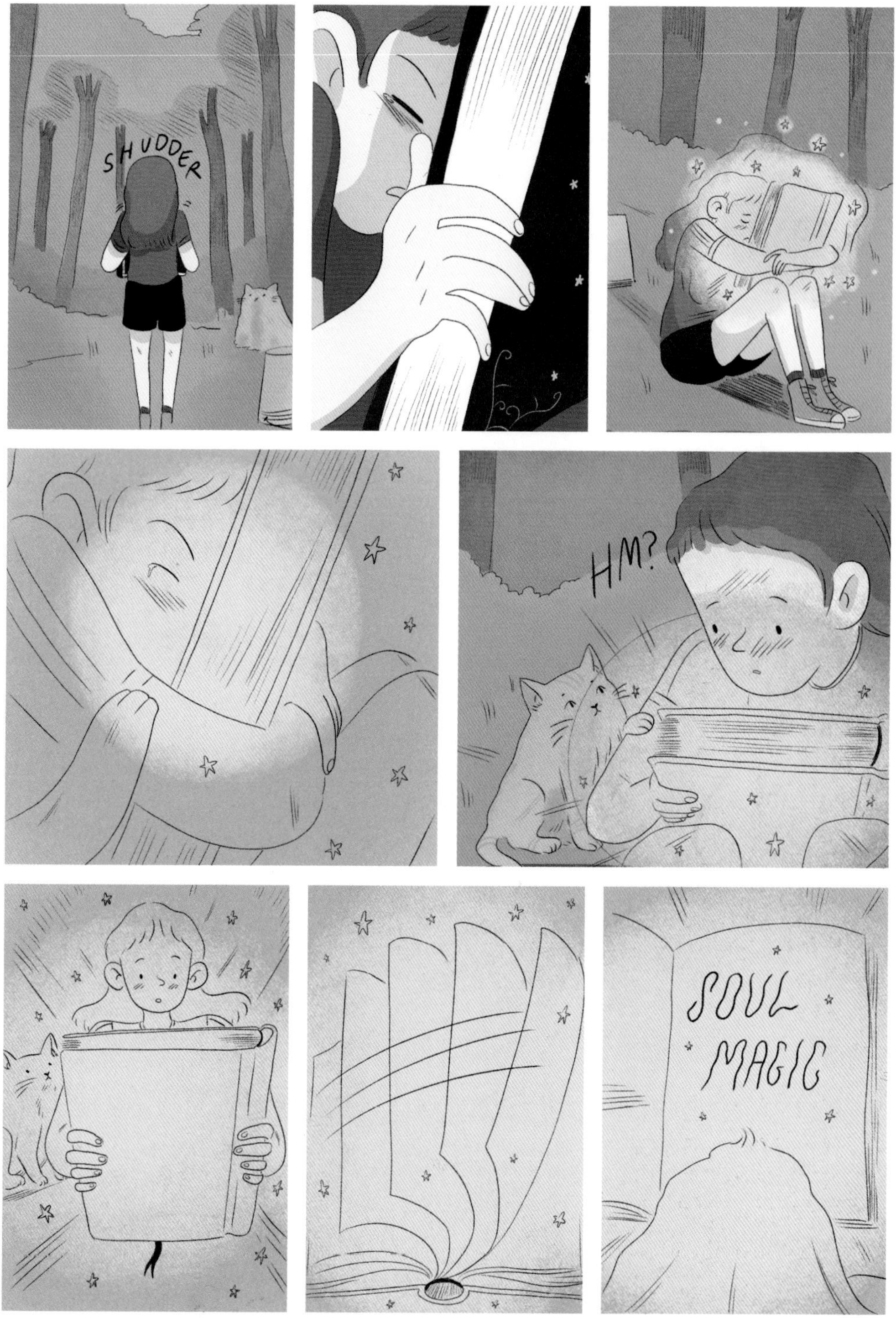
SHUDDER
HM?
SOUL MAGIC

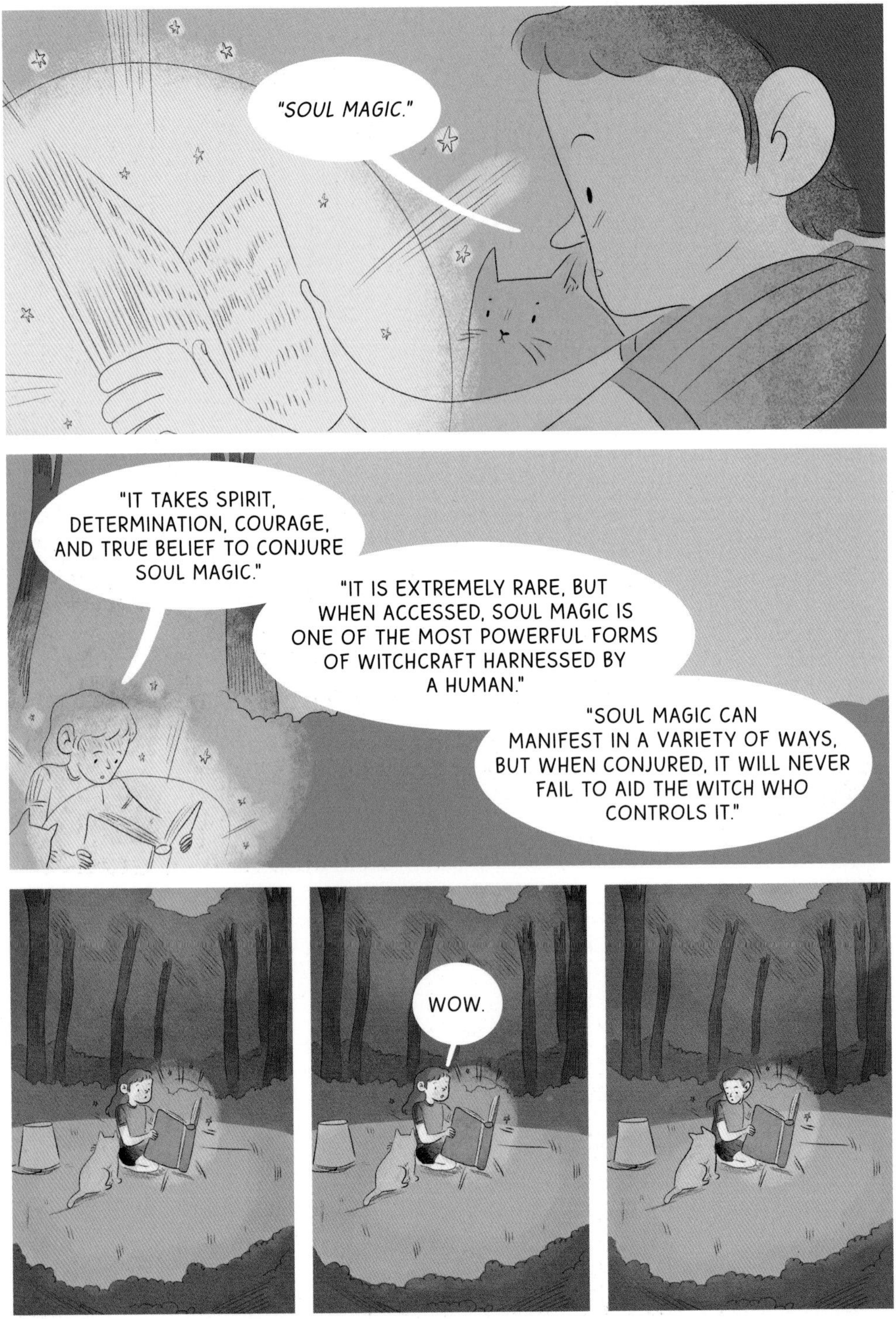
"SOUL MAGIC."
"IT TAKES SPIRIT, DETERMINATION, COURAGE, AND TRUE BELIEF TO CONJURE SOUL MAGIC."
"IT IS EXTREMELY RARE, BUT WHEN ACCESSED, SOUL MAGIC IS ONE OF THE MOST POWERFUL FORMS OF WITCHCRAFT HARNESSED BY A HUMAN."
"SOUL MAGIC CAN MANIFEST IN A VARIETY OF WAYS, BUT WHEN CONJURED, IT WILL NEVER FAIL TO AID THE WITCH WHO CONTROLS IT."
WOW.

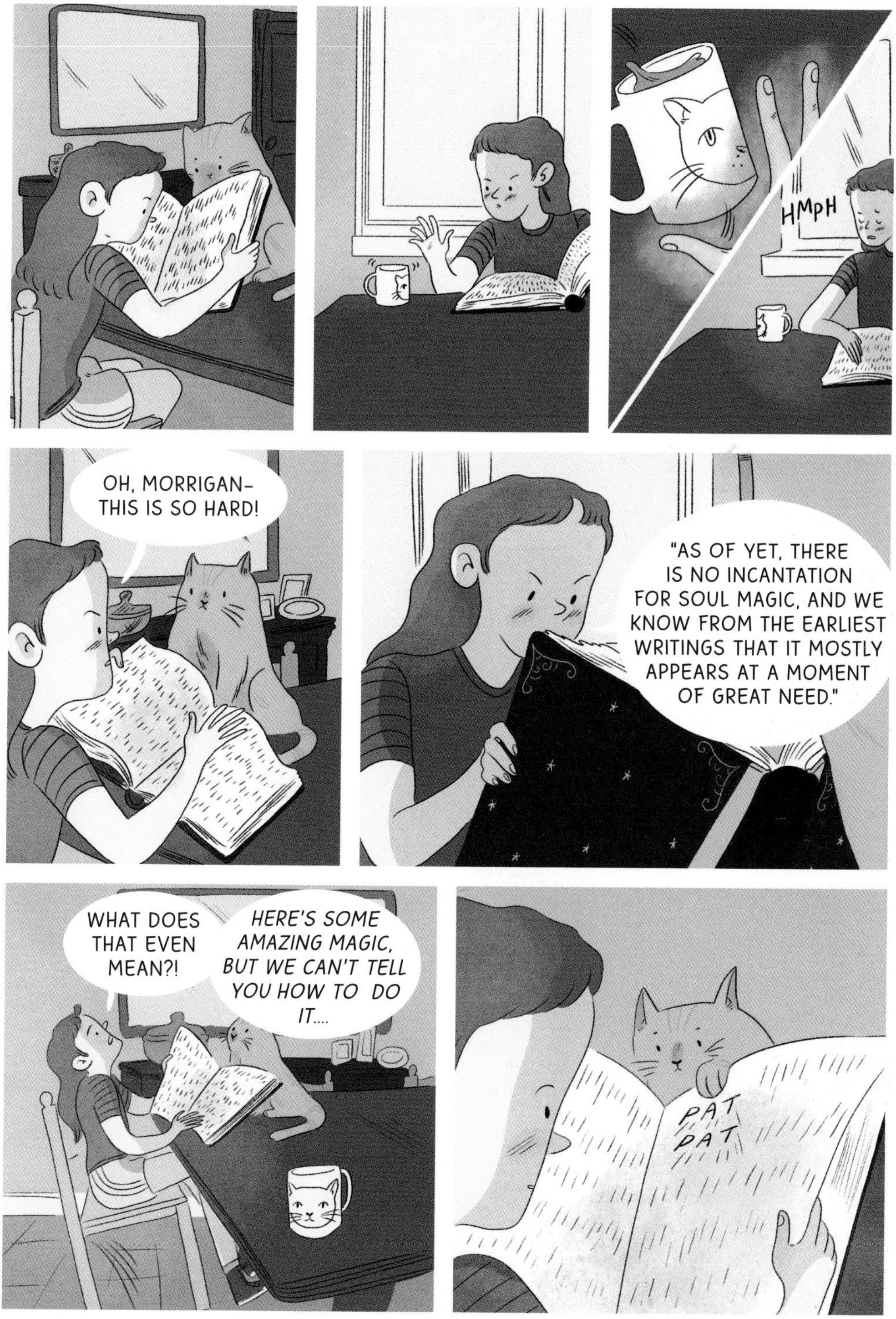
HMPH
OH, MORRIGAN-
THIS IS SO HARD!
"AS OF YET, THERE IS NO INCANTATION FOR SOUL MAGIC, AND WE KNOW FROM THE EARLIEST WRITINGS THAT IT MOSTLY APPEARS AT A MOMENT OF GREAT NEED."
WHAT DOES THAT EVEN MEAN?!
HERE'S SOME AMAZING MAGIC, BUT WE CAN'T TELL YOU HOW TO DO IT....
PAT PAT

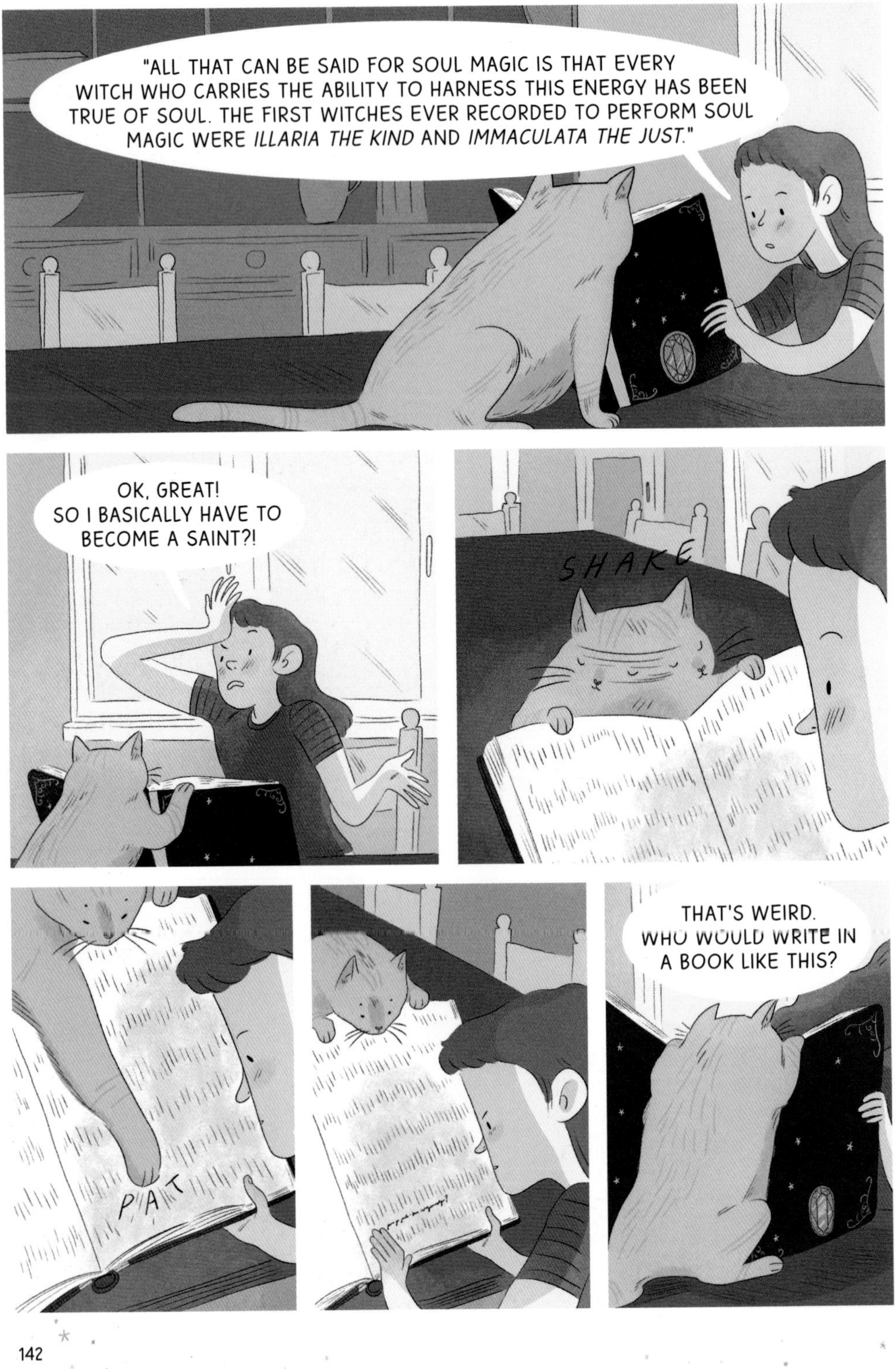
"ALL THAT CAN BE SAID FOR SOUL MAGIC IS THAT EVERY WITCH WHO CARRIES THE ABILITY TO HARNESS THIS ENERGY HAS BEEN TRUE OF SOUL. THE FIRST WITCHES EVER RECORDED TO PERFORM SOUL MAGIC WERE *ILLARIA THE KIND* AND *IMMACULATA THE JUST*."
OK, GREAT! SO I BASICALLY HAVE TO BECOME A SAINT?!
SHAKE
PAT
THAT'S WEIRD. WHO WOULD WRITE IN A BOOK LIKE THIS?

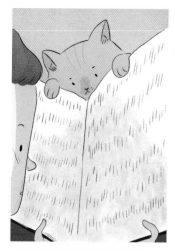

"PURE OF SOUL—TRUE TO YOURSELF?"

HMMMMMMMM

WELL...I THINK I CAN DO THAT. BEING TRUE TO YOURSELF IS KINDA ACKNOWLEDGING THE THINGS YOU LOVE AND WHO YOU ARE....

THERE'S MY PARENTS, DANI, LULU—I LOVE ALL OF THEM...AND DRAWING—THAT'S THE BEST!

MY ZIA, SHE'S SO COOL. AND BEING OUT HERE MAKES ME FEEL REALLY FREE...

...FREE LIKE LUDO FEELS FREE...

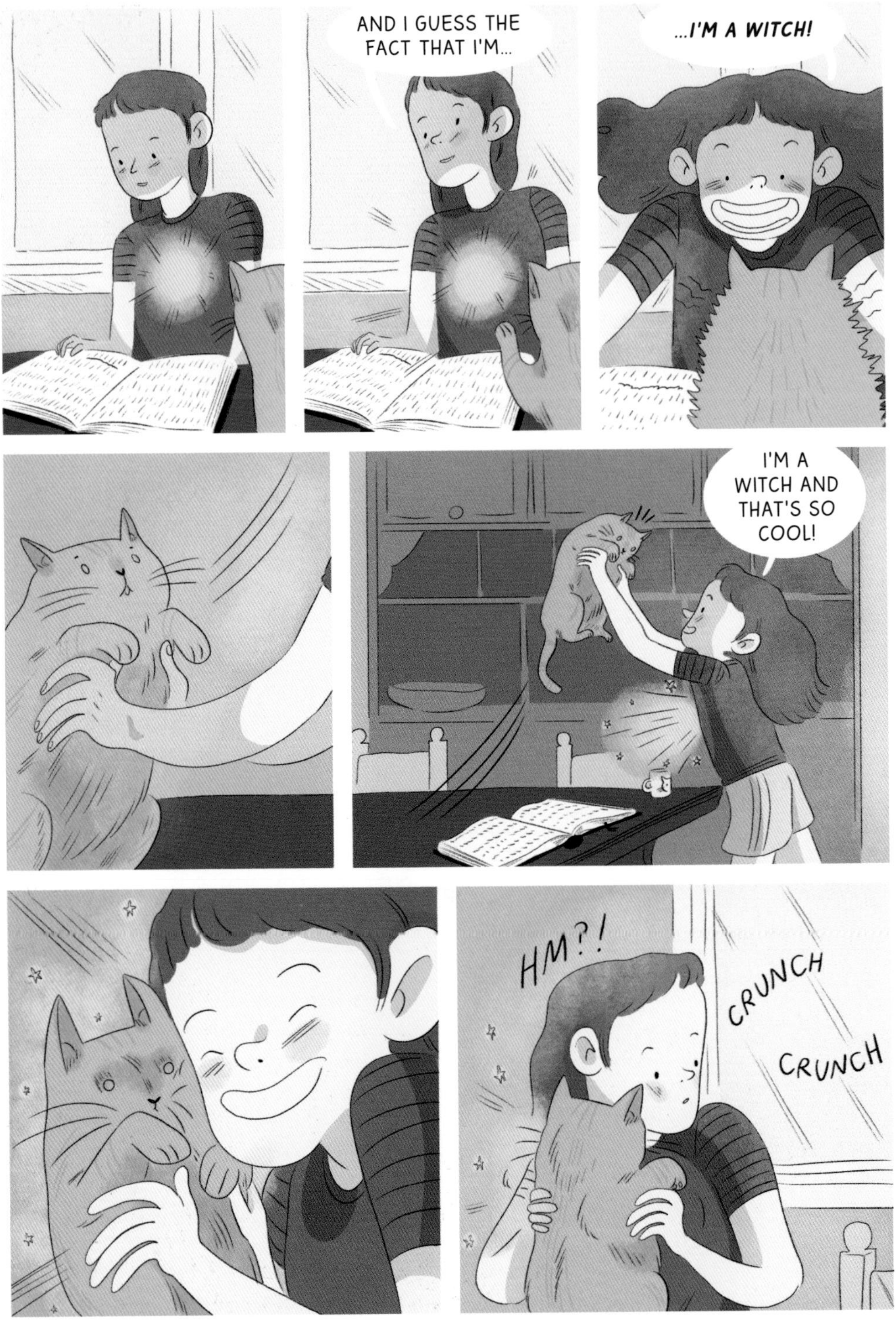
AND I GUESS THE FACT THAT I'M...
...I'M A WITCH!
I'M A WITCH AND THAT'S SO COOL!
HM?!
CRUNCH
CRUNCH

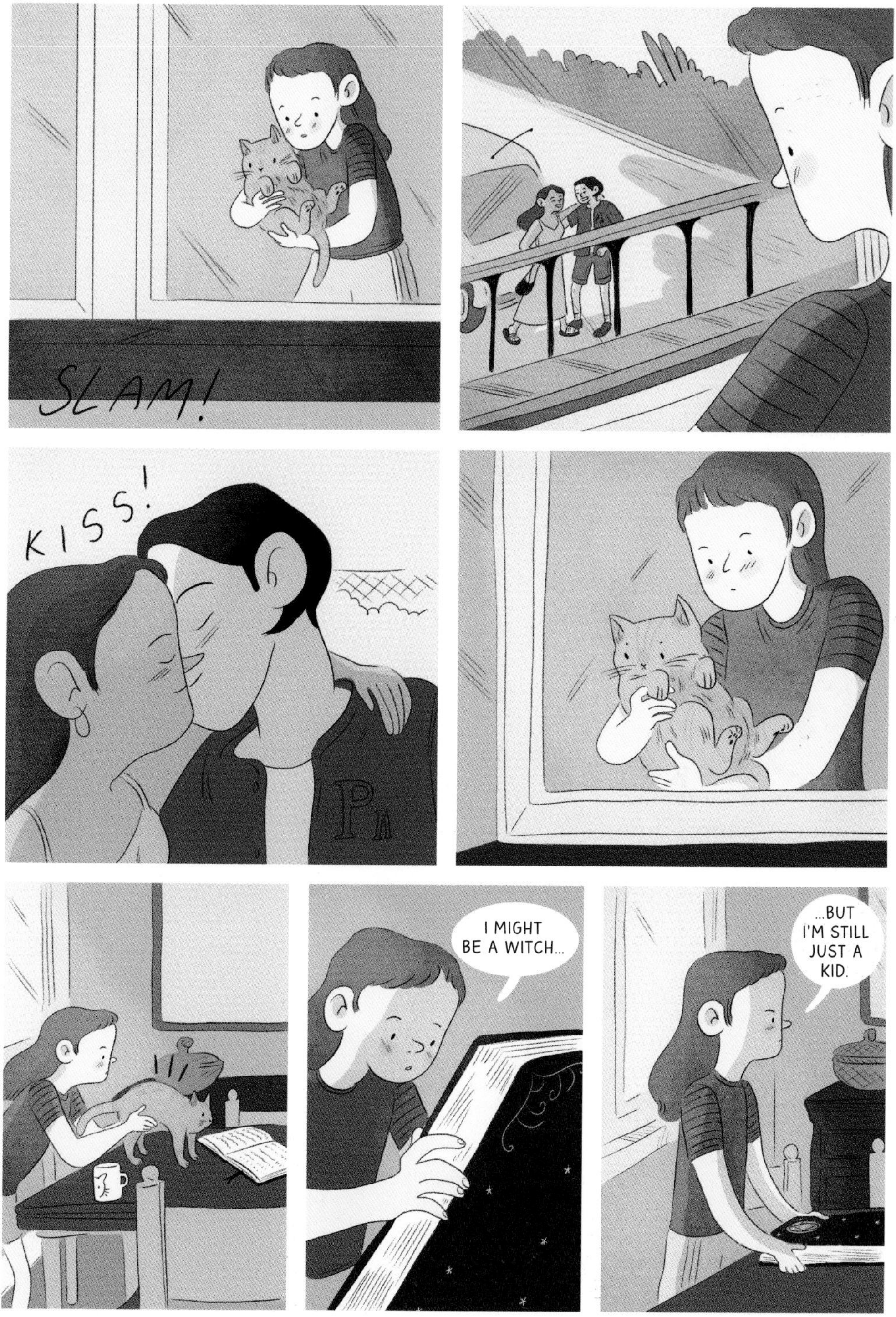
SLAM!
KISS!
I MIGHT BE A WITCH...
...BUT I'M STILL JUST A KID.

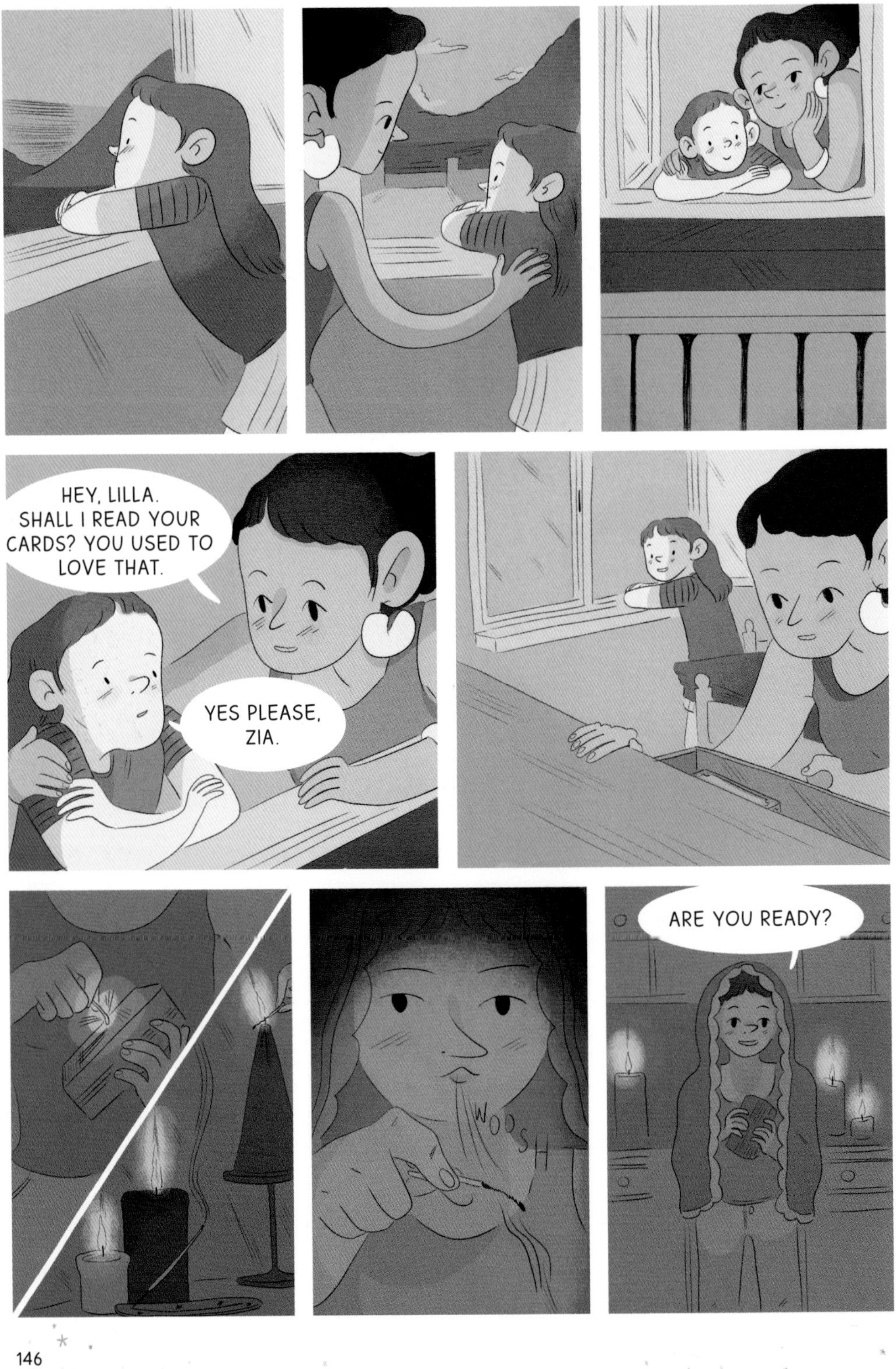
HEY, LILLA.
SHALL I READ YOUR CARDS? YOU USED TO LOVE THAT.
YES PLEASE, ZIA.
WOOSH
ARE YOU READY?

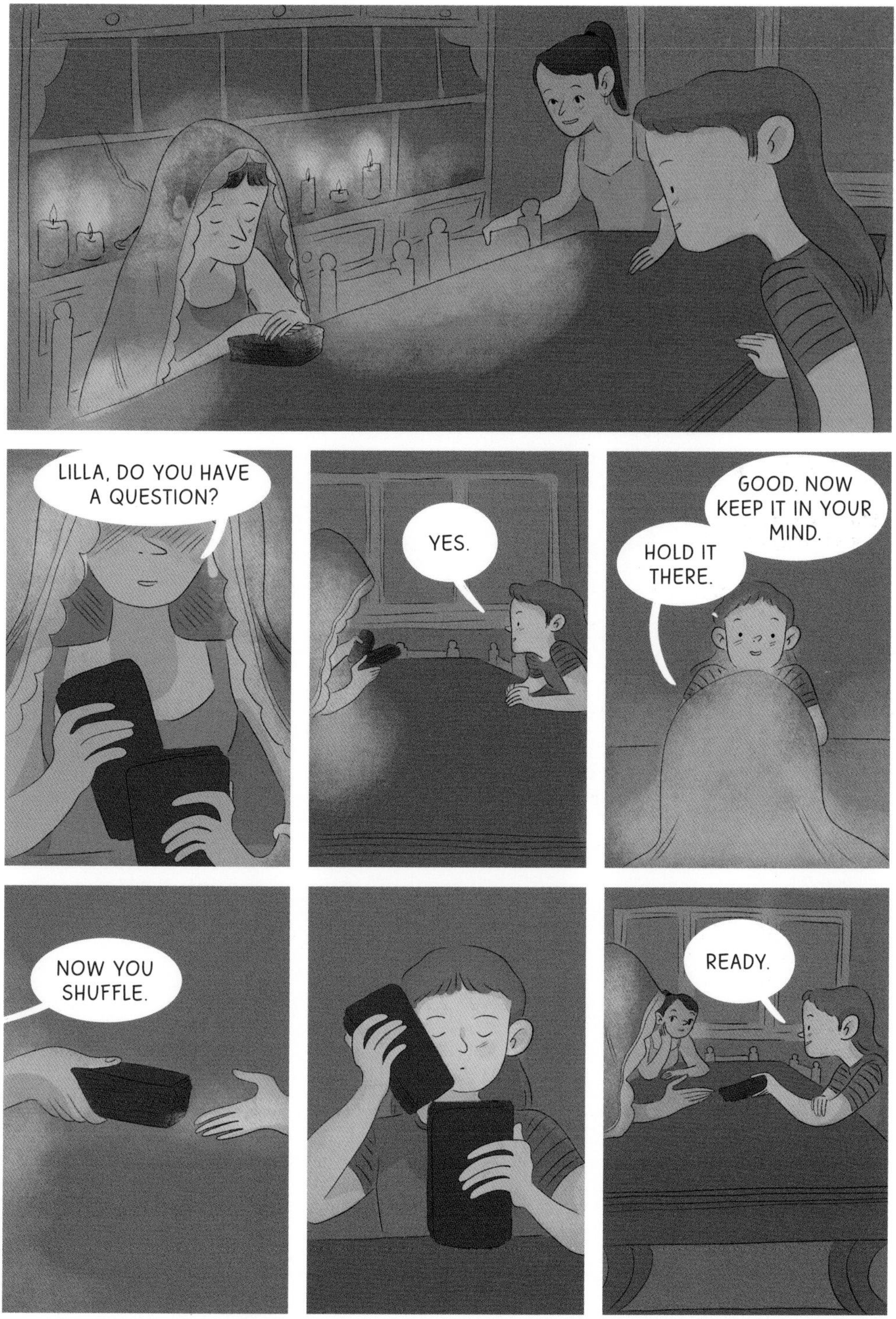
LILLA, DO YOU HAVE A QUESTION?
YES.
HOLD IT THERE.
GOOD. NOW KEEP IT IN YOUR MIND.
NOW YOU SHUFFLE.
READY.

THE MAGICIAN.

SIX OF CUPS.

TWO OF SWORDS.

THREE OF SWORDS.

NINE OF WANDS.

THE LOVERS.

LET'S SEE....

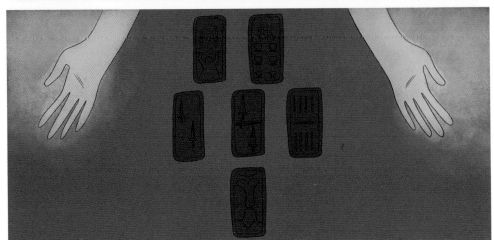

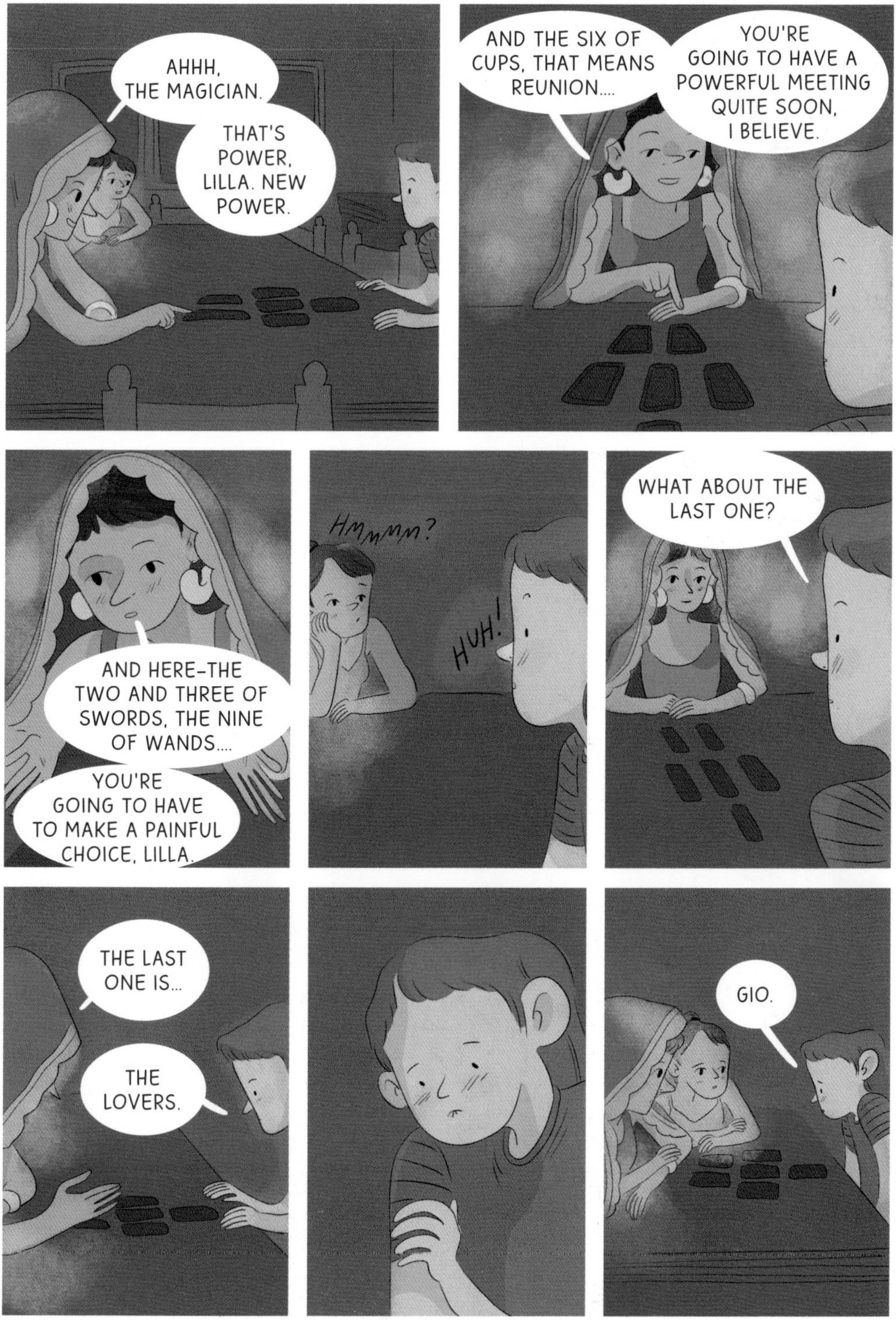
AHHH, THE MAGICIAN.
THAT'S POWER, LILLA. NEW POWER.
AND THE SIX OF CUPS, THAT MEANS REUNION....
YOU'RE GOING TO HAVE A POWERFUL MEETING QUITE SOON, I BELIEVE.
AND HERE—THE TWO AND THREE OF SWORDS, THE NINE OF WANDS....
YOU'RE GOING TO HAVE TO MAKE A PAINFUL CHOICE, LILLA.
HMMMM?
HUH!
WHAT ABOUT THE LAST ONE?
THE LAST ONE IS...
THE LOVERS.
GIO.

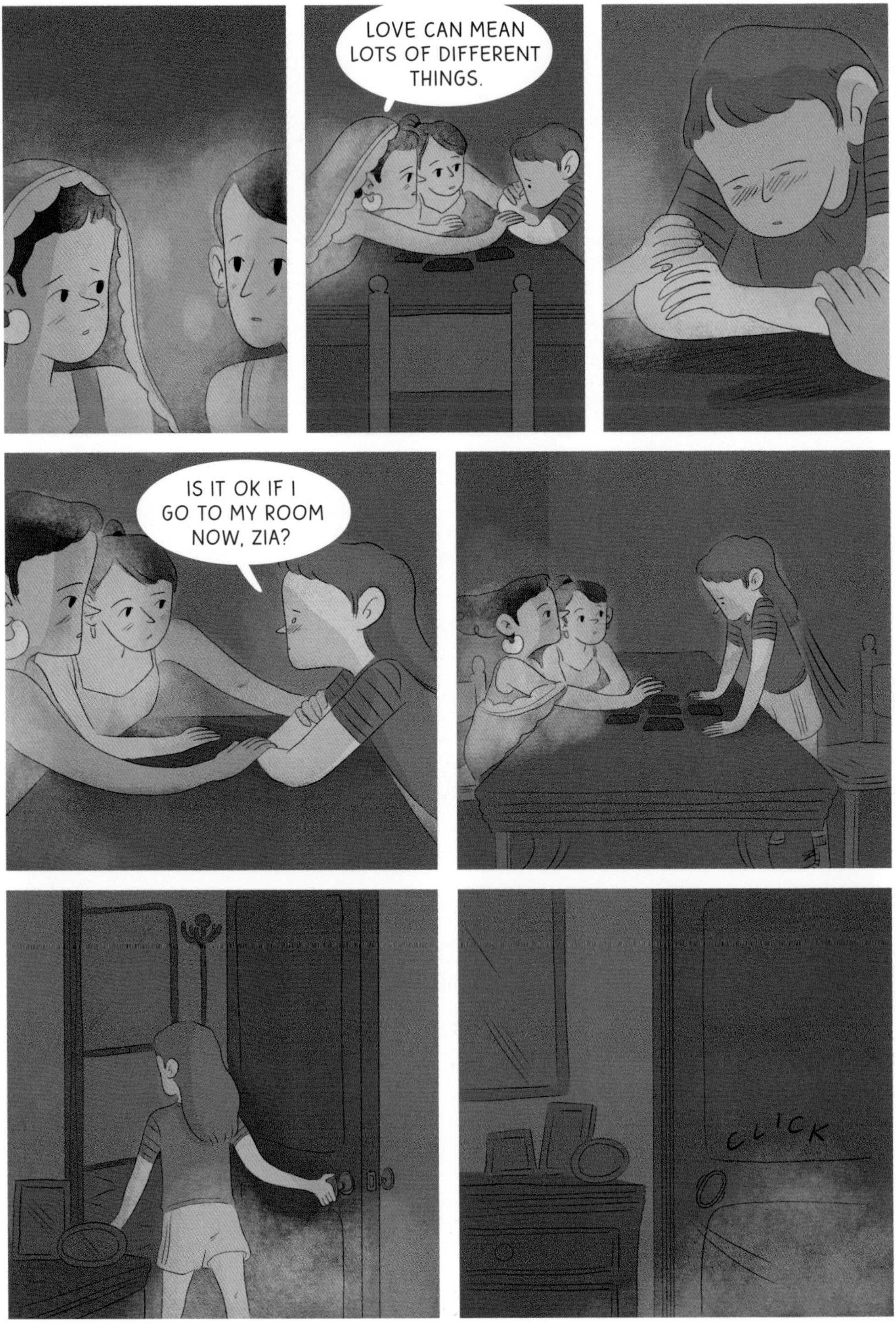
LOVE CAN MEAN LOTS OF DIFFERENT THINGS.
IS IT OK IF I GO TO MY ROOM NOW, ZIA?
CLICK

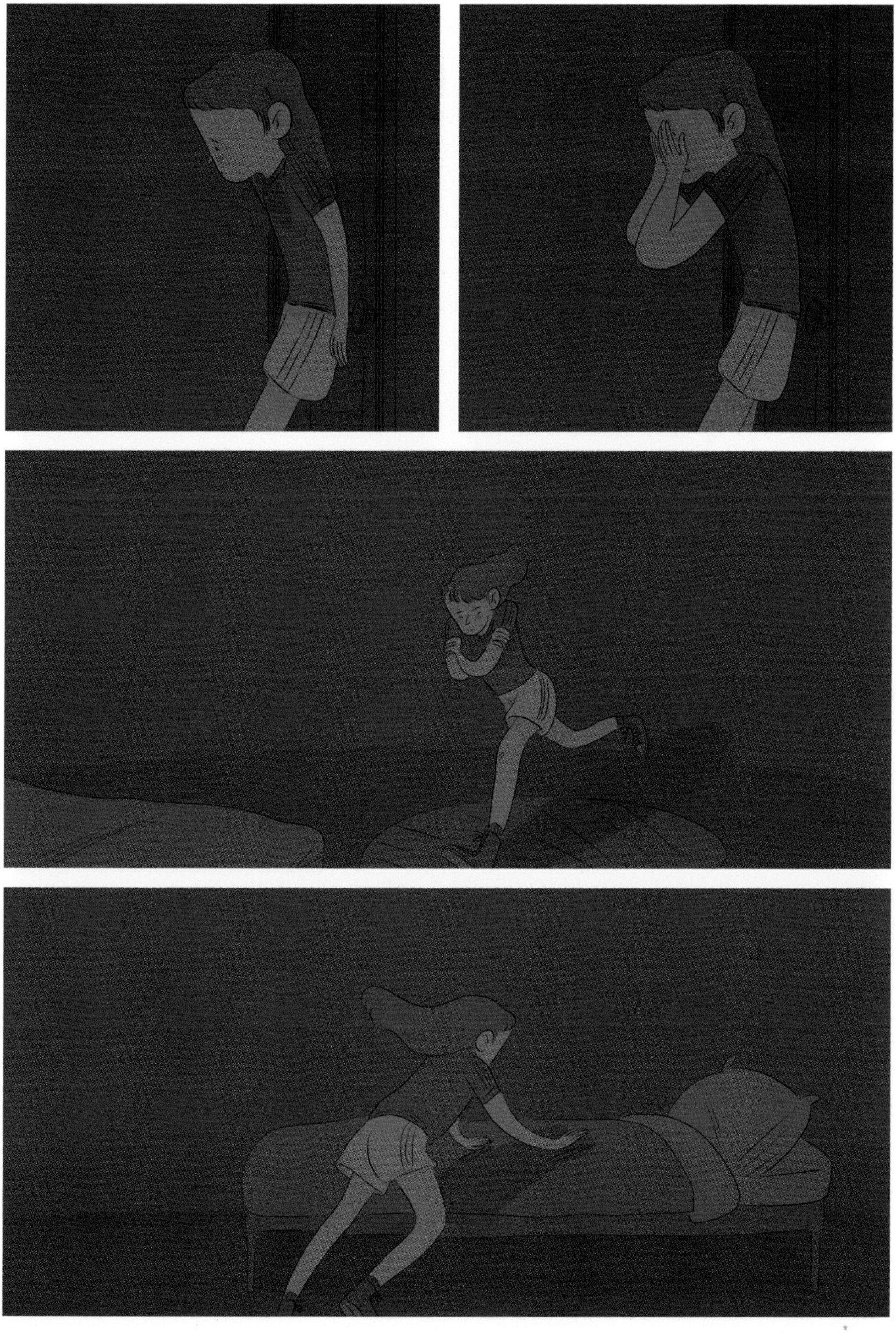

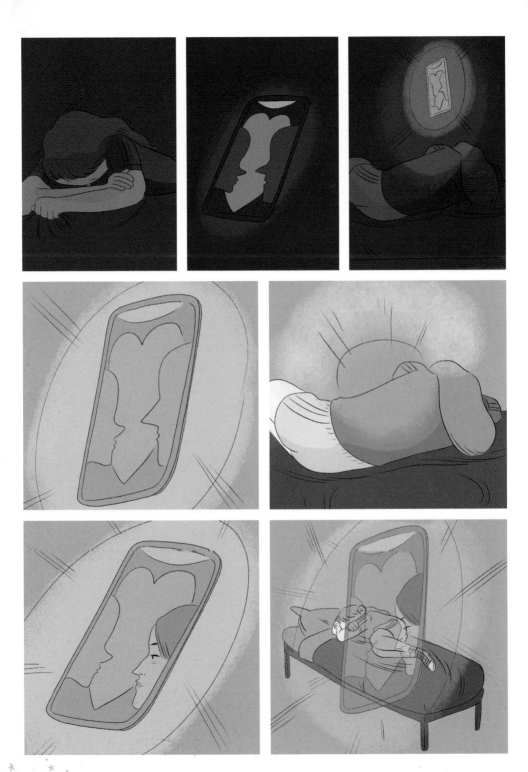

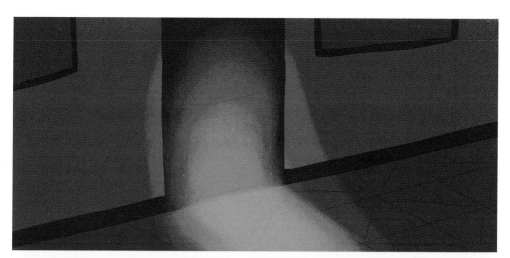

PAD-PAD-PAD

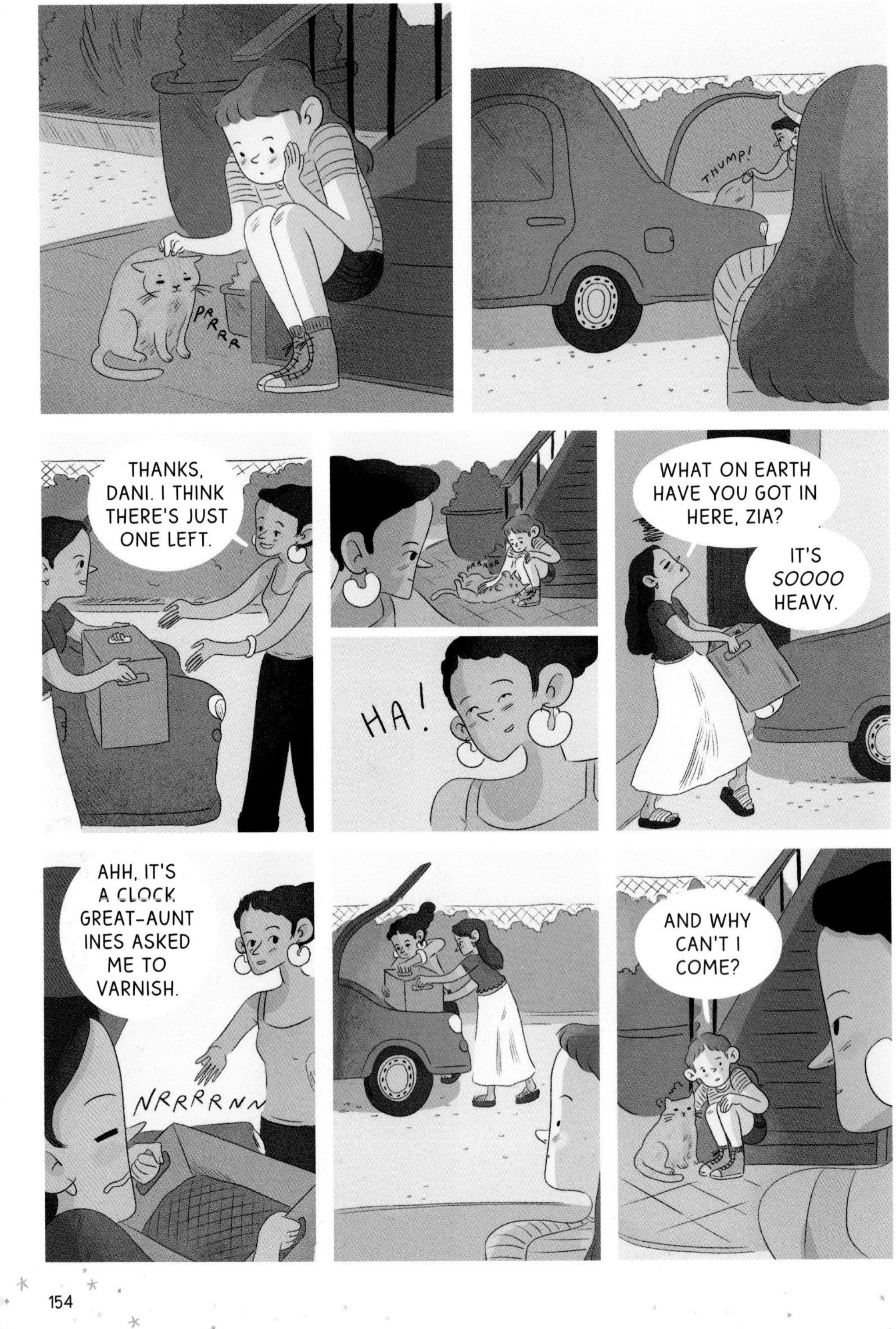
PRRRR
THUMP!
THANKS, DANI. I THINK THERE'S JUST ONE LEFT.
PRRRR
HA!
WHAT ON EARTH HAVE YOU GOT IN HERE, ZIA?
IT'S *SOOOO* HEAVY.
AHH, IT'S A CLOCK GREAT-AUNT INES ASKED ME TO VARNISH.
NRRRRNN
AND WHY CAN'T I COME?

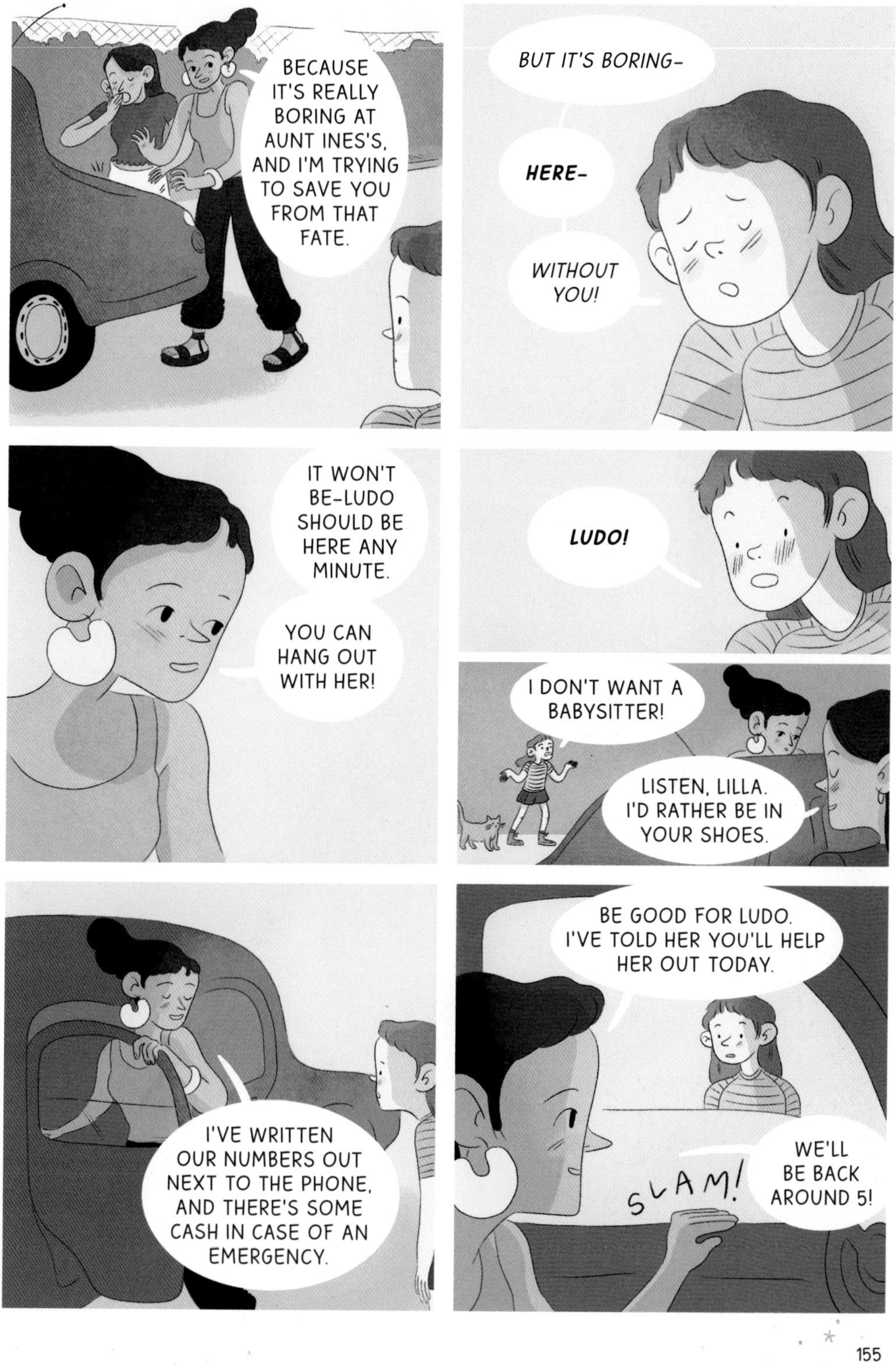
BECAUSE IT'S REALLY BORING AT AUNT INES'S, AND I'M TRYING TO SAVE YOU FROM THAT FATE.
BUT IT'S BORING-
HERE-
WITHOUT YOU!
IT WON'T BE-LUDO SHOULD BE HERE ANY MINUTE.
YOU CAN HANG OUT WITH HER!
LUDO!
I DON'T WANT A BABYSITTER!
LISTEN, LILLA. I'D RATHER BE IN YOUR SHOES.
I'VE WRITTEN OUR NUMBERS OUT NEXT TO THE PHONE, AND THERE'S SOME CASH IN CASE OF AN EMERGENCY.
BE GOOD FOR LUDO. I'VE TOLD HER YOU'LL HELP HER OUT TODAY.
SLAM!
WE'LL BE BACK AROUND 5!

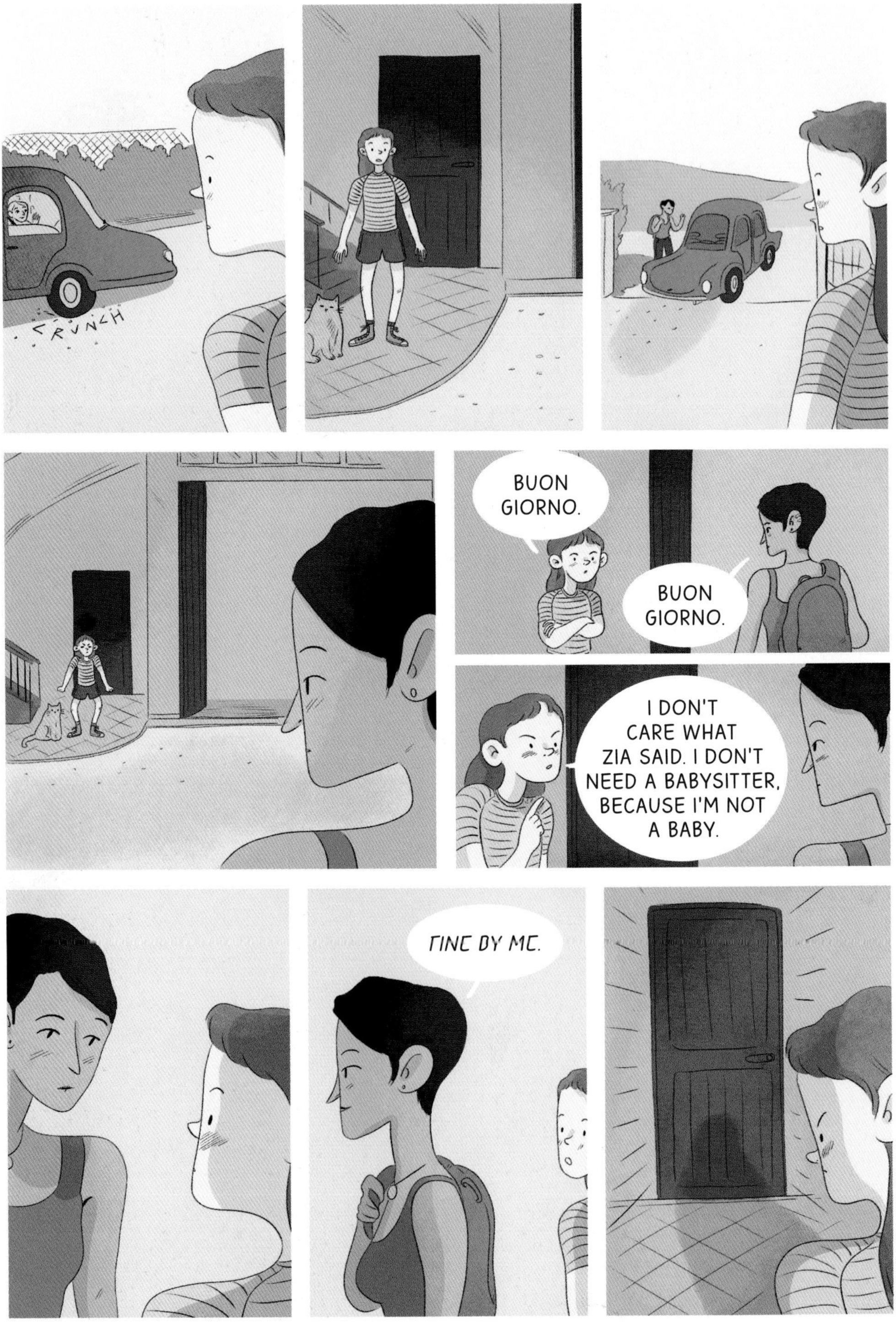
CRUNCH
BUON GIORNO.
BUON GIORNO.
I DON'T CARE WHAT ZIA SAID. I DON'T NEED A BABYSITTER, BECAUSE I'M NOT A BABY.
FINE BY ME.

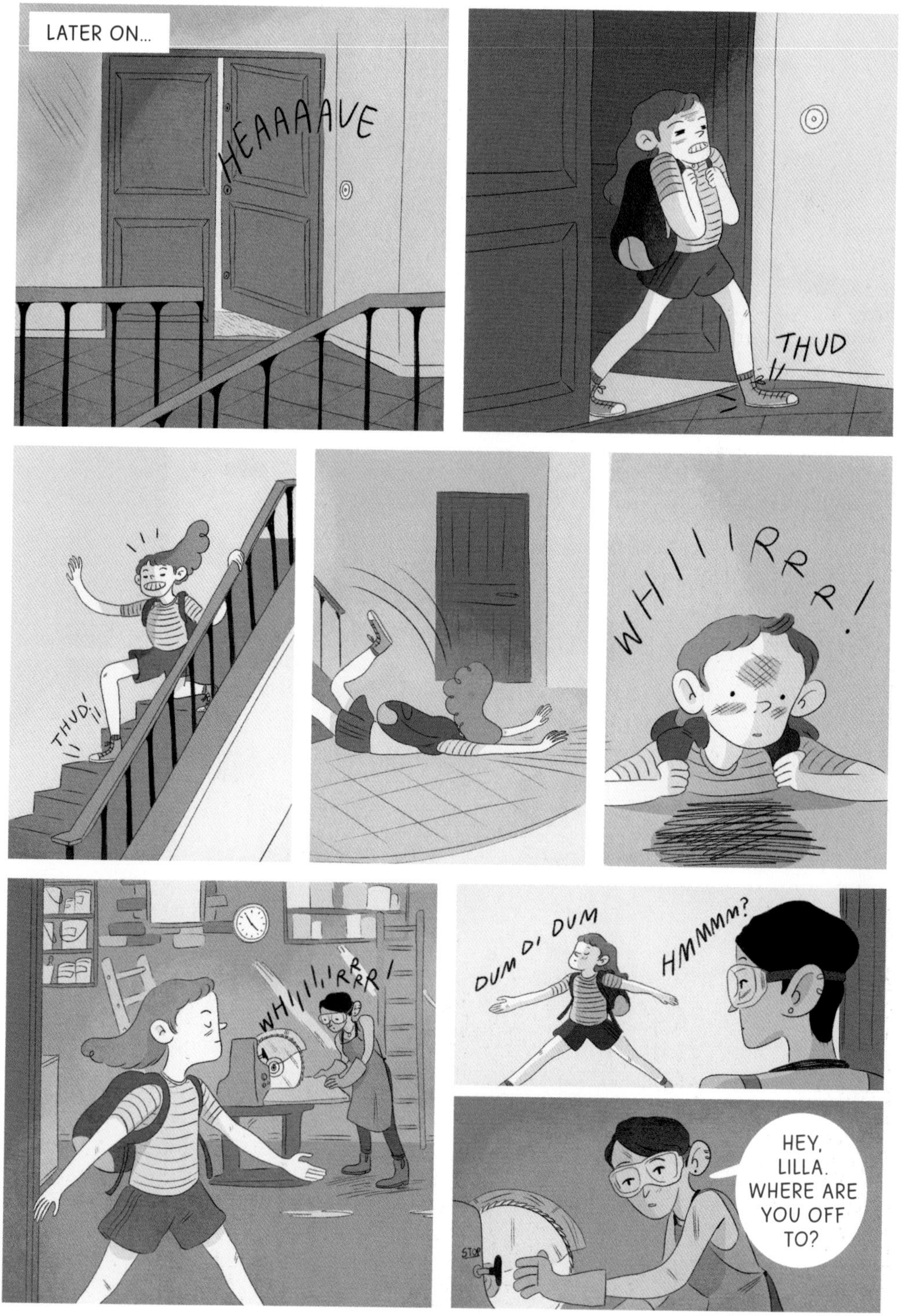
LATER ON...
HEAAAAVE
THUD
THUD!
WHIIIRRR!
WHIIIIRRR!
DUM DI DUM
HMMMM?
STOP
HEY, LILLA. WHERE ARE YOU OFF TO?

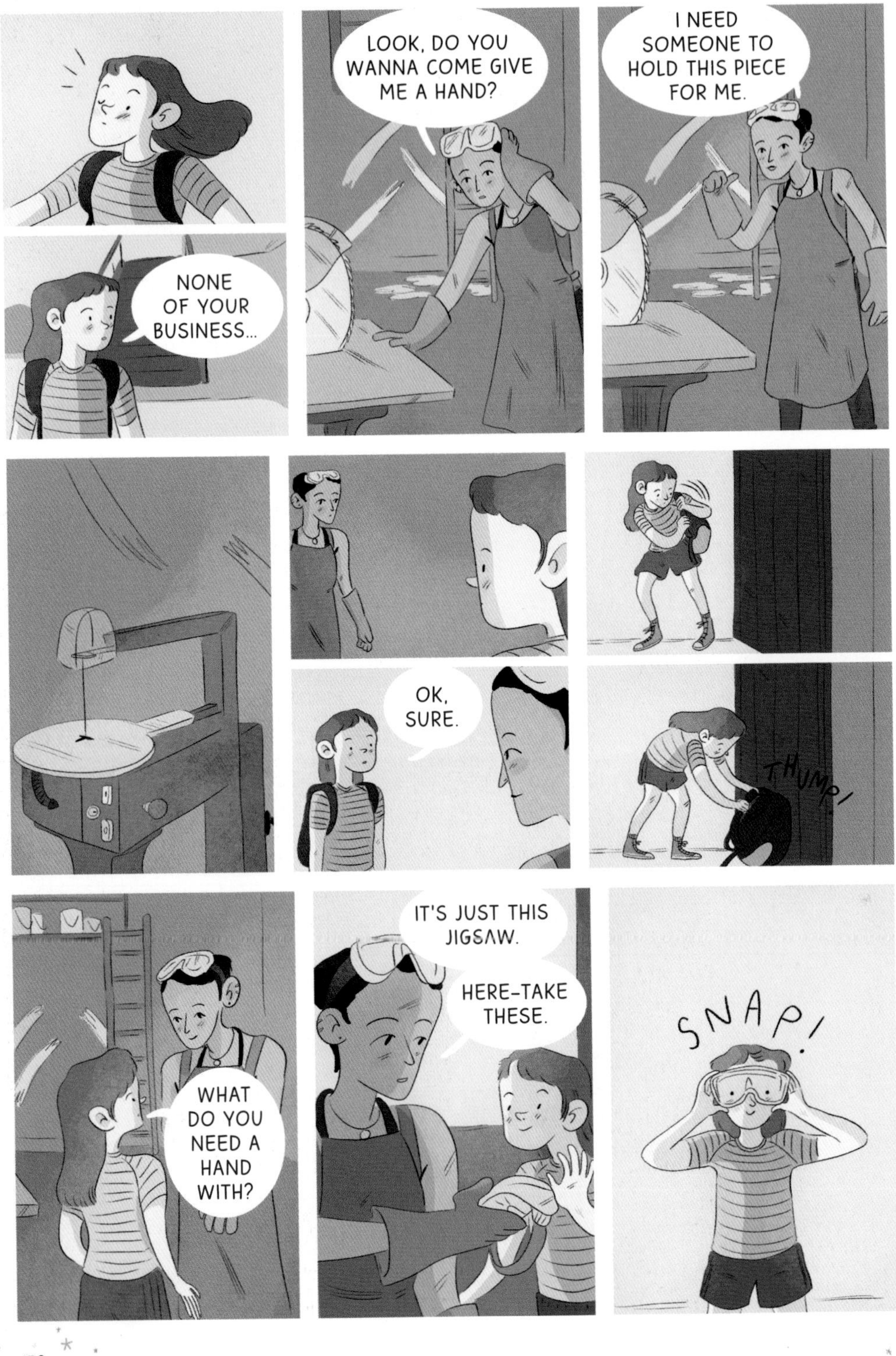
LOOK, DO YOU WANNA COME GIVE ME A HAND?
I NEED SOMEONE TO HOLD THIS PIECE FOR ME.
NONE OF YOUR BUSINESS...
OK, SURE.
THUMP!
WHAT DO YOU NEED A HAND WITH?
IT'S JUST THIS JIGSAW.
HERE-TAKE THESE.
SNAP!

CAN YOU HELP ME GUIDE THIS THROUGH? THE SAW SEEMS REALLY SCARY, BUT AFTER A MOMENT YOU'LL BE FINE!

OK, I THINK I CAN DO IT. I'M NOT VERY STRONG....

YOU'RE STRONG ENOUGH!

USE THESE GLOVES— THEY'LL MAKE IT EASIER.

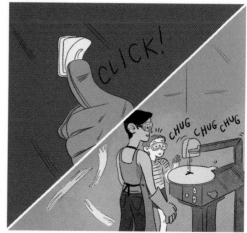

CLICK!

CHUG CHUG CHUG

READY?

I'M GONNA START SLOW....

LET'S GO!

CHUG CHUG

LOOKING GOOD!

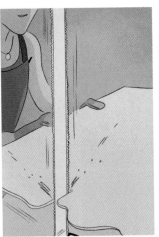

CLICK!

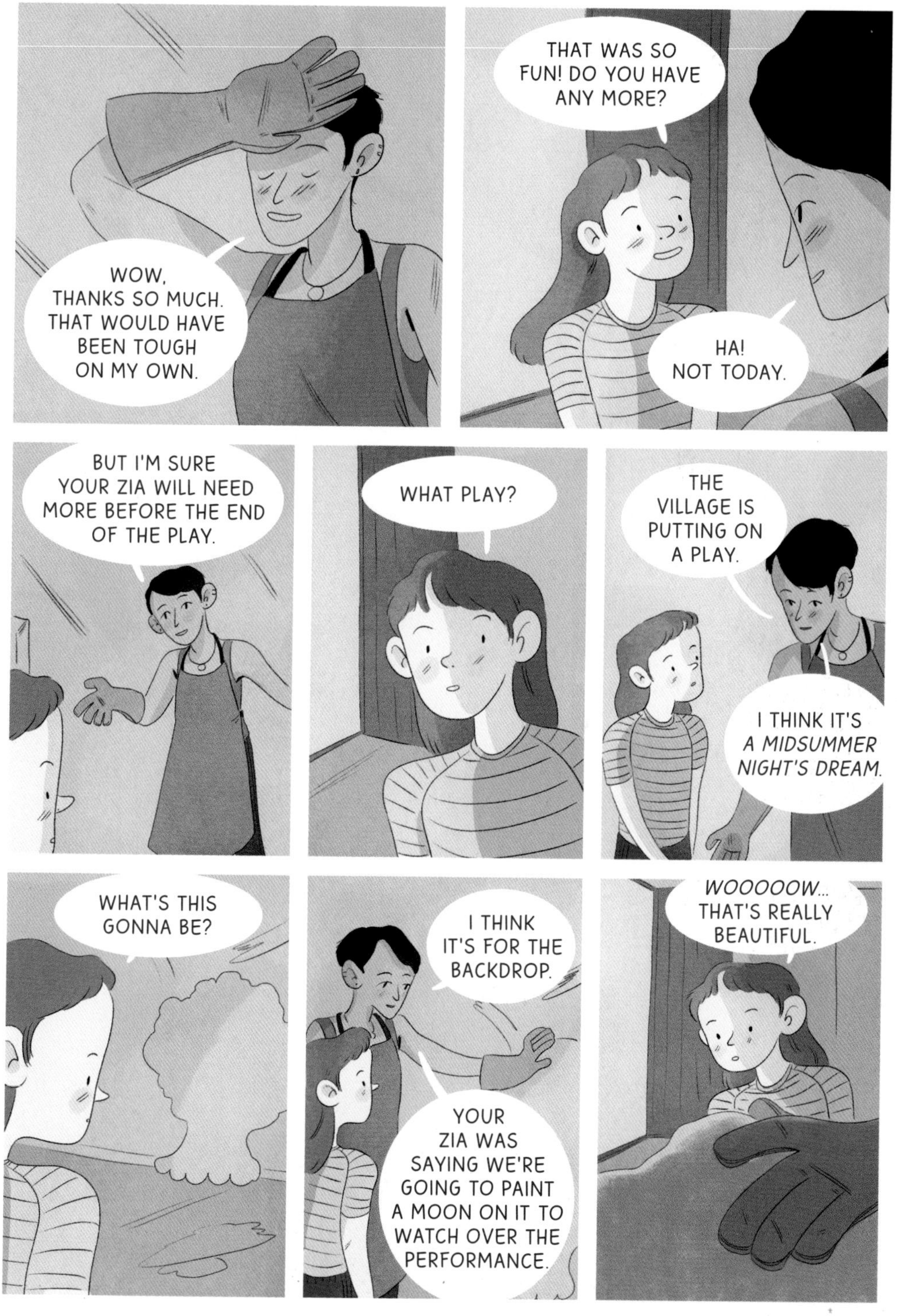
WOW, THANKS SO MUCH. THAT WOULD HAVE BEEN TOUGH ON MY OWN.
THAT WAS SO FUN! DO YOU HAVE ANY MORE?
HA! NOT TODAY.
BUT I'M SURE YOUR ZIA WILL NEED MORE BEFORE THE END OF THE PLAY.
WHAT PLAY?
THE VILLAGE IS PUTTING ON A PLAY.
I THINK IT'S *A MIDSUMMER NIGHT'S DREAM.*
WHAT'S THIS GONNA BE?
I THINK IT'S FOR THE BACKDROP.
YOUR ZIA WAS SAYING WE'RE GOING TO PAINT A MOON ON IT TO WATCH OVER THE PERFORMANCE.
WOOOOOW... THAT'S REALLY BEAUTIFUL.

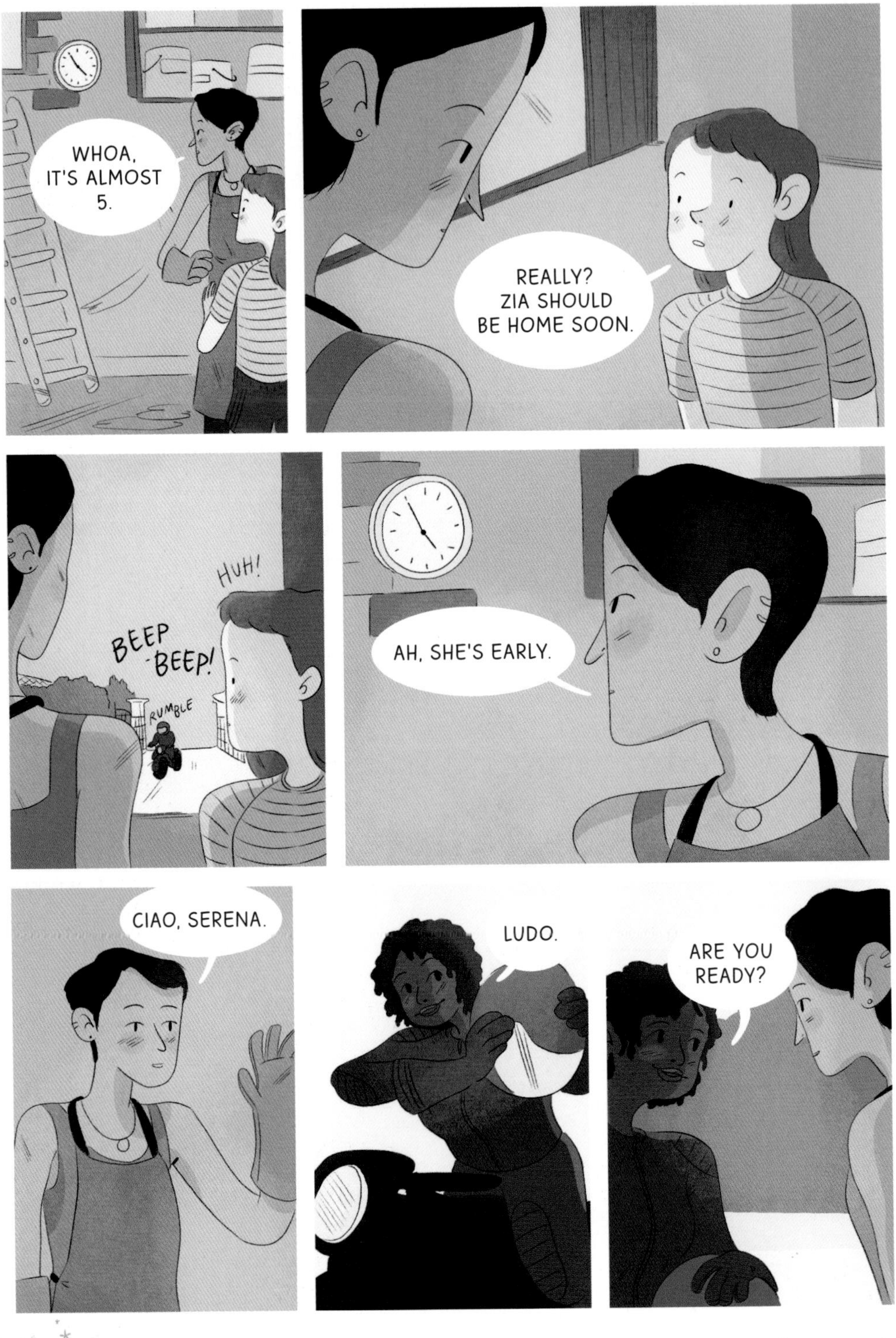
WHOA, IT'S ALMOST 5.
REALLY? ZIA SHOULD BE HOME SOON.
HUH!
BEEP-BEEP!
RUMBLE
AH, SHE'S EARLY.
CIAO, SERENA.
LUDO.
ARE YOU READY?

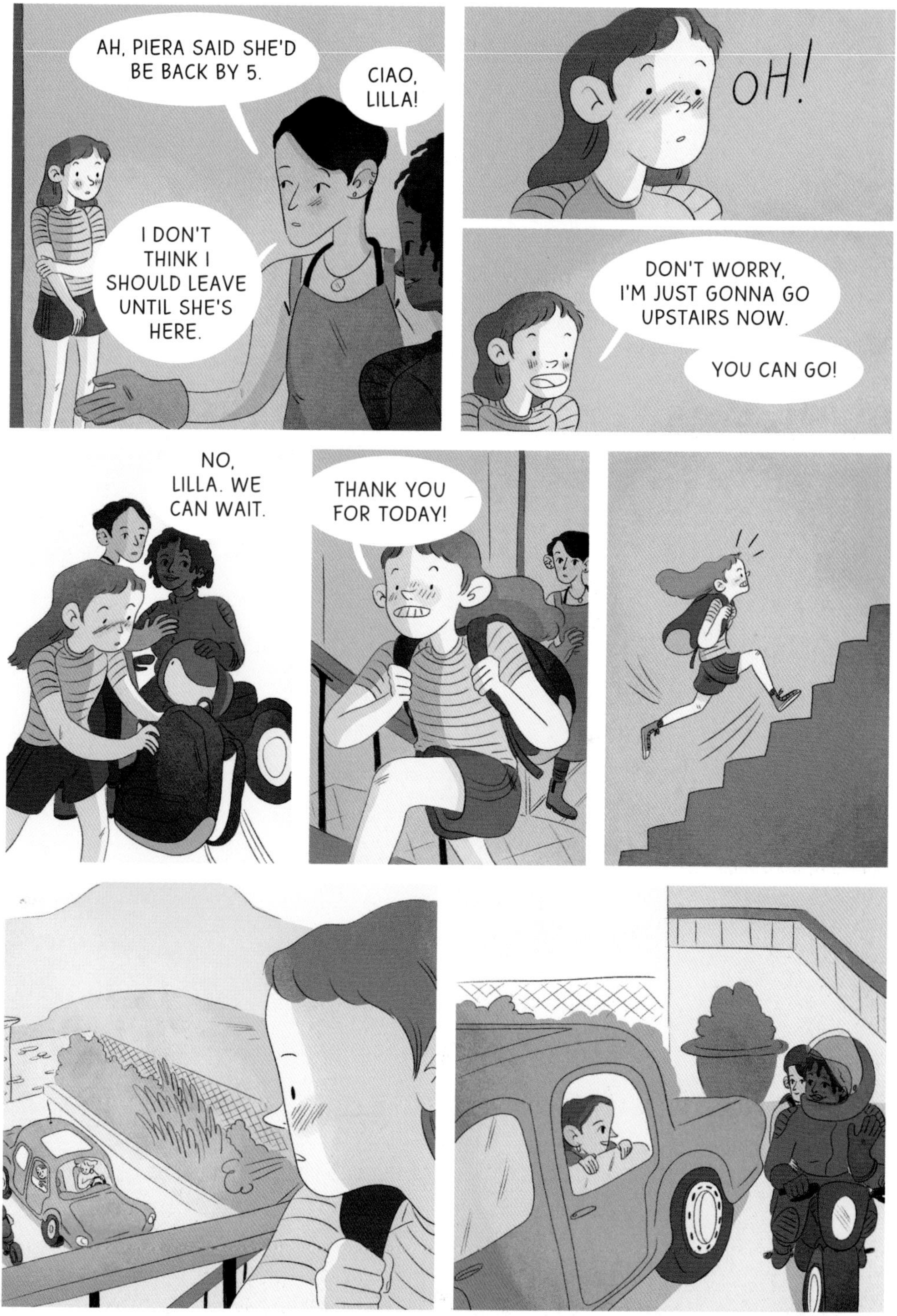
AH, PIERA SAID SHE'D BE BACK BY 5.
CIAO, LILLA!
I DON'T THINK I SHOULD LEAVE UNTIL SHE'S HERE.
OH!
DON'T WORRY, I'M JUST GONNA GO UPSTAIRS NOW.
YOU CAN GO!
NO, LILLA. WE CAN WAIT.
THANK YOU FOR TODAY!

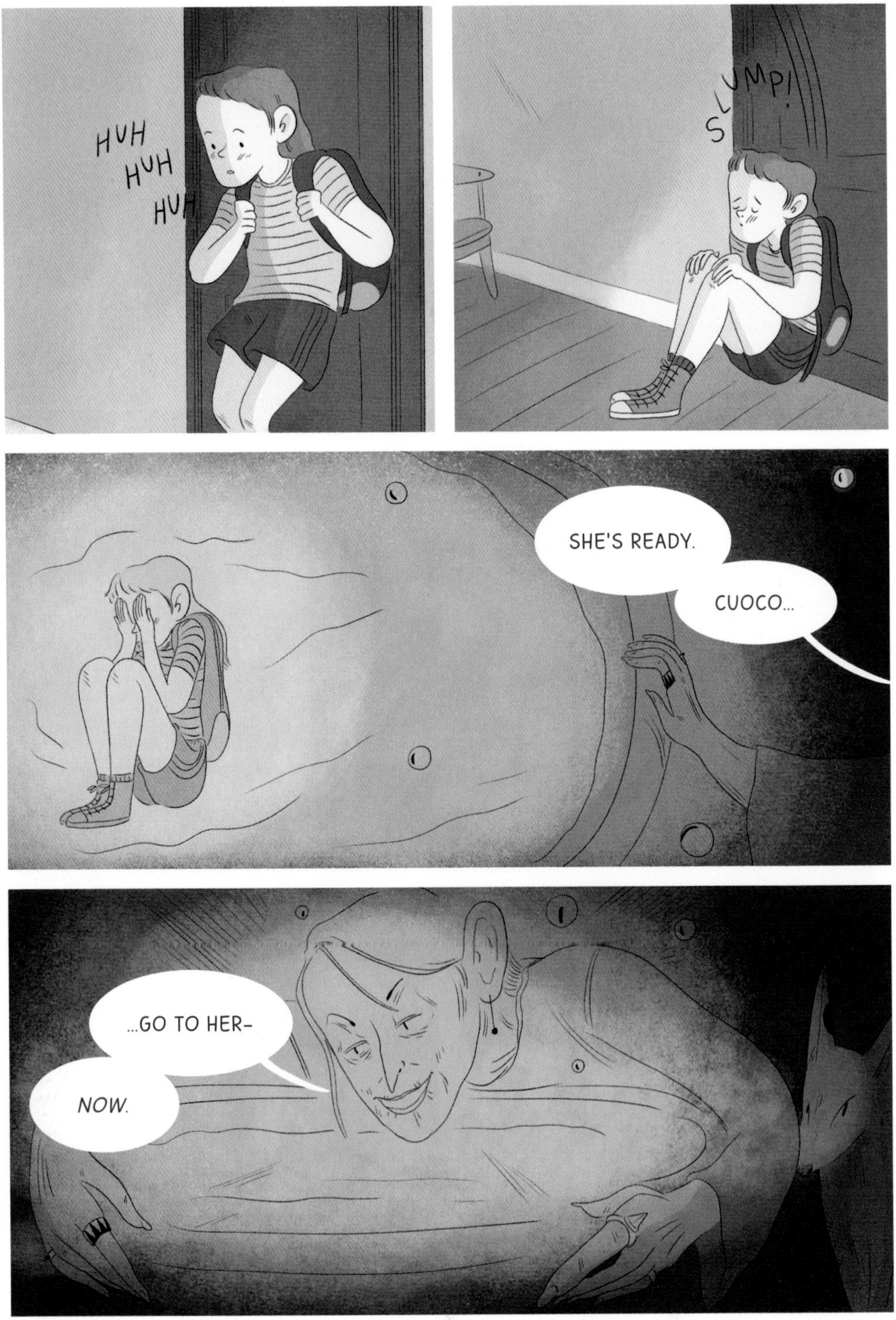
HUH
HUH
HUH
SLUMP!
SHE'S READY.
CUOCO...
...GO TO HER-
NOW.

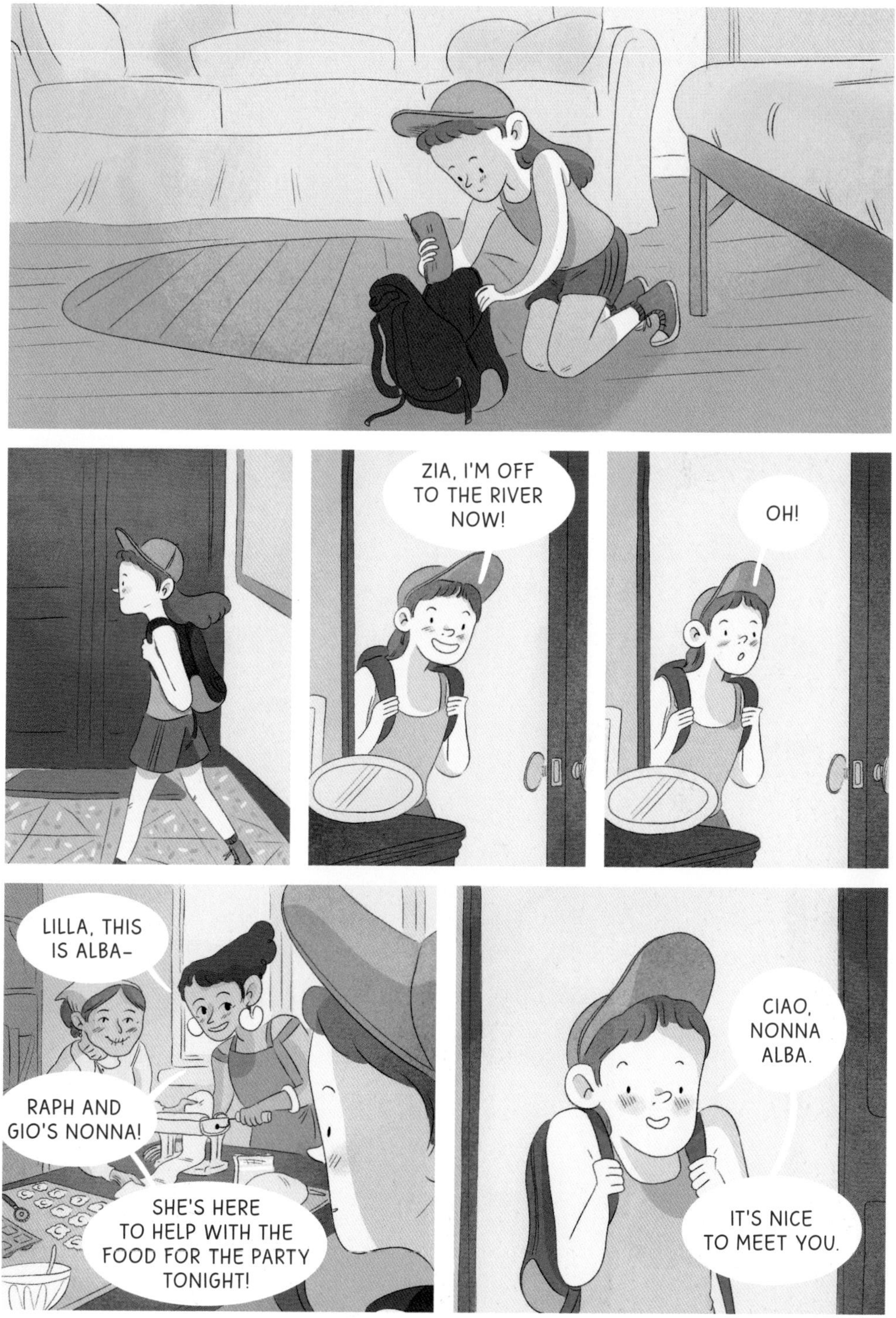
ZIA, I'M OFF TO THE RIVER NOW!
OH!
LILLA, THIS IS ALBA-
RAPH AND GIO'S NONNA!
SHE'S HERE TO HELP WITH THE FOOD FOR THE PARTY TONIGHT!
CIAO, NONNA ALBA.
IT'S NICE TO MEET YOU.

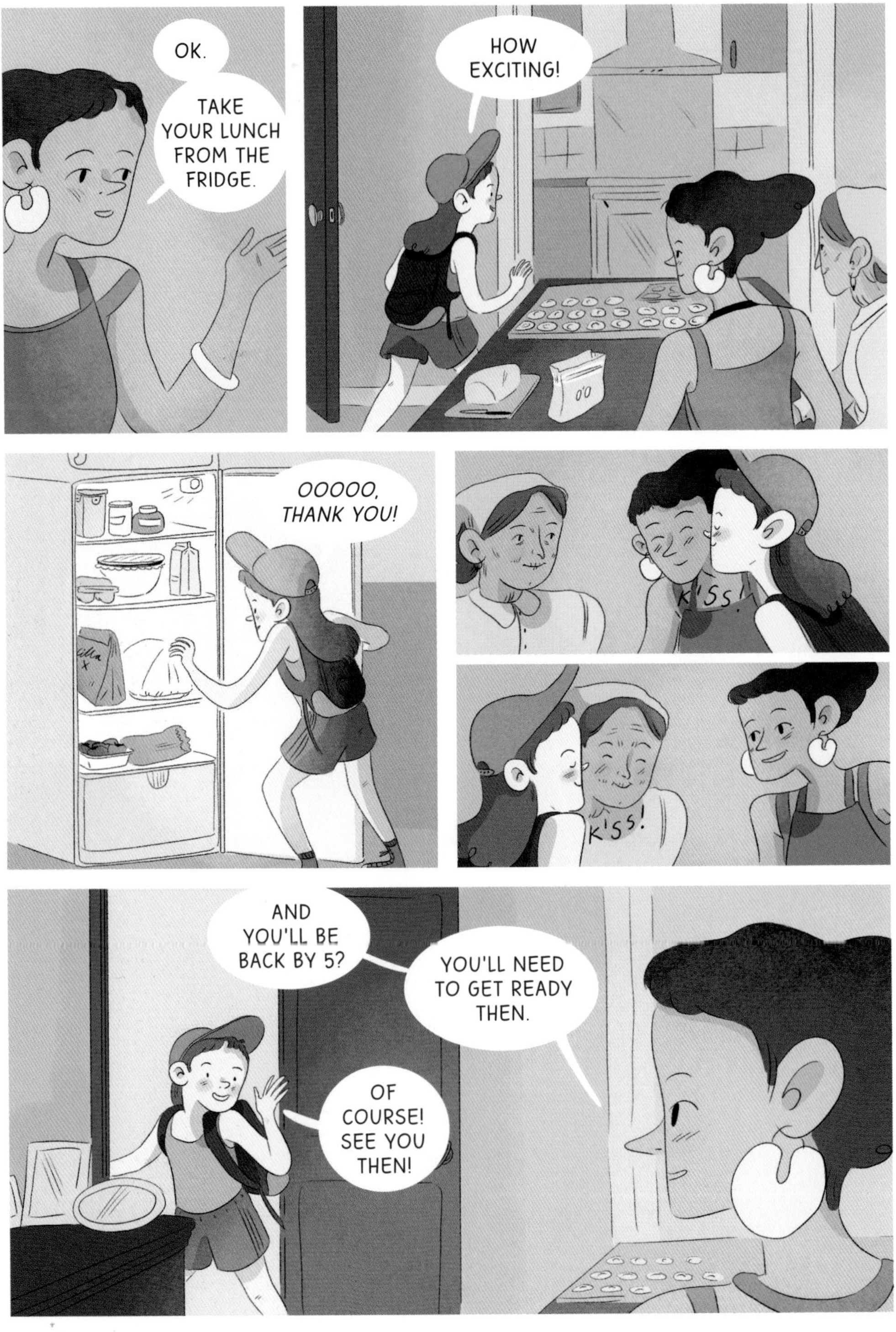
OK.
TAKE YOUR LUNCH FROM THE FRIDGE.
HOW EXCITING!
OOOOO, THANK YOU!
KISS!
KISS!
AND YOU'LL BE BACK BY 5?
YOU'LL NEED TO GET READY THEN.
OF COURSE! SEE YOU THEN!

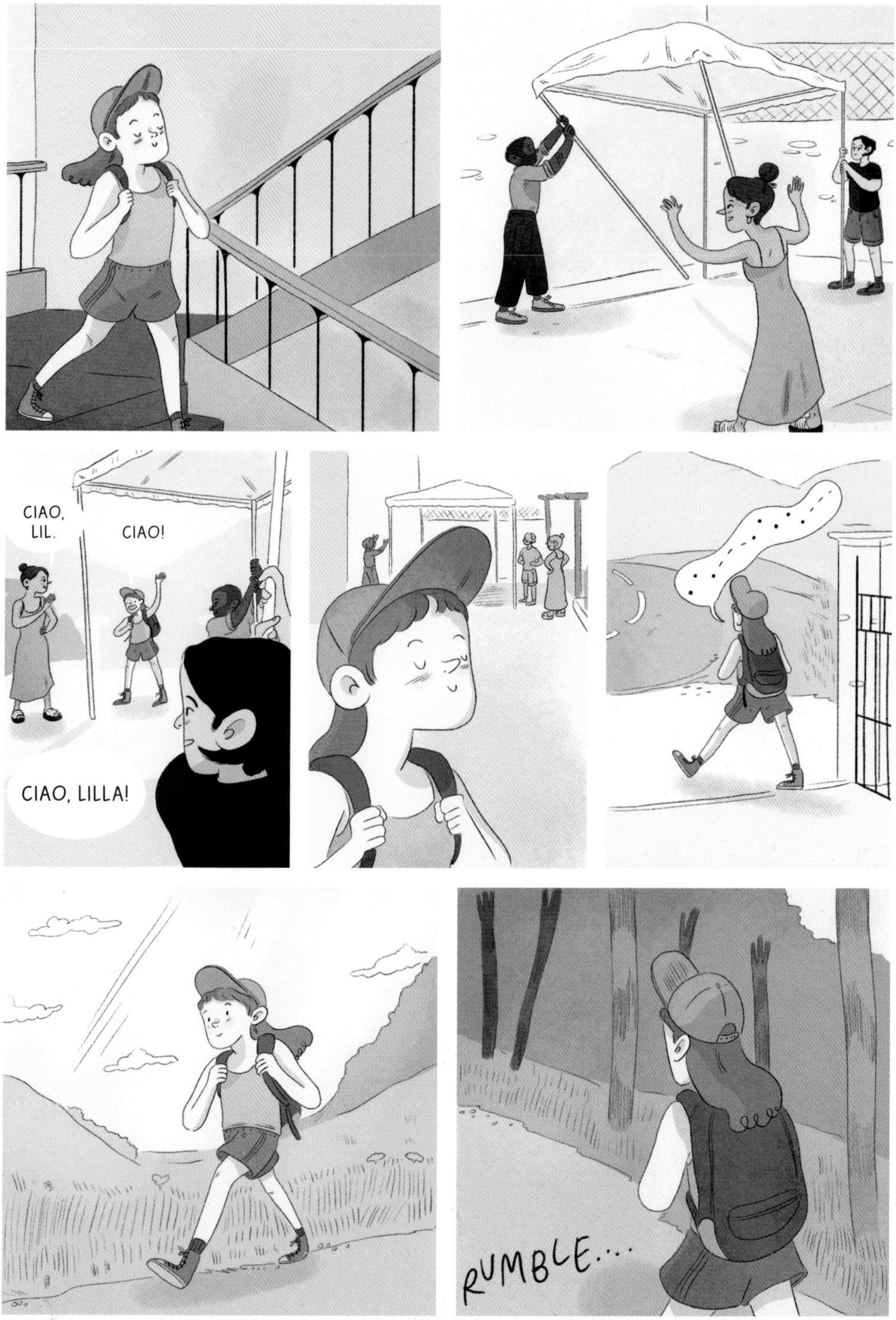
CIAO, LIL.
CIAO!
CIAO, LILLA!
RUMBLE....

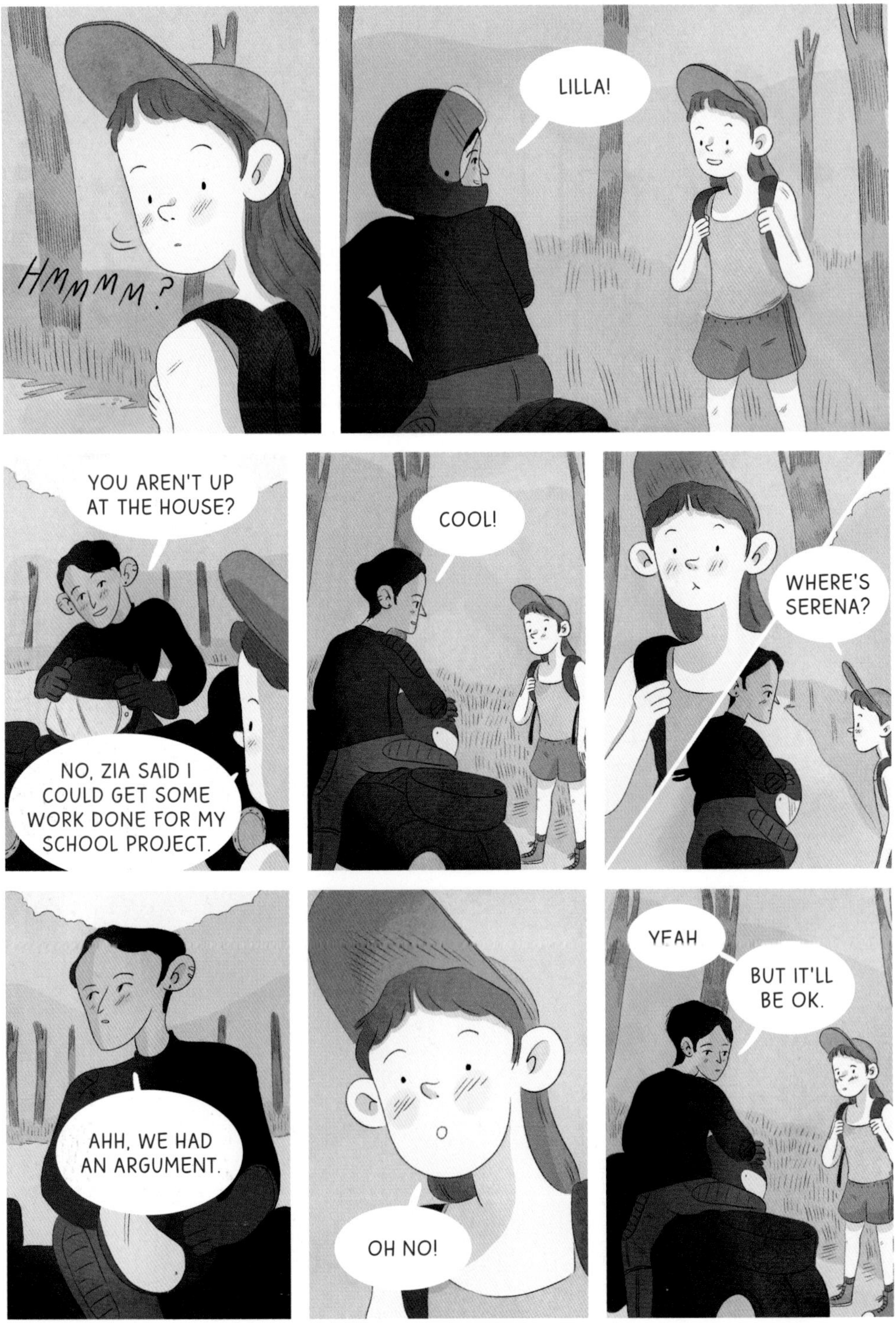
HMMMM?
LILLA!
YOU AREN'T UP AT THE HOUSE?
NO, ZIA SAID I COULD GET SOME WORK DONE FOR MY SCHOOL PROJECT.
COOL!
WHERE'S SERENA?
AHH, WE HAD AN ARGUMENT.
OH NO!
YEAH
BUT IT'LL BE OK.

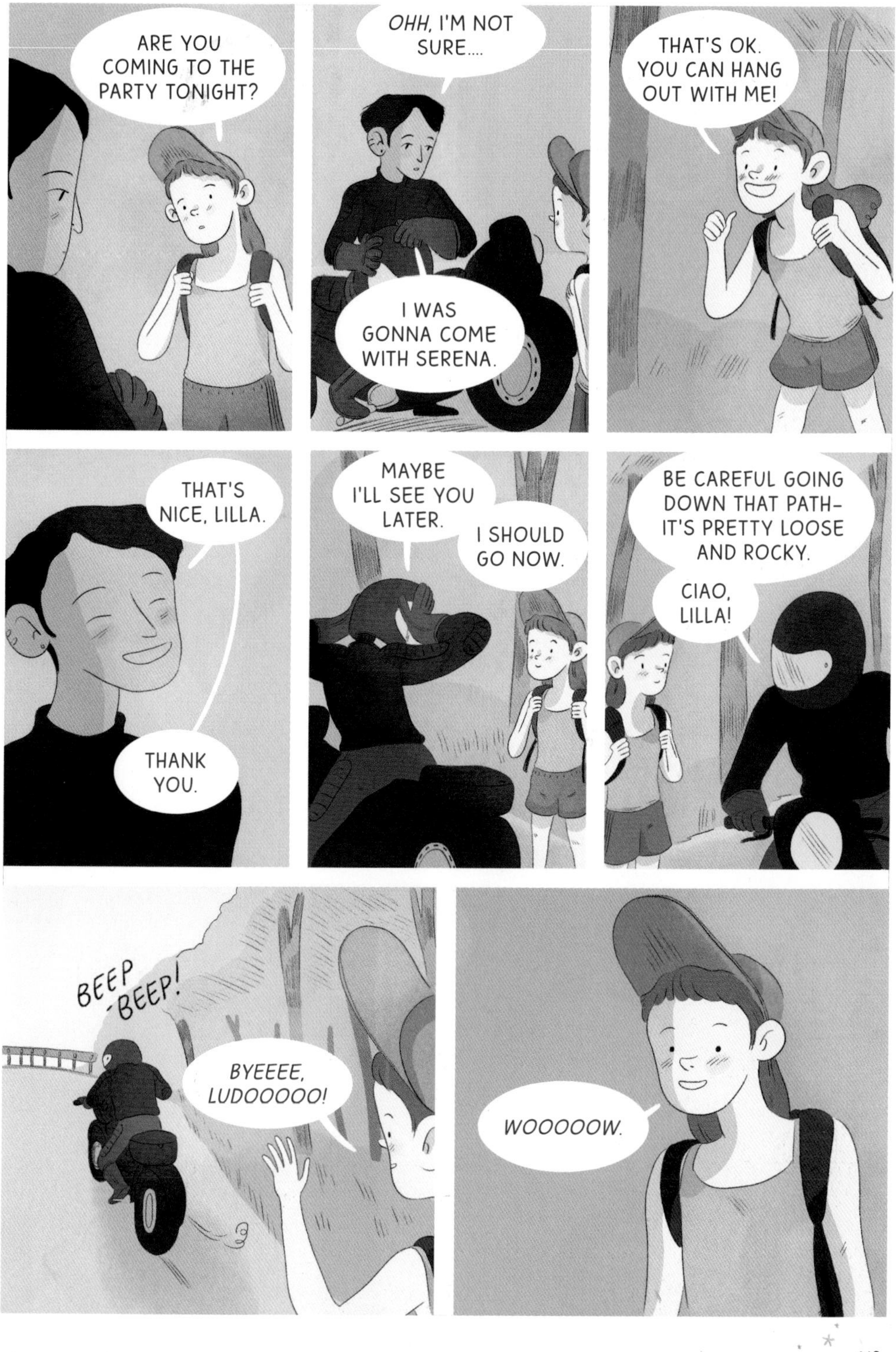
ARE YOU COMING TO THE PARTY TONIGHT?
OHH, I'M NOT SURE....
I WAS GONNA COME WITH SERENA.
THAT'S OK. YOU CAN HANG OUT WITH ME!
THAT'S NICE, LILLA.
THANK YOU.
MAYBE I'LL SEE YOU LATER.
I SHOULD GO NOW.
BE CAREFUL GOING DOWN THAT PATH– IT'S PRETTY LOOSE AND ROCKY.
CIAO, LILLA!
BEEP -BEEP!
BYEEEE, LUDOOOOO!
WOOOOOW.

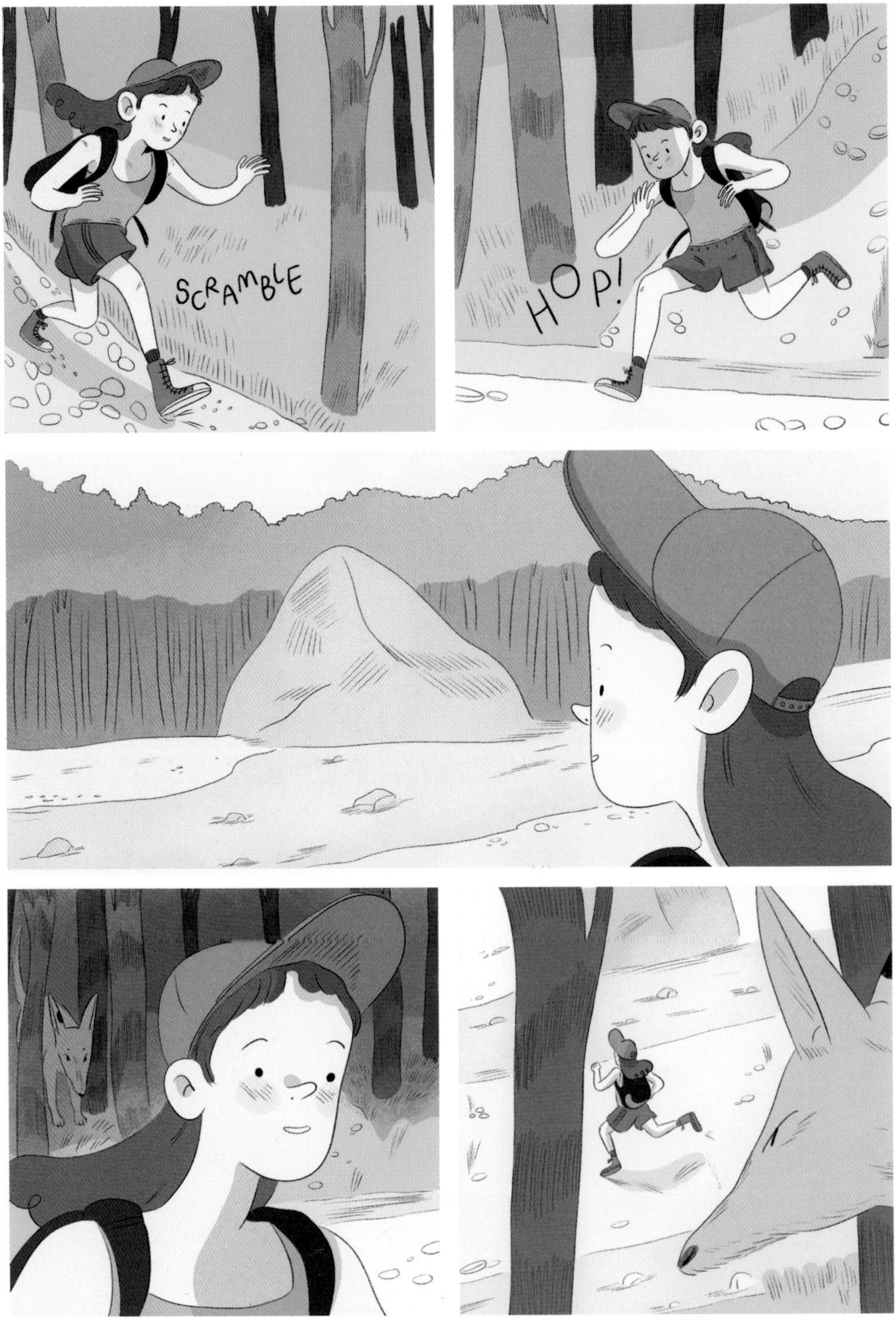
SCRAMBLE
HOP!

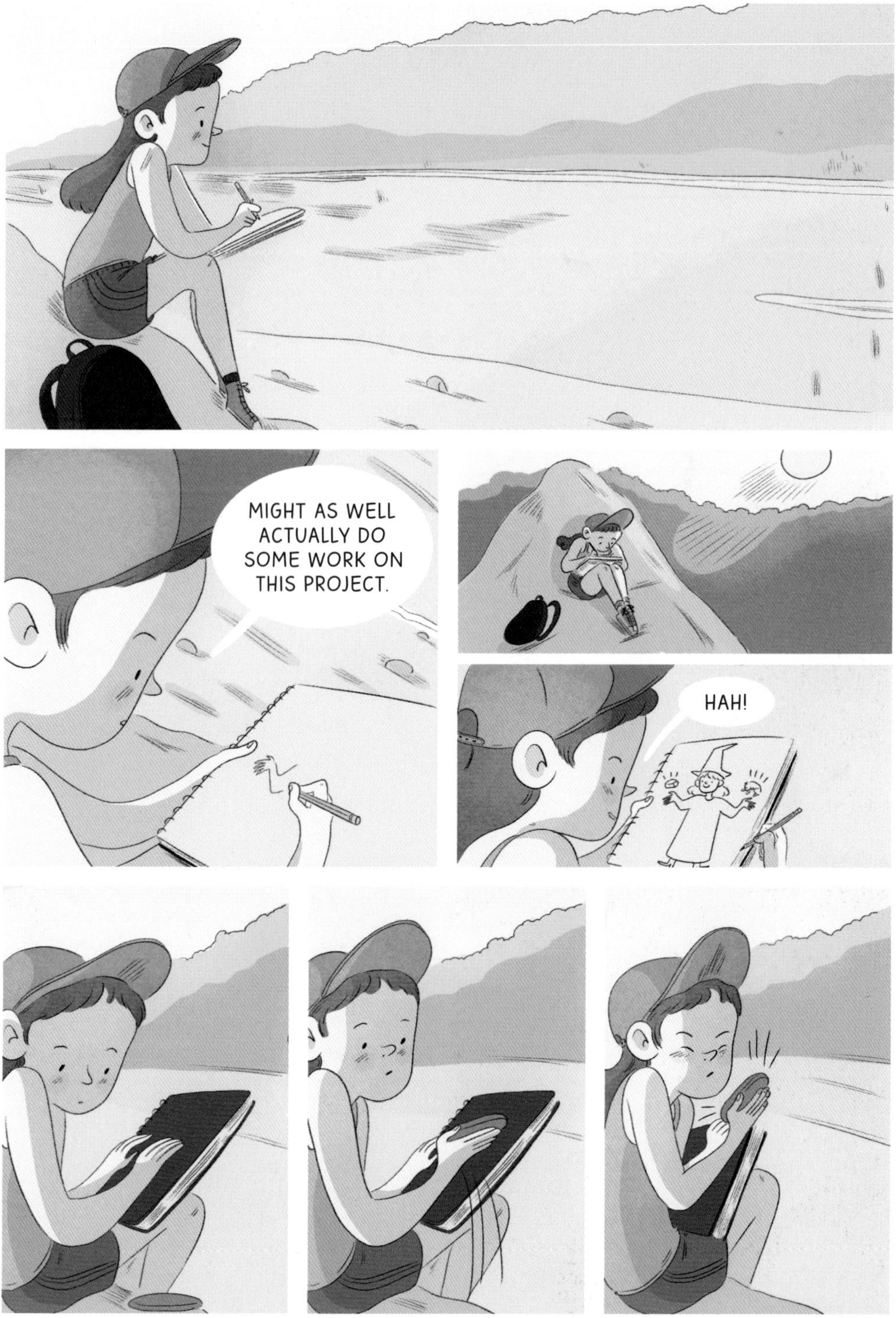
MIGHT AS WELL ACTUALLY DO SOME WORK ON THIS PROJECT.
HAH!

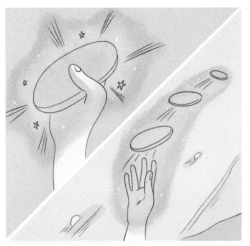

HUH!

WOW, LILLA, THAT WAS **AMAZING!**

HOW DID YOU DO IT? I DIDN'T EVEN SEE YOUR HAND MOVE.

HEY, GIO!

OH, MY DAD TAUGHT ME— HE'S REALLY GOOD.

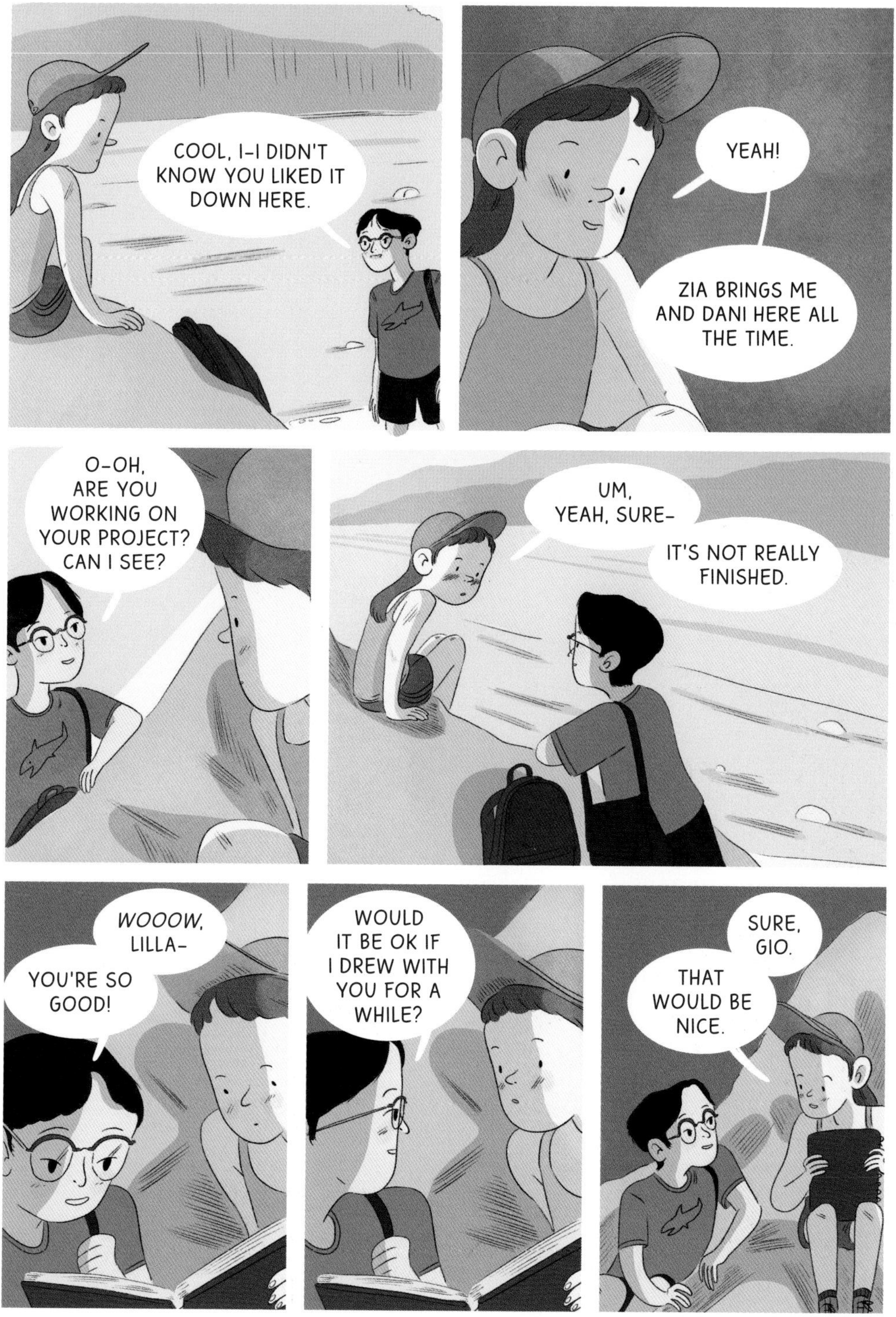
COOL, I-I DIDN'T KNOW YOU LIKED IT DOWN HERE.
YEAH!
ZIA BRINGS ME AND DANI HERE ALL THE TIME.
O-OH, ARE YOU WORKING ON YOUR PROJECT? CAN I SEE?
UM, YEAH, SURE-
IT'S NOT REALLY FINISHED.
WOOOW, LILLA-
YOU'RE SO GOOD!
WOULD IT BE OK IF I DREW WITH YOU FOR A WHILE?
SURE, GIO.
THAT WOULD BE NICE.

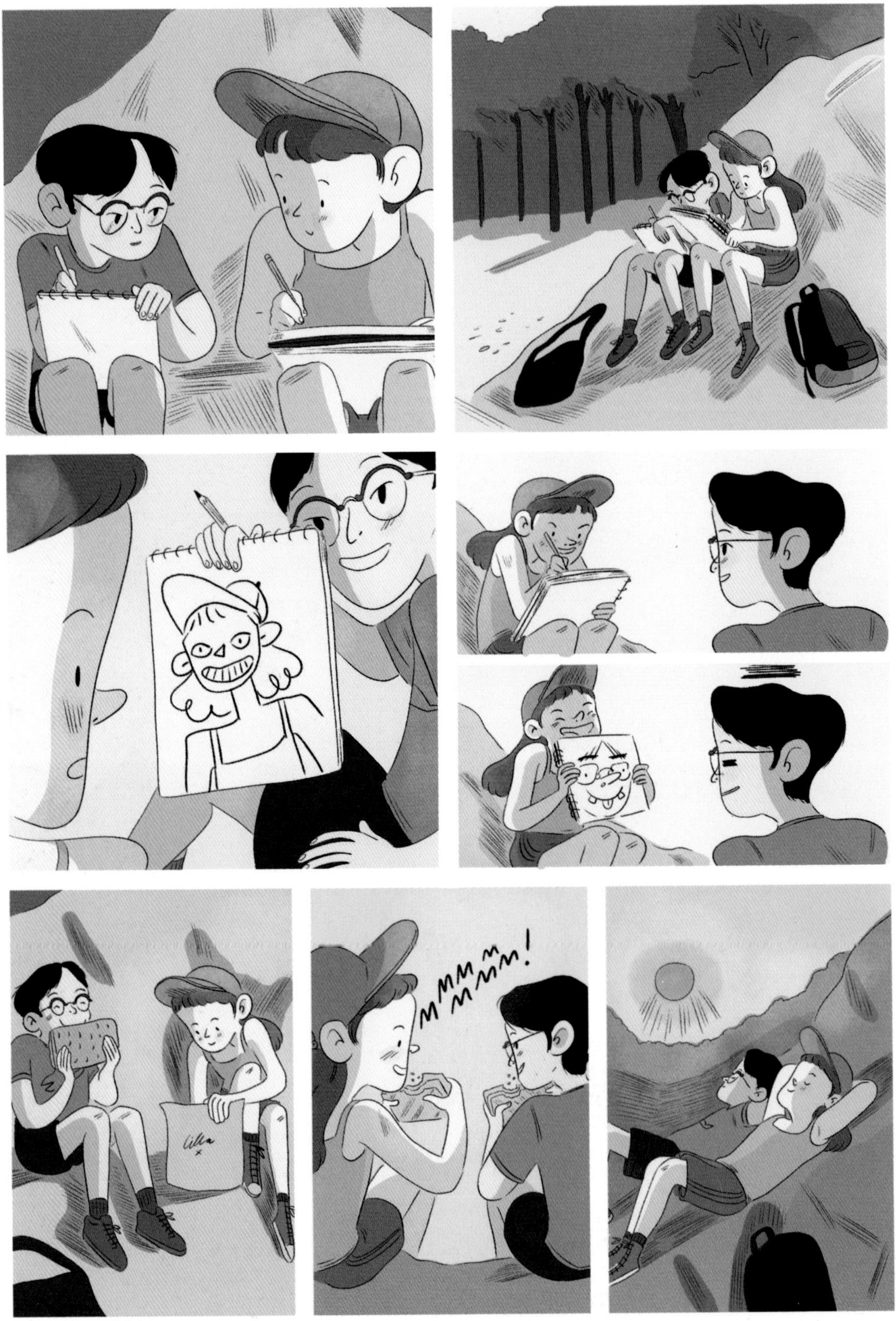
Lilla x
MMMM MMM!

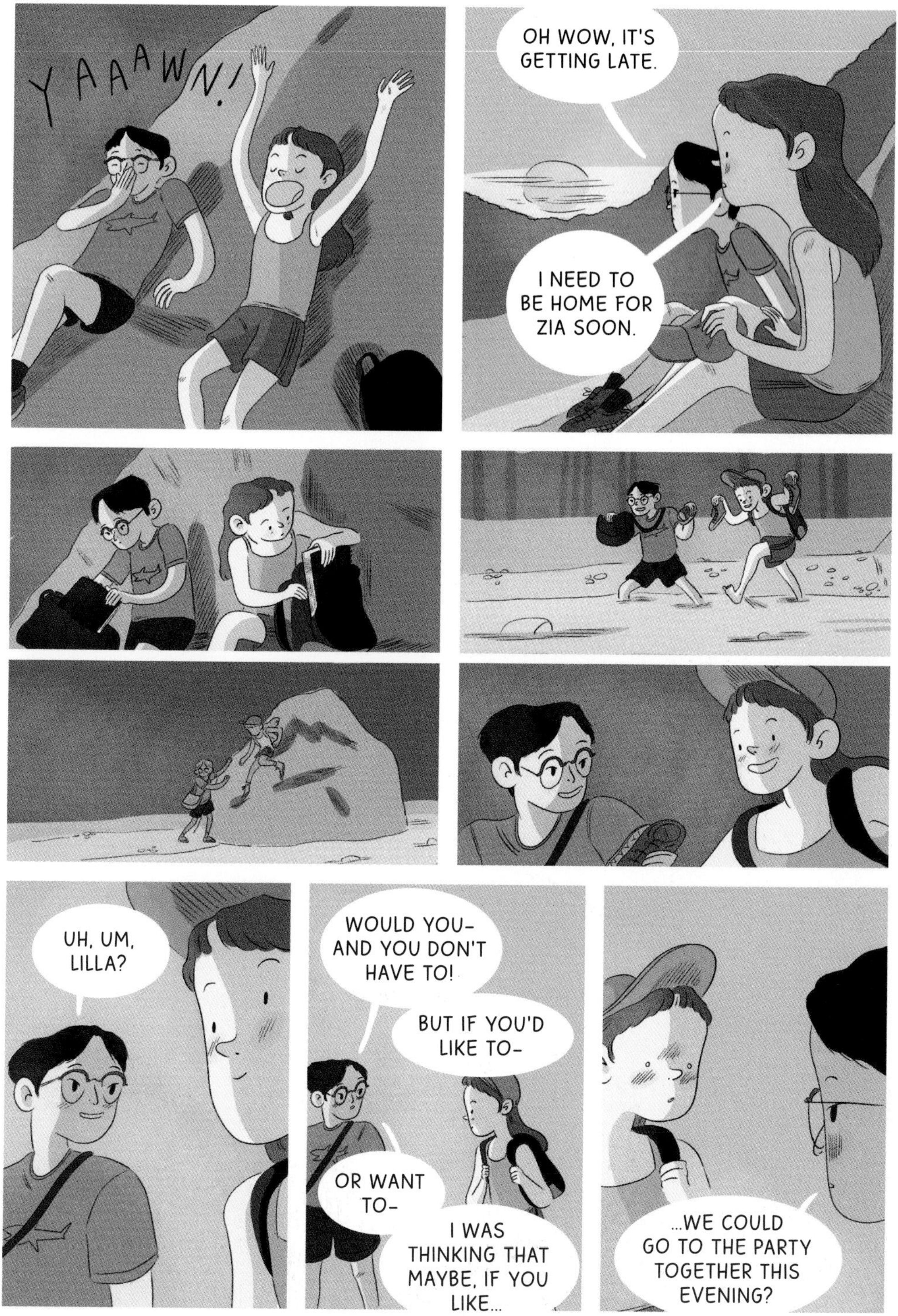
YAAAWN!
OH WOW, IT'S GETTING LATE.
I NEED TO BE HOME FOR ZIA SOON.
UH, UM, LILLA?
WOULD YOU- AND YOU DON'T HAVE TO!
BUT IF YOU'D LIKE TO-
OR WANT TO-
I WAS THINKING THAT MAYBE, IF YOU LIKE...
...WE COULD GO TO THE PARTY TOGETHER THIS EVENING?

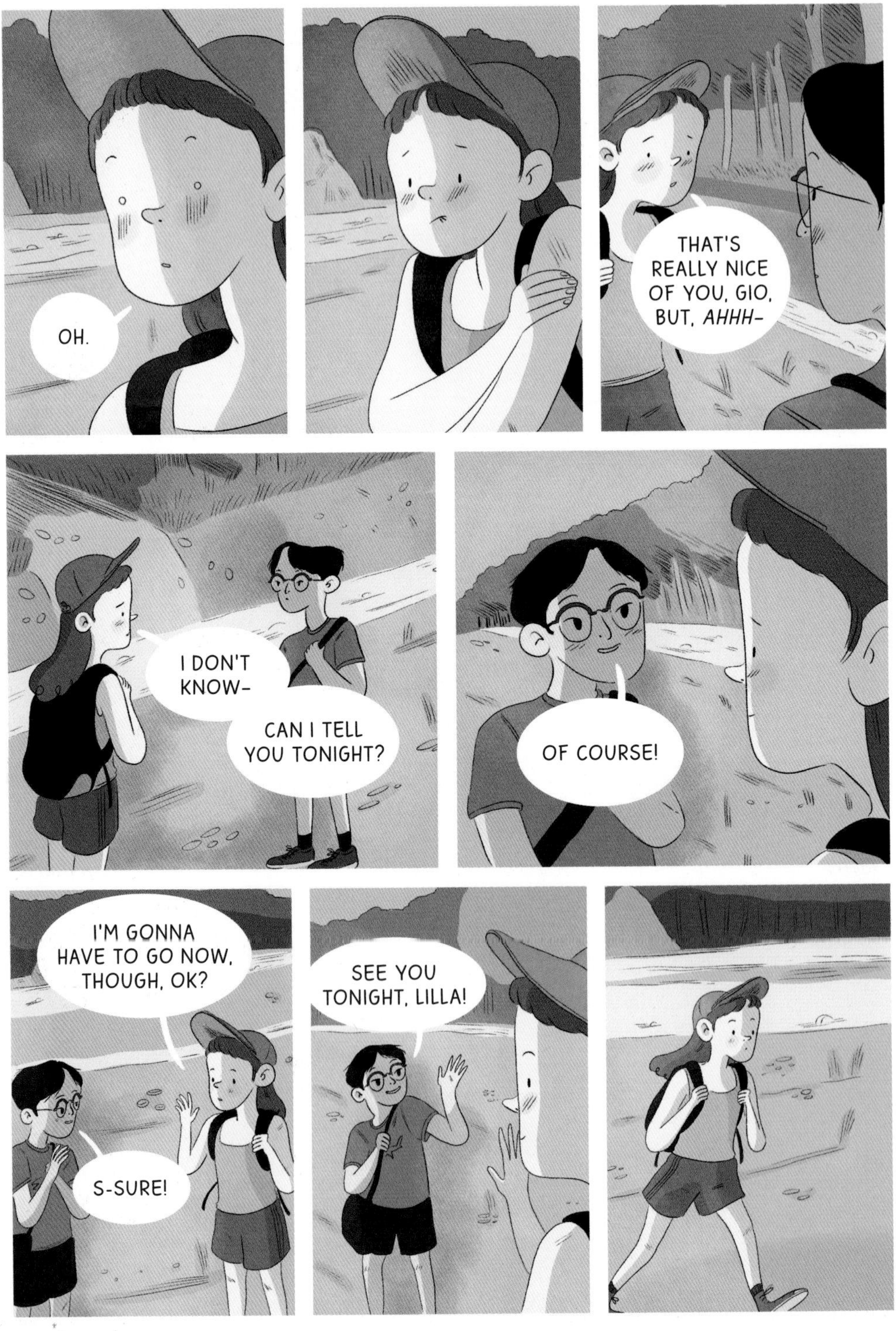
OH.
THAT'S REALLY NICE OF YOU, GIO, BUT, *AHHH*-
I DON'T KNOW-
CAN I TELL YOU TONIGHT?
OF COURSE!
I'M GONNA HAVE TO GO NOW, THOUGH, OK?
S-SURE!
SEE YOU TONIGHT, LILLA!

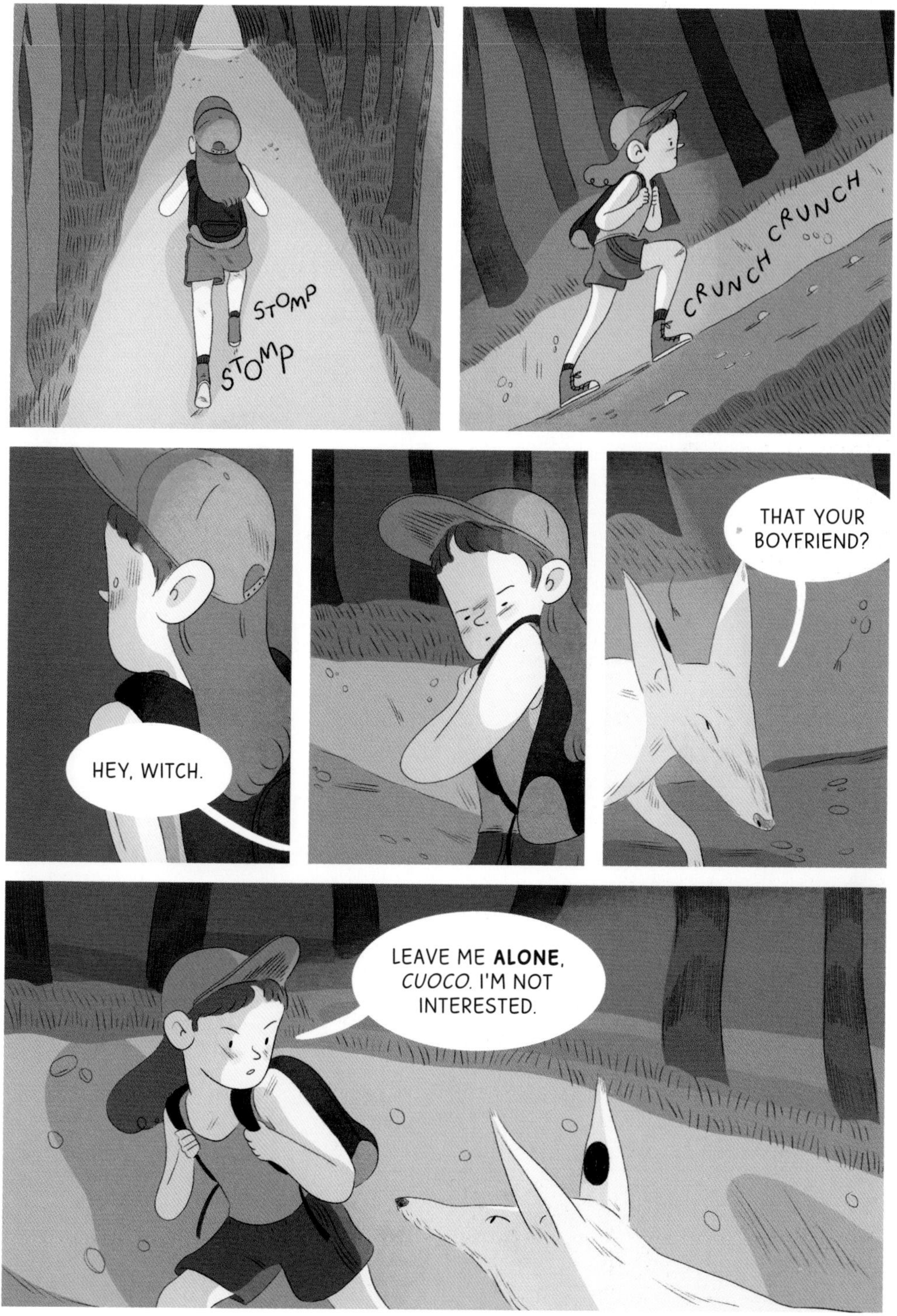
STOMP
STOMP
CRUNCH CRUNCH
HEY, WITCH.
THAT YOUR BOYFRIEND?
LEAVE ME **ALONE**, *CUOCO*. I'M NOT INTERESTED.

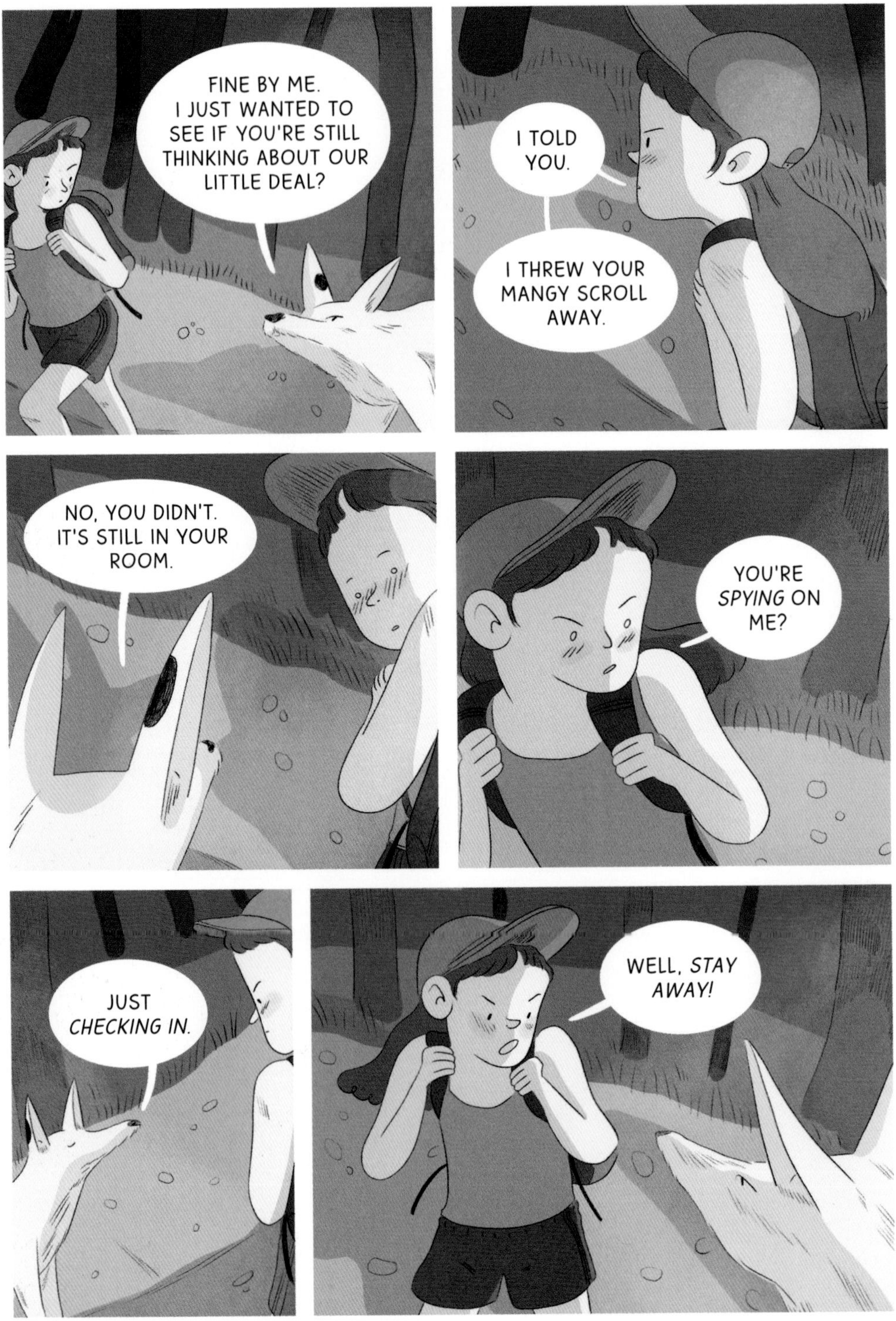
FINE BY ME. I JUST WANTED TO SEE IF YOU'RE STILL THINKING ABOUT OUR LITTLE DEAL?
I TOLD YOU.
I THREW YOUR MANGY SCROLL AWAY.
NO, YOU DIDN'T. IT'S STILL IN YOUR ROOM.
YOU'RE *SPYING* ON ME?
JUST *CHECKING IN.*
WELL, *STAY AWAY!*

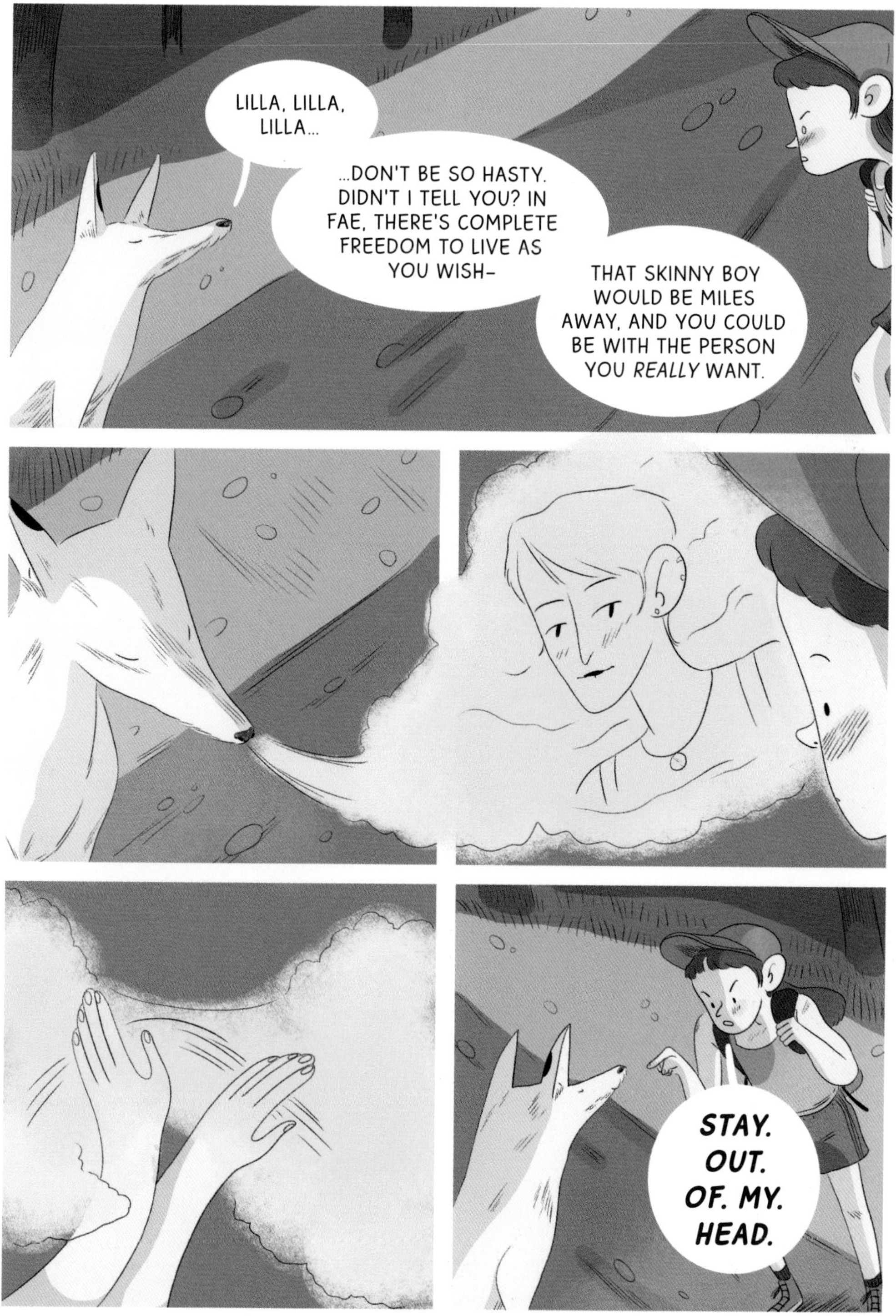
LILLA, LILLA, LILLA...
...DON'T BE SO HASTY. DIDN'T I TELL YOU? IN FAE, THERE'S COMPLETE FREEDOM TO LIVE AS YOU WISH-
THAT SKINNY BOY WOULD BE MILES AWAY, AND YOU COULD BE WITH THE PERSON YOU *REALLY* WANT.
STAY. OUT. OF. MY. HEAD.

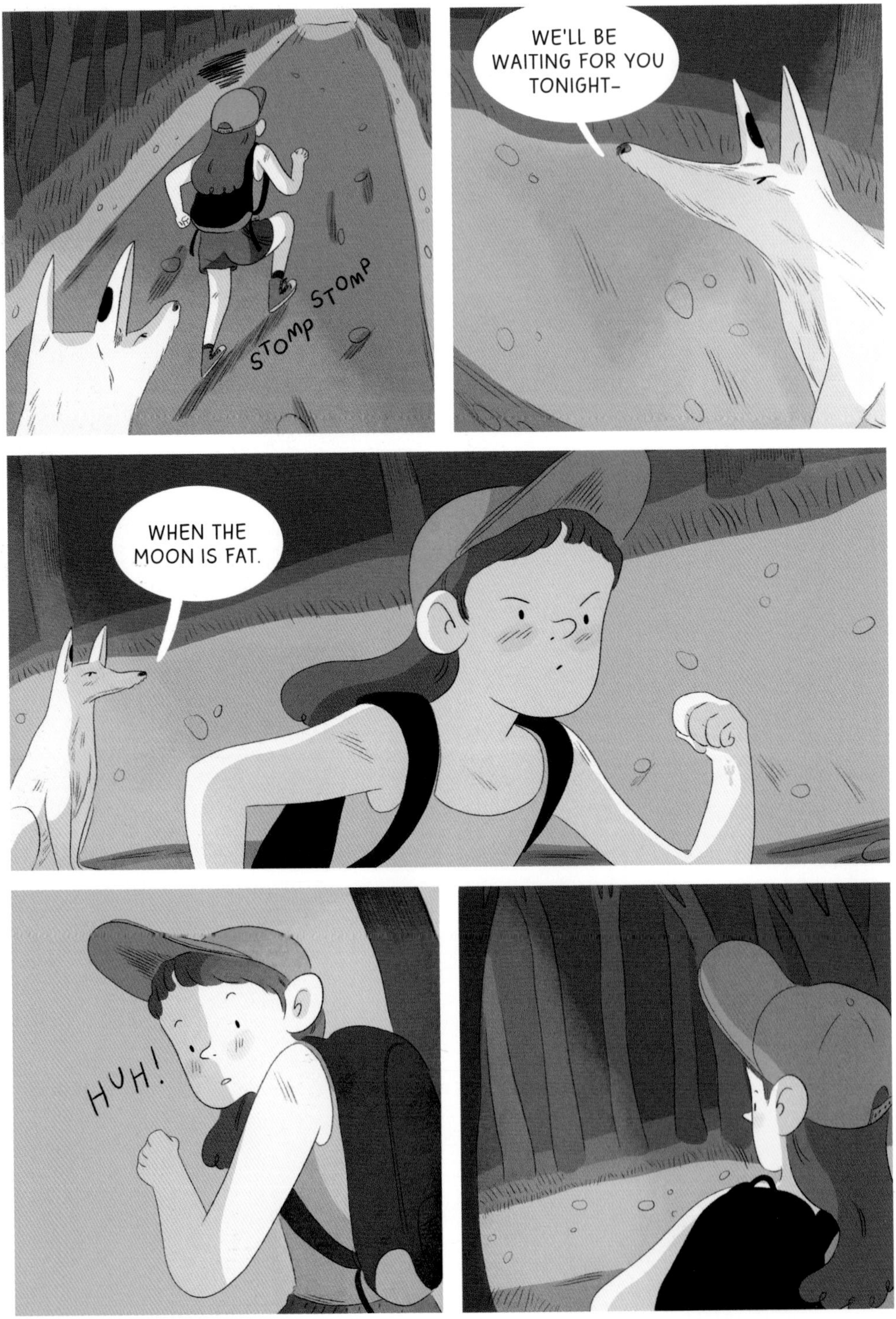
STOMP STOMP
WE'LL BE WAITING FOR YOU TONIGHT–
WHEN THE MOON IS FAT.
HUH!

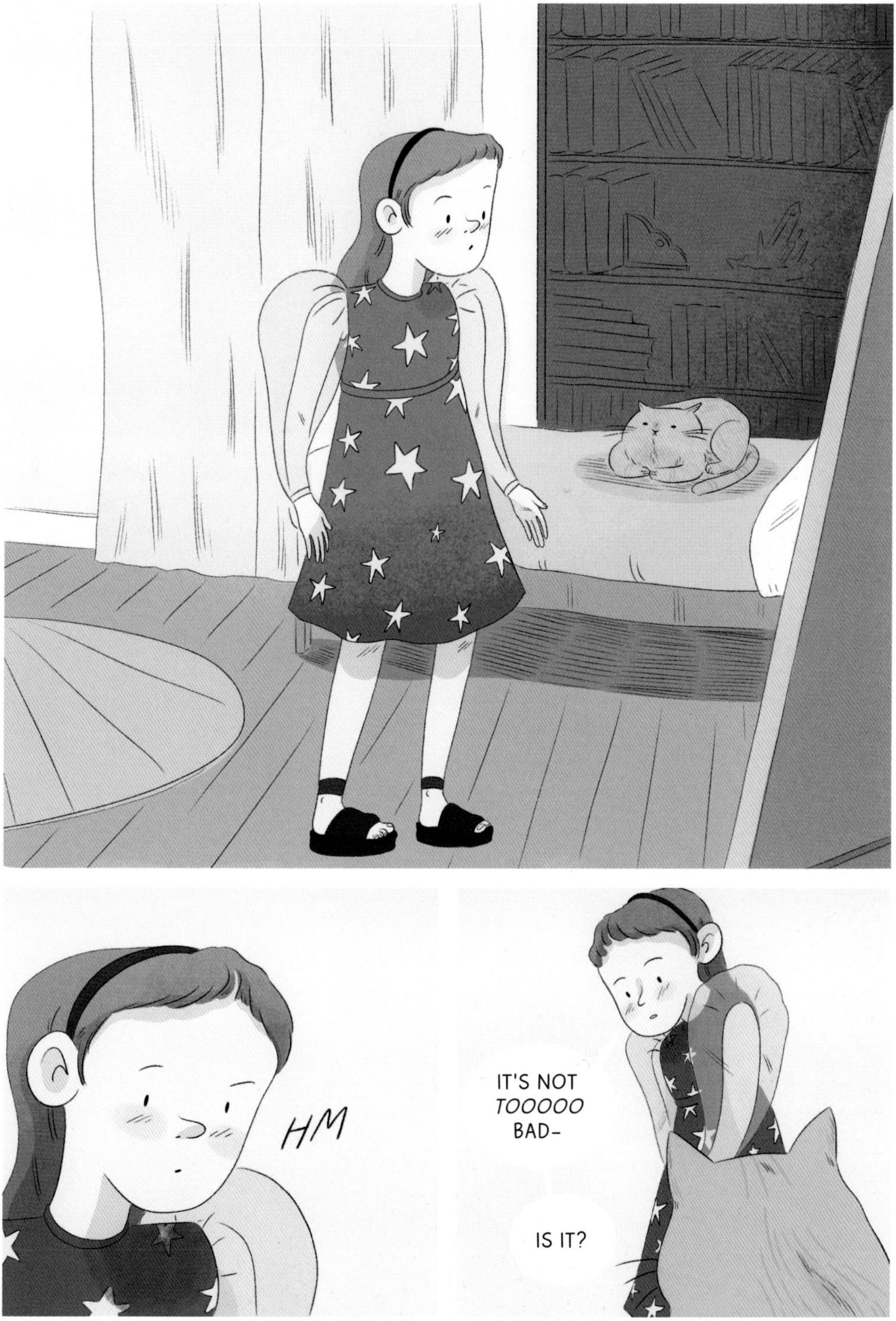
HM
IT'S NOT *TOOOOO* BAD-
IS IT?

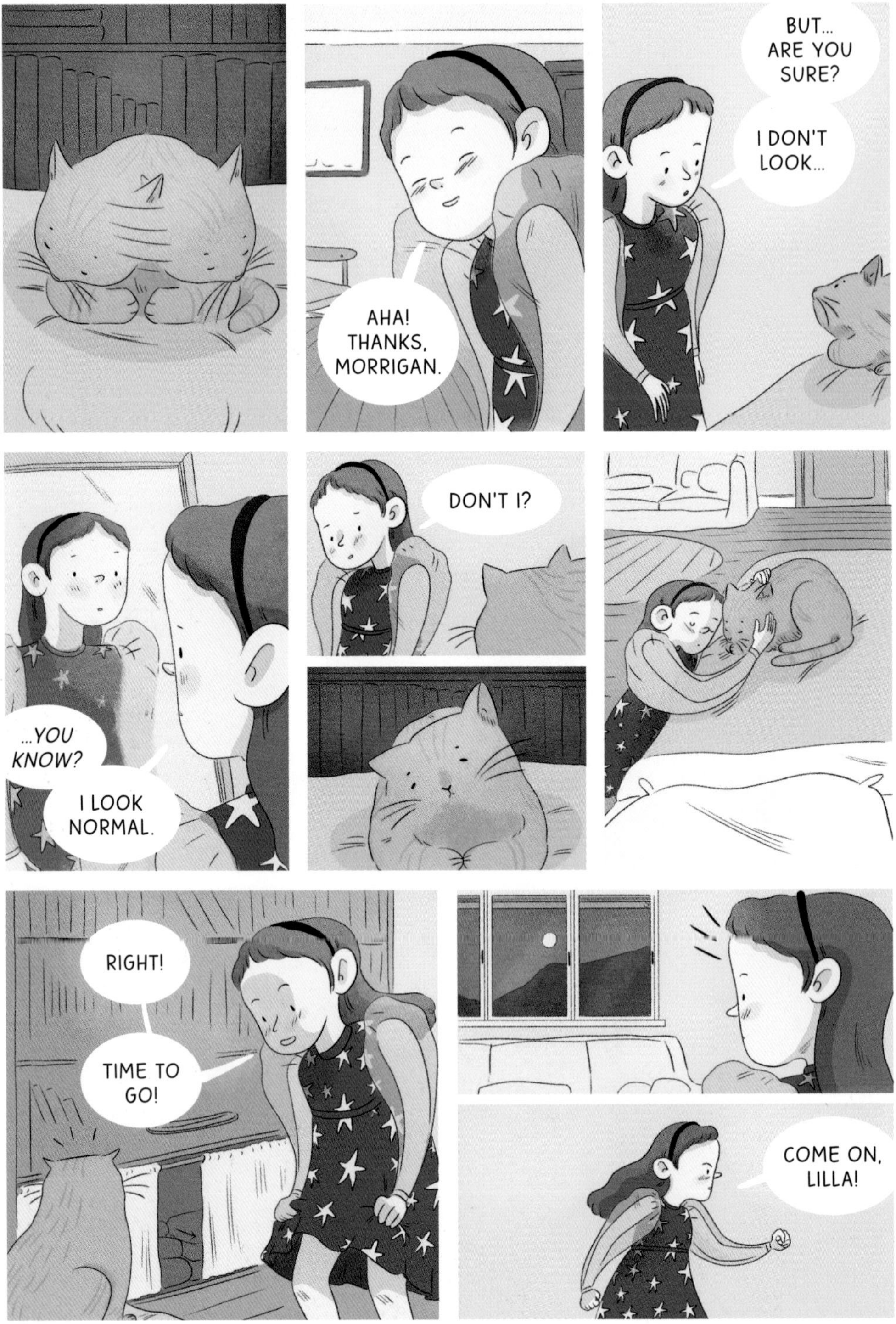
AHA! THANKS, MORRIGAN.
BUT... ARE YOU SURE?
I DON'T LOOK...
...YOU KNOW?
I LOOK NORMAL.
DON'T I?
RIGHT!
TIME TO GO!
COME ON, LILLA!

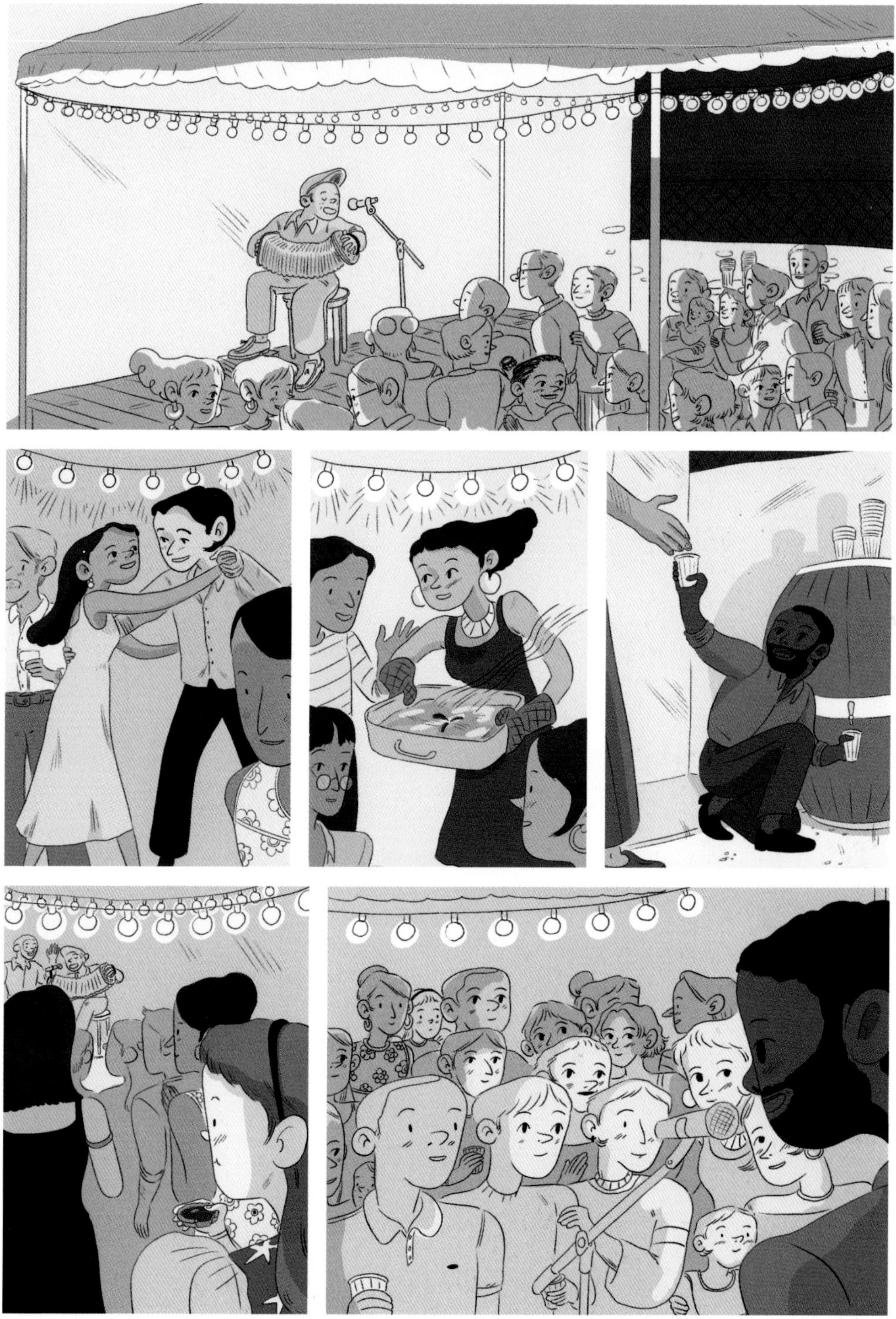

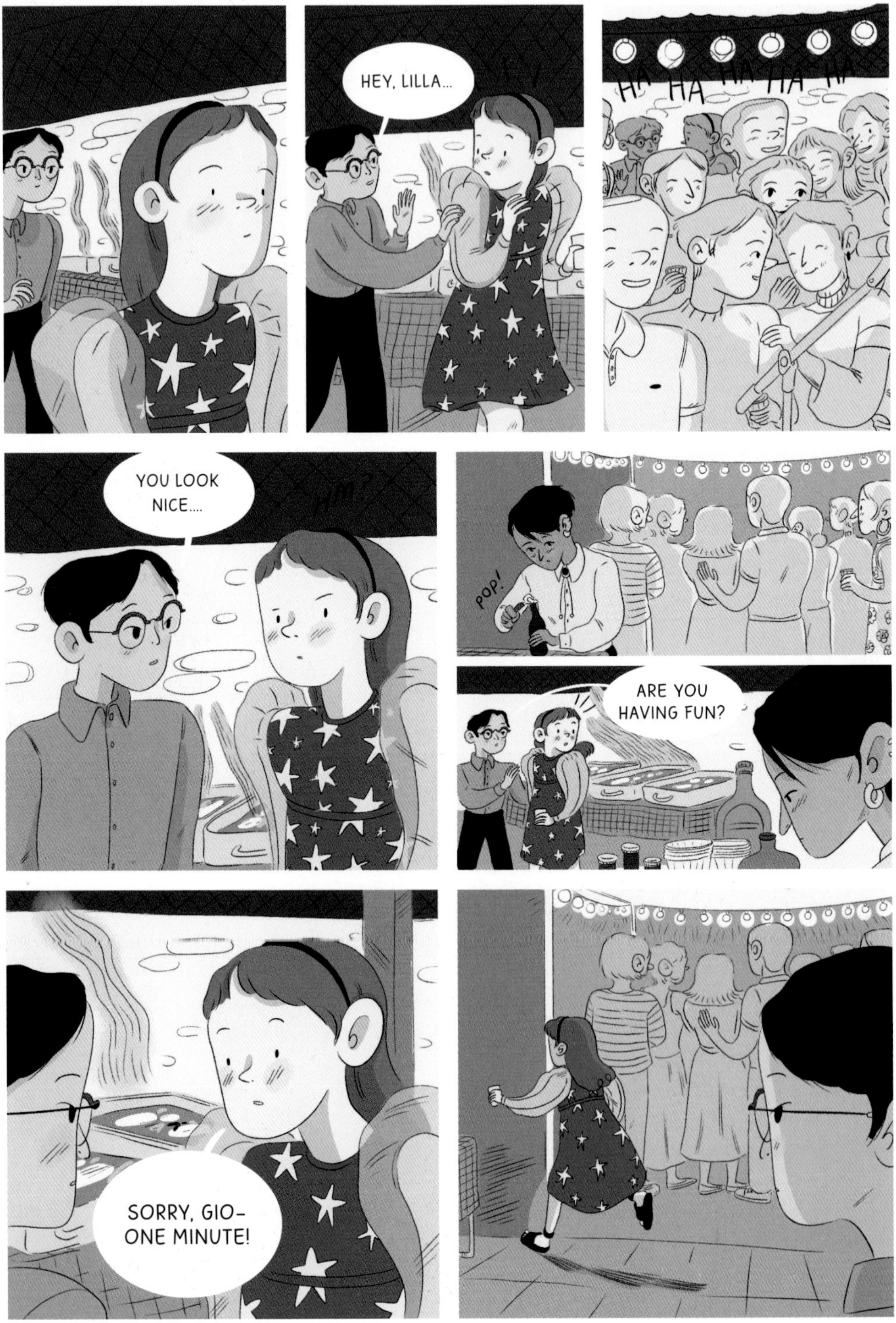
HEY, LILLA...
HA HA HA HA HA
YOU LOOK NICE....
HM?
POP!
ARE YOU HAVING FUN?
SORRY, GIO-
ONE MINUTE!

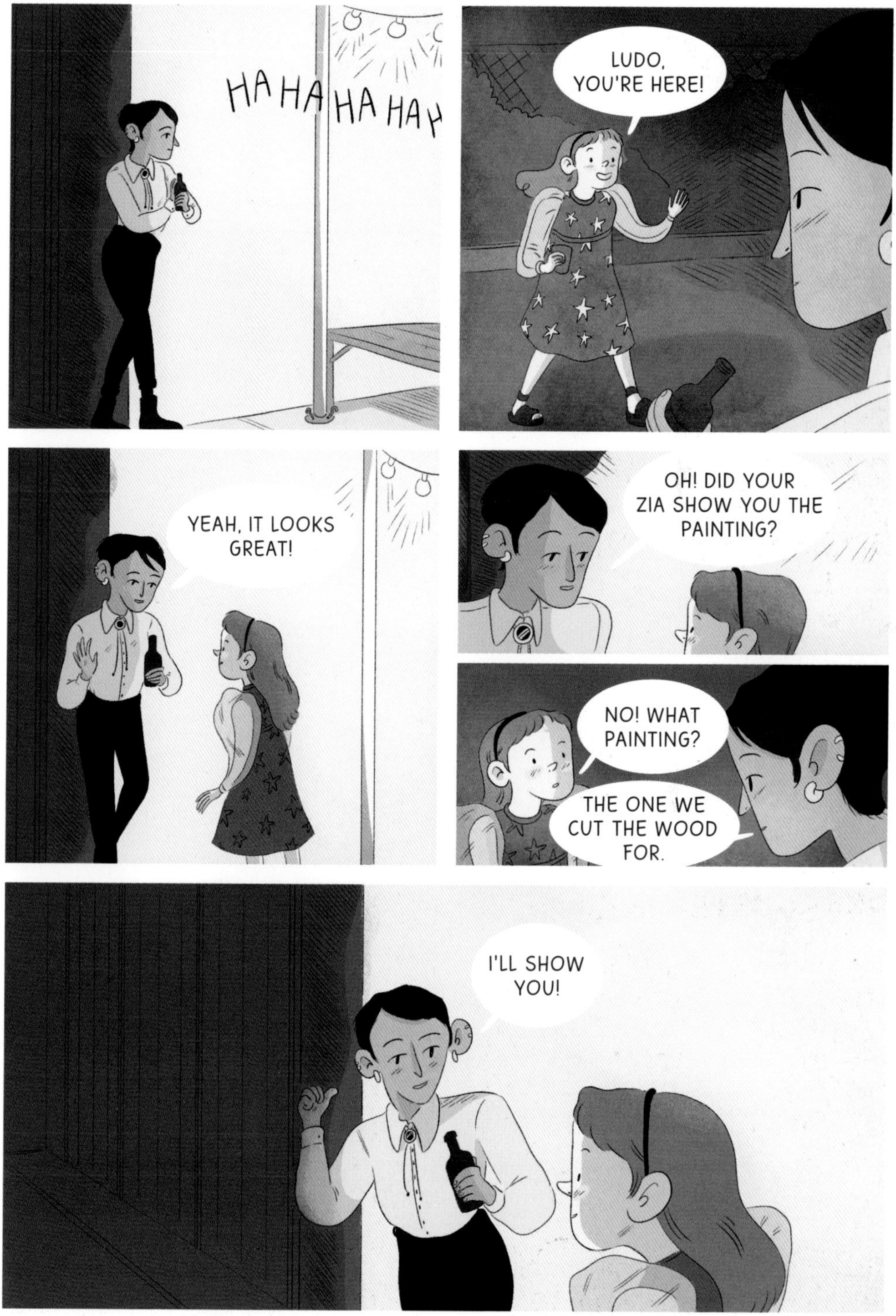
HA HA HA HA
LUDO, YOU'RE HERE!
YEAH, IT LOOKS GREAT!
OH! DID YOUR ZIA SHOW YOU THE PAINTING?
NO! WHAT PAINTING?
THE ONE WE CUT THE WOOD FOR.
I'LL SHOW YOU!

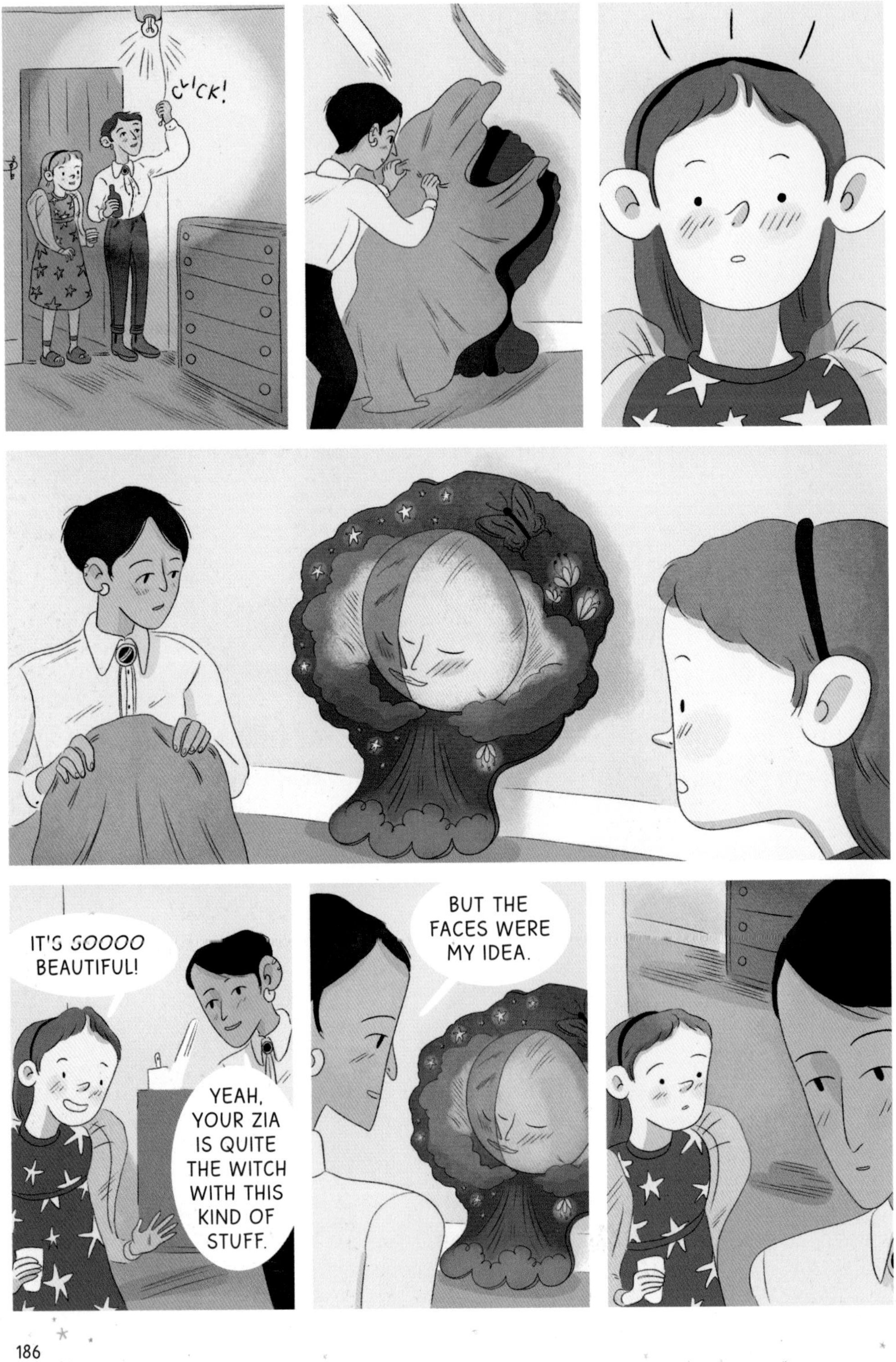
CLICK!
IT'S SOOOO BEAUTIFUL!
YEAH, YOUR ZIA IS QUITE THE WITCH WITH THIS KIND OF STUFF.
BUT THE FACES WERE MY IDEA.

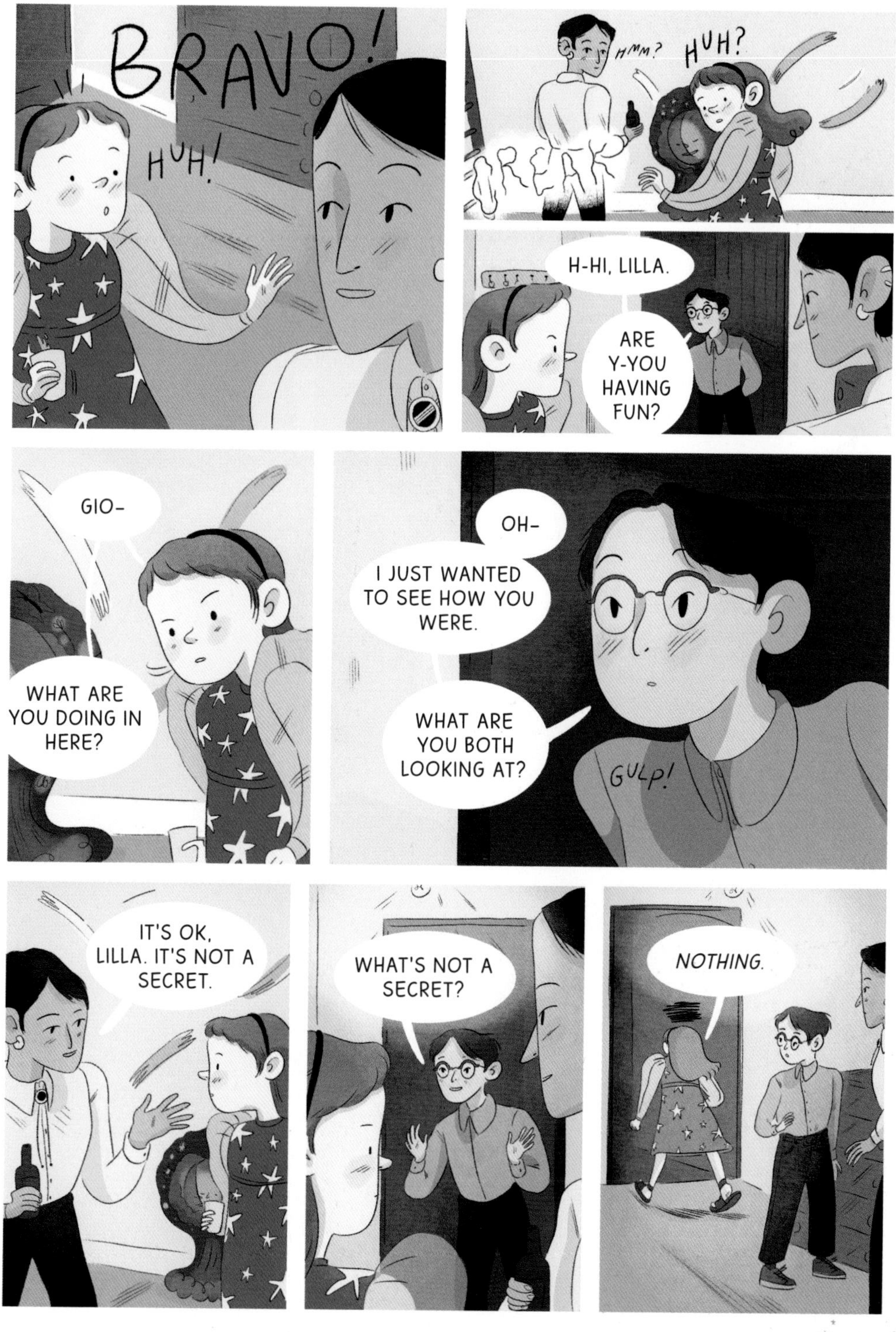
BRAVO!
HUH!
HMM?
HUH?
CREAK
H-HI, LILLA.
ARE Y-YOU HAVING FUN?
GIO-
WHAT ARE YOU DOING IN HERE?
OH-
I JUST WANTED TO SEE HOW YOU WERE.
WHAT ARE YOU BOTH LOOKING AT?
GULP!
IT'S OK, LILLA. IT'S NOT A SECRET.
WHAT'S NOT A SECRET?
NOTHING.

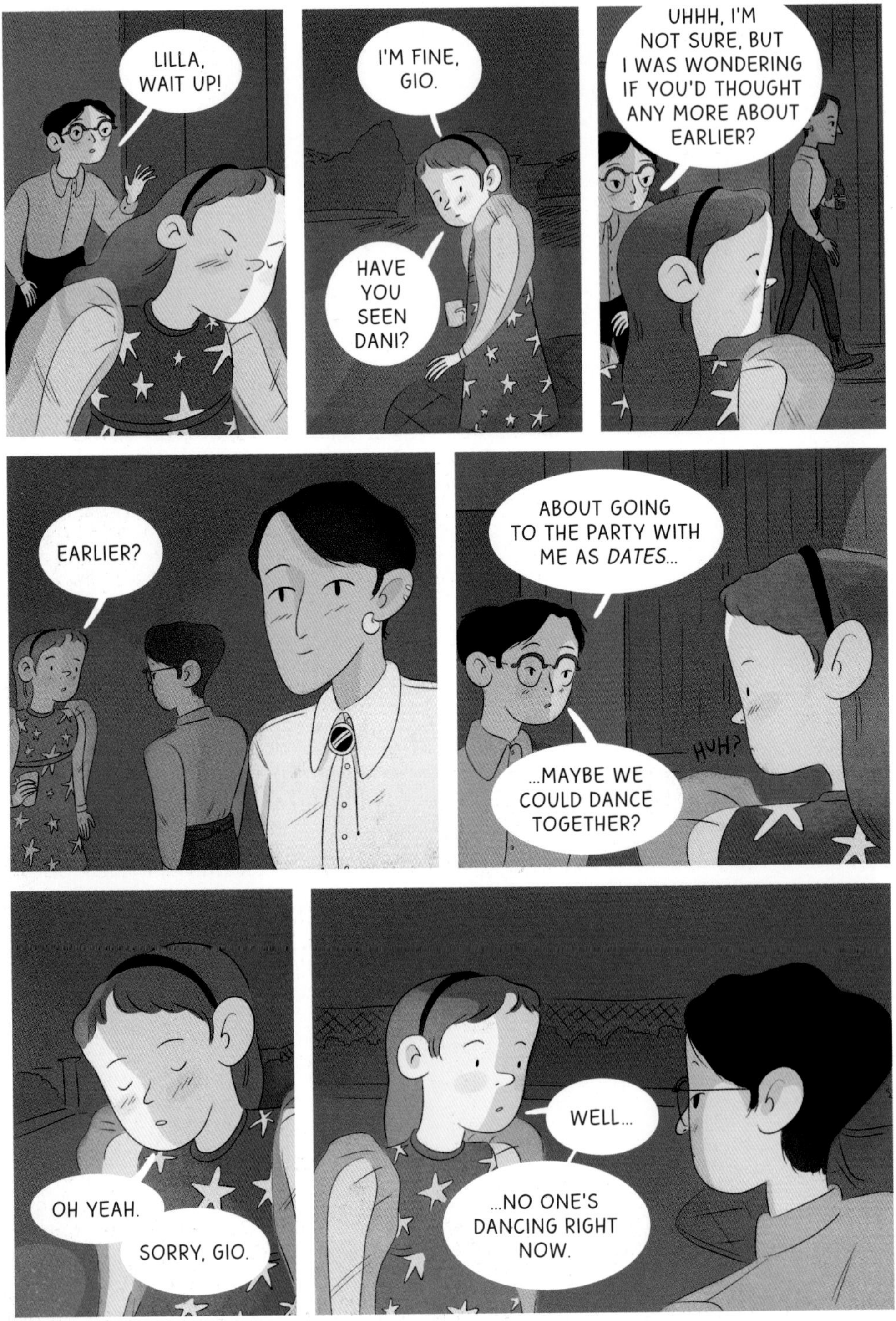
LILLA, WAIT UP!
I'M FINE, GIO.
HAVE YOU SEEN DANI?
UHHH, I'M NOT SURE, BUT I WAS WONDERING IF YOU'D THOUGHT ANY MORE ABOUT EARLIER?
EARLIER?
ABOUT GOING TO THE PARTY WITH ME AS *DATES*...
...MAYBE WE COULD DANCE TOGETHER?
HUH?
OH YEAH.
SORRY, GIO.
WELL...
...NO ONE'S DANCING RIGHT NOW.

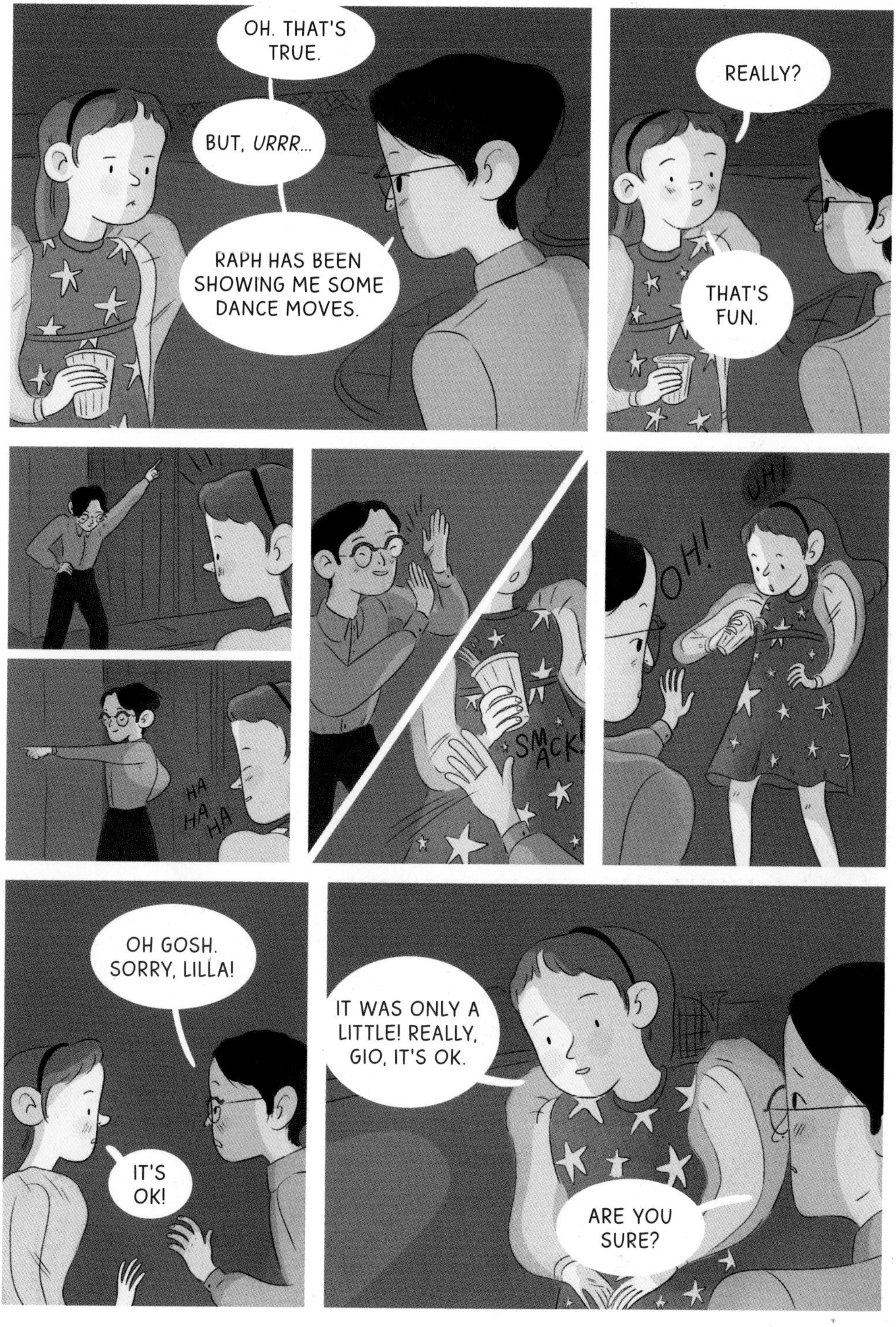
OH. THAT'S TRUE.
BUT, *URRR...*
RAPH HAS BEEN SHOWING ME SOME DANCE MOVES.
REALLY?
THAT'S FUN.
HA HA HA
SMACK!
OH!
UH!
OH GOSH. SORRY, LILLA!
IT'S OK!
IT WAS ONLY A LITTLE! REALLY, GIO, IT'S OK.
ARE YOU SURE?

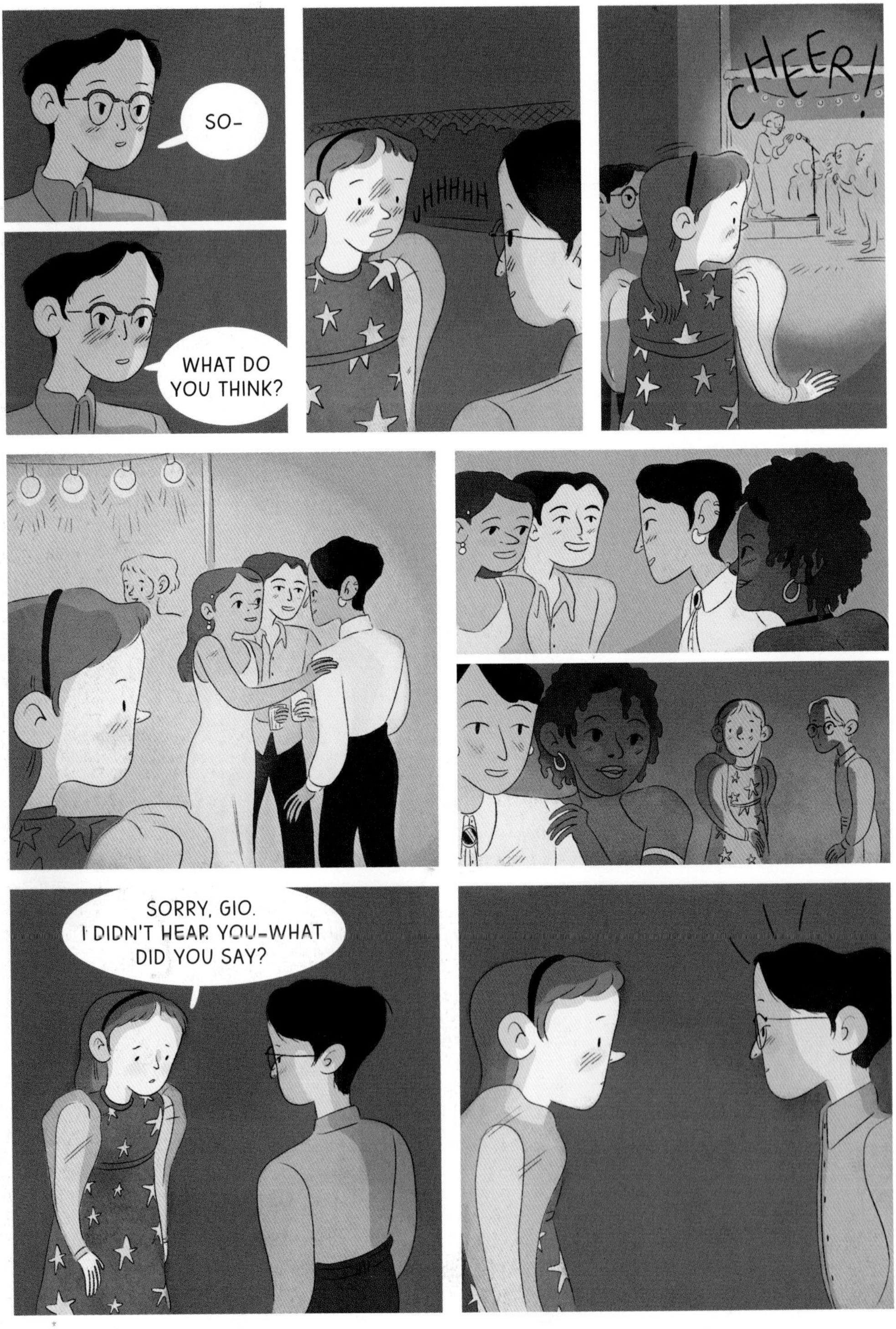
SO-
WHAT DO YOU THINK?
UHHHHH
CHEER!
SORRY, GIO. I DIDN'T HEAR YOU–WHAT DID YOU SAY?

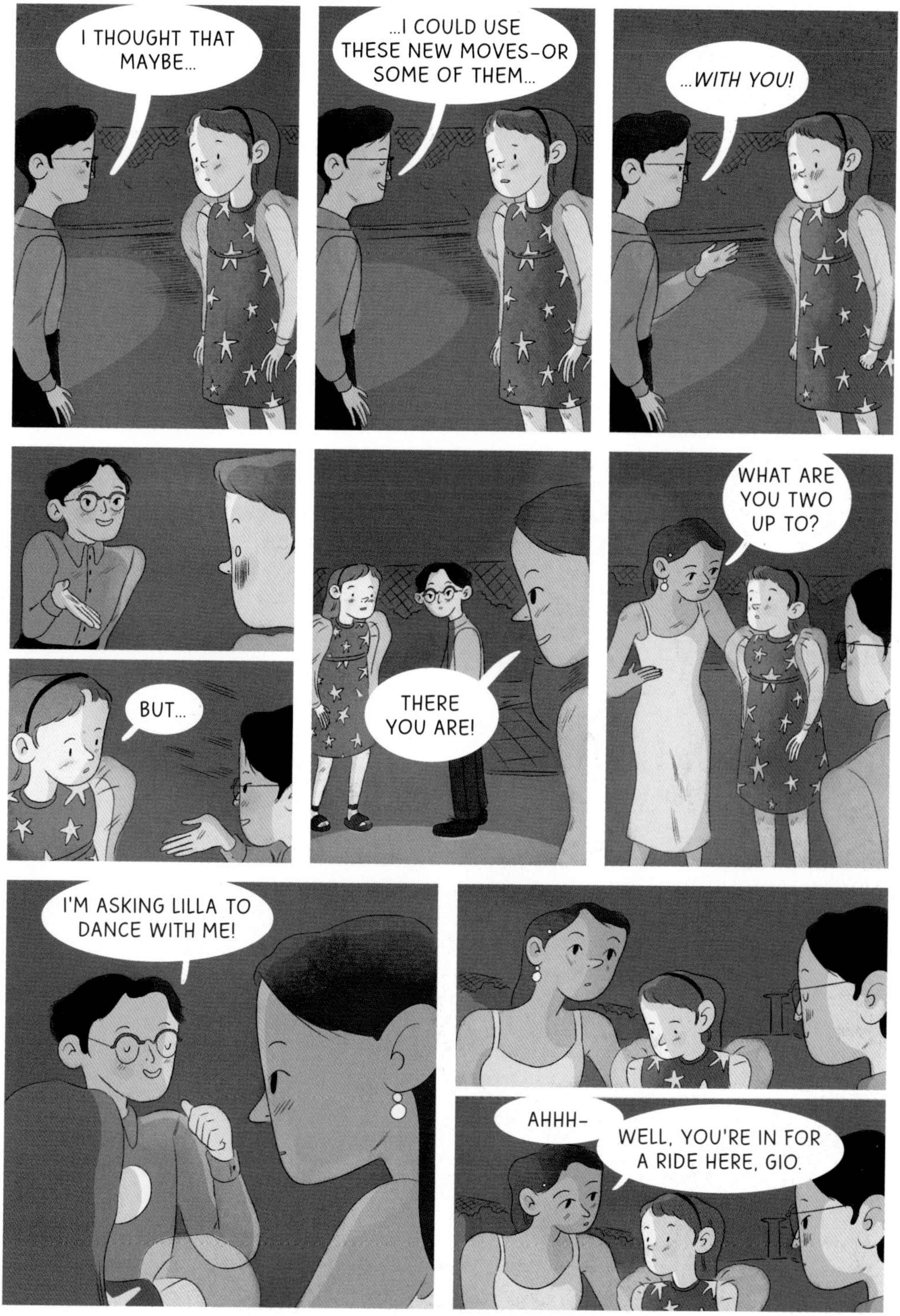
I THOUGHT THAT MAYBE...
...I COULD USE THESE NEW MOVES-OR SOME OF THEM...
...WITH YOU!
BUT...
THERE YOU ARE!
WHAT ARE YOU TWO UP TO?
I'M ASKING LILLA TO DANCE WITH ME!
AHHH-
WELL, YOU'RE IN FOR A RIDE HERE, GIO.

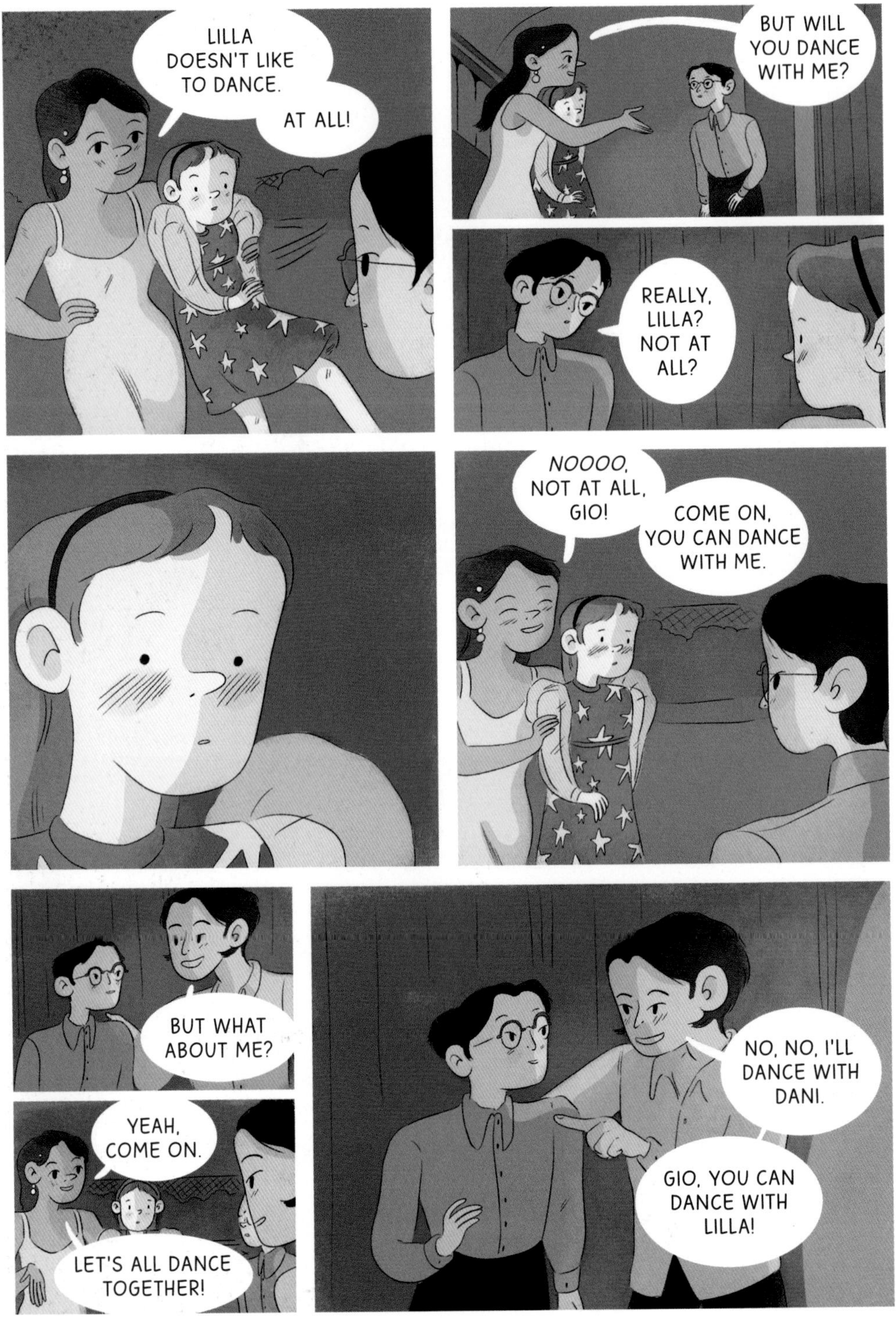
LILLA DOESN'T LIKE TO DANCE.
AT ALL!
BUT WILL YOU DANCE WITH ME?
REALLY, LILLA? NOT AT ALL?
NOOOO, NOT AT ALL, GIO!
COME ON, YOU CAN DANCE WITH ME.
BUT WHAT ABOUT ME?
YEAH, COME ON.
LET'S ALL DANCE TOGETHER!
NO, NO, I'LL DANCE WITH DANI.
GIO, YOU CAN DANCE WITH LILLA!

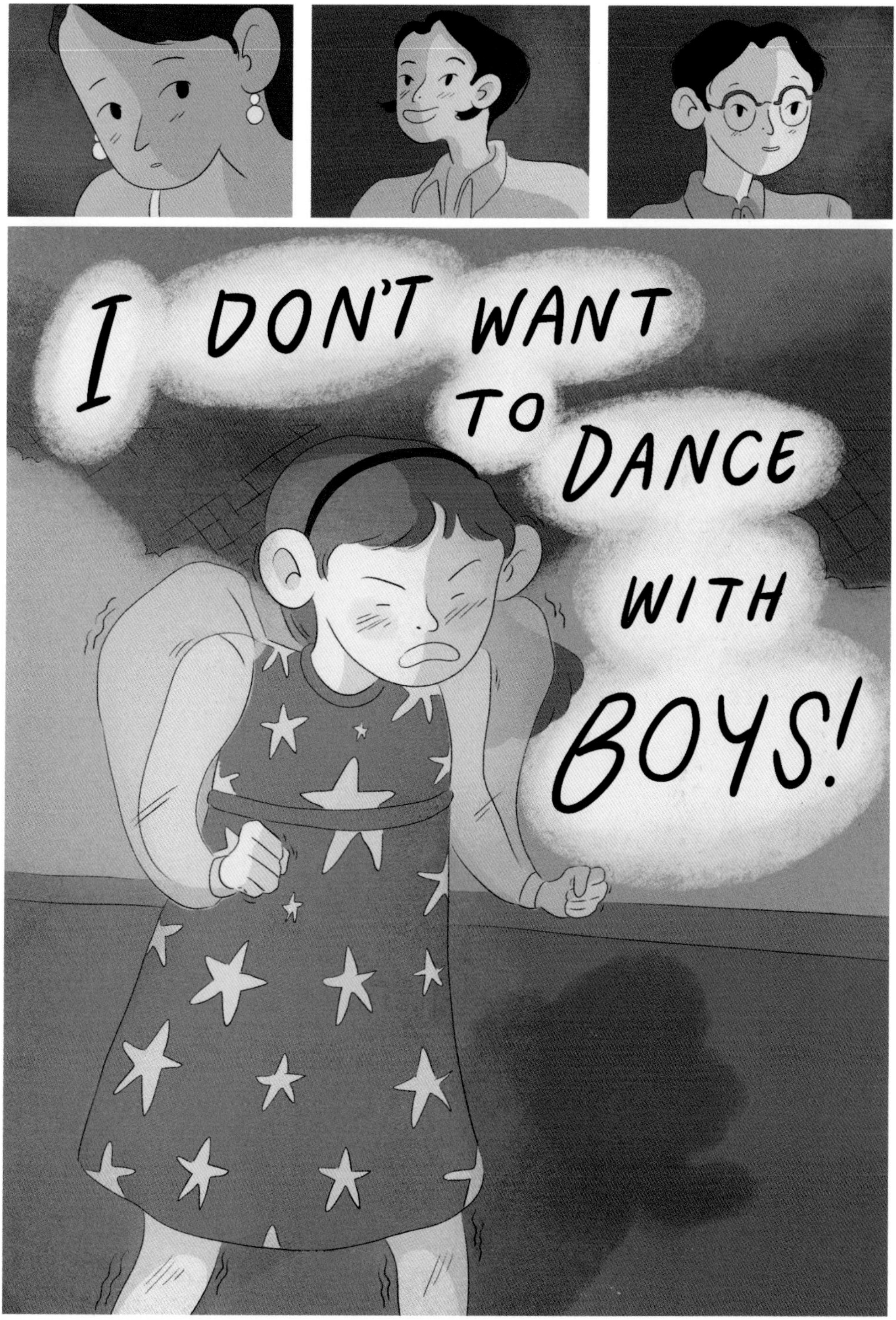
I DON'T WANT TO DANCE WITH BOYS!

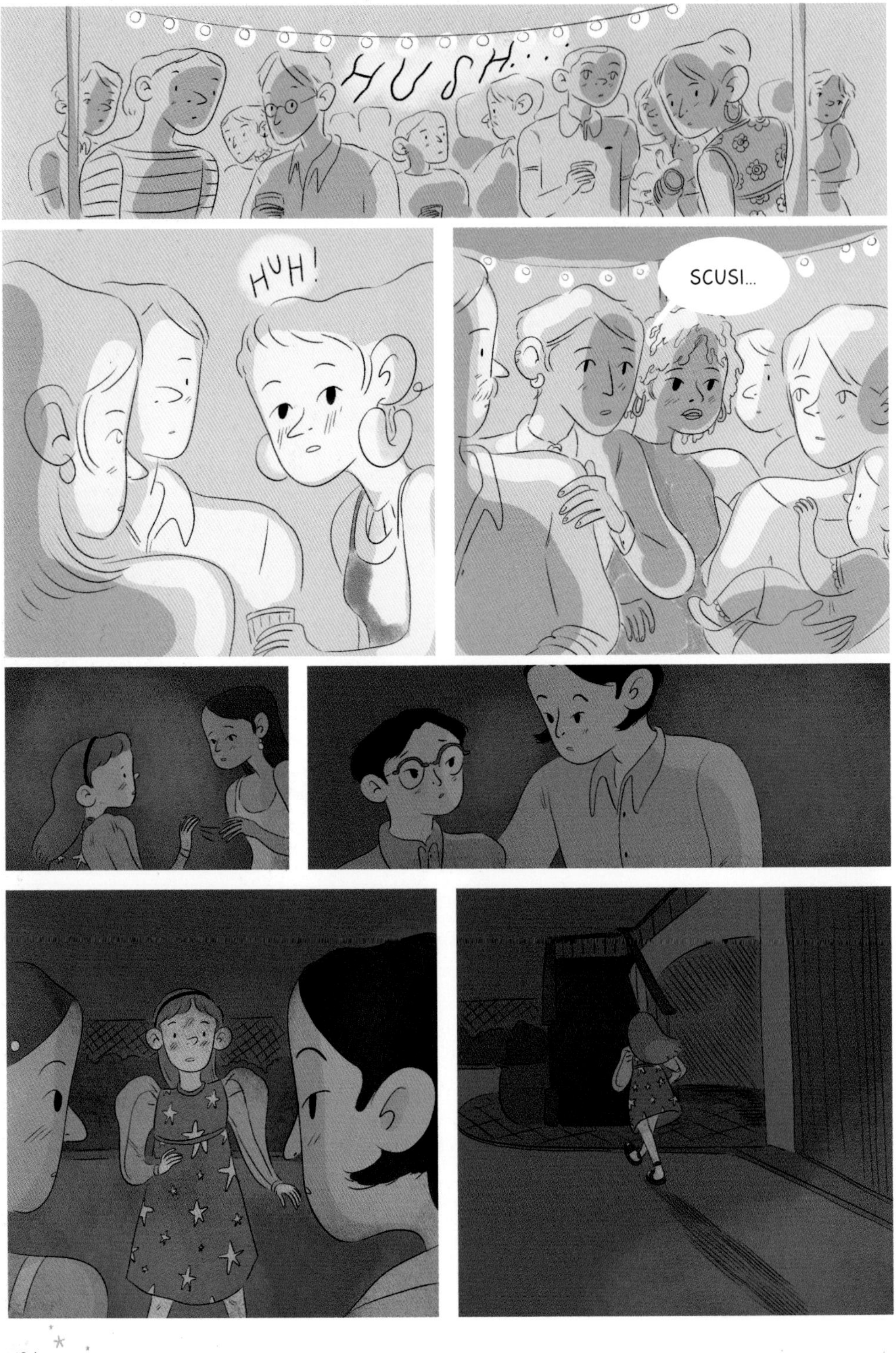
HUSH...
HUH!
SCUSI...

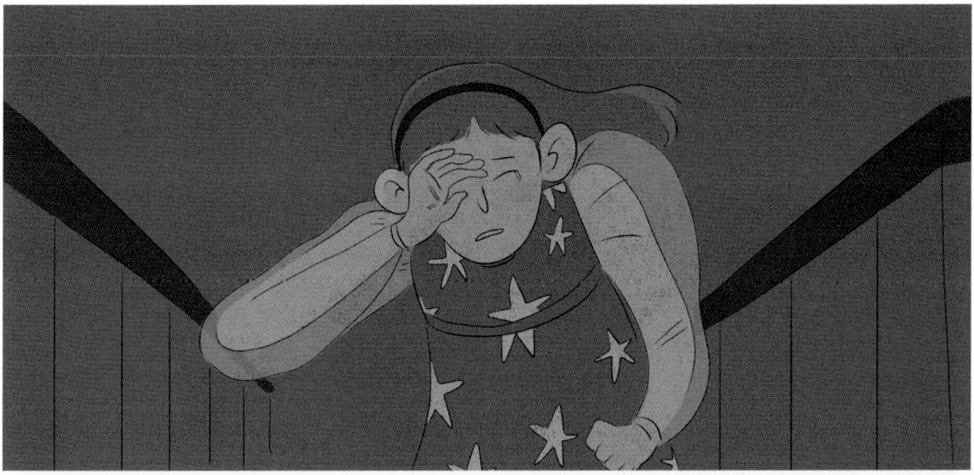

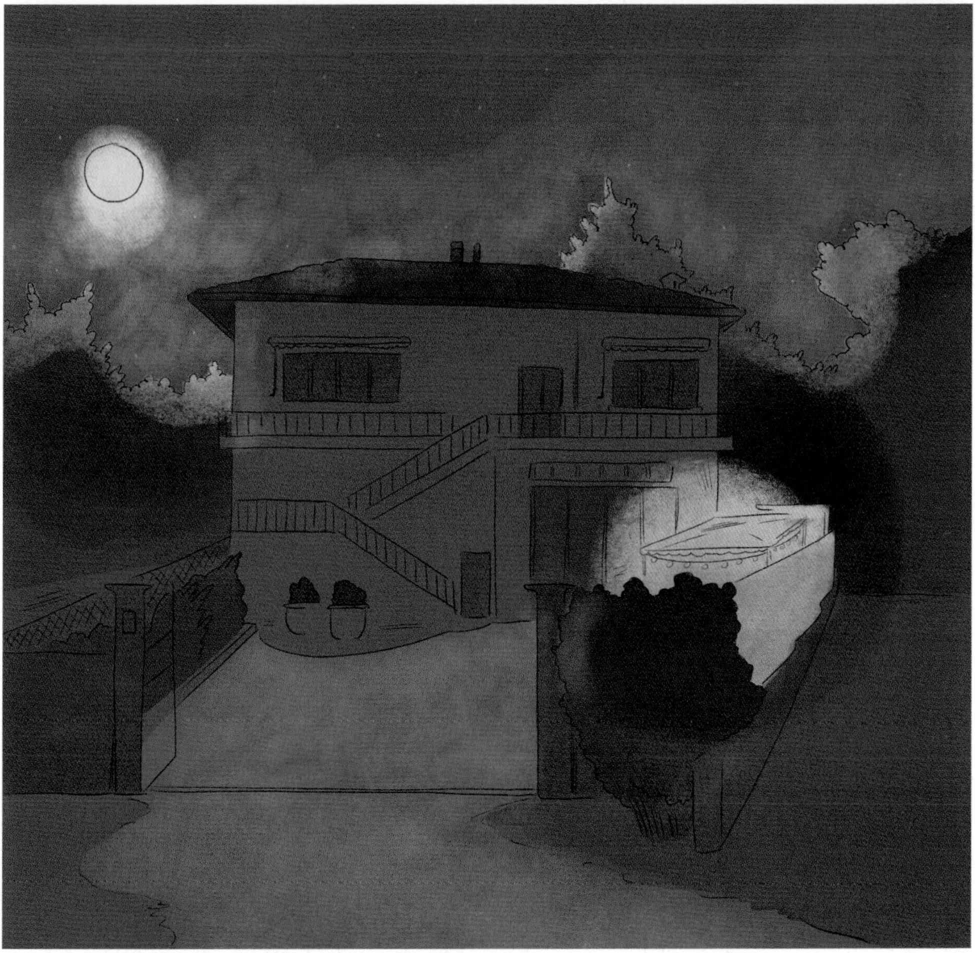

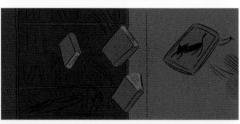

WHERE IS IT?!

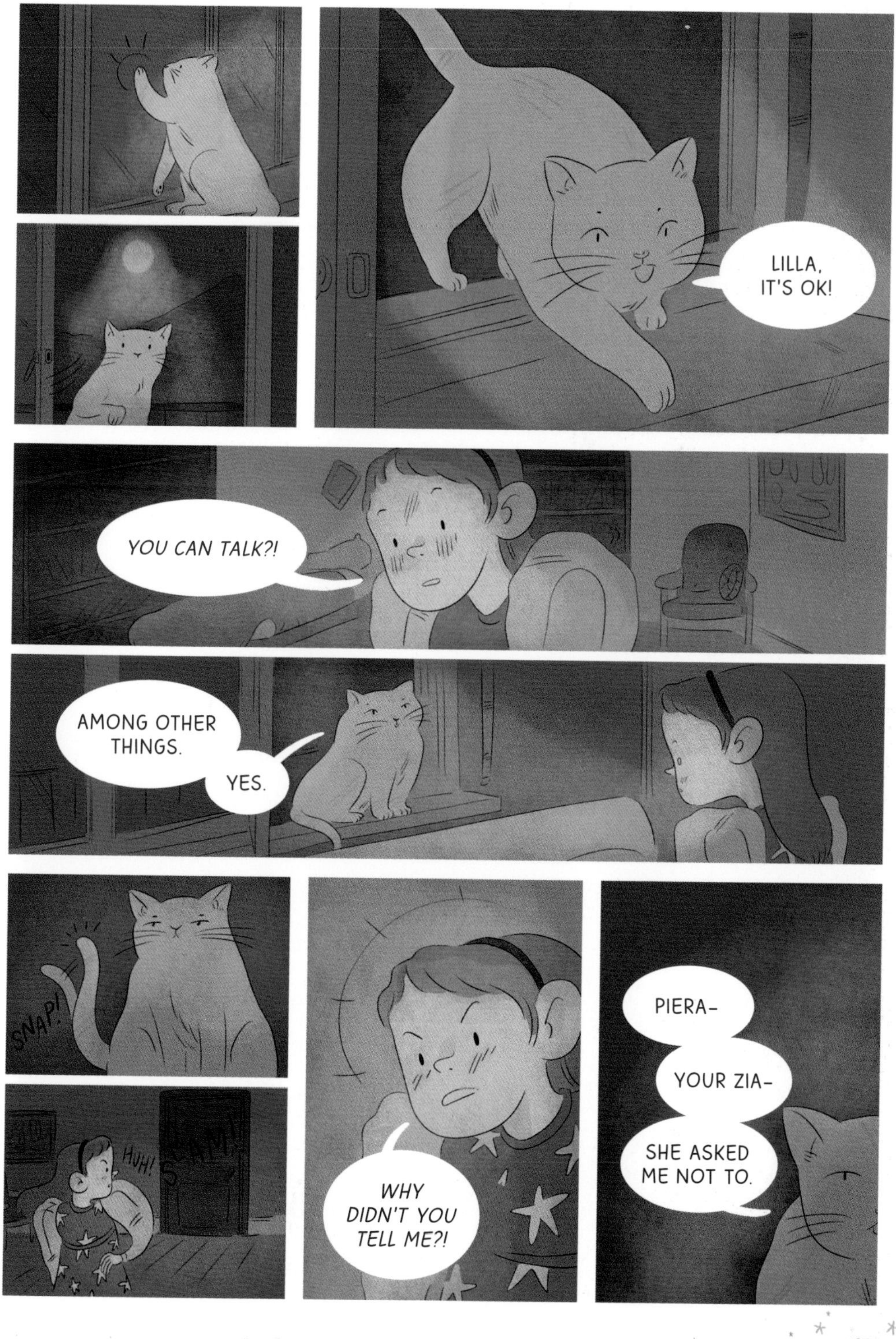
LILLA, IT'S OK!
YOU CAN TALK?!
AMONG OTHER THINGS.
YES.
SNAP!
HUH!
SLAM!
WHY DIDN'T YOU TELL ME?!
PIERA-
YOUR ZIA-
SHE ASKED ME NOT TO.

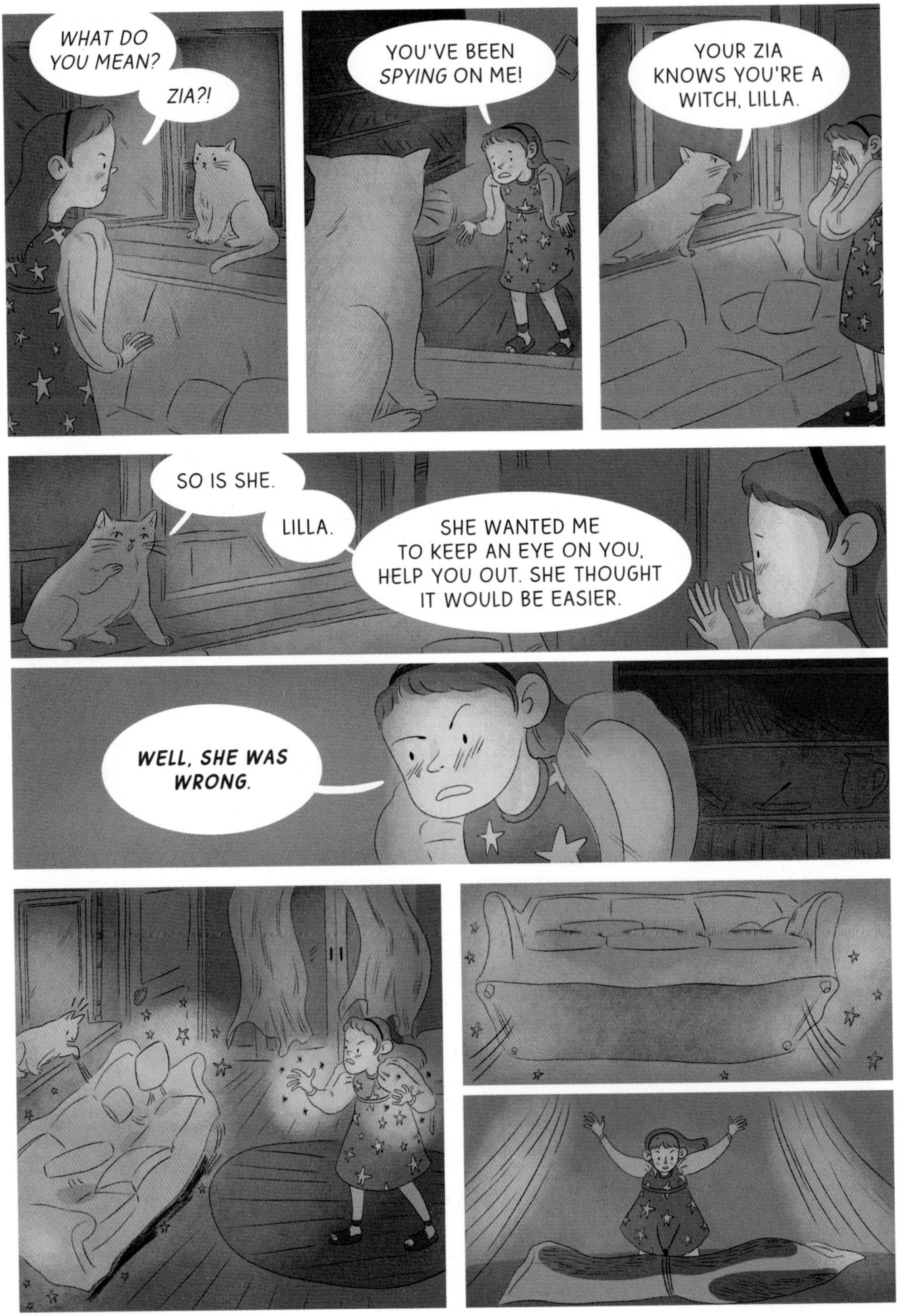

WHAT DO YOU MEAN?
ZIA?!
YOU'VE BEEN *SPYING* ON ME!
YOUR ZIA KNOWS YOU'RE A WITCH, LILLA.
SO IS SHE.
LILLA.
SHE WANTED ME TO KEEP AN EYE ON YOU, HELP YOU OUT. SHE THOUGHT IT WOULD BE EASIER.
WELL, SHE WAS WRONG.

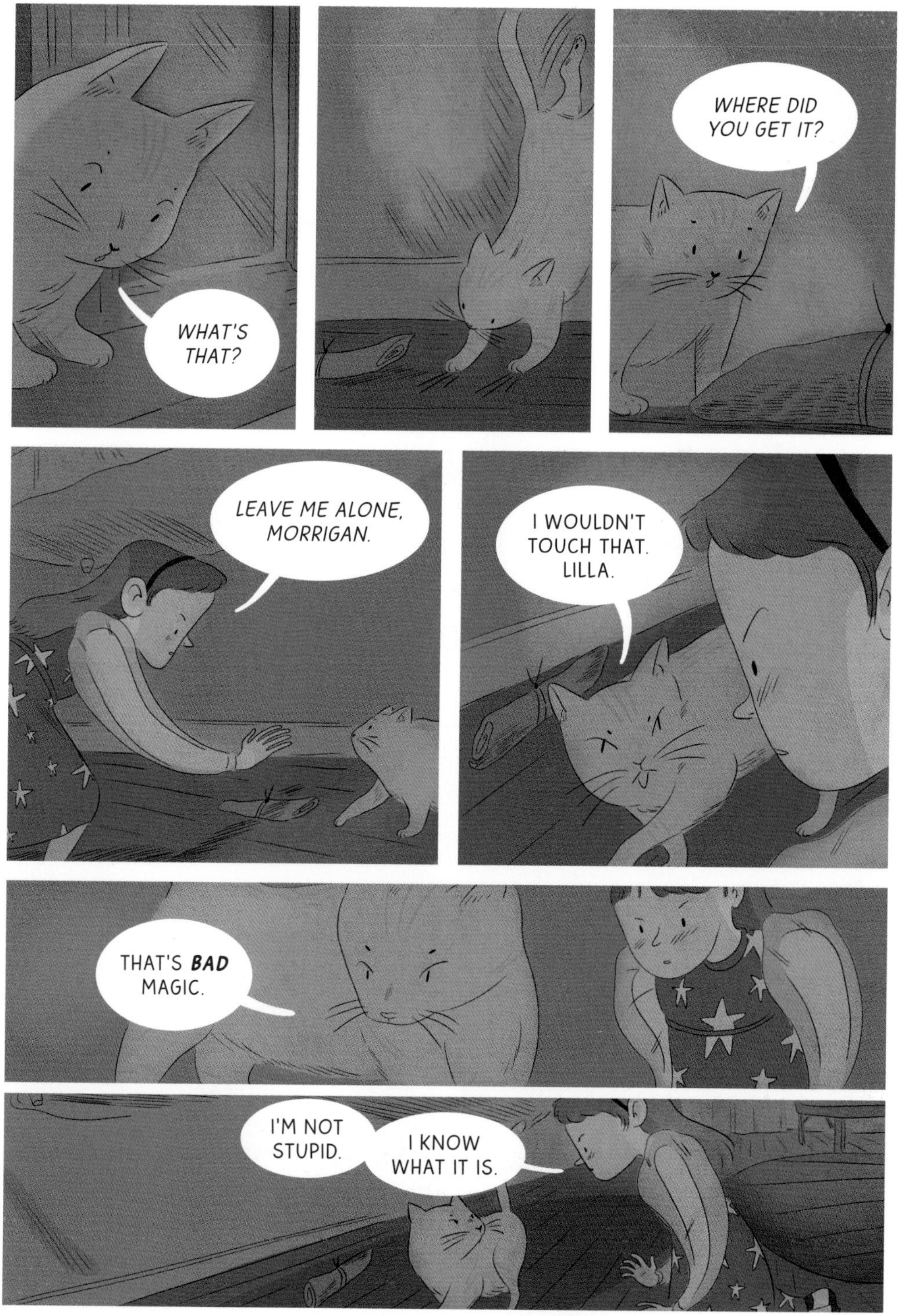
WHAT'S THAT?
WHERE DID YOU GET IT?
LEAVE ME ALONE, MORRIGAN.
I WOULDN'T TOUCH THAT. LILLA.
THAT'S **BAD** MAGIC.
I'M NOT STUPID.
I KNOW WHAT IT IS.

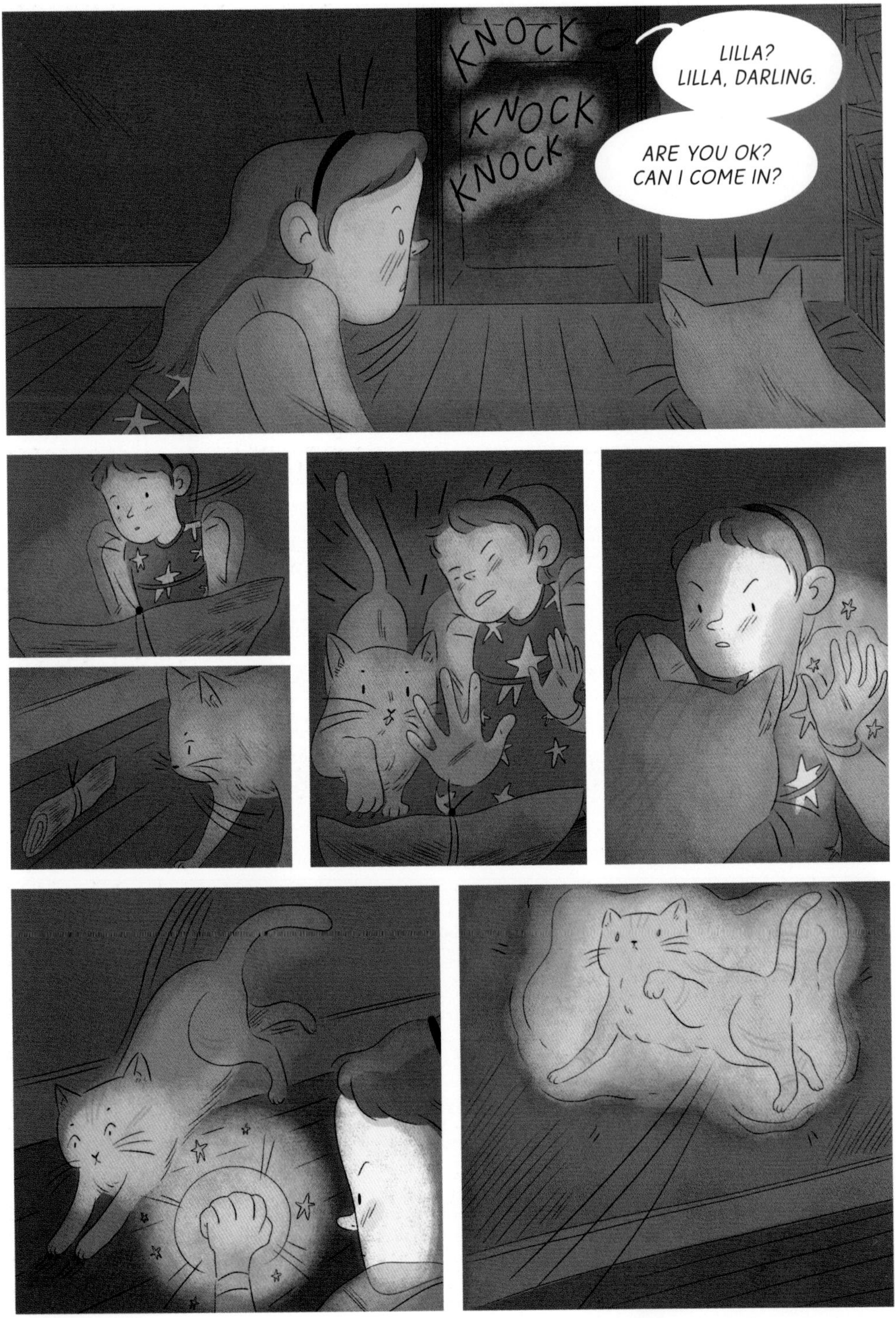
KNOCK
KNOCK
KNOCK
LILLA?
LILLA, DARLING.
ARE YOU OK?
CAN I COME IN?

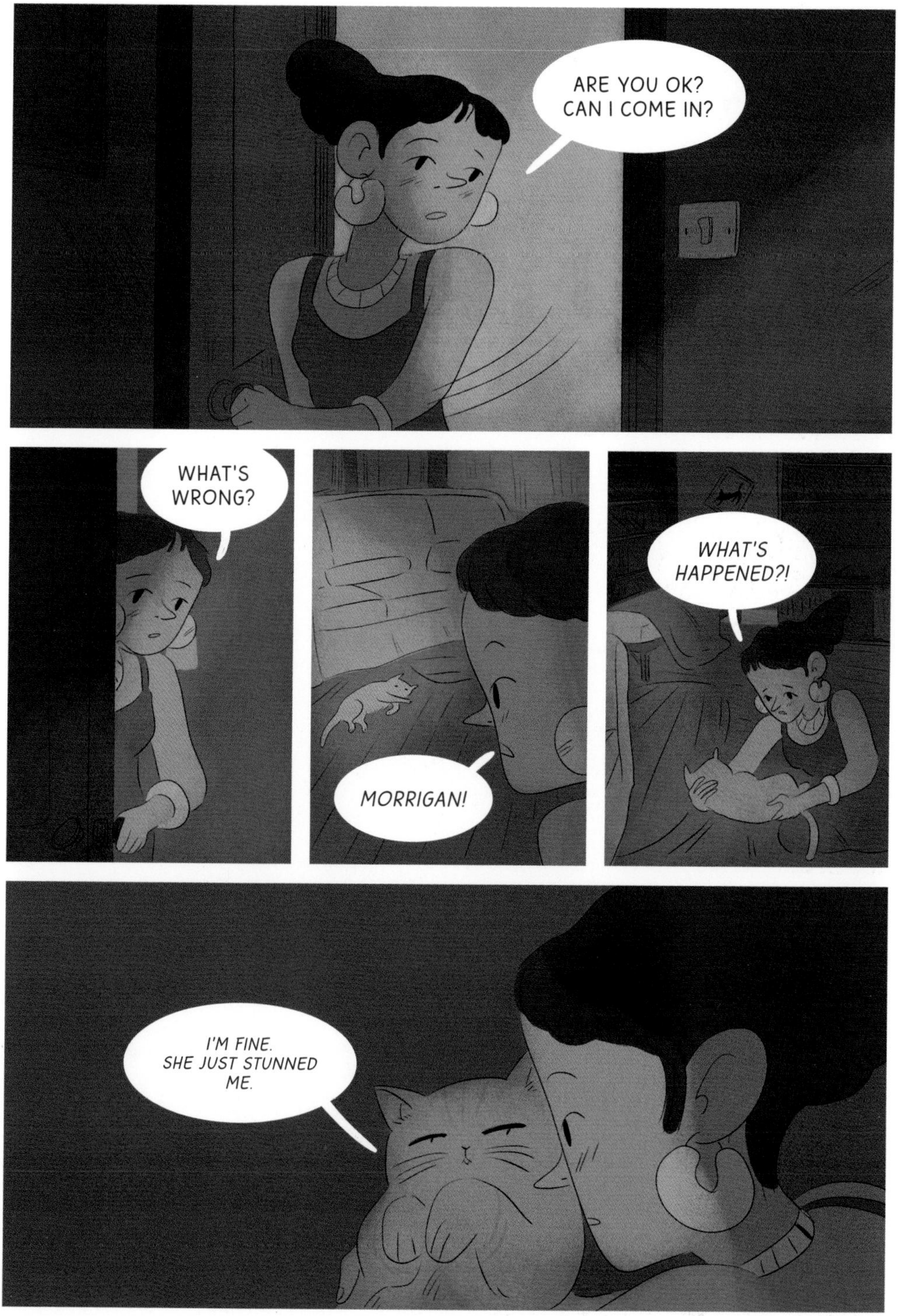
ARE YOU OK?
CAN I COME IN?
WHAT'S WRONG?
MORRIGAN!
WHAT'S HAPPENED?!
I'M FINE. SHE JUST STUNNED ME.

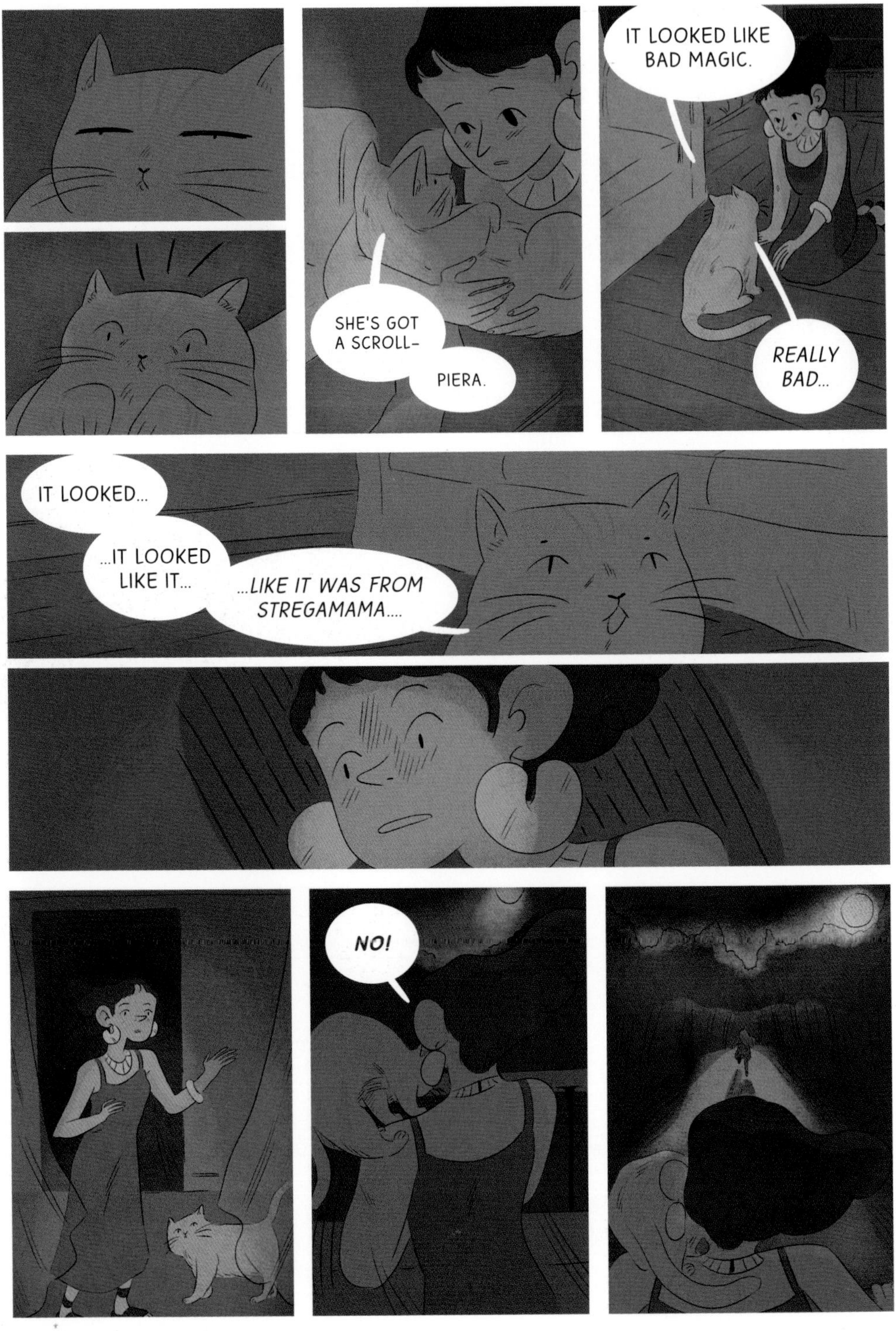
SHE'S GOT A SCROLL–
PIERA.
IT LOOKED LIKE BAD MAGIC.
REALLY BAD...
IT LOOKED...
...IT LOOKED LIKE IT...
...LIKE IT WAS FROM STREGAMAMA....
NO!

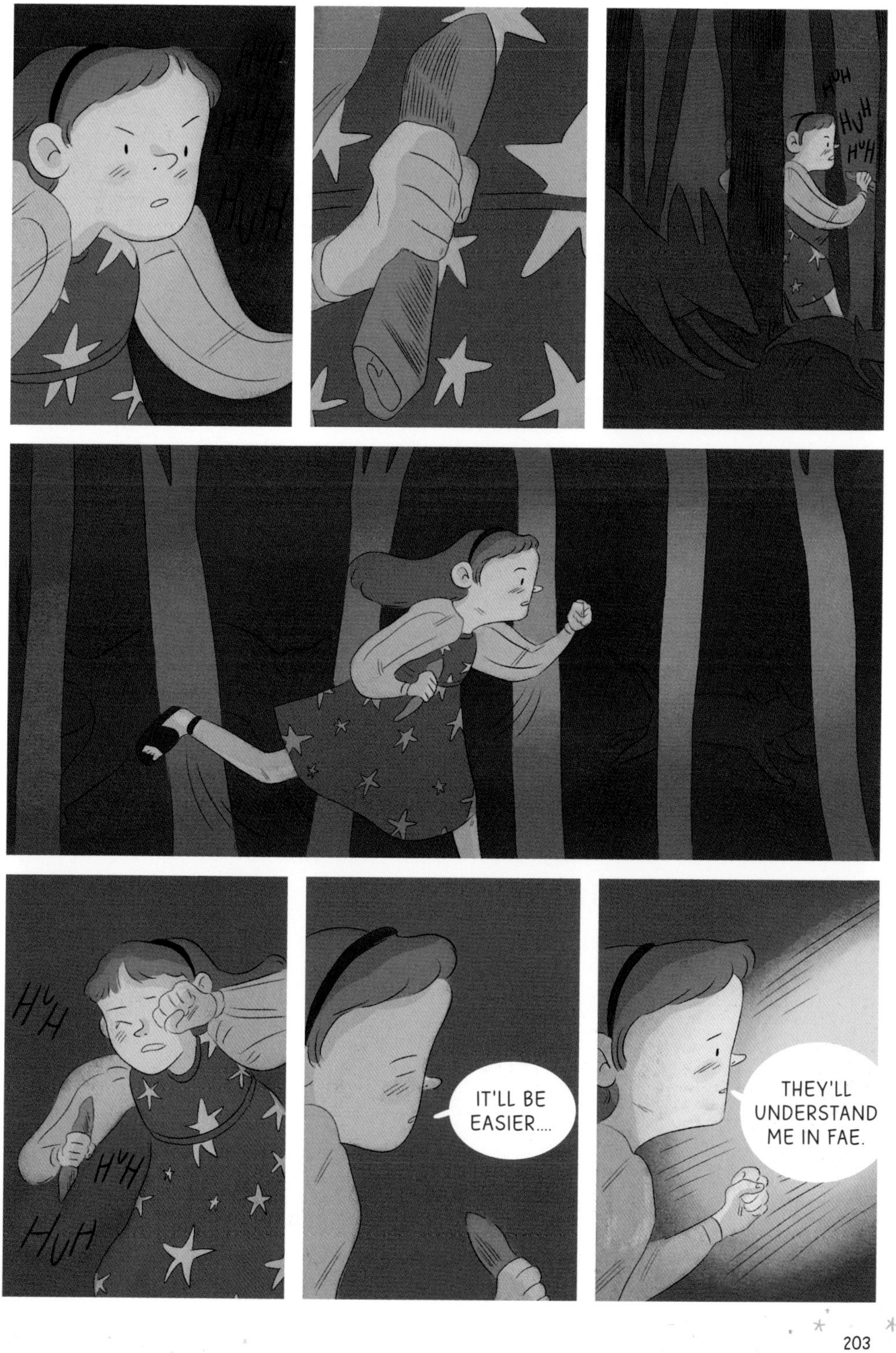
HUH
HUH
HUH
HUH
HUH
HUH
HUH
HUH
HUH
IT'LL BE EASIER....
THEY'LL UNDERSTAND ME IN FAE.

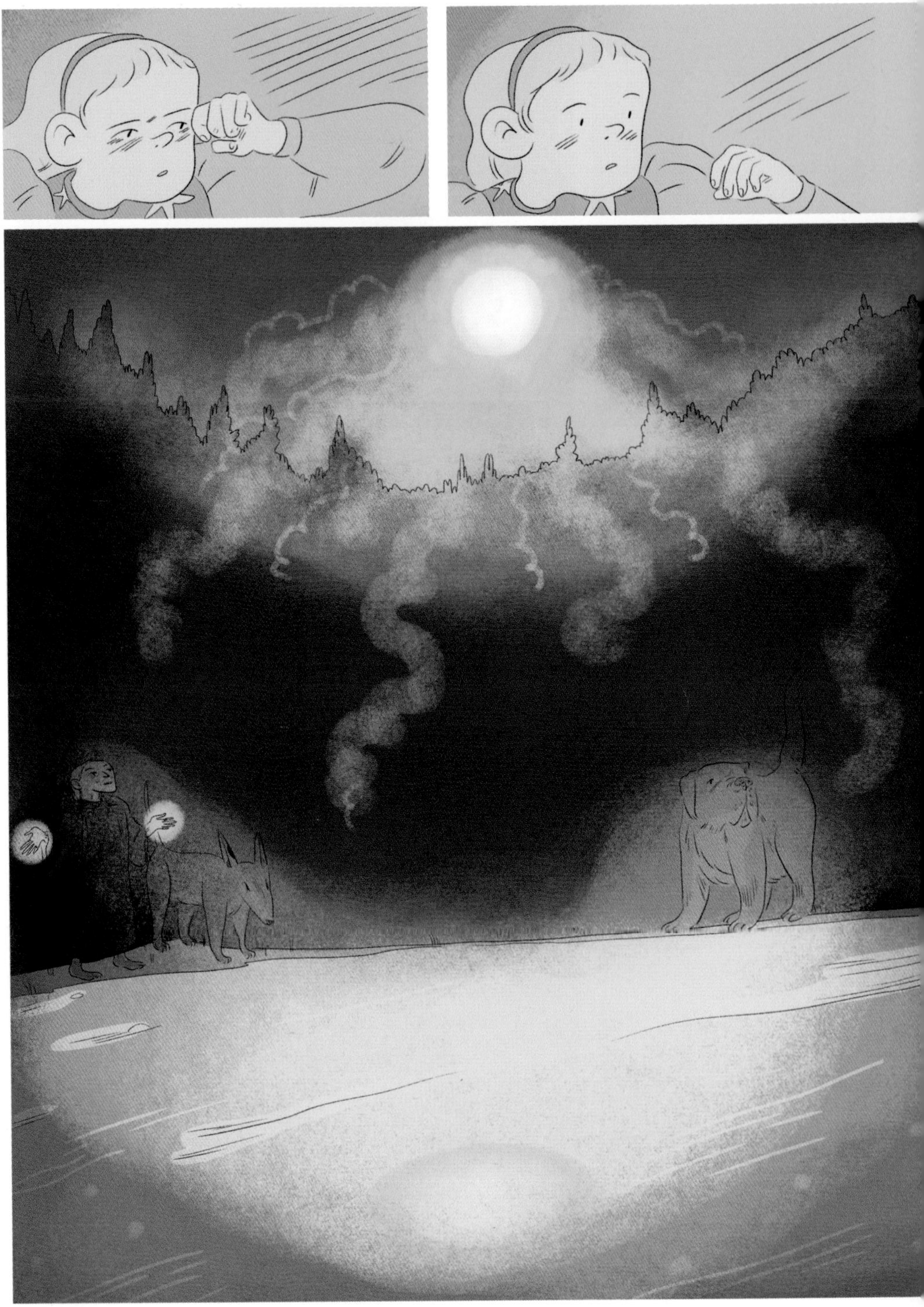

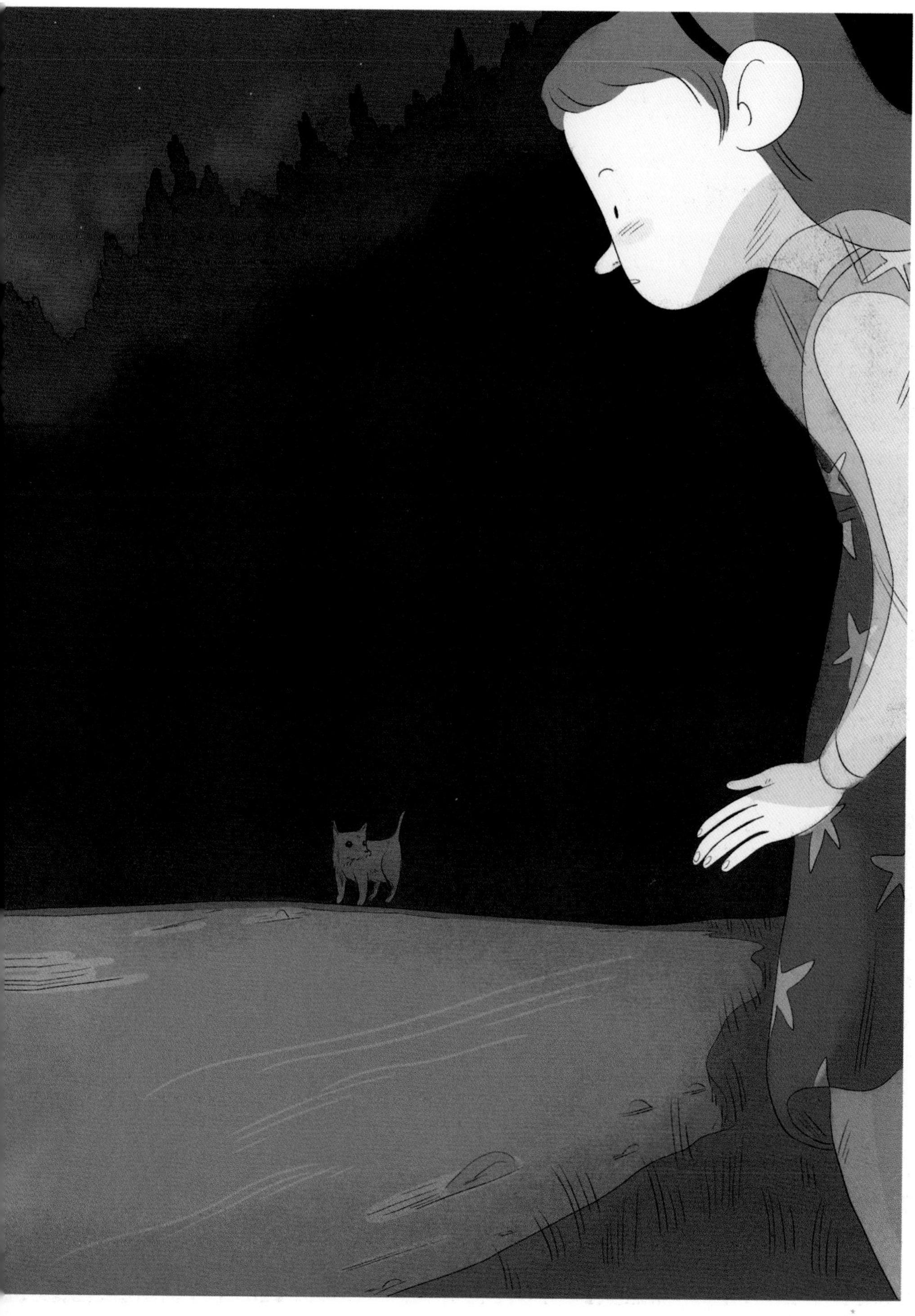

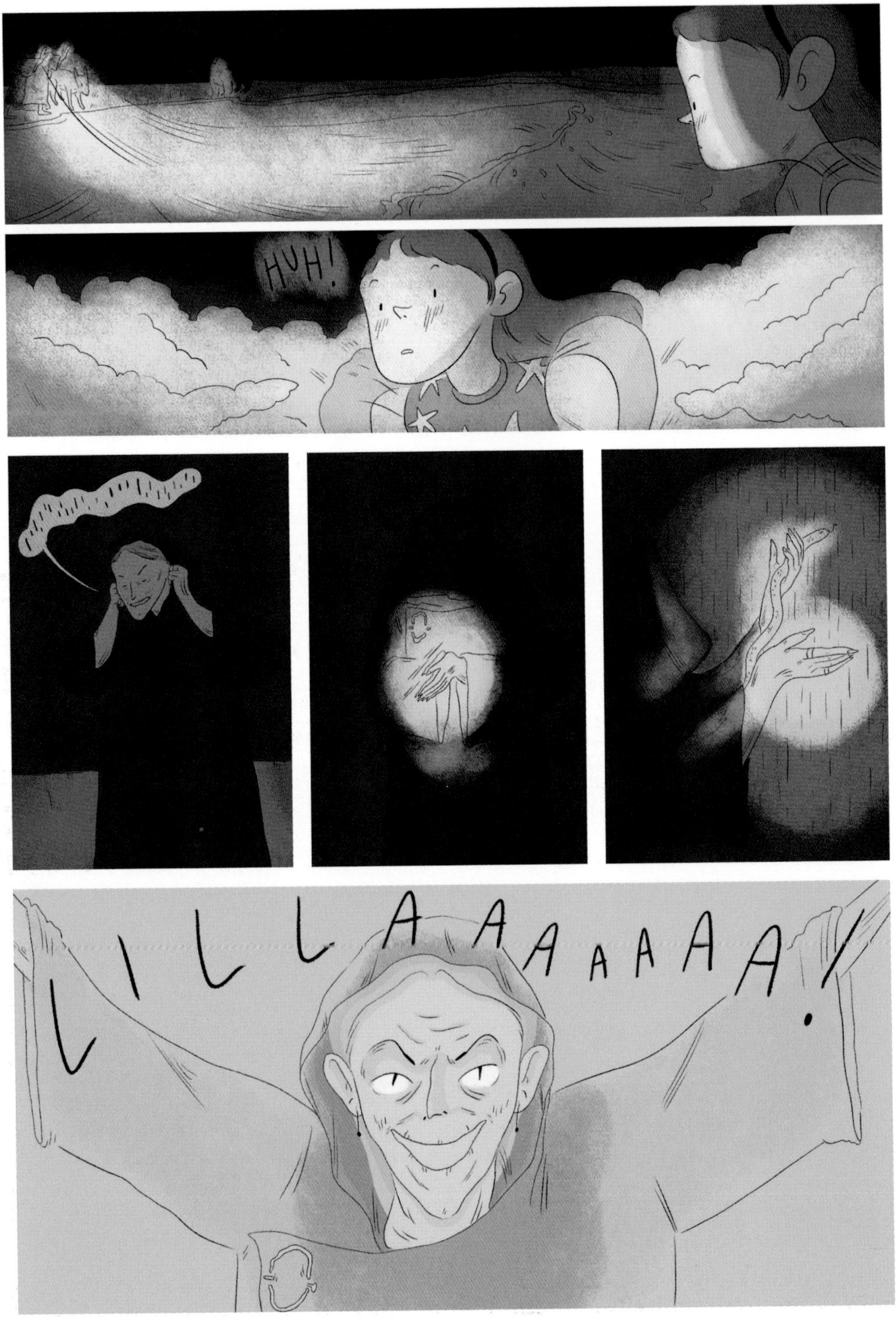
HUH!
LILLAAAAAAA!

WE
HAVE
BEEN
WAITING!

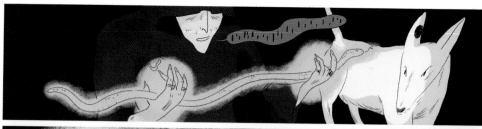

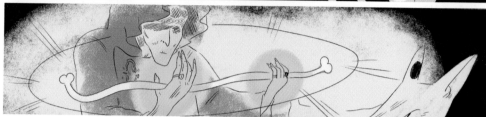

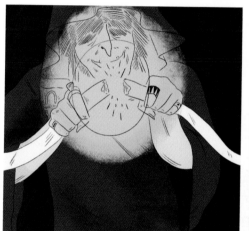

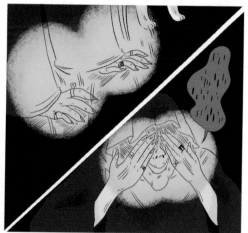

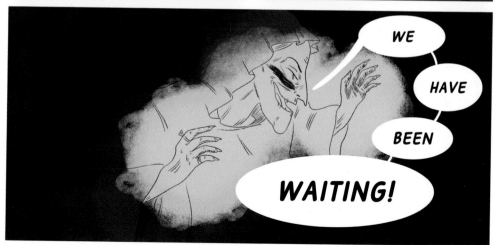

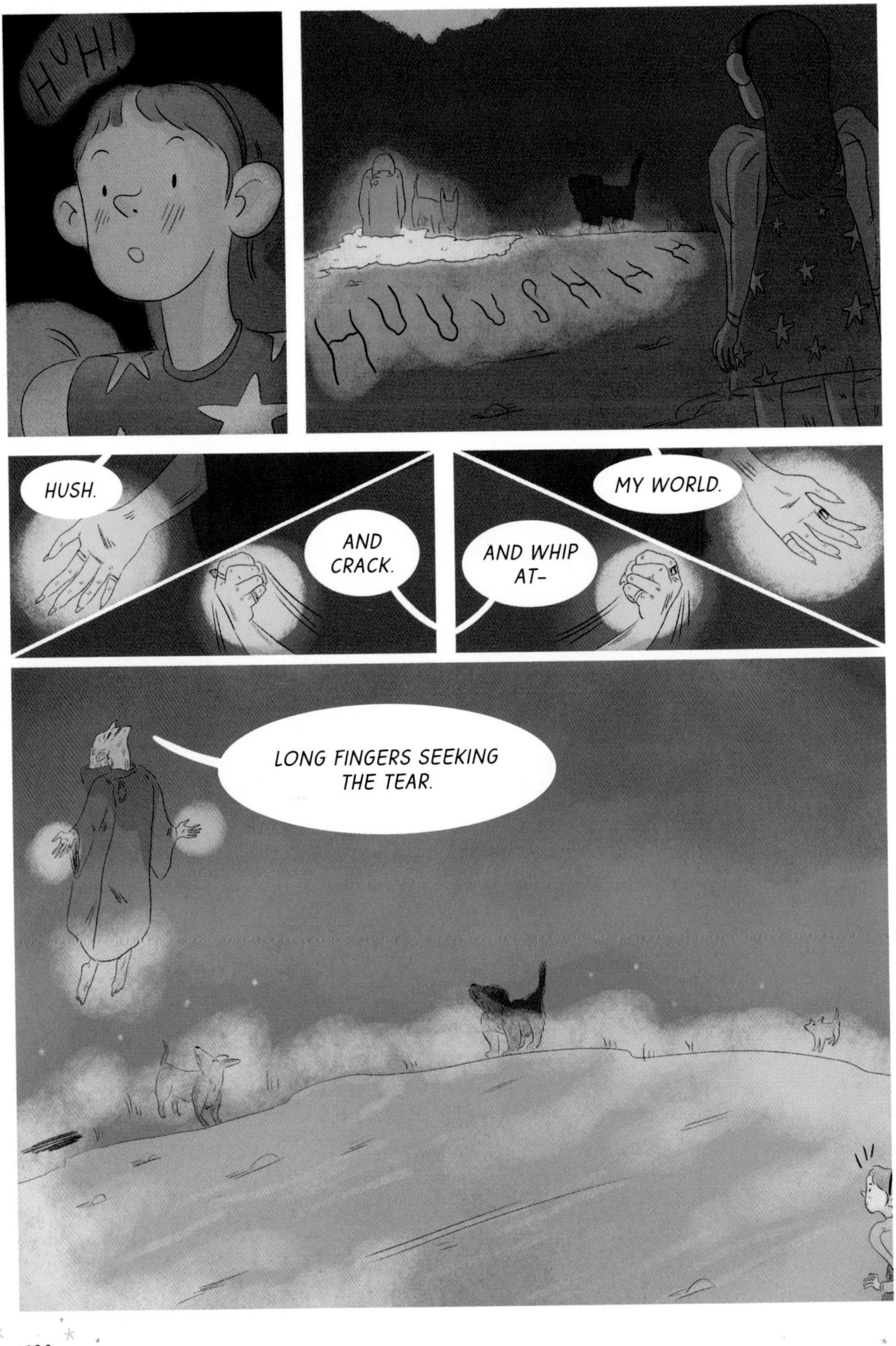
HUH!
HUUUSHHH
HUSH.
AND CRACK.
AND WHIP AT-
MY WORLD.
LONG FINGERS SEEKING THE TEAR.

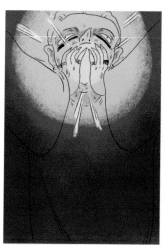
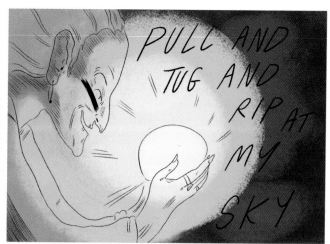

PULL AND TUG AND RIP AT MY SKY

I CALL TO YOU

MOTHER

MY CHILD

SHALL PASS THROUGH YOU!

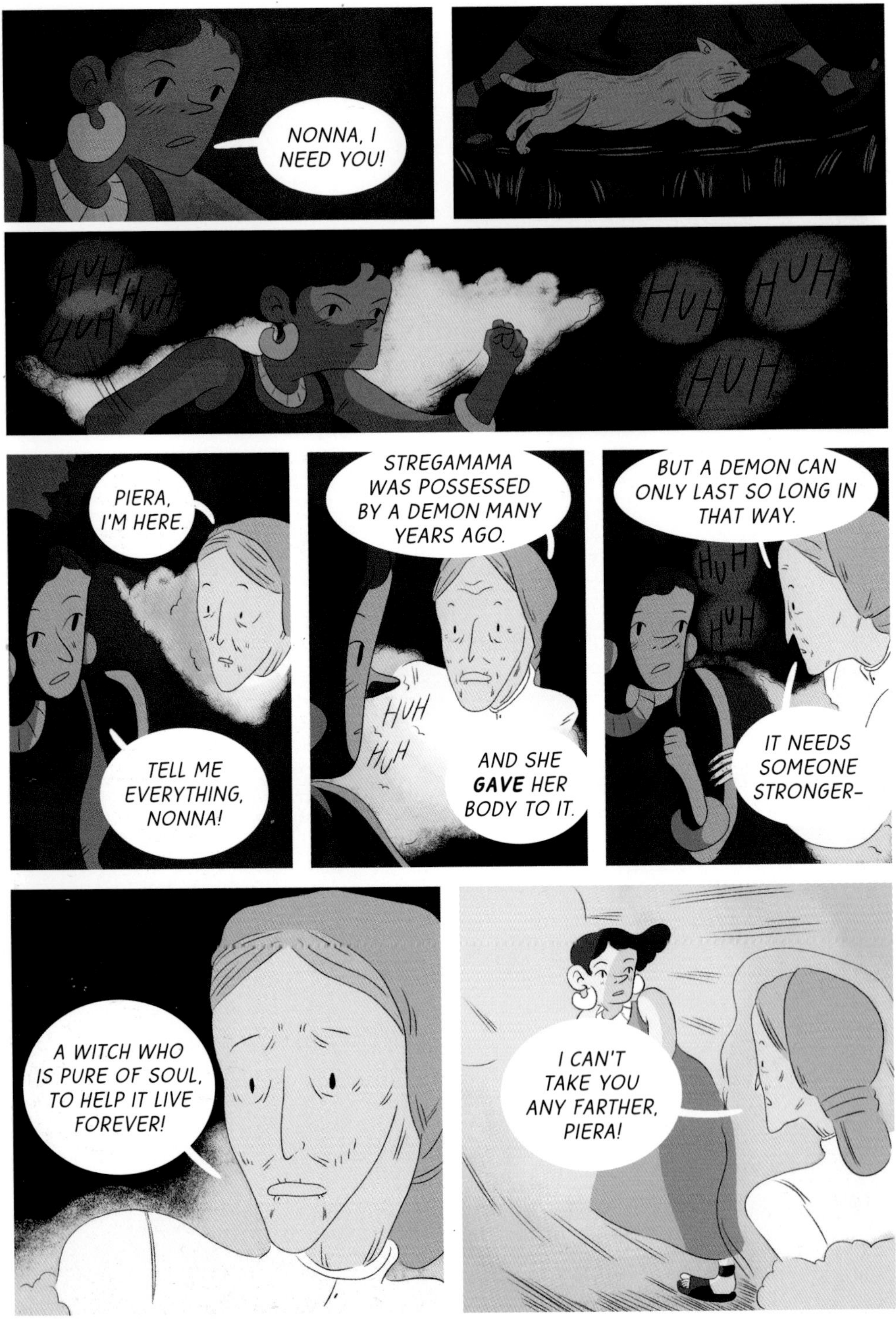
NONNA, I NEED YOU!
HUH HUH HUH HUH
HUH HUH HUH
PIERA, I'M HERE.
TELL ME EVERYTHING, NONNA!
STREGAMAMA WAS POSSESSED BY A DEMON MANY YEARS AGO.
HUH HUH
AND SHE **GAVE** HER BODY TO IT.
BUT A DEMON CAN ONLY LAST SO LONG IN THAT WAY.
HUH HUH
IT NEEDS SOMEONE STRONGER-
A WITCH WHO IS PURE OF SOUL, TO HELP IT LIVE FOREVER!
I CAN'T TAKE YOU ANY FARTHER, PIERA!

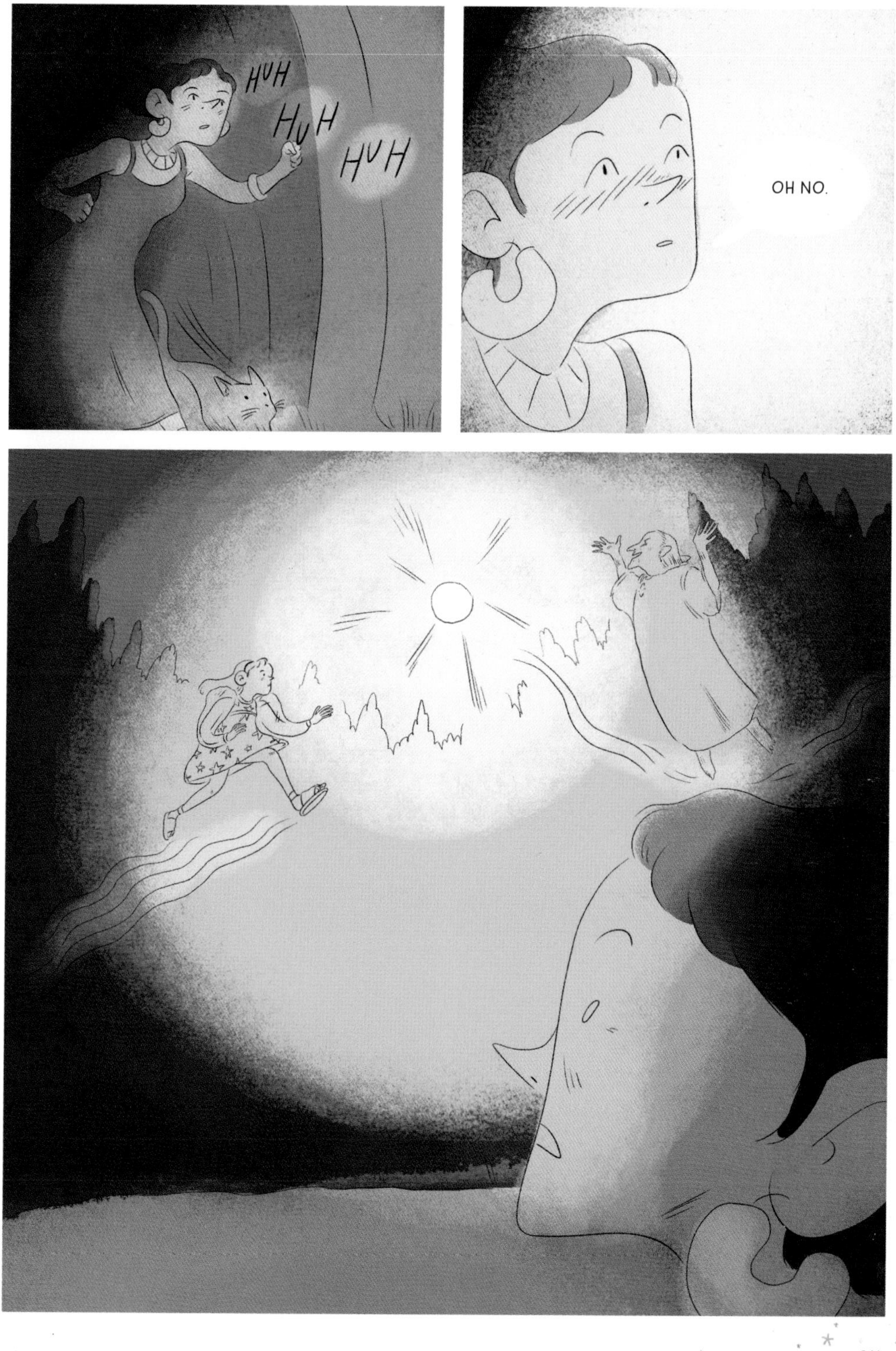
HUH
HUH
HUH
OH NO.

HUH!

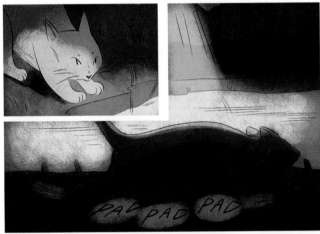

PAD PAD PAD

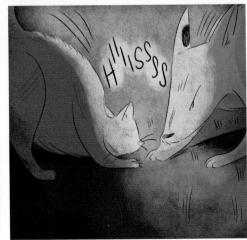

H'ISSSS

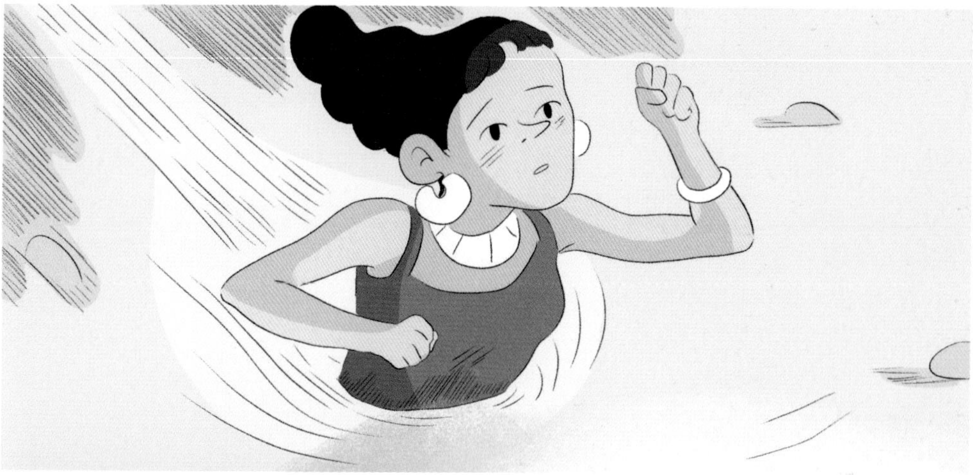
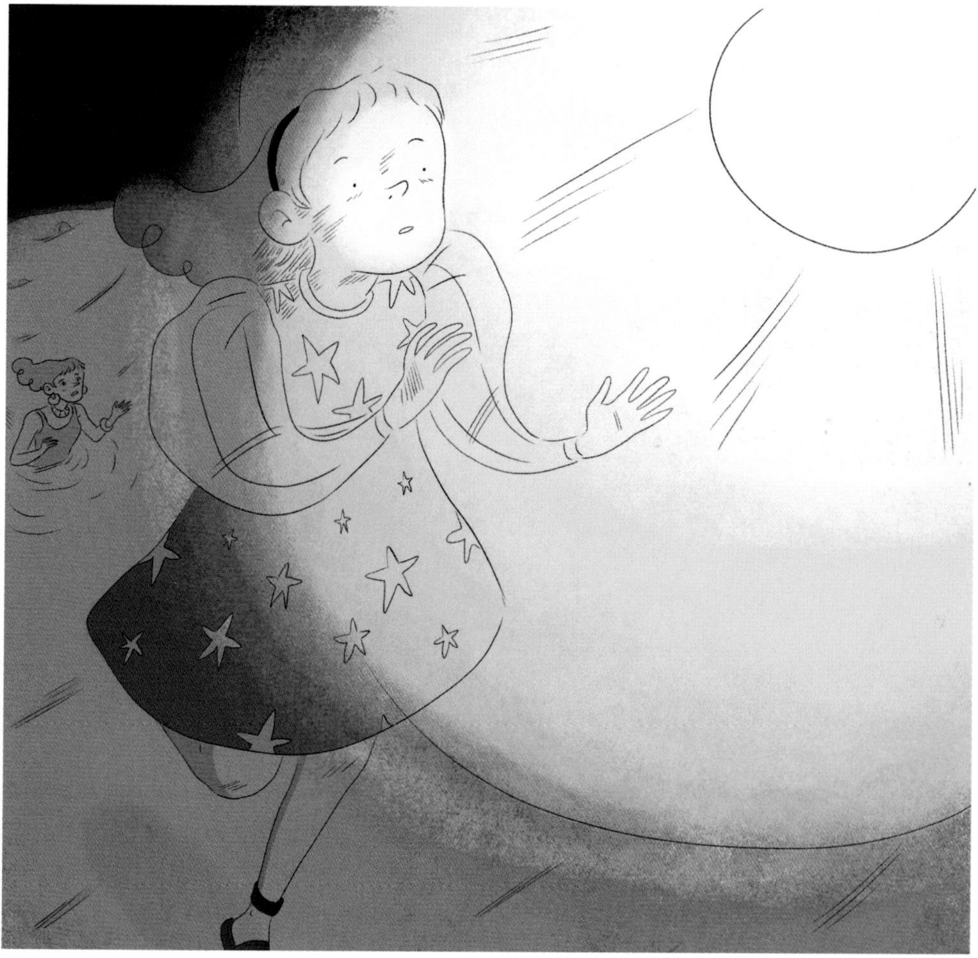

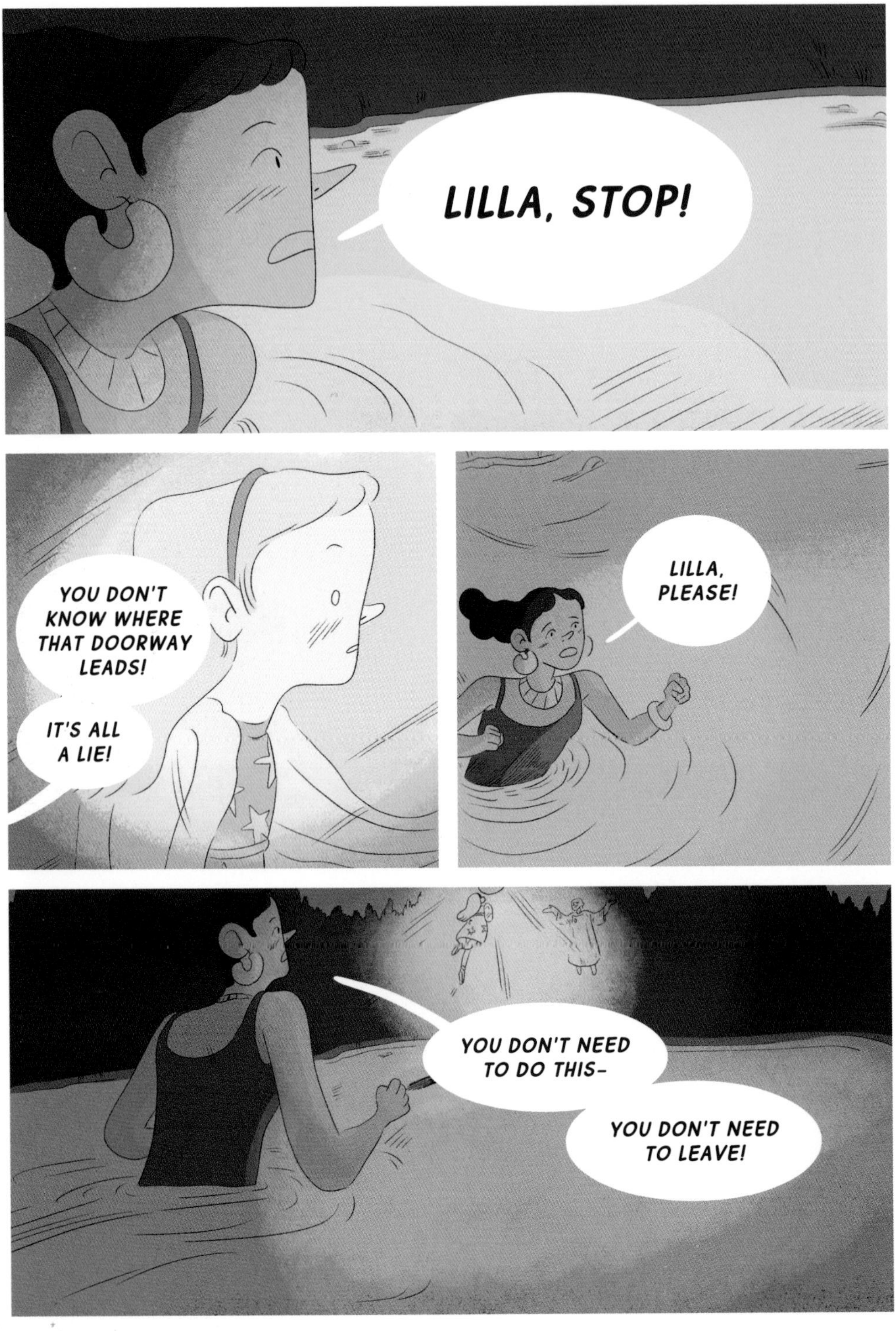
LILLA, STOP!
YOU DON'T KNOW WHERE THAT DOORWAY LEADS!
IT'S ALL A LIE!
LILLA, PLEASE!
YOU DON'T NEED TO DO THIS-
YOU DON'T NEED TO LEAVE!

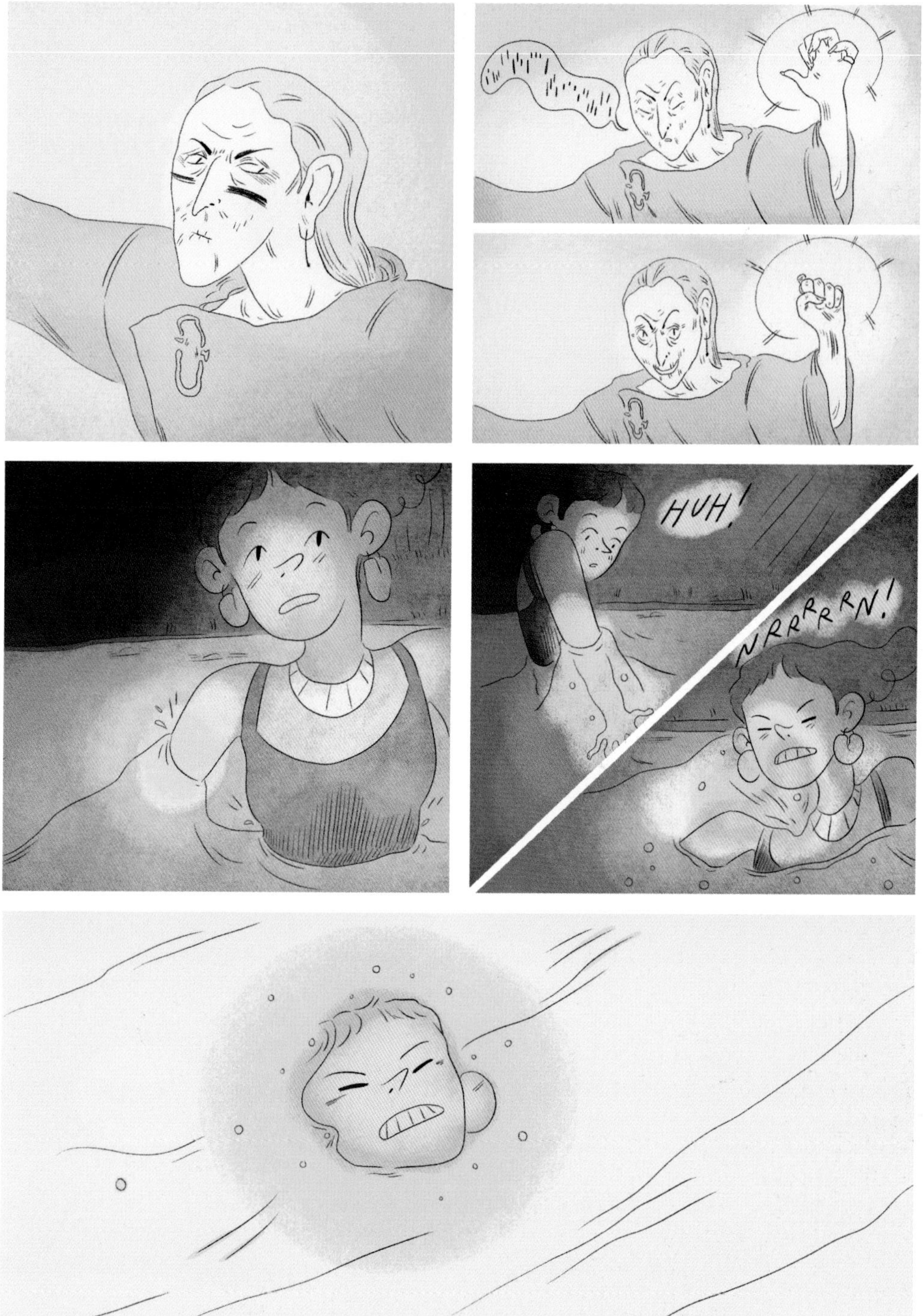
HUH!
NRRRRRN!

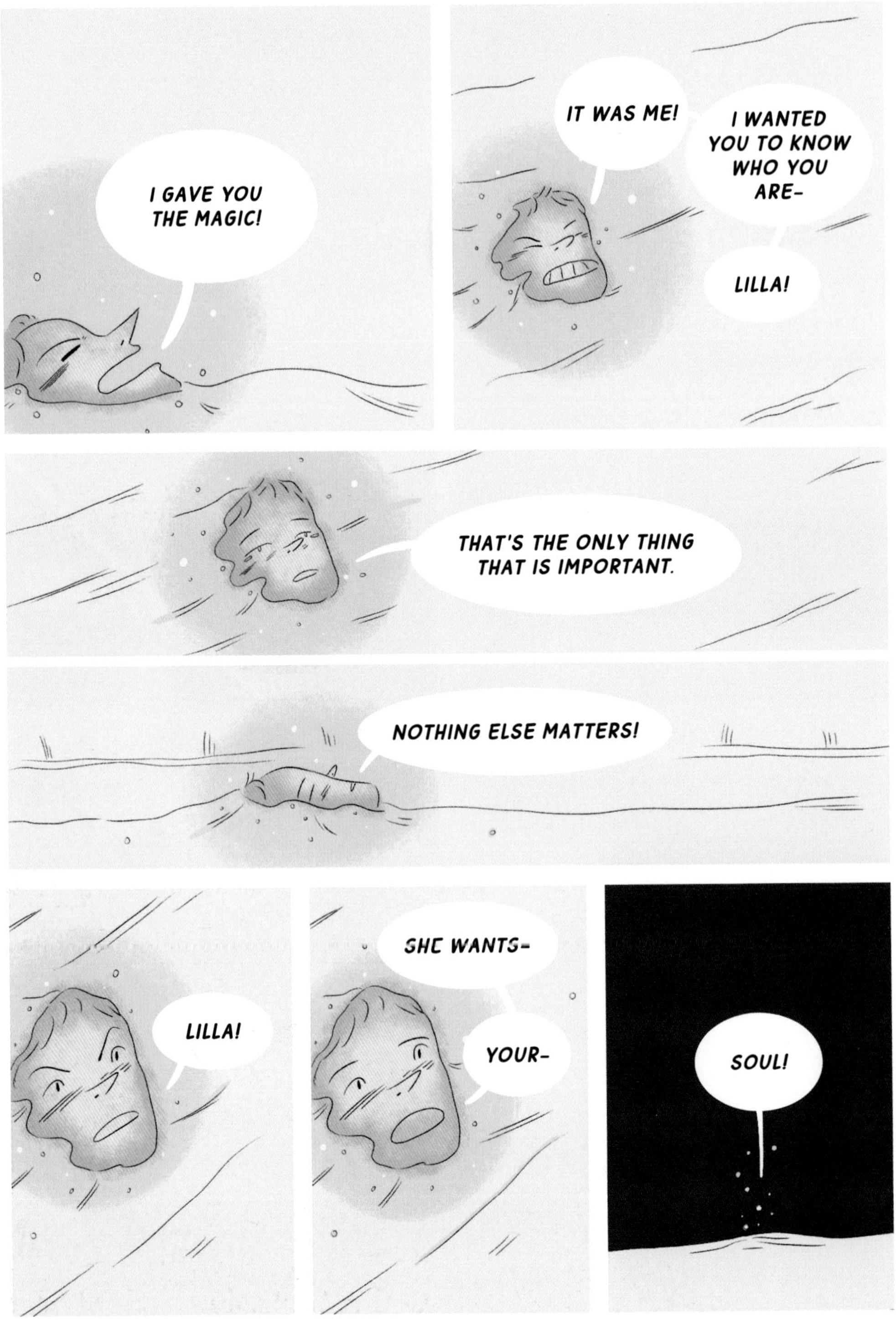
I GAVE YOU THE MAGIC!
IT WAS ME!
I WANTED YOU TO KNOW WHO YOU ARE-
LILLA!
THAT'S THE ONLY THING THAT IS IMPORTANT.
NOTHING ELSE MATTERS!
LILLA!
SHE WANTS-
YOUR-
SOUL!

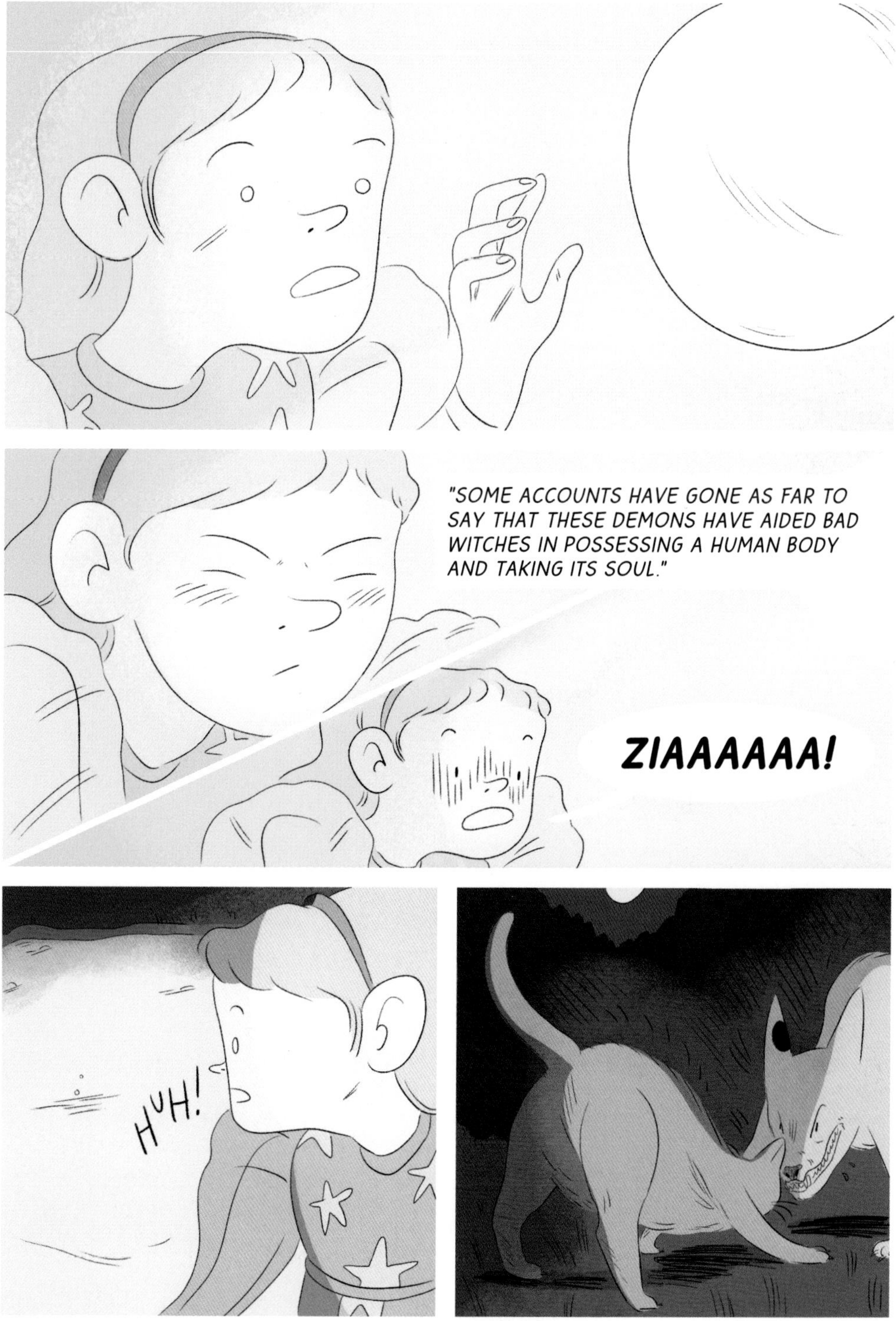
"SOME ACCOUNTS HAVE GONE AS FAR TO SAY THAT THESE DEMONS HAVE AIDED BAD WITCHES IN POSSESSING A HUMAN BODY AND TAKING ITS SOUL."
ZIAAAAAA!
HUH!

NRRRRRN!

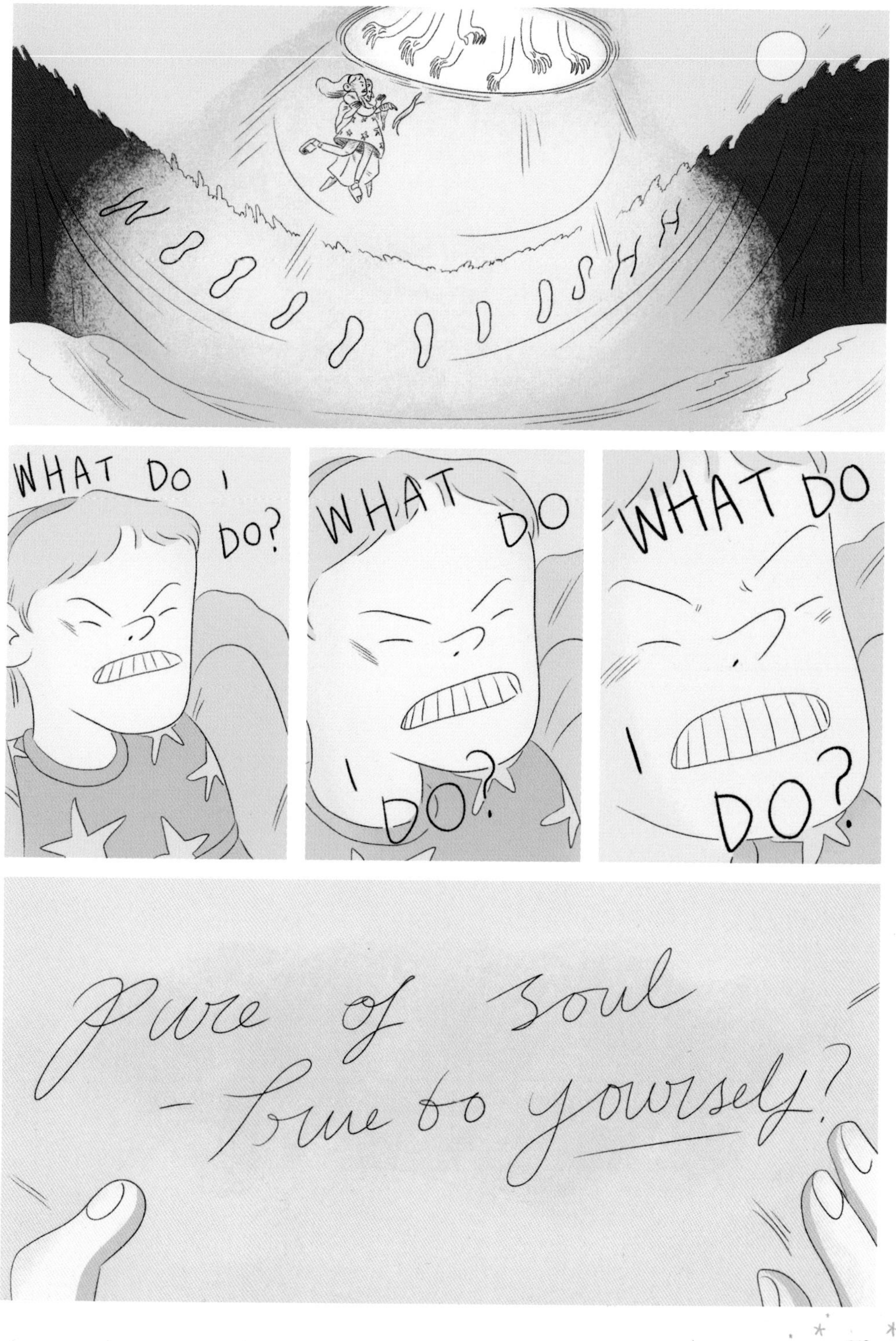
WOOOOOOSHH
WHAT DO I DO?
WHAT DO I DO?
WHAT DO I DO?
pure of soul - true to yourself?

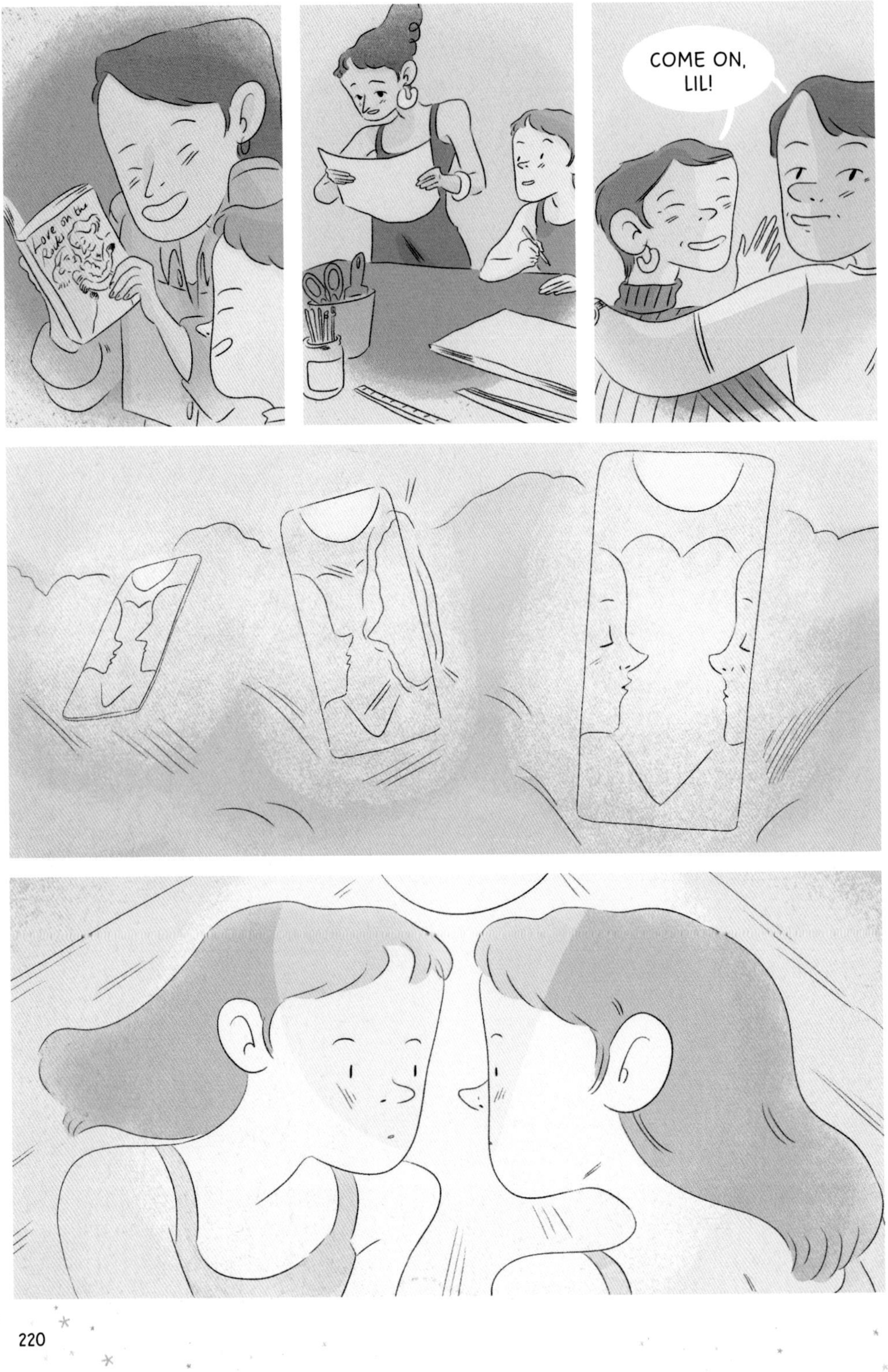
Love on the Rocks
COME ON, LIL!

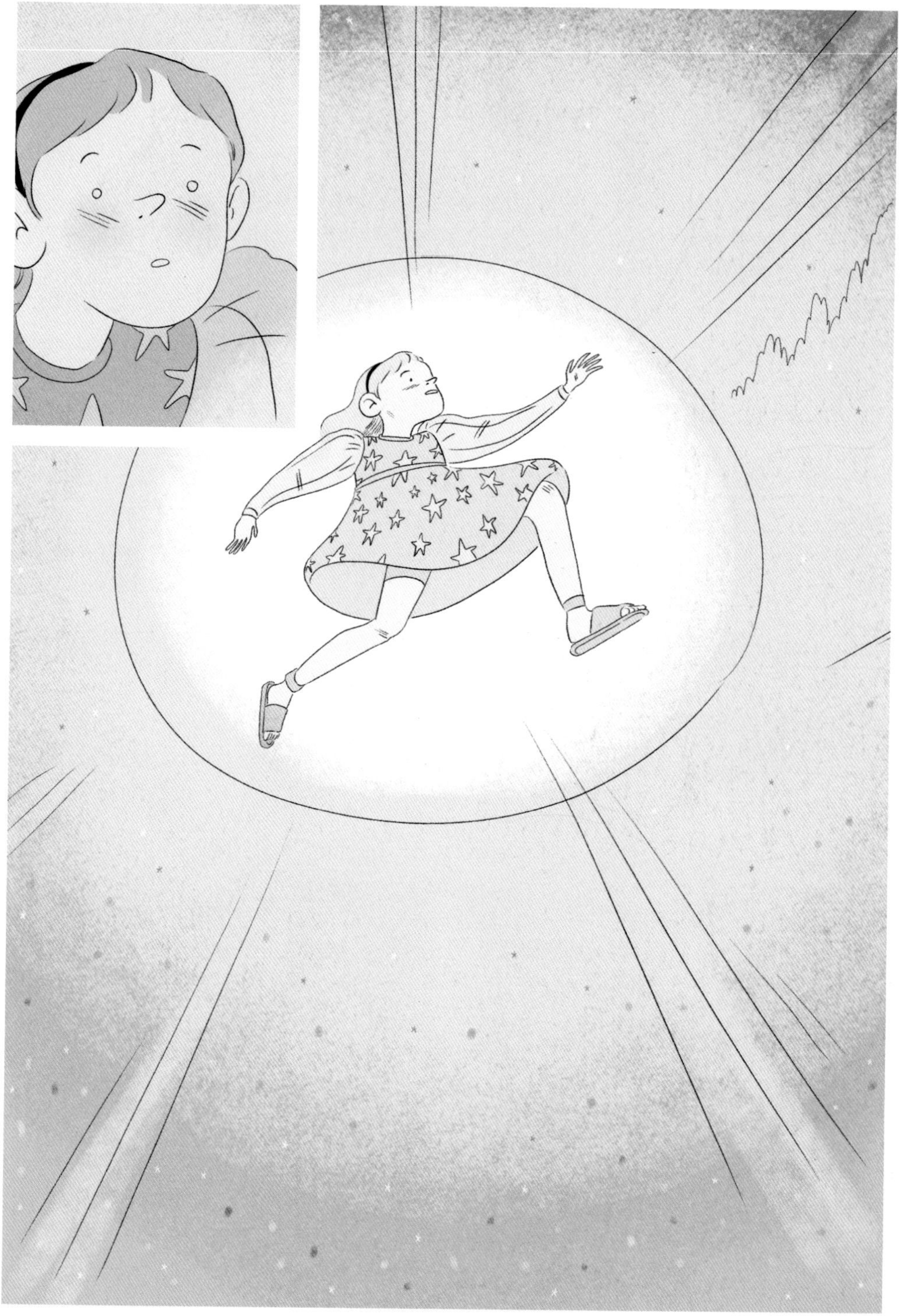

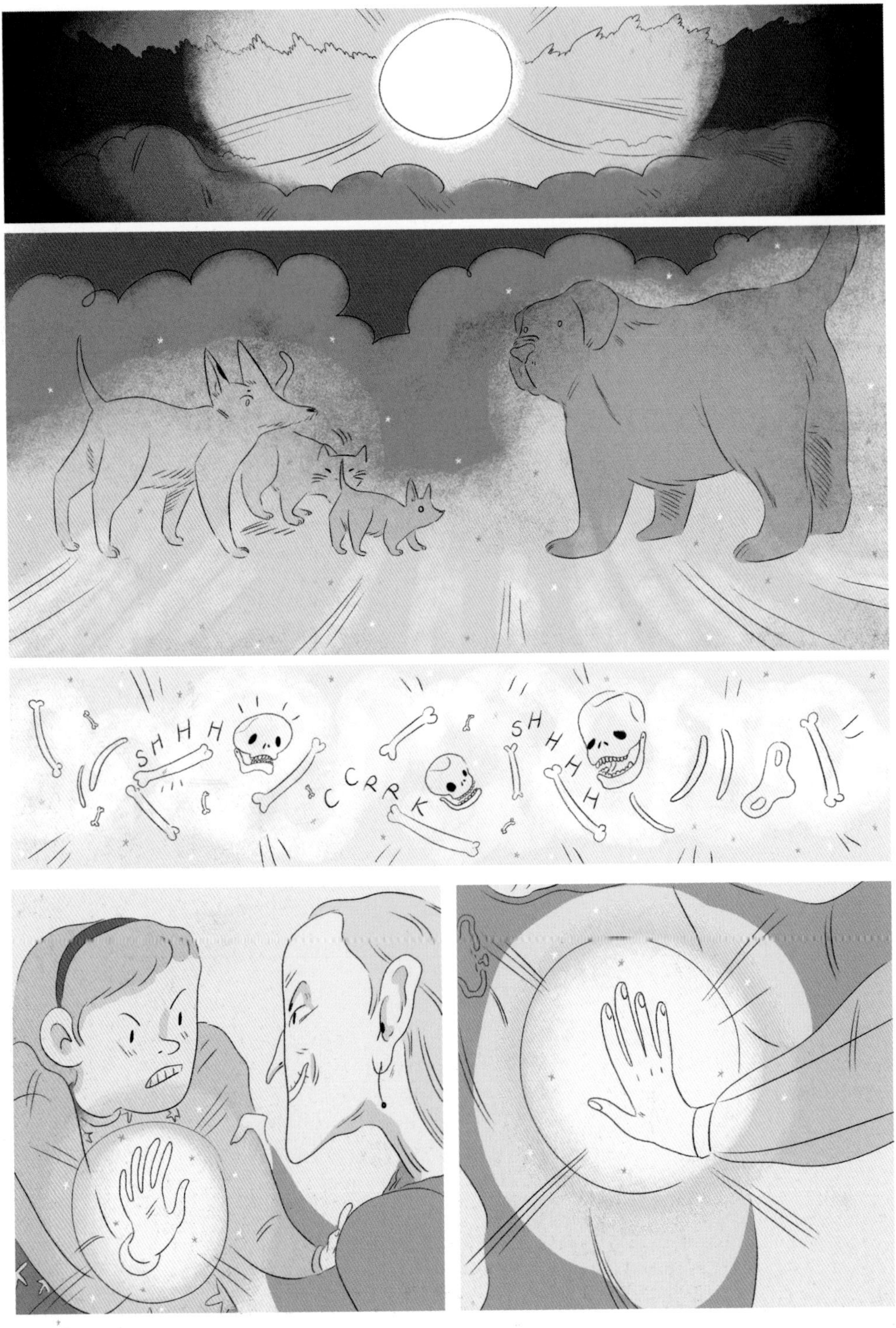
SHHH
CCRRK
SHHHH

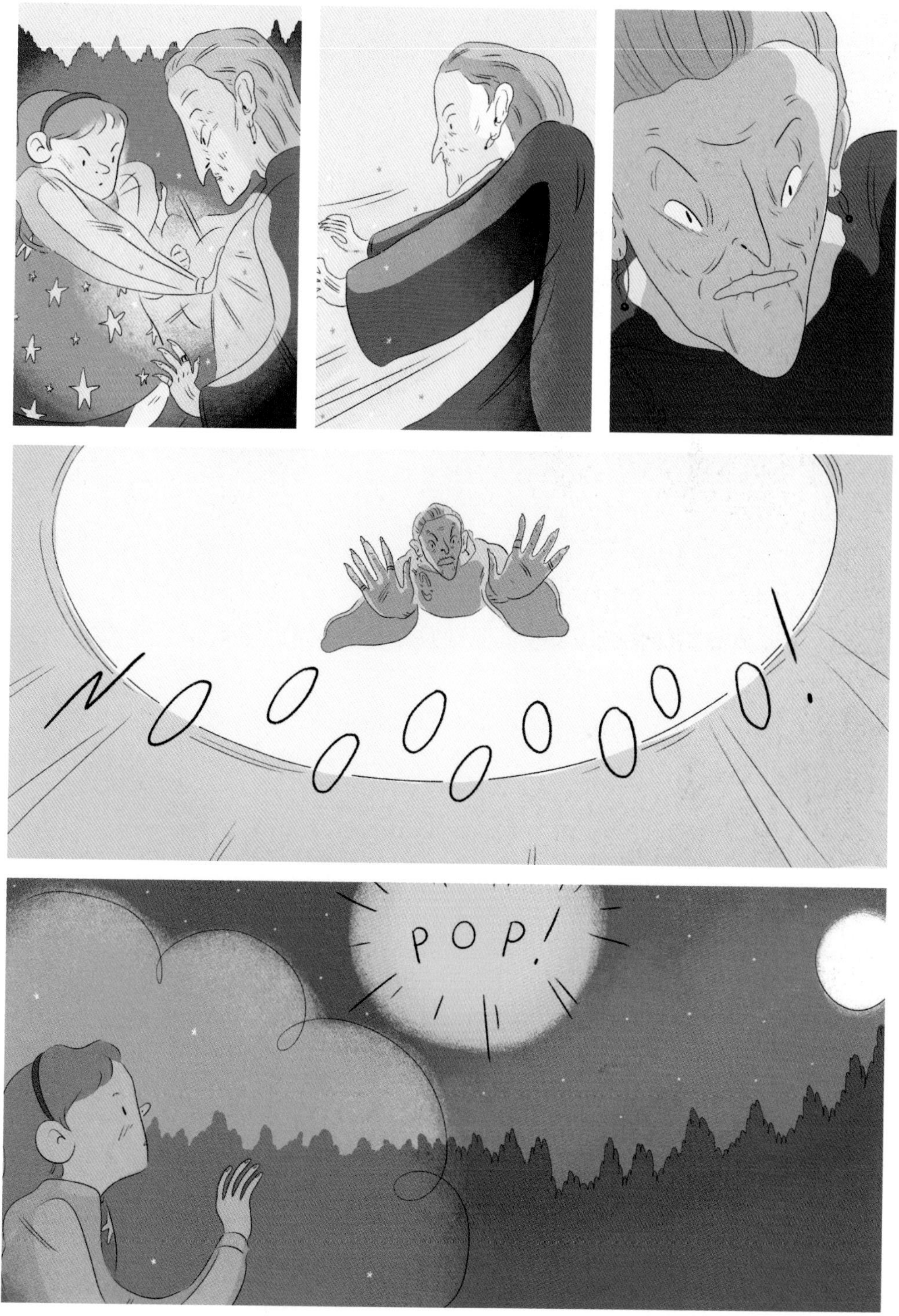
NOOOOOOOOOO!
POP!

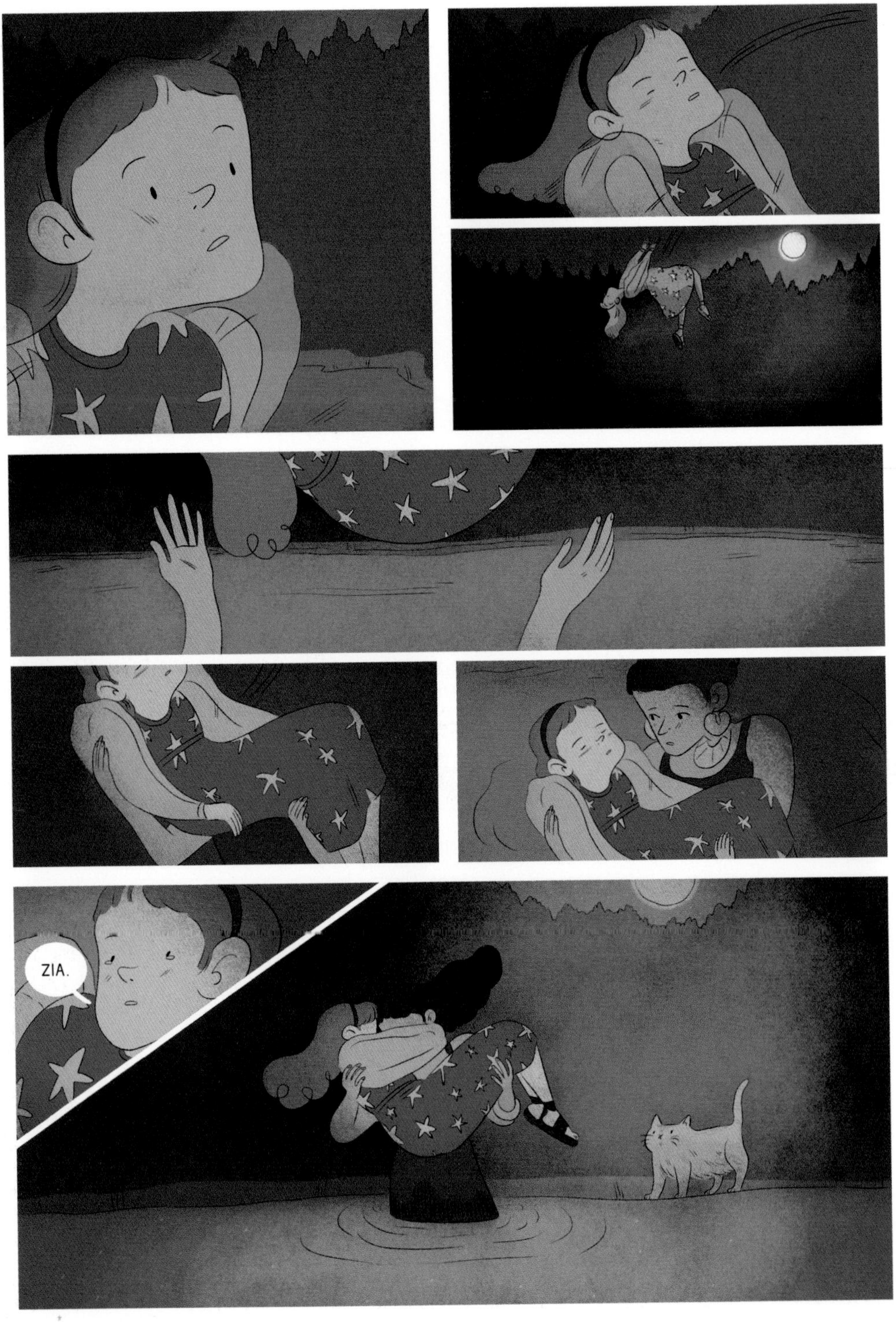
ZIA.

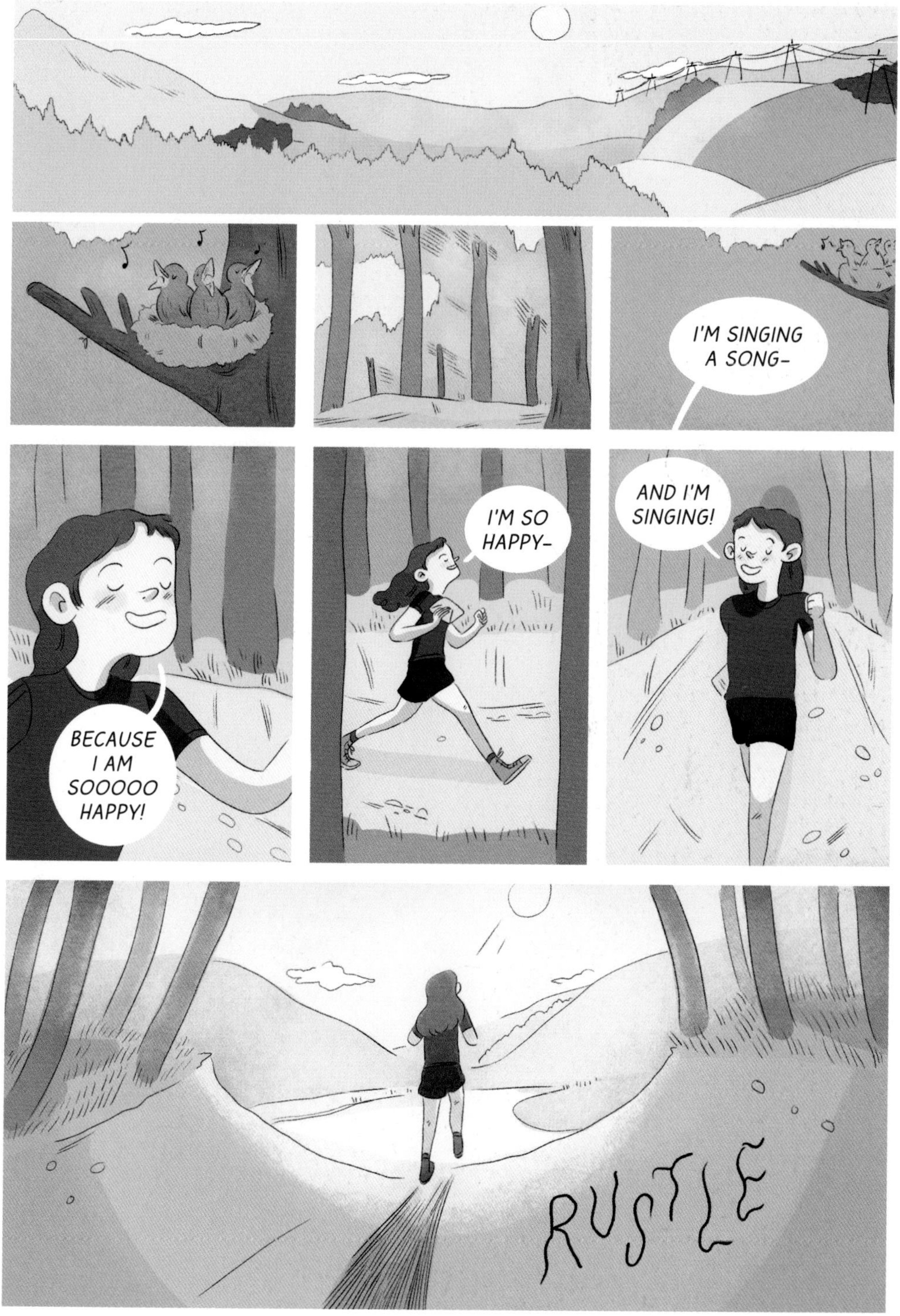
I'M SINGING A SONG-
AND I'M SINGING!
BECAUSE I AM SOOOOO HAPPY!
I'M SO HAPPY-
RUSTLE

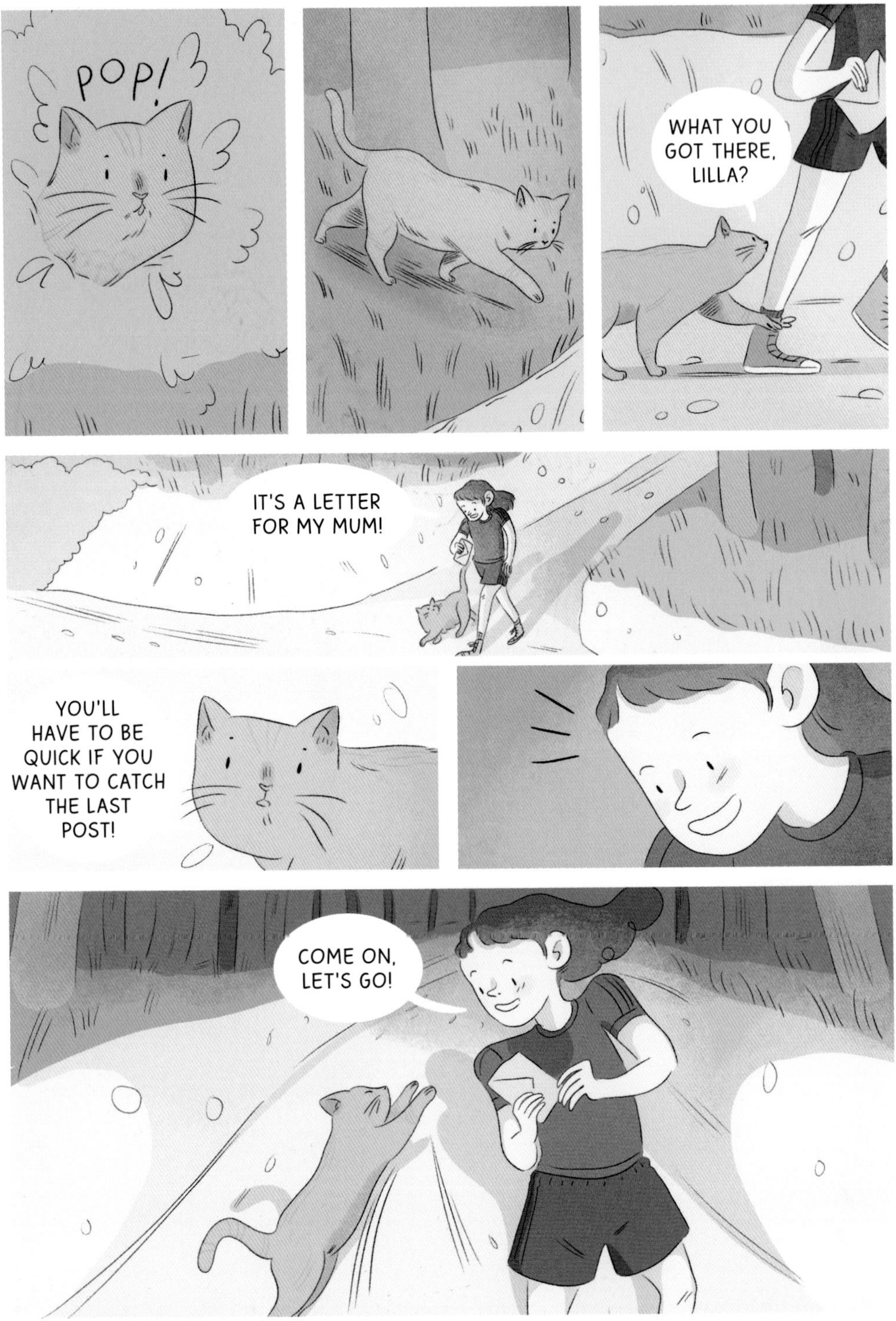
POP!
WHAT YOU GOT THERE, LILLA?
IT'S A LETTER FOR MY MUM!
YOU'LL HAVE TO BE QUICK IF YOU WANT TO CATCH THE LAST POST!
COME ON, LET'S GO!

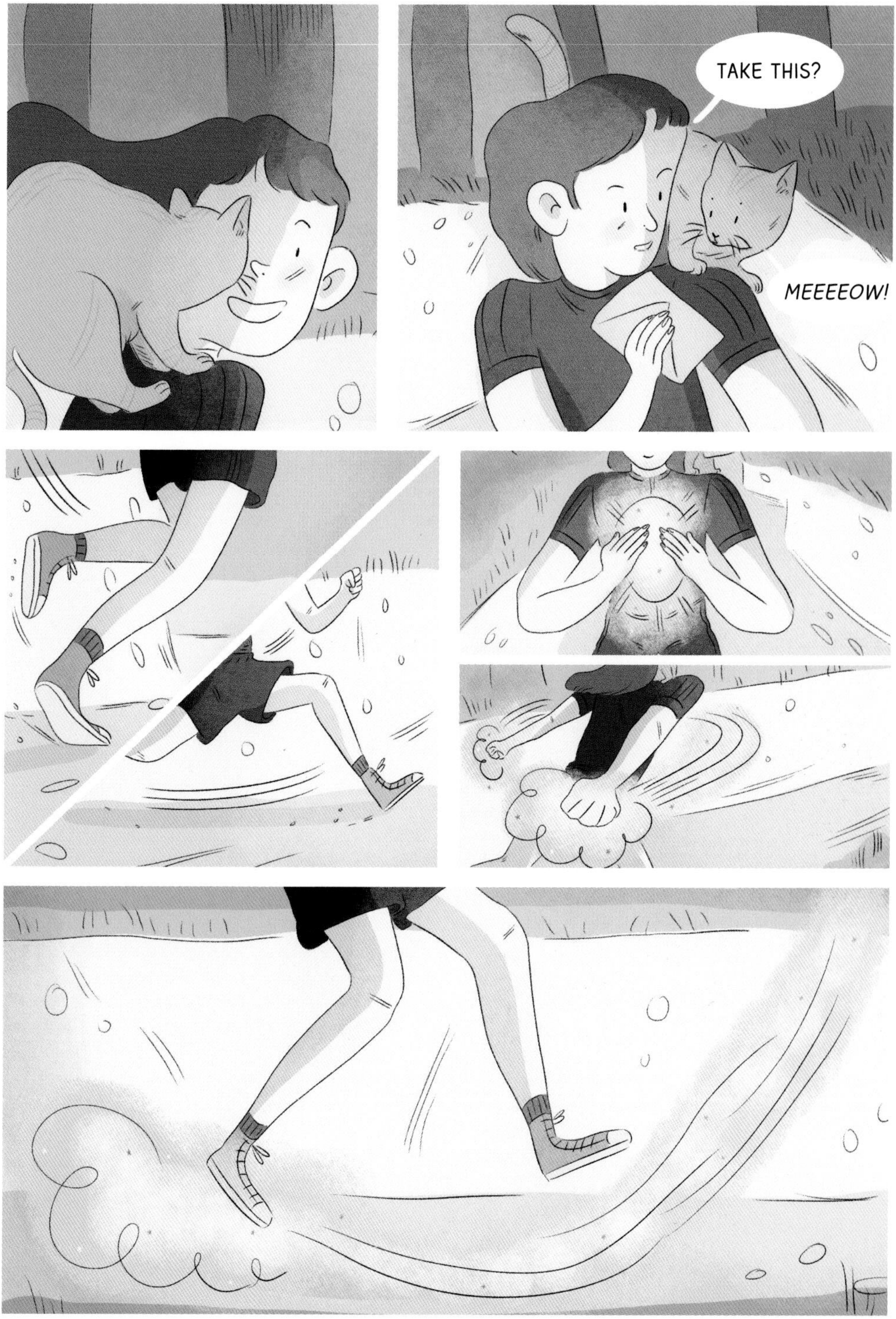
TAKE THIS?
MEEEEOW!

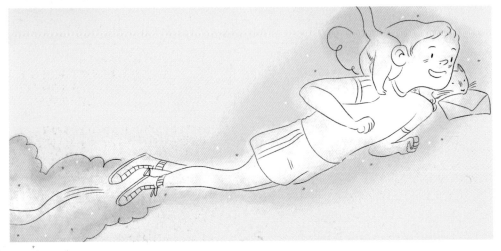

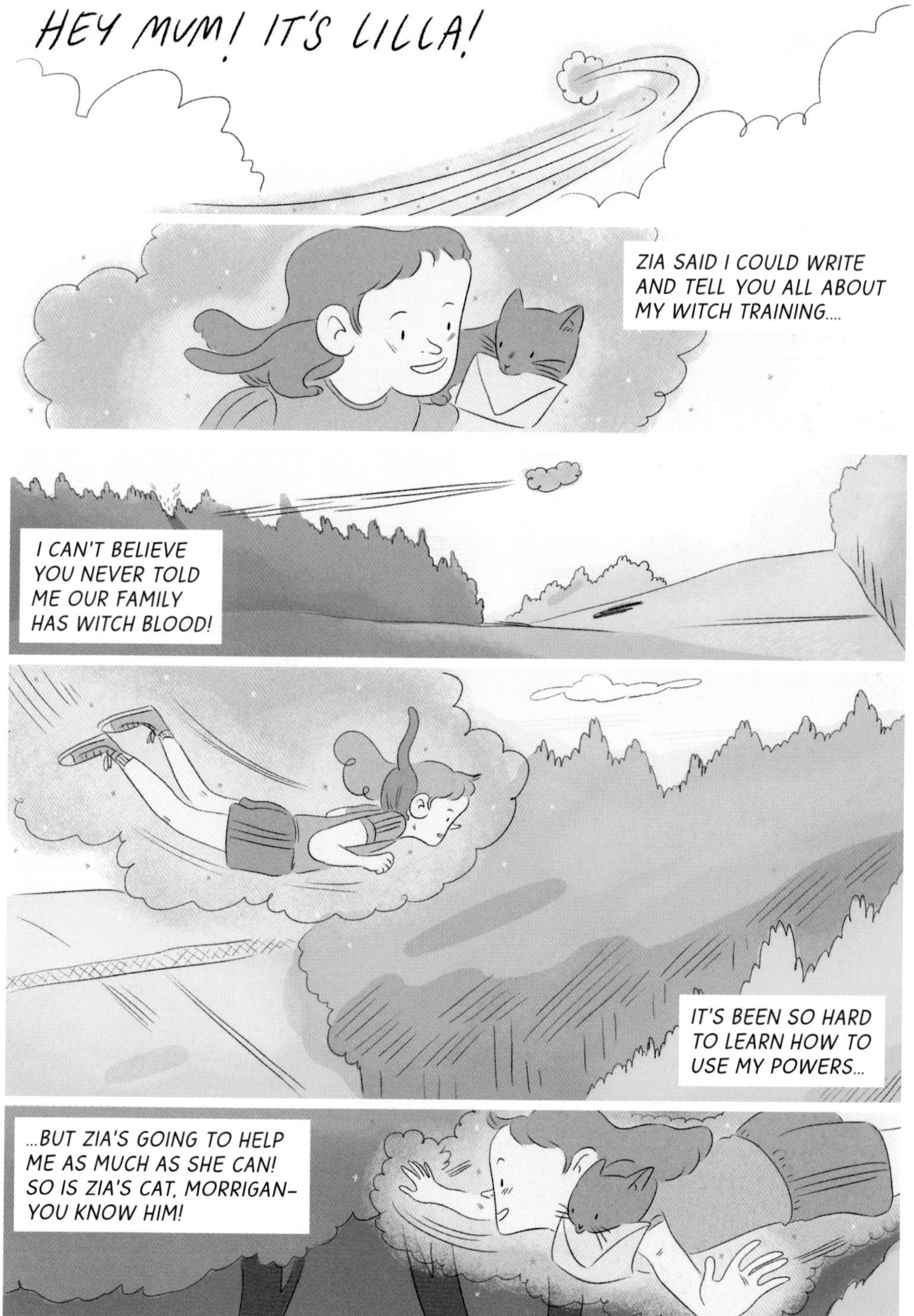
HEY MUM! IT'S LILLA!
ZIA SAID I COULD WRITE AND TELL YOU ALL ABOUT MY WITCH TRAINING....
I CAN'T BELIEVE YOU NEVER TOLD ME OUR FAMILY HAS WITCH BLOOD!
IT'S BEEN SO HARD TO LEARN HOW TO USE MY POWERS...
...BUT ZIA'S GOING TO HELP ME AS MUCH AS SHE CAN! SO IS ZIA'S CAT, MORRIGAN- YOU KNOW HIM!

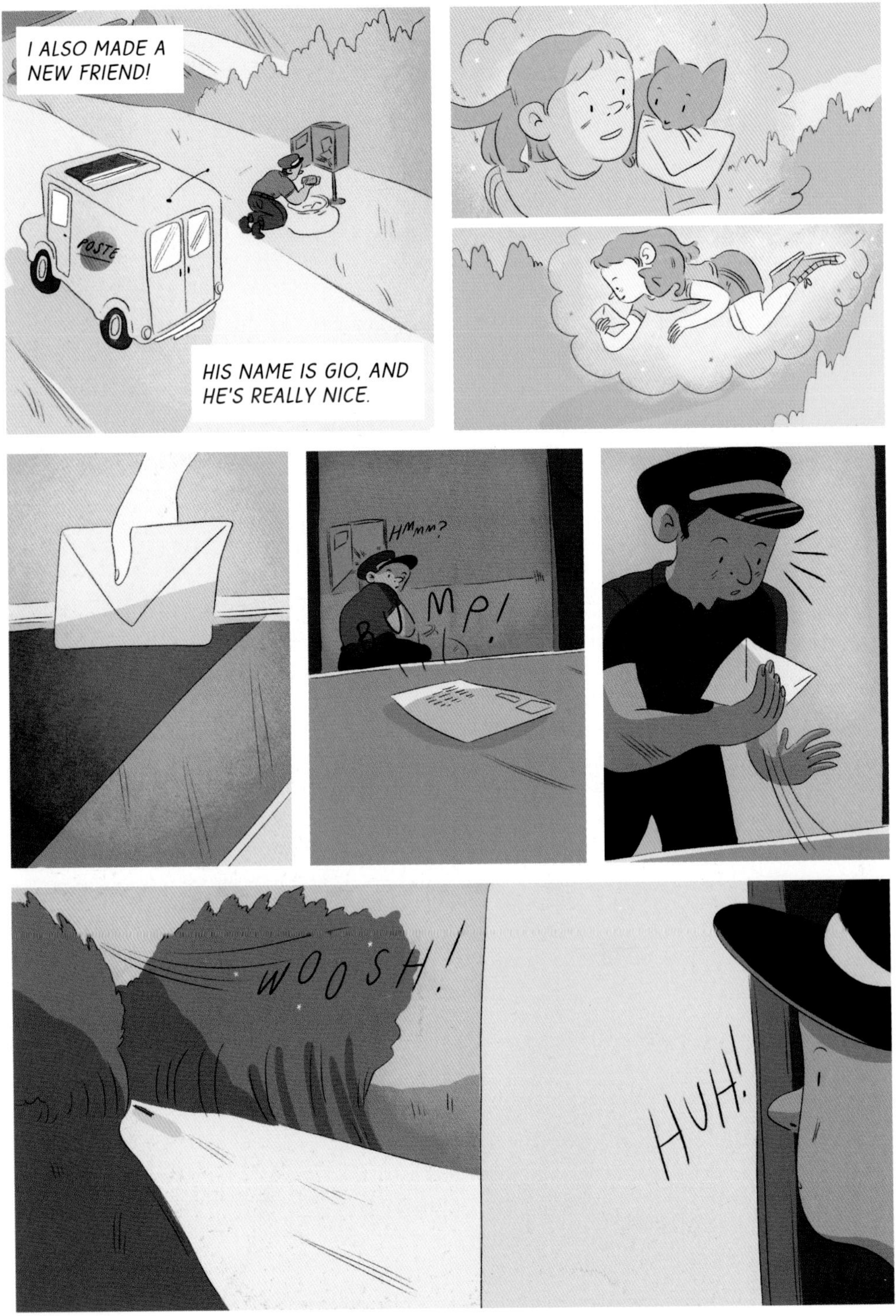
I ALSO MADE A NEW FRIEND!
POSTE
HIS NAME IS GIO, AND HE'S REALLY NICE.
HMmm?
MP!
WOOSH!
HUH!

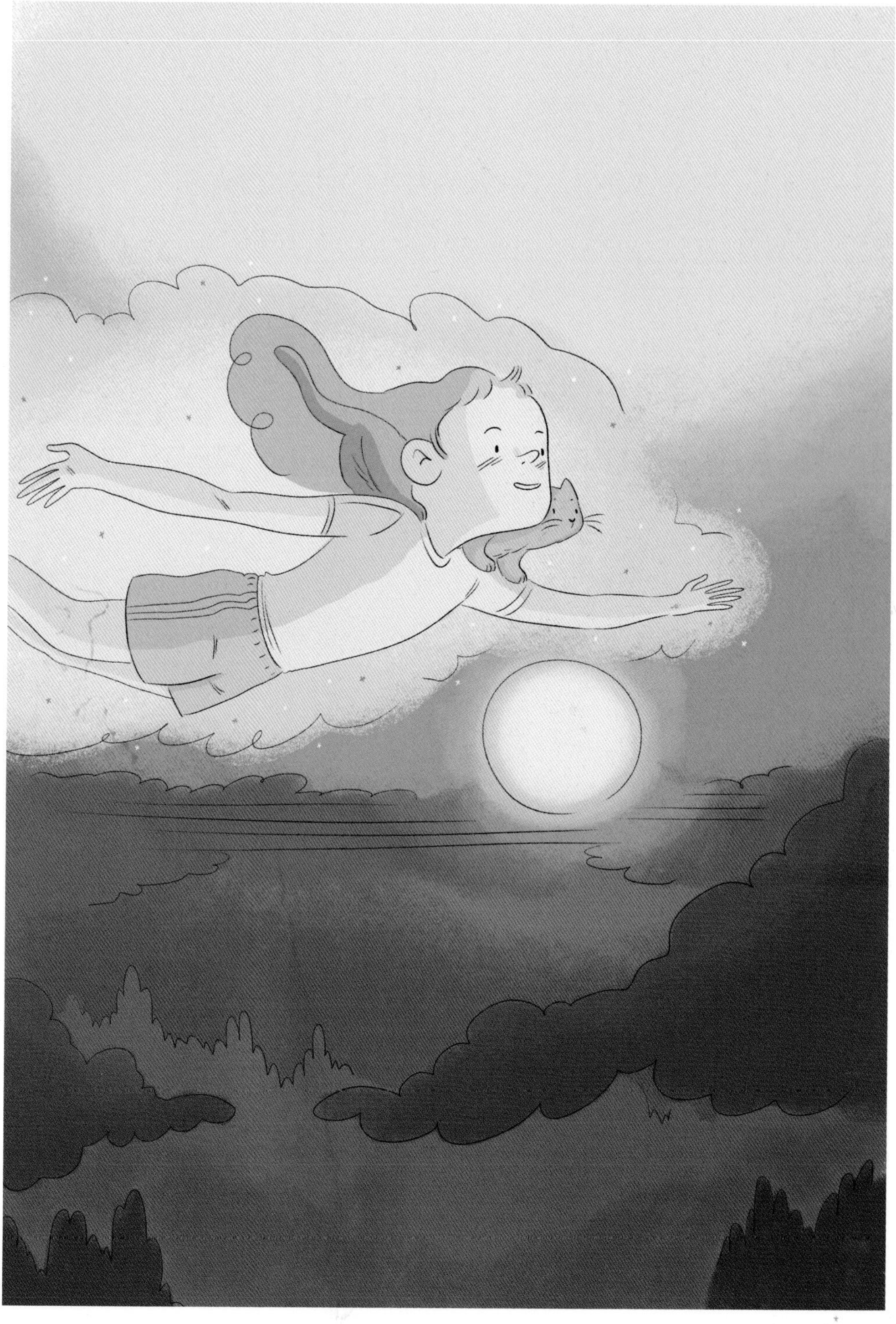

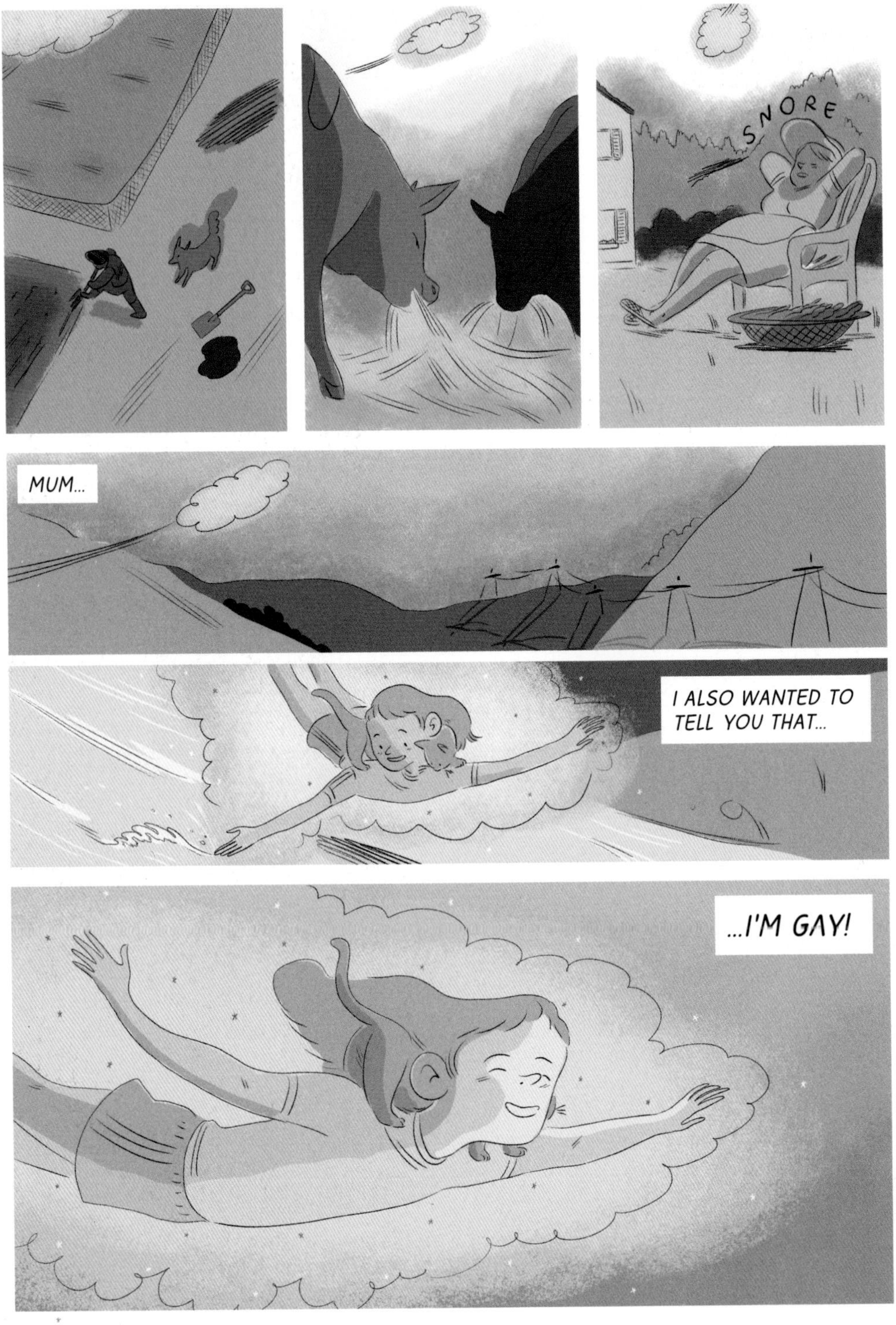
SNORE
MUM...
I ALSO WANTED TO TELL YOU THAT...
...I'M GAY!

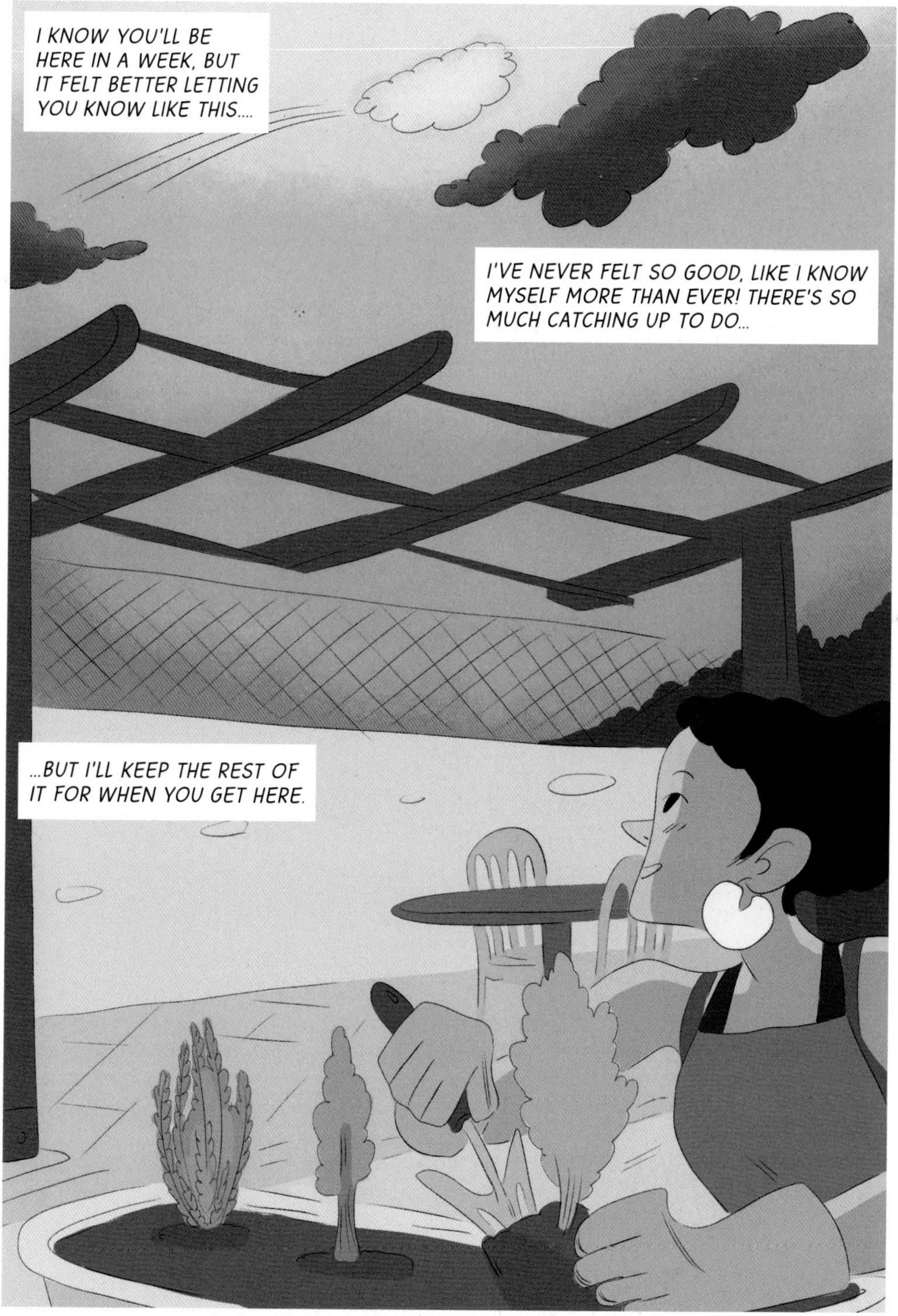

I KNOW YOU'LL BE HERE IN A WEEK, BUT IT FELT BETTER LETTING YOU KNOW LIKE THIS....
I'VE NEVER FELT SO GOOD, LIKE I KNOW MYSELF MORE THAN EVER! THERE'S SO MUCH CATCHING UP TO DO...
...BUT I'LL KEEP THE REST OF IT FOR WHEN YOU GET HERE.

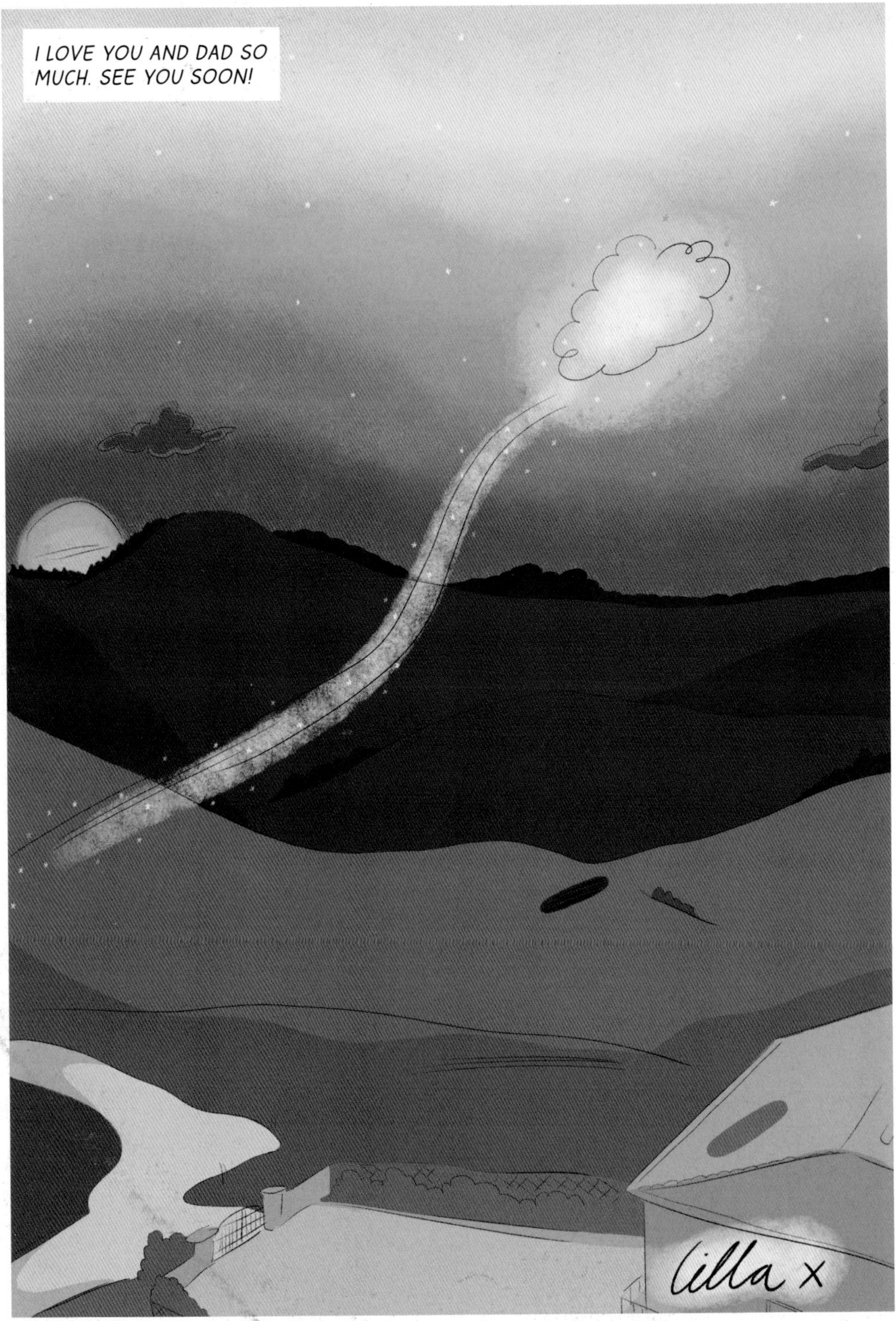
I LOVE YOU AND DAD SO MUCH. SEE YOU SOON!
Lilla x

Acknowledgments

The name *Lilla* comes from the dialect spoken by my family in northern Italy. It's a nickname they've called me since I was born, and it means "little darling girl." Like me, Lilla the character grew up in England, but this book is Italian through and through—the setting, the people, the food, the heightened emotions!

Lilla the Accidental Witch was developed and drawn during the COVID-19 pandemic. I'd planned to spend weeks in the hillsides of my family's village, but instead, every place you see within this book was drawn from my own memories of being in Italy as a little (darling) girl. During a year in which we couldn't travel, drawing the landscapes inside this book allowed me to revisit some of the places that are most special to me.

I began working on this story in 2018, and it took a lot of searching, transatlantic phone calls, and emails to find the right home for her. With that in mind, I'd like to thank my agent, Anna Power; my editor, Andrea Colvin; and my designer, Ching Chan; all of whom played such a big part in telling this story. I'd also like to thank my partner, T, and our wonderful families. I worked on this book across north London in both our family homes, and I know that all their love has made its way into this book.

About the Author

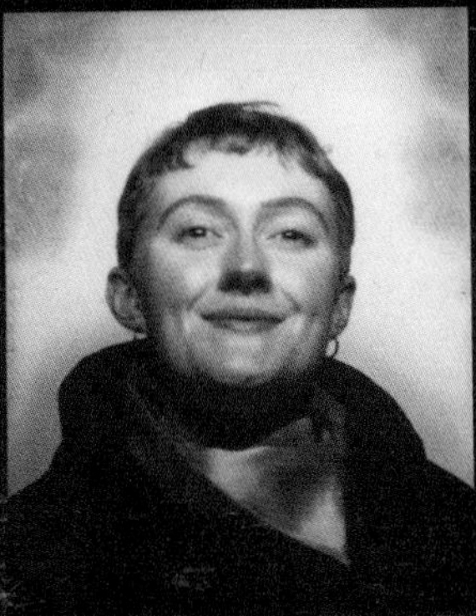

Photo by Eleanor Crewes

Eleanor Crewes

is a graphic novelist who specializes in queer autofiction. Her debut graphic novel, *The Times I Knew I Was Gay*, was published in the UK by Virago and the US by Scribner in 2020, and was featured in *O, The Oprah Magazine* and *The Guardian*. She lives in London with her partner and enjoys cooking her mother's Italian recipes.